TO KILL AN AMERICAN . . .

AS THE RAIDING PARTY QUICKLY DEPLOYED TO cover, DeLuca crouched low beside the Humvee. Two MPs rushed to where the translator had fallen, and then one made a cursory slashing gesture to signal what everybody already knew—the young man was dead. A team of MPs unfolded a body bag at the edge of the garden.

An infantryman approached DeLuca with a piece of a paper he'd found tacked to the tree, about a quarter of a mile off, from which the sniper had apparently fired. It was the wanted poster DeLuca had seen earlier that morning.

DeLuca knew full well what the attack had meant. Most Iraqi snipers were incompetent, poor marksmen who rarely allowed for windage or calculated for elevation, and few ever used sniper rounds. Judging from the severity of the damage done, this was clearly a large-caliber soft-pointed shell fired from a high-velocity rifle. Someone had wanted to claim the reward. And that meant that someone had been given information about the mission.

In other words, there was a traitor on the post . . .

CI:Team Red

DAVID DeBATTO
and PETE NELSON

WARNER BOOKS

NEW YORK   BOSTON

Cover design by Jerry Pfeiffer
Cover photos by AP Wide World Photos
Book design by Stratford Publishing Services

Warner Books

Time Warner Book Group
1271 Avenue of the Americas
New York, NY 10020
Visit our Web site at www.twbookmark.com

Printed in the United States of America

First Paperback Printing: May 2005
10 9 8 7 6 5 4 3 2 1

Acknowledgments

To my lovely wife Brenda, who is still not exactly sure what a counterintelligence agent really does, and I want to keep it that way.

To all of the real-life Army CI agents fighting in the GWOT. Stay safe. We need you more than ever.

To my co-writer and mentor, Pete Nelson. I cannot thank you enough. The muses have surely thrown us together, for you are the perfect complement to my many literary shortcomings, which are legion.

To Dan Ambrosio and Warner Books. Thank you, thank you for taking a chance on an untested, unpublished writer in an already overcrowded genre. May your trust in me, Pete, and our concept bear the fruit we all feel it will.

Lastly, to my literary agent, Todd Shuster, of Zachary, Shuster, Harmsworth. You were there from the very beginning, held my hand and guided me through the crazy world of publishing. All that may come from this incredible journey will be mostly due to you my friend, and I will always remember that. Thank you.

—*David DeBatto*

Pete Nelson would like to thank Dave DeBatto, his collaborator, for all his hard work and input, comments, advice, e-mails, downloads, elaborations, speculations, and for tolerating me when I made him back up and explain all things military, and for his efforts to make this book as true to the experience of the Iraq war as a work of fiction can be —I would like to thank him as well for his sacrifice and for the contributions he made in Iraq. I'd like to thank Todd Shuster, the agent on this project who steered it in the right direction and shepherded the proposal through so many different versions and configurations—thanks for your endless patience, your foresight and your vision of where this could go. Thanks to editor Dan Ambrosio for his enthusiasm, his painless editing, and for his ongoing support during the writing process. I'm grateful for the feedback I got from my wise circle of critics, including Jeannie Birdsall, Bluey Diehl, Cammie McGovern, Sarah Metcalf, Karen Osborne, Tony Maroulis, and in particular for the read I got from David Stern, good friend and master of the macabre. Thanks to Gordon Bigelow and Dick Duncan for advice on sailing and sailboats, and thanks to Dr. Chris Otis for talking to me about pathology. Big big thanks to Samar Moushabeck for supplying me with Arabic translations (not to mention coffee and baked goods), and to her husband Gabby, whose bookstore, Booklinks, served as one of my primary resources (e-mail: booklinker@aol.com). Antepenultimate thanks to whoever invented Google, without which I could not have pretended to know half as much as I pretend I do, both in print and in real life. Penultimate thanks to my son Jack for keeping my spirits up and for sleeping through the night so that Daddy had some time to write, and finally thanks to Jennifer Gates, my finest collaborator, for all her reads, thoughts, insights, patience, support, and understanding.

—*Pete Nelson*

CI:Team Red

Prologue

OUT THE WINDOW, THE DOCKWORKER COULD hear children playing and laughing.

He lay back on the bed and threw his arm over his eyes to block the light that filtered in through the dirty window. He fumbled for his cigarettes on the nightstand. To say he felt terrible was an understatement. He found the remote and turned on the television, then turned it off again, too ill to watch it. On the end table next to the bed, he saw an empty bottle of tequila. He couldn't remember finishing it. It probably explained a lot. Either that, or God was punishing him, but he couldn't believe God would punish him for stealing one lousy bottle of olive oil—not after all the other times when God had looked the other way.

He didn't feel much better when the phone woke him up again around four. This time he screened the call. A man's voice said: "This is O'Brien down at the hall. Look, we got two ships coming in on Monday and we're going to need a full crew so I was hoping you could make it . . ."

The dockworker had half a mind to pick up the phone and tell O'Brien to go screw himself, asking for favors after the way he'd ridden him all week. If he felt better by

Monday, maybe he'd go in, but right now it wasn't looking so likely.

He managed to walk to the bathroom, though he felt dizzy and leaned heavily against the sink. This was more than a hangover. He looked at himself in the mirror. The handsome devil he usually saw looked awful. His eyes were red, and his skin was the color of oatmeal. At six foot four and a muscular 250 pounds, only thirty-three years of age, he was a strong man who'd done a bit of goon work for the union from time to time, but right now he felt too weak to blow the fuzz off a dandelion. He popped two Alka-Seltzers in a glass of water, drank it, and immediately felt worse, barely turning in time to kneel before the toilet, where he vomited for the next ten minutes, including a violent series of dry heaves toward the end that left him feeling even weaker.

He went back to bed. His lower back ached, which he assumed was from all the lifting he'd done during the week, but soon the muscles in his arms and legs began to ache, and his head hurt. He felt utterly fatigued. When he took his temperature, he found he had a fever of 101 degrees.

"Well that's fucking great," he said to no one.

He didn't have any health insurance, and he wasn't about to blow the nine hundred dollars he'd earned that week on a doctor, so he covered himself with a blanket, took three Tylenol and went to bed. He had chills during the night, and he vomited several more times.

By noon of the following day, Sunday, he'd changed his mind about seeing a doctor. He was reluctant to call the hospital emergency room at Massachusetts General because he still owed them five hundred dollars for a prior visit, but he had to talk to somebody, so he placed a block on his phone to prevent the advice nurse from using caller ID and gave a fake name when she finally came on the line. He told her he felt like crap and wondered if she could prescribe him something.

"We'd really have to see you in person before we could do that," she said.

"I don't have any insurance," he told her.

"Can you answer a few questions?"

"I guess," he muttered.

"Do you have a fever?" she asked.

"Uh-huh."

"Can you tell me what it is?"

"One hundred two point four."

"How long have you had a fever?"

"It was a hundred and one yesterday."

"Did it go down last night?"

"I don't know," he struggled to say. "I don't think so."

"Muscle aches?"

"Uh-huh."

"Where?"

"Everywhere."

"Backache?"

"Yeah."

"Headache?"

"Uh-huh."

"Vomiting?"

"Yeah."

"How many times?"

"I don't know. Twenty?"

"Diarrhea?"

"Yeah," he said. "I was thinking maybe I had food poisoning."

"What's the last thing you ate?"

"Spaghetti with white clam sauce. Do you think it's food poisoning?"

"It's possible, with clams, though usually if it's food poisoning, you feel better after you vomit. Anything else? Any other symptoms. Sore throat?"

"No," he said. "I think I've got a rash, though."

"Where?" she inquired.

"On my chest," he said.

"How large is the area?" she asked.

"Maybe the size of my hand."

"Is the area raised and slightly puffy or just red?"

"I don't know. Just red, I think."

"That sounds erythematous," she said as if she was thinking out loud.

"What does that mean?" he asked.

"It could be a negative reaction to medication. Have you taken any drugs?"

"Not lately," he said. The dog downstairs was yapping again.

"Aspirin? Motrin? Tylenol . . . ?"

"Tylenol," he said weakly.

He waited while she added it all up. His head was pounding as he shivered beneath his blankets.

"And you said your fever is one-oh-two point four?"

"Uh-huh."

"I think you should probably be seen by a doctor," she said at last. "Do you think you'd be able to drive?"

"I don't have a car," he said. He had a car, just no license after his third DWI.

"Is there somebody you could call who could give you a ride?" she asked.

He told her there wasn't anybody he could call. He thought again of the five hundred dollars he owed. If he paid it, he might as well not have worked at all the previous week. He told himself that it was just a bug of some sort, and that no matter how bad he felt, he could tough it out.

By Sunday evening, he realized he was wrong about that, but by then he was too sick to move, utterly prostrate and barely able to sit up. He'd brought a hand-held mirror to bed, and when he looked in it, he saw that the rash had spread up his chest and neck to the left side of his face. The rash on his face was simply red, but the rash on his chest had indeed become puffy and tender to the touch.

When the dockworker finally called a cab to give him a ride to the hospital, he got a busy signal. He tried again a while later, but with his fever raging at nearly 104 degrees, in a state of only partial lucidity, he dropped the phone on the floor and was too sick to reach down and pick it up. He never made it to the hospital.

By midnight on Monday, his rash had become vesicular, the red nodes distending into erumpent bladderlike sacs filled with pus and lymphatic fluids, each whitehead excruciating to the touch, the largest about the size of a dime, though they were fairly uniform in size and evenly distributed. His fever stabilized in the night at 102.5 degrees as his thymus, spleen, liver, lymph nodes, and bone marrow began to run out of the raw materials needed to produce antibodies. He spent the next day, Tuesday, lying in bed, groaning and wishing that someone would knock on the door and find him, the mailman, an errant pizza delivery man, anybody. He prayed to God for help, holding in his hands the Bible he'd found in the back corner of his bedstand drawer.

"I know maybe I never gave you enough credit," he said in his prayers, "and I never done much for the church or whatever, but if you could do me this one favor and make me better, I swear I'll change stuff . . ."

Tuesday night (though he could no longer tell how fast or slow time was passing) his condition worsened. His joints throbbed with pain, while lightning bolts of gastrointestinal anguish doubled him over, leaving him in a fetal position most of the time. The whiteheads on his skin began to split and burst. Within hours, full-blown lesions covered his entire body, seeping and staining the sheets upon which he was dying as his air passage narrowed, making him feel like he was suffocating.

In the final throes, he trembled and gnashed his teeth and shook violently, his skin a mat of bubbling rubber as he bled out, hemorrhaging both internally and externally, blood coming from his rectum, his fingernails, his nose, ears, eyes, mouth, and gums. Where he clawed at his skin, the skin tore as easily as tissue paper. The hair on his head fell out in clumps when he grabbed at it. The lining of his brain was inflamed with encephalitis, causing him to hallucinate. In his last uncontrolled thrashing, he knocked over the lamp and lacked the strength to right it. He lost consciousness entirely shortly before midnight. The smoke alarm went off half an hour later when the heat from the light bulb in the overturned lamp set fire to the pages of the Bible he'd hoped would be his salvation.

Firefighters blamed the intensity of the flames on the fact that the old couple they'd rescued from the first floor were packrats who hadn't thrown out a newspaper or magazine in the last twenty years, providing fuel for the inferno. When firefighters finally got to the dockworker—his name was Anthony Fusaro—his body was burned beyond recognition and mostly ash.

Chapter One

IT WAS ONE OF THOSE DAYS THAT STARTED lousy and went rapidly downhill, beginning when DeLuca was called in to meet with Lieutenant Colonel Stanley Reicken in a conference room at the Tactical Operations Center for a briefing. The desert sun had yet to rise, but even at that predawn hour the TOC was jamming, a fifty-foot-square canvas enclosure ringed by armored transports and Bradley fighting vehicles backed up to form a protective cordon, the whole structure roofed with heavy dark green canvas tarps dating back to the Korean War, full of techies, aides, assistants, staff flunkies, translators, and brigade combat team leaders, as well as a handful of DeLuca's fellow counterintelligence agents. He paused before entering to blouse his boots, because Reicken cared deeply about such things, grabbed a cup of coffee from the five-gallon pot by the door, then made his way to the brightly lit room at the far end of the expansive hall, taking care not to trip over any of the cables duct-taped to the floor. The "Star Wars Tent," as some people were calling it, was always impressive to him, perhaps because he was something of a technophobe, with banks of computers crunching numbers and accessing databases, the latest communications equipment with satellite uplinks, electronics of all kinds, the walls alive with real-time UAV imagery sent from drones no bigger than model airplanes, streaming 24/7 on an array of flat-screen plasma televisions, the main screen a four-by-six-foot job hanging at the far wall. A tech officer had told him they had more computer power than NASA had when they put a man on the moon. DeLuca had been led to believe he was going to meet to discuss security needs for the day's mission. Instead, Reicken surprised him by throwing a crude wanted poster down on the table, a photocopy of a pencil drawing of DeLuca that, to his mind, wasn't all that close a resemblance, with the words "MR. DAVID" and "$10,000 AMERICAN" and "CIA" written in inch-high block letters.

"Apparently you're a marked man, DeLuca," Reicken said with a kind of smirk on his face. "Looks like you're doing your job a bit too well. Take it as a compliment. Probably put out by some Ba'ath party poohbah who's getting tired of you arresting all his boys."

DeLuca picked up the drawing and looked at it. The drawing took a good fifteen or twenty years off him. His hairline was wrong, his jaw a bit squarer, his nose not bent where an angel-dusted punk he'd arrested in Chelsea had broken it, and it wasn't an accurate enough rendering that anybody could pick him out of a crowd from it, but it gave him the willies all the same.

"Where'd you find this?" he asked. It would make a nice keepsake, assuming he got home in one piece. Something to frame for the study, assuming he still had a home, back in the world.

"Somebody brought it in," Reicken said casually. "You know, I wouldn't get a big head about it, but I think ten thousand may be a new record for a guardsman." Reicken hated guardsmen. Most of the guardsmen DeLuca knew found the feeling mutual. DeLuca had half a mind to call his old friend Phil—General Phillip LeDoux, to Reicken— and tell him what a horse's ass Reicken was, though that would be operating outside of channels, and he'd gotten in trouble for going outside channels on both his previous enlistments. DeLuca had known the general since the two of them had sat in a freezing cold Quonset hut on the German border back in the late seventies, listening to frantic East German government officials making telephone calls about how the Americans were going to call off the Olympics. DeLuca had joked, over the years, that Phillip only got into Officer's Candidate School because DeLuca turned them down. LeDoux was an excellent example of what good a man could do committing his life to the military. Reicken was a paper-pushing bureaucrat who couldn't carry LeDoux's shorts.

"Anyway," Reicken said, "I thought you should have a heads-up. It's up to you if you want to go out or ride a desk for a few days until we find out who's doing this."

DeLuca decided not to react to the insult. As MacKenzie had told him before, "You're older than him, you're smarter than him, you're better looking and you're six inches taller than he is—he's totally jealous of you, and if you let him get to you, he pulls you down to his level." She was right, at least the part about not letting Reicken get to him.

"No thanks, but I'd appreciate it, Colonel, if we could keep this between ourselves for as long as possible. I wouldn't want to worry anybody on the team."

*   *   *

Two hours later, DeLuca was riding in an up-armored Humvee next to a man who apparently hadn't showered since the first Gulf War. They were fifteen klicks from base, headed for a compound on the outskirts of the town of Ad-Dujayl. The raiding party, operating out of the Balad Army Air Field, popularly known as Camp Anaconda, fifty kilometers north of Baghdad, consisted of three Bradley fighting vehicles and seven Humvees. Each Humvee carried five MPs, two in the front and two in the back, armed with M-16s and 9mm Beretta semiautomatic pistols, and a Squad Automatic Weapon or SAW gunner protruding from a hole in the roof, seated in a canvas sling between the rear passengers with only his upper torso exposed, manning a roof-mounted M-60 machine gun. DeLuca reached across his flak jacket to check his revolver, hoping he wouldn't have to use it. He wasn't one of the gunslingers. Counterintelligence didn't do security. That's what the MPs and the Bradleys were for.

"Eyes on," he radioed to MacKenzie in the lead Humvee.

"Gotcha," she chirped back. "Too bad Doc and Dan have to miss the party," she added, referring to the two other members of DeLuca's team, currently interviewing the mayor of Balad to see if he could explain why they'd found two hundred mortar rounds in the basement of the police station. It was called a THT, or Tactical Human-Intelligence Team, though sometimes he thought Strategic Human Intelligence Team might have made for a more apt acronym. He didn't like it when the team was split. They'd been working well together for months, and had started to anticipate each other's thoughts and needs. He'd said it a million times, beginning when he'd been the top instructor at Intelligence School at Fort Huachuca: "Counterintelligence is a state of mind." Splitting the team disturbed the collective state of mind.

DeLuca thought about the wanted poster. Maybe he could turn it into a positive—having a little celebrity status might help, the next time he was negotiating with a sheikh or tribal leader. MacKenzie had told him he was better looking than Reicken. Was that a flirt? Colleen was attractive, no question, but she was also twenty years his junior, and half the time, he pissed her off. Doc was probably right. "Dave," he'd said, "if you knew half as much about women as you know about counterintelligence, your marriage wouldn't be in the trouble it's in."

"Is bad road," interrupted the man with a thick Arab accent sitting next to DeLuca. The man's name was Adnan, and he'd been with the battalion since they'd left Kuwait, an Iraqi exile and former Intelligence Service liaison with the Republican Guard who'd surrendered during the first Gulf War, after Saddam Hussein's regime had killed his wife and family. He'd worked for the past ten years as a houseboy for a wealthy Kuwaiti family, but he'd jumped at a chance to go back as an informant. Adnan was filled with hatred for the regime, that was clear, but that didn't mean DeLuca trusted him.

"What?" DeLuca could hardly hear Adnan over the din of the Humvee's engine and the rocks and gravel pounding beneath the vehicle.

"Bad road," Adnan shouted again. "The people who live here are all thieves, I think."

DeLuca checked his weapons again. He was armed with a regulation 9mm fifteen-round Beretta model 92S, which he carried in a "Mr. Mike" leg rig, but just in case, he also carried, in a shoulder holster, the same six-inch stainless-steel Smith and Wesson model 66 revolver, loaded with .357 magnum full-jacketed hollow points, that he'd carried during his twenty years on the Boston police force. He carried the revolver because he knew it worked, and because he had a relationship with the piece, a feeling something like, "We've done this before, and we can do it again."

"They're all bad roads," he told Adnan.

The countryside was actually rather lovely, the road lined with date palms and vineyards, and irrigation canals with their water pumps sounding a steady chik-chik-chik. Every house they passed made him nervous, because you never knew who was peeking from the windows, or what sort of arms they might be aiming at you.

"I am ready to die," Adnan said, more or less out of the blue.

"Oh yeah?" DeLuca said.

Adnan nodded.

"Well I'm not," DeLuca told him. "I'm still paying off a dining-room set we got at Filene's."

DeLuca saw women harvesting crops under the hot sun, cultivating with hoes, swinging sickles, even wielding shovels to dig trenches while covered head to toe in full *burquas,* with only the faces of girls under twelve showing. He saw young boys in shorts or *dishdashas* herding goats or sheep. Everybody had ugly feet. It was a nation of people with ugly feet.

"Commence waving and smiling, everybody," he said into the radio. "Sunglasses off if you're looking at anybody. Pearly whites, front and center. Hug hug hug . . ."

Two of the younger boys working in the field waved back at him. It was silly to a lot of people, to Doc and to Dan in particular, but DeLuca firmly believed in presenting a friendly face to the people whose hearts and minds it was their task to win over. Getting tough only created more enemies, and as his mother used to say, "You catch more flies with sugar . . ."

"I think you should ask the CIA for a raise," Adnan said. DeLuca operated "sterile" on CI missions, in a uniform devoid of any insignia that might indicate name, rank, or even branch of service. Most of the people he met, including American officers, assumed he worked for the CIA, calling him only "Mr. David." It was a common misconception that invariably worked in his favor.

"Maybe if we find Saddam's fortune, we can split it," DeLuca said in jest.

"I would spit on Saddam's money," Adnan said.

"So would I," DeLuca said. "Then I'd wipe it off and spend it."

He checked his weapon again. On his very first raid, DeLuca had compulsively double-checked his automatic to make sure he'd chambered a round, imagining fedayeen gunmen with RPGs popping up from behind the stone walls and palm trees like the bad guys in the Desert Storm video games his son played during his sullen teenager period. He was slightly more used to it now.

"Hey Joan-Claude," he radioed to VanDamm, using his nickname for her. "Ask Khalil there how much farther." Khalil was a Kurd, younger than Adnan by ten years and smaller, thin and wiry where Adnan was more solidly built. Khalil was from Sulaymaniyah, on the Iranian border, and a bit of an entrepreneur who'd worked for his uncles smuggling cigarettes and alcohol into Iran as a teenager, leading pack trains through the Zagros mountains, but he'd come south after Operation Iraqi Freedom made it safe for him to do so, looking for opportunities. Khalil supposedly knew the area and had been to Ad-Dujayl before. DeLuca looked ahead, where Mack ("Miss Colleen") and his translator, Sergeant Linda VanDamm, rode in the lead Humvee.

"You should have thought of that before we left," she radioed back. "I'll ask him." She'd served in Frankfurt at the same time DeLuca had, though he hadn't known her there. She was in many ways a seasoned professional, yet she hadn't brushed up on her Arabic since graduating from the Defense Language Institute in Monterey, California. She was married with three kids and should have been home making sandwiches, not pounding down a dirt road between Iraq and a hard place, DeLuca thought.

"He's not sure," she finally said.

"He's not sure how much farther it is?"

"That's what he just said," she replied.

"*Ausgezeichnett,*" DeLuca said. "*Sagt wir sind nicht verloren.*"

"*Wir sind nicht verloren,*" VanDamm radioed back, matching his pidgin German. "*Nür ein bischen upgefucked.* Look at it this way—we don't know where we are, but at least we're making good time."

It was too hot to laugh, nearly 115 degrees in the shade, with a wet-ball of 96 on a 1–100 scale, according to the weather station set up opposite the circle of tents they called home. Everybody had to carry extra water if the wet-ball was above 85. One of the MPs, an undersized kid with a bad complexion, had already taken a bag of glucose just to get himself started. DeLuca had worked as a cop in Yuma, Arizona, after getting out of the service the first time, and thought he knew heat. He didn't. He was dark enough that he didn't sunburn easily, but Colleen, with her fair Scotch-Irish complexion, had to slather on sun block four or five times a day, which made her smell surfer-girlish and reminded DeLuca of all the hotties he'd lusted for as a kid at Jones Beach during summer breaks. The flak vest DeLuca wore only made it worse, adding another fifteen to twenty degrees.

He wiped the sweat from his eyes with his sleeve and opened the Velcro strips on the front of his vest to let the marginally cooler air blow across his drenched DCU blouse. It was standard operating procedure to keep your flak jacket closed on missions, but nobody did. It was also SOP that everybody was supposed to wear their seat belts, but nobody did that either, the common wisdom being that if your vehicle were to come under attack, the faster you could get out of it, the better.

They turned off the main highway and vectored south on a dirt road that paralleled an irrigation canal that drained the Tigris. DeLuca studied his map, trying to figure out where they were. He was tempted to use the sat phone to call his son at IMINT and ask him where they were. Lieutenant Scott DeLuca led a team monitoring imagery collected by one of the many surveillance satellites the Defense Department had quietly placed in orbit above the Middle East after the first Gulf War, and could give DeLuca a precise fix if he wanted one, but DeLuca didn't want to abuse the privilege.

"You look a bit like Tony Orlando," DeLuca told Adnan. "Anybody ever tell you that? You remember Tony

Orlando and Dawn? *Tie a yellow ribbon . . .* No? You ever been to Branson, Missouri?"

"No," Adnan said, shaking his head apologetically.

"You'd love Branson," DeLuca said. He'd taken a vacation there with his wife and hated every minute of it, a fake smile plastered to his face the entire time. "Tony Orlando has his own theater there. People would treat you like a big shot, but you'd have to wear a tuxedo."

They'd dressed Adnan, for his own protection, in an American uniform complete with a camouflaged Kevlar helmet and full battle-rattle and American sunglasses, cheap Ray-Ban knockoffs. DeLuca felt sorry for him, considering what he'd been through. He couldn't imagine losing your wife and child. Adnan had been brought along today because he'd spied for the Iraqi Intelligence Service or "Mukhaberat" back when he'd been a member of the Republican Guard, reporting on any officers showing any disloyalty to the regime. Today they were looking for a man named Omar Hadid, a high-ranking Ba'ath party member and former Mukhaberat official. Hadid was also a sheikh, the tribal leader in Ad-Dujayl and the grandson of the great sheikh Husseini Hadid. DeLuca did not want Omar as much as he wanted the information he could provide. DeLuca's team's mission, for the month since he'd left Kuwait, had been to dismantle what remained of the Mukhaberat—find them (or anybody else on the army's blacklist he happened to come across), arrest them, and start them on their way to Abu Ghraib or Gitmo as captured enemy combatants or, if appropriate, offer them leniency in return for more useful information. He'd popped forty-one former blacklist members so far, including eight faces from the fifty-five on the famous "Deck of Cards." In the opinion of CENTCOM, putting away the Mukhaberat leadership was as crucial to rebuilding Iraq as finding Saddam had been, because of the reputation the agency had earned during Saddam's rule. The head of the Mukhaberat, Izzat Mohammed Al-Tariq, had been killed in the opening days of the war, his compound near the center of Baghdad reduced to a sunken pile of rubble when a half-dozen JDAMs and cruise missiles slammed into it. "The Butcher of Kuwait" was responsible for half the bodies that were still being found in the mass graves surrounding Baghdad. He'd given the order to gas the Kurds during the Anfal campaign in 1988 that killed over one hundred thousand people when Saddam wanted revenge against the Kurds who'd sided with Iran during the Iran-Iraq War. Al-Tariq had personally ordered the torture of thousands of individuals, particularly during and after the invasion of Kuwait in 1990, such that the government of Kuwait had put a bounty on his head, one-365th of Kuwait's gross national product, or about $30 million, to the man who assassinated him. His preferred method of torture, according to reports, was to disembowel his victims in front of their families. Another story, unconfirmed, said Al-Tariq had kept thousands of his victims' body parts preserved in formaldehyde jars in a private collection, and that he'd often gotten his victims to reveal what they knew simply by walking them through it. Some of the things Al-Tariq had done were said to have sickened Saddam himself—he was the psychopath Saddam kept on a chain to intimidate the other madmen under his command. Adnan had been one of Al-Tariq's bodyguards, but only for a month.

Even with Al-Tariq gone, DeLuca's mission remained important because the Mukhaberat had been the only agency Saddam had trusted to hide his weapons of mass destruction. The men who'd worked for Al-Tariq would know where Saddam's WMD—if he had any—had gone.

DeLuca was taking a drink from a bottle of water— "From the Cool Springs of Saudi Arabia," the label said— when suddenly the convoy stopped.

After a few seconds, he got on his radio.

This was no place for something to be wrong.

"What's up, Mack?" he asked. "Why are we stopped?"

"We're here, I think," Mack said. He heard VanDamm's Arabic in the background.

"What do you mean, 'We're here'? We're where?"

"That's the house," Mack radioed back. "Right in front of us."

It took him a split second to realize what had happened. Standard procedure was to stop well away from a target to study the "falcon view" first, a composite photograph of the latest satellite imagery, enlarged so that each squad leader had a picture. The next step was to reconnoiter from at least half a kilometer away with binoculars, then form a 360-degree cordon with an armored vehicle on each side, and *then* move in. What you didn't want to do, if you could help it, was drive right up to a house full of trouble in broad daylight and stop. There'd evidently been a communication failure.

"Out of the vehicles, everybody!" he commanded.

He pushed Adnan out the door and bailed out his own side, scrambling twenty yards to the wall surrounding the compound. He looked back toward the vehicles. Nobody was moving.

"Get the fuck out and take cover!" he shouted again. "Now!"

Mack and VanDamm exited the lead vehicle, dragging Khalil with them. Mack was quick and light on her feet. VanDamm wasn't. The MPs were slow to react, their progress hastened when somebody on the top floor of the house suddenly opened fire on them from a window with what appeared to be a Kalashnikov.

As he ducked, DeLuca heard a burst of shots ring out and felt pieces of splintered wall rain down on him.

The SAW gunner on the second Humvee swung his M-60 around and opened up on the house, shattering brick and mortar, sending up a shower of stucco and ceramic roof tiles, soon joined by the gunner on the third vehicle, both men firing so rapidly that there was not the staccato stutter familiarly associated with WWII-era machine guns, just a steady horrific roar, until DeLuca could see daylight coming through a hole in the top right corner of the building where the gunman had been.

DeLuca took the opportunity to run to where the MP noncommissioned officer in charge (NCOIC), a first sergeant named Carter, had taken cover.

"Sergeant Carter—who's got the back of the house?" DeLuca asked.

"No one," Carter said, as if the idea of surrounding a house you were trying to capture was something that hadn't occurred to him.

"Where are the Bradleys?" DeLuca asked.

Again, the MP didn't know. DeLuca turned and saw them, holding position a quarter klick up the road.

Somebody had to do something.

"As of now, I'm in charge of this mission," DeLuca said. "Do you understand?"

Carter nodded.

DeLuca pointed to Mack and to VanDamm, used two fingers to point to his own eyes, then pointed to the Hummers, finally gesturing with his Beretta to tell them they were to stay with the vehicles. "Keep our friends with you," he added into his team radio, one of six walkie-talkies he'd purchased out of pocket at Radio Shack at $150 a pair before leaving Massachusetts, knowing how the army tended to underequip the National Guard.

VanDamm held up her walkie-talkie to indicate it wasn't working, which made no sense since he'd put fresh batteries in before leaving Balad. He scrambled over to where they were crouched with the two informants. The SAW gunner opened up on the house again as he ran, though no further shots came from the residence.

"I'm sorry," VanDamm shouted when DeLuca reached her. She looked terrified on this, her first mission away from post, but she was holding it together. "It got turned off somehow. It's working now." Mack looked frightened but was trying hard not to show it, her dark eyes darting behind her goggles as she bit her lip, her nostrils flared. "Do you need me inside?" Linda VanDamm asked.

"I'll take Ciccarelli," DeLuca said, referring to the young specialist fresh out of DLI whom they'd picked up for the trip. "I need you and Mack to stay here and make sure our boys don't get scratched up." Adnan did not seem frightened. Perhaps he truly was prepared to die. DeLuca turned to Khalil. "You're sure this is the house? One hundred percent positive?"

"Yes," Khalil said.

"Well, that's a fucking relief," DeLuca muttered under his breath. The SAW gun opened up again. DeLuca stayed down, taking the opportunity to scramble back to the MPs, where he shouted above the roar.

"Sergeant Carter—pick five people to secure the rear of the compound, and put three on each side. On the wall. Pick two more per and tell them to secure the vehicles. My girls are going to be staying with them—I don't want to see a hair on their heads out of place when I get back. I want the SAWs manned, and cordon the house. If they had RPGs, they would have used them by now." He pointed to the armored personnel carriers. "Bradleys, one behind the house and one on each side. That's one, two, and three," he pointed. "Do it now! Tell the rest of your MPs to come with me."

He scrambled to the front gate, where he was met by Specialist Ciccarelli, his translator, and the remaining MPs. Ciccarelli looked like a younger version of himself. A few of the MPs were so baby-faced they could have been carded on a Ferris wheel. Nearly all of them were either Army Reserve or National Guard, most of them with families and all of them probably wondering what the hell they were doing in Iraq while all the regular army military policemen were back home writing traffic tickets at stateside army bases.

The weapons fire from the house seemed to have stopped. DeLuca's intuition told him it was a single shooter and not an organized defense.

"I want you and you at the front window, you on the right, and you on the left," he said. "Everybody else goes in with me. Spread out. On my signal. Who's the kicker?"

A Latino MP the size of an NFL lineman with the name Arroyo on his breast raised his hand. At five feet ten inches and 185 pounds, DeLuca was not his own first choice for the job, though he'd done it before. Ordinarily he used Dan, a six-foot-four, 230-pound karate instructor from San Francisco.

"Where'd you learn?" DeLuca asked the MP.

"LAPD academy, sir."

"Okay. You're on the door. I'm first in. Carter, you're high, I'm low. On the window, stun then cover. Go!"

The MPs spread out down the compound wall, about six feet high with smaller gates at the corners, the wall the same cocoa brown stucco as the house, topped by ceramic tiles. DeLuca tossed his canteen across the front gate to make sure it didn't draw fire. He backed up a few feet and gave the signal, holding three fingers high, checking to make sure all eyes were on him. He surveyed the building one more time, held up two fingers, then one, and then he pointed toward the house.

Chapter Two

PAST THE GATE, DELUCA CROUCHED LOW AND rushed the thirty yards until he found cover behind a black Mercedes 750SL. Parked behind it was a white Toyota pickup truck with a red stripe running along the molding. Word at the post was, always hide behind the Mercedes. The tires shone and smelled of Armor-All. DeLuca's heart thumped in his chest. He took a deep breath, then rushed the door.

His back against the wall, he caught his breath. The others were right behind him.

"You okay?" Arroyo asked him.

He looked at the man. When he'd decided to reenlist after 9/11, he'd gotten into the best shape of his life, lifting weights and running five miles a day, dropping twenty pounds in the process, but all the same, the younger guys looked at him like they expected him to keel over any minute. Maybe it was the hint of gray in his hair.

"Ask me that again and I'll beat you like a piñata," he said, smiling.

He signaled the soldiers at the window to ready their stun grenades, each set with a five-second delay. DeLuca looked at Arroyo, who nodded and told him with his eyes that he was ready. The key to kicking in a door was to hit it one-fifth of the distance between the bolt and the opposite jamb. Too close to the center and the door bends to absorb the shock. Too close to the bolt and you'd break your foot.

The windows were open. There was no screen.

DeLuca gave the ready signal.

He thought a moment, then sent Ciccarelli to the window, where the translator shouted, as per DeLuca's orders, "Women and children clear the room now!"

DeLuca signaled go. Even through the door, the percussion from the stun grenades hurt his ears. He hoped whoever was inside had heeded his warning.

At the same moment, Arroyo stepped back a few feet from the front door, then kicked.

The door collapsed inward. DeLuca jumped across the frame from right to left, his sidearm leading the way, as Carter X'ed in behind him. He covered the room quickly. His eye fell on a shape in the corner of the room. He nearly fired before realizing he would have shot a large urn, mounted on a pedestal. They were in the house's great room. He saw a tan leather couch, a table with six chairs, a grand piano, a Persian rug, and a massive swamp cooler in the back window braced by a pair of potted palms. The house smelled of cordite and dust, the air stirred by a slowly rotating ceiling fan.

"Clear," Carter shouted.

A door led to a kitchen, another to what appeared to be a library. DeLuca pointed to six MPs and told them with sign language to investigate, three to each room. Once the dust settled, he thought he smelled food cooking in the kitchen.

There was a staircase against the far wall leading upstairs. He'd just assigned four MPs to search the upstairs when he heard a noise from above. He had raised his weapon, about to fire, when an AK-47 came clattering down the steps, momentarily startling him.

"Don't shoot!" a voice upstairs said. "Please."

"Do you speak English?" DeLuca called out.

"I speak English. Please, don't shoot. We are not armed. Please."

DeLuca moved to the bottom of the stairs and stood off to the side, his Beretta raised, and looked up, where he saw a man, about forty, and a young boy, perhaps eleven or twelve, trembling and terrified, both with their hands high in the air. He kept his Beretta trained on them, looking behind them to see if anyone else was there.

"How many people in the house?" he asked.

"Just us," the man said. "And the women."

"How many women?"

"Four," the man said. "Two are my wives. And a sister-in-law, and a daughter."

DeLuca looked over as three MPs exited the library.

"It's clear," one said.

DeLuca spoke into the walkie-talkie he'd bought at Radio Shack. "Miss Colleen, I'm going to need you in here to search the women. You four, upstairs when Miss Colleen gets here—only she touches the women."

He returned his attention to the men at the top of the stairs.

"I want you to come down with yours hands on the railing. Now! Don't take your hands off the railing." He turned to Specialist Ciccarelli. "Tell the women they have to go to the library. Quickly."

Ciccarelli translated, shouting up the stairs.

The man descended with his son. DeLuca made them lie on the floor, searched them, and bound their hands behind their backs with flex cuffs. He elected not to throw sandbags over their heads because he wanted the older man to see that none of his women were touched or otherwise harmed.

Ciccarelli gave another order and four figures descended the stairs, clad in black *burquas* and sandals. DeLuca kept his gun trained on them. Only the daughter's face showed. She was about eight, an exquisitely beautiful child with long dark eyelashes. DeLuca held the library door open for them, making sure not to scrutinize them too closely. He posted an MP to stand in the doorway and guard the women.

The four MPs who'd searched the upstairs came down and told him it was clear. He asked them to search the entire compound, thoroughly and carefully, but to respect the property. Too many infantry division squads with ID methods and ID mentalities had trampled crops, broken dishes, driven Bradleys through people's front doors, or crushed Mercedes-Benzes with their tanks while on missions, operating with a brutishness as old as war itself, but that didn't help DeLuca win the confidence of the people he questioned.

He left Carter to stand guard just inside the front door. He looked in the kitchen, then took off his flak vest and his helmet, dropping them on the floor by a back door that led out onto a patio. In a small bathroom off the kitchen, he closed the door behind him, then splashed water on his face, ran his wet hands over the top over his close-cropped scalp, and dried himself with a hand towel. When he looked in the mirror, he noticed anew the resemblance he bore to his twin sister, Elaine, and then he remembered why he was here. She'd been one of the best legal secretaries the law firm of Eslen & Winnicott ever had, but Eslen & Winnicott happened to have their offices on the ninety-seventh floor of the south tower of the World Trade Center, where she'd been working the morning of September 11, 2001. "Look at this view," she'd told him when he'd visited her office to take her out to lunch on their last birthday. "You don't get much closer to heaven than this."

Well, he'd thought after the towers went down, *actually, you do, Elaine—you do.*

He picked up his gun and returned to the great room, where Mack told him the women had been searched. He helped the man and the boy to their feet, handling them roughly because he wanted them to understand that he was angry. It was a simple enough idea, a technique he'd learned during his time on the job back home, starting an interrogation in anger and calming down. It worked much better than the other way around, and it seemed to work on Iraqi bad guys as well as it worked on all the crackheads, car thieves, and burglars back in Massachusetts.

"Let's sit over here where we can talk," he said, holstering his weapon as he gestured. He drew a deep breath. "Please."

The man and the boy sat cross-legged on the Persian rug. DeLuca let them stew a minute while he examined the photographs on the wall, portraits of old men in *agals* and *dishdashas* holding swords and one grainy old sepia-tone of an Iraqi wearing a heavy wool British WWI doughboy uniform, standing in the bright sunlight next to an elegantly dressed white woman in a pith helmet. He pointed to the photograph and looked to the man, who informed him it was a picture of his grandfather with Dame Edith Warner, the last British governor of colonial Iraq. DeLuca raised his eyebrows to say he was impressed, knowing how much Iraqi men liked to brag about their ancestors.

Finally he sat opposite them, taking care not to show his prisoners, who were technically also his hosts, the soles of his feet, which was considered a serious insult. It was also considered bad manners to get directly to the point without a certain amount of banter first. He'd lectured on the need to make small talk when he'd been an instructor at counterintelligence school at Fort Devin, and he'd even given a briefing at the post when it was clear that some guys weren't getting it—talk about their families, talk about women to the men and children to the women, talk about the hardships everybody suffered during the boycott, establish a relationship first. Don't act like you're in a hurry.

"You must be very proud of your family's accomplishments," he said at last.

"My grandfather was with the British at Gallipoli," the man said. "He was a great sheikh."

"These are your family vineyards?" DeLuca asked. "And the grapes you grow are for wine?"

"Yes," the man said. "We sell them to the French."

"Was the weather favorable this year?"

"The weather, yes. But we have had trouble keeping the pumps for the irrigation going, with the power outages."

"Are you Omar Hadid?" DeLuca asked.

"I am Ali ibn Hadid al Dujayl," the man replied. "I am chief of police. Omar is my brother."

"And who is this?"

"This is my son Kamel," Ali Hadid said. "Omar is his uncle." Kamel was a good-looking kid with big ears and a spray of freckles across his nose. His head lowered, he looked up at DeLuca. Kamel wore a long one-piece white tunic. Ali wore black pants and a white shirt.

"Please," the older man said. "We are of no danger to you."

When the older man spoke, he glanced around and leaned forward conspiratorially as if the room was bugged, a fairly common habit, DeLuca had come to understand, in a country where one out of every twenty people had been employed in the security apparatus, and everybody seemed quite comfortable snitching on everybody else.

"Where'd you learn English?"

"I lived in London for a time," Ali said. "I was in college there."

DeLuca turned his attention to the boy.

"Were you the one who was shooting at us, Kamel? Was he the one shooting at us?" he said to Ali. "You tell me you pose no threat and yet your son was shooting at us." Neither father nor son spoke, but from their silence, DeLuca knew it had been Kamel. "Were you trying to kill me and my friends?"

"Please," Ali said. "He did not know."

"What do you mean, he didn't know? Don't try to tell me he didn't know. Are you a terrorist, Kamel? Are you Al Qaeda? Are you Fedayeen Saddam?"

"Please, no," the father said. "He is just a boy."

DeLuca summoned his fiercest glare. The fact was, the kid was just protecting his home and family. DeLuca's intuition told him Kamel was not a terrorist or potential suicide bomber, yet each interrogation dealt you a different hand of cards, and these were the cards DeLuca had to play. The father feared for his son. That fear was something DeLuca could use.

"Well," he said. "Boy or not, he fired a weapon at us and he'll need to account for that. Sergeant Carter. Take the prisoner, please. Get him ready for transport."

This was another trick of the trade—never specify a threat. Leave a blank and let the person being interrogated fill it in. They were bound to imagine something worse than you could.

Ali watched his son leave. The look on his face was beyond concerned.

DeLuca asked him to give him the names of the women who were locked up in the library. Ali's daughter was named Nida. The sister-in-law was named Suher.

"And you have two wives?" DeLuca asked.

"Amina and Samir," Ali Hadid said.

"You must have great endurance," DeLuca said. "I don't know how you Iraqi men do it."

Ali smiled.

DeLuca had yet to meet an Iraqi male who didn't respond to having his machismo sensibilities flattered. Sometimes the best approach was to ask direct questions, while other times, the wiser course was to kick back and wait for the subject to volunteer information. DeLuca had Kamel cooling his heels in a Humvee. Ali wanted him back.

"Do you think you'd find it easier to talk to me if I unbound your hands?" he asked.

"Please," Ali said.

DeLuca took the Gerber knife from his belt pouch and used it to cut away the flex cuffs, plastic strips not unlike the ties used to close garbage bags but with a loop at both ends.

"Would you like something to eat or drink?" Ali asked, once his hands were free. "If you would let Amina and the others from the library, I will have them bring you something. Please."

DeLuca knew that one mistake a lot of American officers had been making had been to refuse offers of hospitality, saying, "I don't have time for this." The principle of hospitality in Arab cultures was ancient, derived from the harsh desert climate, where anybody was likely to find himself suddenly in need of shelter or water. For DeLuca, it was just common sense to go along with local customs.

"Thank you," DeLuca said. "Just something to drink, though." He told Ciccarelli to let the women out of the library.

"Is he your son?" Ali asked.

DeLuca shook his head.

"All us Italians look alike. This is a beautiful house. Is it yours?"

"No," Ali admitted. "It is my brother's."

"Omar's?"

"Yes. We have been watching it for him while he is away. Since the war began. You know, there have been looters. Many places are not safe."

Through the window, DeLuca saw the MPs searching the yard. To his chagrin, one of the Bradleys had driven up to the compound's wall, but the soldiers from the Fourth Infantry who occupied it hadn't gotten out of the vehicle. What were they waiting for?

One of Ali's wives returned with a pitcher of water and a basin. She set the basin on the floor before the American. DeLuca held out his hands and let the woman pour water over them. She offered him a towel, and he dried his hands, and then the woman went and did the same for her husband. A second woman brought a tray bearing two glass teacups, an inch of refined sugar in the bottom of each, and then she filled the cups with hot chai from a teapot. Ali added another three or four tablespoons of sugar to his cup. When he was offered a glass of ice water, DeLuca accepted even though they'd been warned not to drink the water. He could always take an extra doxycycline later.

Mack knocked on the door to report that the grounds had been secured. DeLuca asked her to stay by snapping his fingers and pointing to a spot by the door. He saw her stiffen when he snapped his fingers. Ali smiled in appreciation at the way DeLuca commanded his female. It was a ruse DeLuca and MacKenzie had worked before, but not one she particularly cared for. He tried to apologize by winking at her when Ali wasn't looking, but she only glared at him. It still wasn't half the look his wife would be giving him under the same circumstances.

"If I could," Ali said. "I would speak to you alone."

"Miss Colleen will stay," DeLuca said. "I may need her help."

"Tell me," Ali said, pausing. "Is it Captain? Or Major? Colonel?"

"You can call me 'Mr. David,'" DeLuca said.

"Do you have children, Mr. David?" Ali asked.

"No, I don't," DeLuca lied.

"If you did, you would know. Boys Kamel's age do foolish things," Ali pleaded. "If I had known he had the weapon . . . he did not know any better."

DeLuca paused, giving Ali time to wonder what his answer was going to be.

"I think we were all very lucky today," DeLuca said. "It would have been very easy for somebody to get hurt. I'm glad no one in your family was hurt, and I'm glad that none of my men were hurt. But when somebody fires at my soldiers, I must protect them. Your son is going to have to go through the system. He'll be processed at Balad and we'll just have to wait and see what happens next," DeLuca said, rising to go.

The fake walk-away was another useful technique, one he'd learned watching his wife dicker for prices at flea markets, the undisputed queen of the tag sale bargain.

"Please," Ali said. "You must understand that I am in a very difficult position. This house is being watched. If I am seen to cooperate with you, there are many who would kill me. But if I don't help you, you will take my son. I care only about my family."

"What I can do for you," DeLuca said, "depends entirely on what you can do for me. I also have to bring what you give me back to my commanders, if I'm going to try to persuade them to help me. It has to be a trade. I need to talk to your brother. We're trying to take apart the Mukhaberat. We're trying to find the people who worked for Izzat Mohammed Al-Tariq."

He thought he noticed Ali visibly flinch. He'd played enough poker to know a tell when he saw one.

"And I know your brother worked with him. And that he was a member of the Ba'ath party. Were you a member of the Ba'ath party, abu Kamel?"

Ali hesitated. By addressing him as Father of Kamel, DeLuca was underscoring the point that Ali needed to cooperate if he wanted to help his son. Ali nodded.

"But we all were. It was the only way to survive under Saddam. It is exactly as you've said. Everything is a trade. If you were not with them, they would assume you were against them. You see."

"I do," DeLuca said. "Was your brother Mukhaberat?"

Again Ali hesitated before nodding.

"But it was not his choice. Under Saddam, one could not appear to stand outside the government. Omar is sheikh. He leads the tribe. For his people's sake, he is Ba'ath, he is Mukhaberat, but not for himself. He is not for Saddam. He saw that Saddam got his payments from the embargo runners who came from Syria. That's all."

DeLuca said nothing. He'd heard this from virtually everyone he arrested, "I wasn't working for Saddam—I was working to overthrow him . . ." yada yada yada.

"We had a report that your brother is starting a new Hezbul Ba'ath. You know we can't allow him to do that, don't you?"

"It is not Ba'ath," Ali said. "He is trying to organize the people of this area, that is all. There is no government here. He works to get electricity and fresh water. They need a place to hold school, so he makes the arrangements. Without my brother, it would be chaos. You will ask him and he will tell you himself."

"Do you know where your brother is?"

Ali didn't answer.

"I want you to tell your brother he has to be at the front gate at Balad Air Force post at noon. Twelve o'clock sharp." He took the notepad from his shirt pocket and wrote on it, ripping the page out and handing it to Ali. "This is a hall pass. Have him show this at the gate and tell him to ask for Mr. David, and someone will bring him to me. And don't try to tell me you don't know how to reach him, because I know that's not true. Do you understand?"

"Yes," Ali said. "Will you arrest my brother?"

"I don't know," DeLuca lied again. "Right now we just want to talk to him."

DeLuca sensed a note of renewed panic in Ali's demeanor.

"Please," he pleaded. "If you take my brother, no one will protect us. Please . . ."

"As I explained, I can't help you unless you help me," DeLuca said. It was just a hunch, but he suspected the man had more to tell him. "You have to give me something I can work with. So far, I have nothing."

"I can do that," Ali said after considering his options, glancing toward the others in the room. "But I must speak with you alone. Please."

DeLuca thought a moment, then gestured to Carter and Ciccarelli to wait for him in the kitchen. He told Mack to go keep VanDamm company. When they were alone, Ali spoke again, choosing his words carefully.

"I am forced to trust you," he said. "I do have information. Valuable information, but I must only give it to somebody in authority. I must be careful who I give it to. I don't mean to insult you."

DeLuca had heard this tune before, too, people trying to play up the importance of what they were about to say, to increase their bargaining power.

"You deal with me," DeLuca said. "I am the ultimate authority in this matter. It doesn't go any higher than me."

"I understand," Ali said. "You are CIA, yes?" DeLuca did not respond. Ali sighed, closing his eyes a moment. "I have no choice, but it is dangerous. In exchange you must promise me you will take care of my family. That is all I will ask. I don't care about myself. You must protect them. Because I no longer can, and if you take my brother . . . My family cannot stay in Iraq. They have no future here. For a while I had hope, but now . . . I want you to take them to the United States. This your government must do for me. I do not ask for my wives or myself. I ask only for my son and daughter."

"I can't make you any promises," DeLuca said. "Other than to promise to try. It all depends on what you give me."

Ali considered his options. DeLuca suspected they were few.

"You say you are looking for Mohammed Al-Tariq. Yes?"

"We're looking for his people," DeLuca said. "Al-Tariq is dead."

Ali stared at him. "He is not dead," he said.

Now DeLuca paused. Despite his skepticism, the enormity of the statement, if true, was significant.

"I'd be interested to know what it is that makes you say that," he said. "Because as far as I know, the proof that he's dead is pretty conclusive."

"Tell me—how do you know?" Ali asked.

The details were still classified, and DeLuca knew better than to reveal them to Ali, but he limned the general facts for the Iraqi policeman. Special Ops had infiltrated Al-Tariq's household and collected both his DNA and his fingerprints before the bombing, to assist in subsequent identification. The Third Infantry follow-on had combed the rubble and discovered Al-Tariq's fingerprints on a shoulder-fired Russian SAM-7 antiaircraft weapon, as well as pieces of human flesh from which they'd taken tissue samples, sent to the Criminal Investigations Division lab at Fort Gillem in Georgia. The CID report came back that the tissue samples matched Al-Tariq's. There were plenty of dubious kills, but this wasn't one of them. Al-Tariq was gone. Of that, there was no doubt.

"I can tell you that we have the DNA," DeLuca said. "There really isn't any question."

Ali shook his head.

"You can believe what your laboratories tell you," he said. "I will believe what my eyes and ears tell me. I know he is alive because he was here, three nights ago. With three of his men. Omar does not know they were here. They move from house to house. They don't ask permission, and they will kill whoever tells of it."

DeLuca couldn't guess what sort of angle Ali was playing.

"So he was here then?" he said. "And three men?" Ali nodded. "Did you learn their names?" Ali shook his head. "You'd never seen them before?" Ali again shook his head. "What did they talk about?"

"This is why I must tell you," Ali said. "Because my son was here, even though I told him to stay away from these men. And they said, 'Kamel, we would like you to be a martyr for Allah.' Would he like to be *a Wajeh*? Would he be one of the Thousand Faces of Allah? But Mr. David, I swear to you, this is not the Islam that Kamel was raised in. My brother and I have both lived in the West. Kamel was born in England. Omar says those who think that to be pro-Islam one must be anti-Western are ignorant of the Koran. So I sent Kamel away. I told him heaven does not admit assassins. This is what Al-Tariq is doing."

"Recruiting suicide bombers?" DeLuca asked.

"Martyrs, yes," Ali said. "He has billions of dollars in United States cash that he has hidden before the war, I think. Years before. It is his money that is training the insurgents now. His money is paying the families of the martyrs. Once it was Saddam and Al-Durri but now Al-Tariq has taken over. He will pay their family half now and half when the thing is done. This is what they said."

"When what thing is done?" DeLuca asked.

"When the Thousand Faces of Allah have become martyrs," Ali said, glancing suspiciously about again, nearly whispering. "I must explain it to you carefully. This you must know. He is not just recruiting them. He is giving them weapons. Weapons of mass destruction. He has done it. You want to know why you cannot find them? They are gone. They are in the hands of a thousand assassins. *Al-Alf Wajeh.* The Thousand Faces of Allah. Did you think they didn't know you were coming? They've known for years this war would come. Did you think they would just sit and wait for you to come find them? What did you think they were doing these last five years, while your inspectors were looking for these terrible things? Now one hundred thousand of you are looking, and you find only empty shells. Where did the contents go? Why did Saddam not use these weapons of mass destruction when your tanks were rolling into Baghdad? Because they have already been deployed. I think perhaps they are already in your country. I don't know the details. But by the way they spoke, I believe it has begun. *Lanatullah.* The curse of God."

All right, DeLuca thought. *Now you're starting to scare me.*

"Lanatullah?" he said. "This is what they were calling it?"

Ali nodded.

"'Laen Allah is in the land of the infidels,'" Ali said. "I heard them say these exact words."

DeLuca considered. There'd been a constant stream of threats, coming from all kinds of sources on virtually a daily basis, saying, in effect, "We will avenge the occupation . . . we will destroy you . . ." etc. Playing the WMD card was nothing new or noteworthy.

This was qualitatively different.

"So why were they telling you all this?" DeLuca asked. "Why confide in you?"

"They wanted my help," Ali said. Ali bit his lip and, for a moment, appeared to be ashamed. "They did not come to me because they thought I was their friend. They came to me because they thought I would be too afraid to say no. I know Al-Tariq. I was interrogated myself by Mukhaberat once. If they knew I was telling you all this . . ."

He didn't have to finish the thought.

"I understand your concerns," DeLuca said. "I can tell that you're trying to be truthful with me, but I also have to consider the proof we have that Al-Tariq is dead. I don't know how to reconcile that with what you're saying."

"Do you want proof that he is alive?" Ali said. "That he was here?"

"You have proof?" DeLuca said.

Ali asked to go upstairs. DeLuca sent Carter with him. When Ali returned, he was carrying a small package, something wrapped inside a white cloth. Ali set the package down in front of DeLuca, who untied the string holding it together and unfolded the white handkerchief. Inside, he found two pieces of paper, rolled into tubes with the ends folded over. Inside the tubes, he found a pair of syringes.

Using the handkerchief, he picked up one of the syringes, holding it to the light. It contained a clear watery liquid. He held the syringe under his nose and sniffed. The syringe smelled strongly of rubber, like a tire's inner tube. It was also the smell of insulin. Elaine had come down with Type 1 juvenile onset diabetes when she was eight. DeLuca knew the aroma because he'd squirted some of his sister's insulin onto his tongue once, thinking it was going to taste like sugar.

According to the files he'd read, Izzat Mohammed Al-Tariq was also diabetic.

"Can I keep these?" he asked. Ali nodded.

"Mr. David," Ali said. "You must promise me you will not fail. I think . . . I think this is a very serious matter."

"I will treat it seriously," he said. "I can promise you that."

"You don't understand," Ali said, leaning forward again and lowering his voice. "I must tell you this. Some years ago, before I was a police officer in Ad-Dujayl, I was in charge of security for a division of the Mukhaberat, at a place called the Muthanna State Establishment. Have you heard of it?"

DeLuca nodded. Muthanna was a biological and chemical weapons plant, second in size only to the Al-Hakam facility that UNSCOM had closed down in 1996. Muthanna, 120 kilometers northwest of Baghdad, had been heavily damaged during the Gulf War and inspected several times thereafter, by UNSCOM and by David Kay's boys. It had at one time been capable of producing weapons-grade biological and chemical material, but it had been shut down since 1994. DeLuca said as much. Ali nodded.

"Yes, it was destroyed," he said. "But only after the equipment was moved, to a place called Al Manal. Also called the Daura Foot and Mouth Disease Facility. Have you heard of this?"

DeLuca shook his head.

"Al Manal was top secret. I do not know what was done there," Ali continued. "But you must ask about the Jamrat Project. The security needs for this were beyond anything else."

"*Rami el Jamrat.* Throwing Stones at the Devil," De-Luca said. *Rami el Jamrat* was the name of the ceremony pilgrims on the hajj performed. Ali nodded. With a finger, he sketched out a diagram on the rug before him of Al Manal to illustrate his story.

"They built a facility. Under the ground. In the southeast part of Baghdad. We were told not to allow anyone near it. It was a top-grade containment laboratory, designed by the Russians. And the men who built it, I believe they were killed afterward. That is how important the secret was. After that, we did not ask. Project Jamrat was something terrible. I don't know what the weapon was, but I believe it was never destroyed, and I believe it is what Al-Tariq intends to use. It was his money that built it. My sense was that it was kept secret even from Saddam. When Saddam's own cousin came, we were told not to let him near it."

"I'll make it my top priority," DeLuca said. Part of him felt as if he'd just been told a ghost story. The other part of him was scared.

The first thing he would do, when he got back to base, would be to read Al-Tariq's file again. The second thing would be to have the syringes tested—if Al-Tariq had used them, they would contain traces of his DNA, which could be analyzed and compared to previous samples. If that suggested Al-Tariq was still alive, *then* he'd worry in earnest.

DeLuca went to the window to assess the situation. A crowd of about thirty people had gathered around the Humvees. He told Ali they were going to need to put on a show, lest onlookers think he was cooperating. Ali understood. DeLuca told Ali that at some point, he was going to have to report to the post and tell his story again. From that point on, he probably wouldn't be able to go home again, so he needed to get everybody ready.

"You've done the right thing," DeLuca told him. "I think we'll be able to work something out."

"I will explain to Kamel," Ali added.

DeLuca summoned Carter and Ciccarelli from the kitchen, asked the translator to open the front door, then threw Ali through it.

"Do *not* shoot at United States soldiers!" DeLuca growled at him dramatically, loud enough for everyone gathered to hear. "Do you *understand* me?"

He manhandled the prisoner into the vehicle, after which he dusted himself off.

He took one last look around the courtyard, then climbed back into the Humvee for the ride home. When Specialist Ciccarelli asked permission to return to the house to retrieve something he'd dropped, DeLuca told him to hurry it up. He watched Ciccarelli stoop down in the garden, stand up again, and hold something above his head to indicate he'd found what he was looking for. He smiled. Through his binoculars, DeLuca could see that Ciccarelli held a photograph of a girl in his hand.

Then Ciccarelli's head exploded, throwing a spray of blood up against the side of the house. A split second later, DeLuca heard the report from the sniper's rifle.

As the raiding party quickly deployed to cover, DeLuca crouched low beside the Humvee, but there was no further gunfire. Two MPs rushed to where the translator had fallen, and one made a cursory slashing gesture toward his own throat to signal that the young man was dead. Carter ordered his men to fan out into the nearby countryside as DeLuca scanned the surrounding hills with his binoculars, to no avail.

When Carter established an "all clear," an infantryman returned to DeLuca with a piece of paper he'd found tacked to the tree, about a quarter mile off, from which the sniper had apparently fired. He showed it to DeLuca. It was the wanted poster DeLuca had seen earlier that morning.

As DeLuca mounted the Humvee and headed back to Camp Anaconda, he knew full well what the attack had meant. Most Iraqi snipers were incompetent, poor marksmen who rarely allowed for windage or calculated for elevation, and few ever used sniper rounds. Judging from the severity of the damage done, this was clearly a large-caliber soft-pointed shell fired from a high-velocity rifle with a telescopic sight, the weapon wielded by someone who knew what he was doing. Someone who wanted to claim the reward.

Ciccarelli had died because the drawing looked more like him than it did like DeLuca. *"Dear Mr. and Mrs. Ciccarelli,"* DeLuca would have to write, *"The United States Army regrets to inform you . . ."* He wouldn't have to tell them how unnecessary or unfair their son's death had been—they would already know that.

DeLuca had been the target.

This meant that whoever shot at him had been given information about his movements and his mission. The only people who'd known what his mission was going to be were the people in the raiding party—but none of them had been told where they were going—and a handful of personnel who'd been in the TOC that morning.

This meant that somebody inside the wire was willing to sell him out.

In other words, there was a traitor on the post.

Chapter Three

WITH HIS NEATLY TRIMMED SALT-AND-PEPPER beard, his silver hair swept back from a receding hairline, his gunmetal three-thousand-dollar Italian-cut Fazioli suit, his silk five-hundred-dollar charcoal Gregg d'Arcy tie, and his pale gray eyes, the man at the center of attention at the Harvard Club, on Commonwealth Avenue in Boston, Massachusetts, looked as if he'd been forged from solid steel. He was, as anyone who met him soon discovered, impressive, despite his short stature, charismatic, a man whom women were drawn to and men envied. Since 9/11, his phones, at home and at the university where he lectured, had not stopped ringing with requests for him to appear on talk shows, news programs, roundtables, think-tanks, panels, and academic seminars, everyone wanting to know the same thing—why did the Arabs hate the Americans so? He'd done his best to explain, though he didn't like trafficking in generalities. What he never said was, "If you have to ask that question, you'll never understand."

"Professor Mahmoud Jaburi," the woman next to him was saying, "I'd like to introduce you to three of my best students. This is Nada Rashad, Buthaina ib-Yaakub, and Shamika Johnson Muhammed. I was just telling Nada . . ." The woman prattled on, while Jaburi pretended to be listening. He smelled alcohol on her breath, even though he'd been quite specific that he would only attend an alcohol-free reception. Had she not been his host as one of the Kennedy School of Government's deans, he would have walked away, but he could not, so he smiled politely as she spoke, twisting the ring on his finger behind his back and shifting his weight from heel to heel.

"I wanted to tell you, professor," the shortest of the three girls said, "that I've found your comparison of the *Muwatta of Ibn Malik* with the *Musnad of Ahmad ibn Hanbal* to be extremely relevant to my own studies in international law. I have been trying to convince my department that it should be a required text."

"That is very kind of you to say," he replied. "Some schools can't even teach the five pillars correctly. I know of one where *Sahih Bukhari* is not part of the curriculum. So first things first, I believe."

"Shamika spent a semester in Riyadh working on the Sunna Project for the HSA," the dean said, putting her hand on the back of a black girl and urging her to step forward. The black girl was wearing a head scarf, like the other two, tan, though black would have been more respectful and appropriate. He hoped she would not be another one of those irritating American Black Muslims who were constantly foisting their opinions on him.

"Do you speak Arabic?" he asked her. She lowered her eyes.

"Oh, no," she said humbly enough. "Very little. But I do speak HTML. I was working with the English translations anyway. Mostly just a lot of coding and data entry, but it was a fascinating experience."

"And whose translations were you working with?" he inquired, referencing the continuing project to create a searchable database of all the sayings and deeds of Mohammad.

"Abdul Hamid Khan and M. Muhsin Siddiqui," the girl named Shamika replied. "And a number of lesser translators."

"Shamika is a published poet," the dean interrupted. "She told me she was surprised at the amount of latitude she was given to utilize her own English language skills." Jaburi considered explaining to the woman that the Koran and its adjuncts were living documents, but he decided instead to ignore her.

"And do you approve of the website currently entering all 880,000 nonauthenticated *Hadith* outside the *Sahih*?" he asked the black girl. The *Hadith* comprised the sayings and deeds of Mohammad. The *Sahih* was the true collection, as agreed upon by scholars through the centuries.

"Only as a source for study by those interested in the *isnad*," she said, referring to the oral tradition by which the *Hadith* had been passed down through the generations, before scholars established the science of *Hadith* study. "I wrote my undergraduate thesis on the oral traditions of politically repressed peoples, using American and Caribbean slave narratives and folk tales. There are parallels between what happened in America and what's been perceived in Islamic nations where religious enculturations have been deprived of the right to free expression. I've also been working on a translation of a Kurdish poet, outside of my doctorate."

At least she spoke proper English, without resorting either to black slang or to the ridiculous forms of elevated diction and pretentious stilted elocution so many American Black Muslims seemed to find so absurdly empowering.

"You speak Kurdish, then?"

"Well, I'm learning," she said. Why anyone would want to learn Kurdish or translate a Kurdish poet was beyond him, though he understood how two low cultures might resonate with each other.

"And where are you from?" he asked her. The third girl edged closer, obviously dying to get a word in, but she was fat and ugly and probably stupid, judging by her vacant expression, and Jaburi wanted nothing to do with her.

"I'm originally from Baltimore," the one called Shamika said.

"May I ask, will you be writing the introduction for the Sunna project? I was told you'd been invited to, but I hadn't heard what your response was."

Jaburi sighed wearily, looking toward the ceiling.

"Yes, I've been asked," he said. "I don't really know if I will have the time. These days I seem to spend all my free hours and minutes on television news programs answering questions about what's going on in the Middle East. But yes, I suppose I will do something for IHSAN, even though we know the Internet represents all that is base and vile."

He smiled as if he were joking.

"Perhaps I'll see you again when the project is formally launched," she said. He wondered briefly if the whore was trying to seduce him. She was probably only trying to represent to him an inflated understanding of her own status, implying that she'd been invited back to Riyadh for the ceremony. This was a problem inherent with educating women—it was never enough for them to merely receive knowledge.

"Yes, perhaps." He smiled.

"May I have a word with you?" someone at his elbow intervened.

Professor Jaburi turned to see the man he'd had an appointment to meet.

"Andrew," he said in greeting, embracing his friend. "*La ilaha ill Allah wa-Muhammad rasul Allah.* I wasn't sure you would make it. Did you hear my lecture?"

"I did," the other said. Jaburi suspected he was lying. "Brilliant as always."

"And what part did you find the most illuminating?"

"Oh, all of it," Andrew said. "*Athabuna wa athubukum Allah.* Did I pronounce that correctly? 'Divine Reward and Punishment in the Hereafter, as Miscegenated by Twenty-first Century Jihad.' Very interesting. And quite relevant. I was just reading Joseph van Ess's thoughts on the subject last week."

Reading an encyclopedia, Jaburi thought. Still, the man he knew as Andrew Timmons was better educated than most of the CIA agents he'd met, and he did seem to take care to inform himself, insofar as that was possible.

"Professor," the third girl interrupted. Jaburi was immediately annoyed. He didn't like to be interrupted. "Can I ask you one question? What do you think of John Ashcroft?"

"What do I think of John Ashcroft?" Jaburi said. This mere girl had the audacity to bait him? Was she currying favor, or trying to impress him? "Let me ask you," he said, "what do you think of him? Have you met him?"

"No, but . . ."

"Well I have," Jaburi snapped. "Several times. I find him a man of astonishing principle and a true and pious believer. I would wish that all people, whether Christian or Muslim, were as true to their beliefs as he is. He understands the significance of correct belief as well as the tenet that it is the combination of God's grace and human intelligence and effort that will save us, as individuals and as nations. Now if you are asking me if I approve of how the rights and freedoms of Arab-Americans or of Muslims traveling or visiting in this country might potentially be abridged by the misapplication of the Patriot Act by zealous enforcement agencies unable to see beyond their own paranoia, I would give you a different answer, but you asked me about my friend John Ashcroft. Excuse me."

He turned and accompanied Agent Timmons, making their way through the crowd to an adjoining library, a wood-paneled room lined with bookshelves stocked with leather-bound volumes. A second CIA agent stood watch at the door, which Timmons closed behind them.

"Do you think I was too rough on her, Andrew?" Jaburi asked.

"Not at all," Timmons said. "That's what education is all about. I got straight A's at Yale but I swear today I only remember the things taught to me by the professors who tried to kick my ass. Pardon the expression."

"Pardon granted," Jaburi said graciously. "I always make allowances for vulgarities when I'm dealing with government officials. What was it you wanted to see me about? Your call sounded rather urgent. I take it this is not a social visit?"

"Actually," Andrew Timmons said, "I wanted to run something by you. Hopefully I won't take up much of your time but I need to test that photographic memory of yours. Just between you and me, my boss at Langley bet me twenty dollars you wouldn't be able to do this but I told him never underestimate that intellect of yours."

"Memory and intellect are two different things," Jaburi said. "And the correct word would be 'hopeful,' not 'hopefully.' Also 'you and I,' not 'you and me.'"

"There you go," Timmons said. "Just kick my ass. It's good for me."

"What is it you have?"

Timmons reached into the inside pocket of his sport coat and extracted a piece of paper, folded into thirds, which he opened and handed to Jaburi. Jaburi set the reading glass hanging from a chain around his neck on the end of his nose and scratched his beard as he read a list of telephone numbers, perhaps twenty in all, with a variety of international country codes preceding them. Jaburi studied the paper for a few moments before handing it back to the CIA agent.

"And what is this from?"

"These," Agent Timmons said, "were found in the call log of a cell phone that was taken off an Al Qaeda operative in Jiddah. We were just wondering if any of the numbers meant anything to you. Would you like to see it again?"

Jaburi shook his head, insulted by the unnecessary offer.

"The Swiss numbers are none I've ever seen," he said, "though I would guess they would be numbers for those who facilitated the May 12 bombings in Riyadh. And the

Saudi numbers would be for those who participated more directly, but you have no doubt already come to the same conclusions. The Sudanese and Omani numbers are not known to me, but the fifteenth number in Yemen is that of a man named Faris al-Farük, whose name I gave you last year when you were asking me about the *Cole* attack. Was that number truly in this person's cell phone or were you testing me?"

Timmons smiled apologetically.

"I'll split the twenty dollars with you if that would make it up to you," he said.

Jaburi smiled again.

"The number I truly would suggest you look into would be the one in Vancouver. The third one on your list in the 604 area code. This is a man named Yasseen ibn-Rezwan. His wife's name is Selwa and he has two sons named Hakim and Hatem, seven and four. He is on the board of the Al-Awda there and he has had me come speak at his fundraisers on two occasions, but the last time I was there, he told me at dinner that he'd been raised in Najaf where his father worked for the Iraq Oil Ministry before coming to this country in the 1950s, even though Iraq did not have an Oil Ministry until much later. He also claimed to have no knowledge of the Ahmed Rezzam incident in 1999. I found that suspicious. Though I believe I informed you of my suspicions at the time."

"You probably did," Timmons said. Rezzam had been a thirty-four-year-old Algerian who'd been arrested while mixing bombs in a Vancouver motel with the intention of blowing up the Los Angeles airport on New Year's Eve of the year 2000. "Unlike you, I don't have a photographic memory. But that's good. Seeing his number on this list should confirm your suspicions. We'll look into it. Anything else?"

Jaburi shook his head.

"Oh—one more thing," Timmons said. "I almost forgot. Where's Osama bin Laden?"

"I believe he has shaved his beard and is working as a busboy at a Denny's in Youngstown, Ohio," Jaburi replied with a smile. It was a joke he and Timmons always made to end their briefings.

"Okay then," Timmons said. "I'll have some of my people look into it. As always, professor, it's been a pleasure."

Professor Jaburi returned to the reception, where he told the dean that he was feeling tired and needed to go to his hotel. There, he used one of the computers in the media center off the lobby to check his e-mail. In addition to all the spam offering him Viagra and penis enlargements, he read one from his travel agent, giving him an updated itinerary for his speaking tour, and another from his wife, Aafia, who told him their son Asgher needed more money for school clothes.

There seemed to be no limit to the amount of money Asgher needed just to get by, and his sister Nesreen was worse, insistent on having all the latest name brands to wear to school. The money wasn't the issue—it was the way they saw the world. It was a question of values, where despite his best efforts, his children had none. He'd given up. The struggle was not worth the effort it took, and it was too late anyway. Things would be different when he was reunited with his family in paradise, which would happen soon enough.

He went to his hotel room, where he lay on the bed. It disturbed him to think of how throughout the Arab nations, any young boy or girl with a computer could, in a matter of moments, see things no grown adult was ever meant to see, women having sex with five or six men, or with each other, or with the common beasts of the field. He turned on the television to see the latest news from his homeland, still occupied by the infidels, the nation dissolving in chaos, impurity, and mediocrity before his very eyes. It was depressing, and yet it made him feel better to know that it would all be over soon enough and that Allah had chosen him to be his agent. It was because of his gifts, Mahmoud knew, that he'd been chosen to be the next prophet, even though he, too, had been corrupted. God's forgiveness knew no limits. In that sense he knew himself to be a savior, the vessel and the mechanism through which this world and all its evil would be obliterated, in order that a new world, true to Islam and created in accordance with the correct teachings of the Koran, could emerge to take its place, occupied by the true believers who survived. God had sent plagues before to purify the world when man had turned to sin and lost his way. He was sending one again.

Al-w'ad wa al-wa'id.

A threat is a threat. A promise is a promise.

La ilaha ill Allah wa-Muhammad rasul Allah.

Before going to bed, he got down on his knees to face Mecca, and then he gave a brief prayer of thanks, and a humble request that Allah would give him strength for the holy mission he was about to embark upon.

Chapter Four

THE COMMAND CENTER DELUCA AND OTHER members of the 419th Military Intelligence Battalion worked out of, the OMT (Operations Management Team), about a five-minute drive from the TOC, was in a converted adobe Iraqi Air Force building, inside of which three rooms had been partitioned. The main room, at the end of the hallway, held tables along the walls where computers and printers sat, one wall featuring a large whiteboard where the names of agents, their missions, and the vehicles they'd check out were charted in grease pencil. In the center of the main room, a large wooden table overflowed with manuals, maps, and files currently in use, which sometimes made it difficult to hold briefings there. Halfway down the hall, on the right, was the TR or "Team Room," where the THTs kept their files and did their reports. The room was full of classified material and therefore off-limits to informants or to agents looking for a place to interrogate suspects. Reicken's office stood opposite.

The secretary at the desk in the reception area outside Lieutenant Colonel Stanley Reicken's office was a specialist named Washington, first name Marilyn, DeLuca had come to learn, a black girl in her early twenties from Georgia who'd joined the National Guard for the educational benefits, she'd told him, adding that it beat working at Waffle House. Lately she'd come to feel less certain of that, she'd said with a weak smile.

He'd gone over the Al-Tariq files as soon as he got back to base, finding a free terminal at the TR and logging on with his team username, THT80, and his personal password, Hazel, the name of his first dog. There were entries regarding Al-Tariq dating back to the fifties—CIA reports, DIA summaries, photographs at various ages, as well as a biography that included where he started his political career, his military background, how he joined the Ba'ath party, how he'd risen through the ranks (including the names of the rivals he'd killed or made disappear), brief bios of his family members, his tribal history, and the names of his tribal allies and/or rivals. DeLuca was most concerned with the sitreps at the end of the folder. The evidence that Al-Tariq was dead was compelling and complete. It was one of the few cases where they actually had a body, with a 100 percent DNA match from tissue samples. They had fingerprints taken before the war that matched fingerprints from the scene after the bombing. They even had part of the face, with a registration of 98 percent according to the NSA's face recognition program. There truly was no reason to doubt that the man was dead. Ali's story was getting harder and harder to believe.

If Al-Tariq were still alive, the syllogism was ominously clear. Saddam's was a regime based on fear, emanating from the top down. U.S. policy, from the very start, held that in a fear-based regime, if you chopped off the

head, the body would die. Al-Tariq had been head of the
Mukhaberat, and the Mukhaberat was in charge of the
WMD. According to the satellite communication intercepts DeLuca found in his file, Al-Tariq had been talking
to Al Qaeda operatives before the war, mostly fielding
calls from men asking him for sanctuary after being
driven out of Afghanistan. The Pentagon's greatest fear
all along had been that Saddam, through Al-Tariq, would
provide Al Qaeda operatives with WMD. If Al-Tariq was
dead, then the Mukhaberat would probably collapse, once
the fear that held it together was gone. That was why his
compound had been so heavily targeted.

However, if Al-Tariq were alive, then the likelihood
that he'd given WMD to Al Qaeda operatives, or trucked
them into Syria, as Ali had suggested, was greater than
ever, particularly now that Al-Tariq had more incentive to
use them and less to lose. Things like sarin, VX, bubonic
plague, smallpox, anthrax, dirty bombs, or even suitcase
nukes could be headed for the United States (or Great
Britain, or any of the other countries in the coalition) in a
kind of shotgun approach, where even if 90 percent of
his agents were caught, another hundred suicide bombers
would get through.

The first thing to do would be to check the DNA on the
syringes DeLuca had in his shirt pocket, each in its own
zip-locked evidence bag.

"Colonel Reicken will see you now," Specialist Washington told him, pointing toward the door with a pencil.
She mouthed the words, "Good luck."

Reicken insisted that subordinate personnel hold their
salutes until he returned them. It was one of the many
things DeLuca found irritating about the man. Another was

that he kept fourteen individually wrapped caramels on a plate on his otherwise fastidiously tidy desk, never thirteen, never fifteen—fourteen. He didn't eat them himself. He didn't offer them to his guests. They were there to make some sort of statement, a humanizing gesture, perhaps. DeLuca had a sense Reicken was dying for somebody to ask him, "Hey, Colonel, what's with the caramels?"

DeLuca wasn't going to be the one to ask.

At a time when DeLuca's team sometimes ran three or four missions a day in 120-degree heat, without cool water to drink, Reicken's office featured an air-conditioner in the window and a refrigerator full of things many of the men dreamed of at night: lemonade, iced tea, Popsicles, ice cream . . . Reicken had initially offered such things to DeLuca during office briefings (as a way to get his men to like him?), but DeLuca turned him down. If his team couldn't have Popsicles, he certainly wasn't going to eat one.

The trick to playing Reicken was to get him to think whatever it was you wanted him to do was his idea, so that he'd get credit for any successes, and to make sure that if there were any risks involved, he wouldn't be blamed for any failures.

"Sergeant DeLuca," Reicken said. "Sit down, please." He scanned the memo DeLuca had sent him, his eyes moving back and forth behind his wire-rimmed self-dimming bifocals. Reicken didn't like to meet with any-body unless he had a memo to read first, telling him what to expect from the meeting.

DeLuca waited.

"So," Reicken said at last. "What is it that I can do for you? Because if I'm reading this right, you want me to reopen a closed blacklist file, when I still have a whole country full of nasty individuals out there trying to kill my soldiers. Have I read that right, Sergeant DeLuca?"

"You have, sir," DeLuca said. "And if you wouldn't mind, sir, if you could just give me the memo back, I was hoping that we could both forget I ever mentioned the idea."

"Have you *seen* Al-Tariq's file?" Reicken asked. "Because as far as I can tell, Sergeant, we have DNA, we have fingerprints, we have humint—we even have tissue samples from the damn body. Do you know how infrequent it is that we get confirmation with 100 percent confidence on blacklist case files? Do you really think it's wise to reopen this case?"

"Not at all, sir," DeLuca said. "I guess the idea that Al-Tariq could still be alive sort of freaked me out at first, but I can see now that I probably overreacted. Personally, it's a little embarrassing."

"Well, don't be too hard on yourself," Reicken said. "These guys have had their whole lives to practice lying. I haven't met one yet I thought I could trust. Just for the record, what was it that this Ali . . ."

"Ali Hadid al Dujayl," DeLuca said.

"This Hadid guy—what was it about him that you found so convincing?"

"I was leveraging his kid," DeLuca said. From the look of confusion on Reicken's face, DeLuca knew the lieutenant colonel hadn't read his report on yesterday's mission. "He took a shot at us, but it was pretty clear he was just defending his family. I was pretending like there was no way I could let him go, so the guy started telling me a story to save his kid. But I realized last night, a guy is going to say anything to save his kid, right? He said Al-Tariq was trying to recruit him."

"Who? Ali?"

"No, his son. Kamel. But when I saw Al-Tariq's file again last night, it became pretty obvious that Ali was talking out his ass. So if it's all the same to you, I'd just as soon not have this go in my file."

"Just a minute," Reicken said. "Let me just play devil's advocate here for a minute. Let's just suppose Al-Tariq was alive—that would be a bad thing, right? You said he said Al-Tariq was trying to recruit the kid. I'd say that'd be a pretty damn good reason to turn the guy in. It's been my experience that the vast majority of these guys are doing their level best to get us to do their dirty work for them. You think Ali might have a beef with Al-Tariq?"

"Well, he used to work security for him. And his brother's Ba'ath party. I'll be talking to him shortly about unrelated matters. You think Al-Tariq is worth going for? If, as you say, there's a chance he's alive? Because I'd hate to waste time . . ."

"Is he *worth* going for?" Reicken said. "If you'd read the file, you wouldn't have to ask. I don't think the Kuwaitis would offer one day's worth of their gross national product if he wasn't worth going after. You think the Al Qaeda connections are solid? You think he's got what he needs to put the Sunnis and the Shiites together?"

DeLuca shrugged.

"What it might take to get the Sunnis and the Shiites together is beyond my expertise. They've been enemies for five hundred years."

"That may be true," Reicken said, "but the enemy of my enemy is my friend."

DeLuca had bet Mack five bucks he could get Reicken to say that.

"He certainly had the resources to throw around," DeLuca said. "But as you say, he's been taken off the list, so why waste our time? Then again, if he's not dead, it wouldn't look bad if we were the ones who got him. Be quite a feather in your cap."

"What's the hard evidence?" Reicken asked. "You say you have a syringe?"

DeLuca was about to correct his commanding officer—he had two syringes—but changed his mind.

"If Al-Tariq used it, it's got to have his DNA on it. And fingerprints, unless somebody else shot him up."

"Better safe than sorry," Reicken said. "I often think of the old saying about the horse that needed the nail and the king couldn't find one so the horse fell down or whatever it was. At the very least, we can send the evidence to Gillem."

DeLuca reached into his shirt pocket and extracted one of the two syringes he'd taken from Ali Hadid. Reicken held the zip-locked bag up to the light and examined the contents.

"And you're certain this is an insulin syringe?" he asked.

"My sister was diabetic," DeLuca said. "I recognized the smell."

"That's tough," Reicken said. "Does she still have it?"

Reicken knew why DeLuca had reenlisted, but apparently he'd forgotten.

"No, sir, she doesn't," DeLuca said.

"Well good, then. I'll see to this. Specialist Washington will give you the forms you need to fill out to request the lab work. I'll review it when you're done."

"Any idea how long it might take to hear back?" DeLuca asked.

"From Gillem? God only knows. I heard somebody say they're running three months behind because of personnel shortages."

"Any chance we could mark this priority and get a rush on it?"

Reicken cocked an eyebrow at him.

"Let's not get carried away, DeLuca," he replied. "You said yourself the man is dead. If all we're doing is throwing another shovel full of dirt on his grave, I don't see where's the hurry. Anything else?"

"Not at this time, sir."

"Dismissed, then. Oh yeah—and congratulations."

"For what, sir?"

"Didn't anybody tell you? You're the new team leader."

"What about Doc?"

"Sergeant Christopher is gone," Reicken said. "I'm not really at liberty to say why, but apparently he's been having some mental problems."

Back at Tent City, the team quarters were deserted, the cot where Doc had bunked stripped and empty, his footlocker gone. This wasn't making much sense. DeLuca hadn't seen anybody the day before when he returned from Ad-Dujayl, and he'd fallen asleep early. Dan Sykes was still sleeping when he went to breakfast, but he was gone now. DeLuca crossed to the "women's quarters": Men and women shared the same large tent, but with one end curtained off with ponchos hung from jury-rigged clotheslines. They shared the same bathrooms and showers as well, though there, a sign was posted listing gender-specific hours. Women had been given three times the hours in the bathroom than the men had, but there wasn't a man in the unit who found that remotely surprising. He called over the curtain and asked for Mack, but she was nowhere to be found.

He returned to his cot. This was his home now, a large dark green canvas wall tent first deployed during the Korean conflict, with holes where the hot desert sun shone through and too many patches to count—nothing but the finest equipment for the National Guard. Tent City so strongly resembled the set from the TV show *M*A*S*H** (save for the wall of sandbags surrounding each tent) that somebody had hung a sign that said "Suicide Is Painless" underneath the wet-ball. The thermometer hanging from the post in the center of the tent said it was 103 degrees, which was nearly subarctic compared to what it had been other days.

What did Reicken mean, Doc's been having some mental problems? There had to be some kind of mistake. Doc (he'd been trained as a medic) seemed to have a lot on his mind sometimes, but who in Iraq didn't? He'd transferred to the 419th from the 431st after "philosophical differences" with his CO, but that had nothing to do with his mental state—Doc was as sane as anybody. There had to be more to it.

He set the syringe on the bed beside him and examined it for a moment. It was obvious that he couldn't afford to go through channels and wait three months or more for the lab reports to get back from Fort Gillem. It was equally obvious how to get around that. In his footlocker, he found the Motorola 9510PP satellite phone he'd taken out a home equity loan to buy before being deployed. It had been a three-thousand-dollar investment, but Bonnie had insisted on it as a condition of his reenlistment and deployment. In the old days, you had to wait in line for your turn to call home, and when your turn came, you only had fifteen minutes, with army censors listening in. Now half the soldiers in country had their own sat phones, on discounted monthly GI Special plans from companies like Iridium or Globalstar or Thuraya. One of the worries counterintelligence had was that any soldier with a traitorous inclination and a sat phone could call in troop positions to the enemy and there was little the army could do about it. Soldiers could transmit messages, photos, e-mail, without any censorship or oversight.

It was going to get somebody into big trouble, DeLuca knew.

DeLuca's phone was the best civilian money could buy, a 1,900 maH high-capacity device with Internet service at 10 kbps, computer connectivity, an IrDA port, Vibracall, voice mail, e-mail, instant messaging, and picture-phone capabilities at 2,400 bps. It had taken him three days just to program it, using the Easy Start Up guide that came with it, and half the time, he still didn't know how to use it.

He looked at his watch. It was just after 1000 hours. That made it two in the morning back in Boston. He dialed a number, figuring his old friend would still be up.

"O'Doherty," she answered. "I hope this is the pizza boy."

"I thought I'd catch you still up," DeLuca said.

"David," she said, a smile evident in her voice. "How are you, dear? I was afraid you'd blown up."

"Not yet," he said. "You're going to, though, if you eat pizza at this hour."

"Just who would I be watching my figure for now, David?" she asked.

"How are the cards treating you?"

"As ever. Last night I had a sixty-five low on the flop and Walter drew a perf' at the river to beat me. I think I lost four dollars on that hand."

Gillian O'Doherty had been the chief coroner and medical examiner for Suffolk County, Boston, since the late seventies. She and her husband, Bobby, had been part of DeLuca's poker group since the group began. Now Bobby, a Vietnam vet, like Walter Ford, and a good cop, was gone, and Gillian spent most of her time working in her laboratory in an old brick building (scheduled for demolition, once a more modern facility could be built) attached to Tufts Medical School at the edge of Chinatown. She'd just finished her final round of chemotherapy for non-Hodgkins lymphoma when she lost Bobby, but she carried on through it all—she could just possibly be the flat-out toughest person DeLuca had ever met, and between the Rangers and the PJs and the SEALS and the Special Ops guys he'd worked with through the years, he'd met some fairly tough individuals. She was planning to retire, once she'd managed to catch up from a backlog of cases. She probably would have been a brilliant surgeon, had surgical positions been offered to women back when the young Irish girl from Quincy graduated from medical school.

"I take it this isn't a social call," she said.

"I wish it was," he said. "Actually I've got a problem I was hoping you could help me with."

He explained the situation, that he had a syringe with DNA on it that he needed identified against DNA taken from the body of a most likely dead Iraqi bad guy, just on the chance that he might still be alive.

"Can you tell how old the DNA sample on the needle might be?"

"They can ballpark it within a few weeks," she said.

"Good enough," he said. "How soon do you think you could get something for me?"

"The FBI lab has always been pretty good to me," she said. "Maybe a week to ten days from when I get the sample. Possibly sooner. How important is it?"

"Hard to say," he told his old friend. "It's likely I'm wrong, and if I am, it's not a big deal, but if I'm right, we might be looking at an EOTFWAWKI scenario."

"I've always hated all your military acronyms. What's that in plain English?"

"E-O-T-F-W-A-W-K-I," he said. "End of the fucking world as we know it."

"Not again. I'll get right on it. I'm going to need the previous findings."

"Check your e-mail. I'll attach the file."

"You can do that? It isn't classified?"

"It is, but I can do that."

"Don't forget the McCallums that's waiting for you," she said, referring to the bottle of fifty-year-old Scotch she'd told him she'd keep to toast him when he returned.

"I haven't," DeLuca said. "Listen, Gillian, did you ever meet my brother-in-law Tom? Miecowski? Elaine's husband?"

"No, but you talked about him. NYPD, right?" she said. "Attached to the DEA?"

"He's with Homeland Security now," DeLuca said. "New York office. I'm going to cc him on this, just so I know I've got somebody there who's up to speed who'll take my back if I need it. I think I know where to get some support from the Army, too. Anyway, I'll send you Tom's e-mail address and tell him you're going to copy him on whatever you find."

"Whatever you say, David. I think my pizza boy is here. My cell phone is ringing and it's most likely him at the door and I'll need to let him in."

"I'm glad you locked it. You were always too close to the Combat Zone for me."

"Robert felt the same way," Gillian O'Doherty said. "He used to come pick me up when I worked late, no matter how late it was."

"I still don't like the idea of you walking to your car all by yourself at this hour," DeLuca said.

"Well, somehow there's almost always a patrol car outside my door occupied by someone who used to work with my husband," Gillian said. "I'm sure it's just a coincidence. But I do appreciate it."

He'd lain back on his cot to think when he heard something beneath his pillow. He reached under it and found an envelope with his name on it. He recognized Doc's nearly illegible handwriting. Inside the envelope, he found a note:

> Dave—first of all, congrats to the new TL. I'm sure you'll do a better job at it than I did, though I think we had our moments, didn't we? I'm off to Bragg to straighten this business out. You're going to hear a number of things

about me that aren't true. For your own good, I'm not
going to tell you what's going on, but I want you to know
that I never lied to you. Best of luck. If Reicken hasn't
told you yet, remember to take special care of Dan.

                                                        Doc

He was rereading the note when Dan Sykes entered the
tent. Doc had explained the situation with Danforth Tay-
lor Sykes, son of Danforth Sykes, Sr., long-term Republican congressman from Palo Alto and the number-two
man on the House Armed Forces Committee (with a senator, a governor of California, and three Army generals
also perched in the family tree). According to Doc, the
plan was to give Dan enough combat experience to make
him electable, down the road, but not enough to get him
killed. DeLuca liked him. Despite his background of privilege, he didn't want to stand apart. He wouldn't have
liked it if he'd known he was being handled with kid
gloves, a directive that had, according to Doc, come down
from the highest levels.

"Where've you been?" DeLuca said, folding the note
and putting it back in the envelope. "What happened to
Doc?"

"That's where I've been. I was at the TOC. Doc's gone."

"Gone?"

"On a plane, if he hasn't landed already. We came back
from talking to the mayor, and there's a memo that
Reicken wants to see him ASAP. I go to dinner, and when
I get back, he's packed up and out of here. I just figured
maybe he'd been transferred or something, but this morning they tell me at the OMT that he's been chaptered out
and now he's being held at Fort Bragg for questioning."

"About what?"

"I don't know. The guy I talked to said there was some question about Doc's mental state."

"What does that mean?"

"Your guess is as good as mine. They're transferring a new guy over from Tikrit today," Sykes said. "Wanna see something else that's interesting?"

He handed DeLuca a piece of paper he had in his back pocket, a color inkjet printout of a photograph of a girl in a pale gray strapless satin evening gown, a corsage in her hands, smiling next to a somewhat dorky-looking young man in a powder blue tuxedo. She was stunning.

"Am I supposed to know who this is?" DeLuca asked.

"That's MacKenzie," Sykes said. "Is that a howl or what? I Googled her and found her high-school website. She tell you she was elected prom queen? I thought it might be good for a laugh or two."

"Do you have any other copies?" DeLuca asked.

"No, but I could print you one out," Sykes said. "I thought you were married."

"I thought you were engaged to a vintner's daughter," DeLuca said. DeLuca refolded Mack's prom picture and stuck it under the envelope from Doc. One of the concerns, bringing women into the military, had been that male commanding officers might feel extra-protective of them and lose their impartiality. DeLuca didn't care. He knew that the strength of any team was its cohesiveness, the willingness of each member to subordinate his (or now her) own needs to the good of the whole. Competitiveness was allowed, and good-natured teasing was, too, but divisive behavior was not.

"Here's my first decision as TL," he told the younger man. "Leave it alone. Just don't go there. Mack is one of us. Okay?"

"Hey, come on," Dan said. "I love Mack. She's one of the boys. I can't bust her balls like everybody else?"

"She doesn't have balls," DeLuca said, "and she's not one of the boys. She's part of the team. So follow the Golden Rule my Italian father taught me—'Do onto others as I fucking say you should do onto others.' All right?"

"I hear you," Dan said. "You gotta admit she cleans up pretty good, though."

"Did you have anything actually useful you were going to do today?" DeLuca said. "Because I have something for you to do. What do you know about Dr. Rihab Taha?"

"Dr. Germ?" Dan said. "Off the top of my head? Mrs. Six of Spades, married to General Amir Rasheed Muhammad al-Ubaydi, Saddam's oil minister and weapons delivery system guy. She's a microbiologist, educated in England, I think—some people call her 'The Bug Lady,' both because she headed up Saddam's bioweapons program and because she was fucking crazy. She used to cry and throw chairs at the U.N. inspectors—serious anger management issues. Apparently she's been completely out of her mind since she was arrested. They can't get anything that makes the first bit of sense out of her."

"I hadn't heard that."

"They got her lab notes when Saddam's son-in-law Kamal defected in 1995 with her handwritten proof that she was testing botulinum and anthrax delivered by artillery shells. It's one of the few bits of hard intel we have that WMD existed."

"Rockets, actually," DeLuca said. "How'd you have such a lousy grade point average at Stanford if you're that smart?"

"I had to work at it," Dan said. "What about Taha?"

"We're looking for anybody who might have worked on a biological warfare program called the Jamrat Project. If it's not in her file, it's gotta be in somebody's. Somebody who worked with her, and/or Hazem Ali. Virologist, also educated in England. Gone-a-missing, supposedly directing a veterinary college, last his official location was given. Search the Blix list and then double-check it against ours. Keyword '*Jamrat*.' Keyword '*Lanatullah*,' for 'God's Justice' or 'God's Curse' or something like that. Keyword *Alf Wajeh*. Keyword 'Thousand Faces.' Keyword 'Al Manal.' Keyword 'Daura Foot and Mouth Disease Facility.' Do your Boolean best. Get Joan-Claude to give you spellings. I think she's got a dictionary somewhere."

"The sooner we can reduce this godforsaken country to one gigantic database, the better," Dan said. "Did something happen I should know about that put biologicals back on the top of the pile?"

"Just something the guy we popped last night said," DeLuca told his younger team member. "Ali Hadid. I'm having a cup of tea with his brother today. At noon. According to Ali, Mohammed Al-Tariq is still alive and putting together a new coalition of shitheads. Possibly armed with biologicals."

"He's dead," Dan said. "They have a whole bag of roadkill to prove it. Don't they?"

"Better to be sure," DeLuca said. "Read my report. Where is Mack, by the way?"

"Last I saw her, she was researching your lunch date for you," Sykes said.

"Excellent," DeLuca said. "I should be back by eleven-thirty. Tell her I'll meet her here then."

"Where you going?"

"To see an old friend," DeLuca said.

The old friend ordinarily worked either at CENTCOM in Doha or in the Green Zone or out of Saddam's former palace in Tikrit. DeLuca had heard he'd be inspecting and briefing the TOC that morning. He saw a small fleet of helicopters parked on the tarmac beyond the TOC, the general's convoy, three Blackhawk HH60s and four fully armed Apaches to fly escort, skimming the treetops at 180 mph. The briefing was for officers only, a discussion of the current ROEs and sitreps, though the situation reports hadn't changed all that much in the last few months, everything still as fucked up as it ever was. DeLuca located one of the general's aides and pulled him aside.

"When he's done, would you please tell the general that Herr Totenbrau would like to have a word with him?"

"Herr Totenbrau" was the name of the beer DeLuca and Phillip LeDoux had brewed in the apartment they'd shared, back when they'd roomed together in Frankfurt in the late seventies and early eighties, translating as "Mr. Death Beer." Their job had been to man a listening post on the East German border, a Quonset hut surrounded by barbed wire atop Mt. Meissner, a twenty-five-hundred-foot forested peak in the Harz range about thirty kilometers east of Kassel, where they spent tedious twelve-hour shifts wearing headphones and eavesdropping on East German telephone conversations, kicking back over bratwursts and beer in the pubs in the local villages when they were off duty. DeLuca and LeDoux had graduated first and second in their class at counterintelligence school at Fort Huachuca, Arizona, both of them posting higher scores than anybody had for the previous twenty years. Both had been offered OCS. The problem DeLuca had with Officer's Candidate School was that when you graduated, you had to be an officer, and he wouldn't have minded the education, but he had no desire to be an officer. LeDoux had gone on to become, in DeLuca's opinion, one of the best generals the army had. DeLuca got out of the army when he realized how detrimental military service was to his married life, or lives. His first marriage, to a Long Island girl named Donna, lasted less than two years. He'd married Bonnie feeling optimistic that things would be different, even took a reassignment as an instructor at Huachuca that kept him home more, but he left the service when he saw the same things happening to his second marriage that had happened to his first, not the drinking or the affairs, but the loneliness. Women, he concluded, needed to feel like you put them first. They were funny that way.

"Langsam nicht sehen," he said.

Phillip looked as fit as ever in his DCUs, six foot two and lean, tanned from the desert sun, with just a touch of gray showing in his close-cropped black hair. With his prescription Ray-Bans in place, he looked like an updated version of Douglas MacArthur, minus the corncob pipe. He had a serious demeanor, but like the Texas high-school football coach who only smiles after the championship game is over, he was only serious because he knew it made his men work harder to please him. He smiled broadly when he saw DeLuca beneath the tree.

"I heard you were lurking around somewhere," the general said, returning the salute with a snap. "I'd hug you but the men are watching."

"Wouldn't want to make them jealous," DeLuca said. "How've you been?"

"Good, good," LeDoux said, looking DeLuca over from head to toe. "Jesus, David—you look great. Last time I saw you, you were . . ."

"Twenty-five pounds heavier," DeLuca admitted.

"How'd you do it?"

"Atkins," DeLuca said. "Like everybody else. Plus I started lifting weights and running five miles a day. I'm in better shape now than I was in Germany. Even then, I had to talk the recruiters into taking me. Regular army wouldn't consider it. I think the Guard guys were impressed when I told them I'd ridden with Patton."

"I got your letter," LeDoux said. "I'm sorry about Elaine."

"She was the best."

"How's Bonnie with you reenlisting?"

"Trying to adjust," DeLuca said. "I don't know how you're doing with bachelorhood, but it does make all this bullshit easier." He nodded toward the TOC.

"Actually, it looks like that part is coming to an end for me," LeDoux said. "I got engaged, right before coming over. Kathryn O'Connor. From a Navy family, believe it or not. Her father's at Annapolis. She's a lawyer."

"Then she knows the deal," DeLuca said.

"It's great to see you, David," LeDoux said. "Anything I can do for you while I'm here? I'm going to have to be getting back to Tikrit pretty soon."

"Actually there is," he said. "Much as I was hoping for a purely social visit."

As briefly as he could, he laid out for LeDoux what he'd learned about Al-Tariq, *Alf Wajeh, Lanatullah,* and the Jamrat Project. LeDoux listened closely, his arms folded across his chest. DeLuca left out the part about there being a price on his own head. By the time he was done, the rotors on all seven helicopters were turning.

"So what's your gut?" LeDoux asked. "You think Ali was telling the truth?"

"My gut is, yeah, he was," DeLuca said. "He was trying to save his son, but there was more to it. I'm talking to his brother in less than an hour, so I might learn more then. You understand what it could mean if Al-Tariq is still out there, right?"

LeDoux nodded.

"I've always trusted your gut, David. What do you need from me?" LeDoux asked.

"Whatever you got," DeLuca said. "I got sort of a problem with my CO. Remember Gillette in Stuttgart? This guy's worse. I just got a feeling he's going to crap on my birthday cake every chance he gets. Plus there could be stuff I need to get done without filling out three hundred forms to do it. You could help me expedite. If you agree that it's important."

"It sounds important to me," LeDoux said. "Could you forward me the report you wrote up on the raid? And keep me posted along the way?"

"Absolutely," DeLuca said. "Look, Phil—I don't want you to take on something new if your plate is already full. As I assume it is."

"I've got more than one plate," LeDoux said. "They make sure of that." He called over his shoulder to an aide, who stepped forward with a salute.

"Yes sir, General, sir," the aide said.

"Captain Martin," the general said. "This is Mr. David, from counterintelligence. Mr. David—what was the name of your dog as a child?"

"My dog?" DeLuca said. "Hazel."

"Hazel," LeDoux repeated. "Captain Martin, you will be my contact with Mr. David. My liaison. When he gives you the password 'Hazel,' you are to do your best to accommodate his every need. If there's something he needs that you can't do, you come to me." LeDoux turned to DeLuca. "Do you need a sat phone?"

"Got one," DeLuca said.

The general turned to his aide.

"Give him your direct number and mine, and take his, and get me a copy." He saluted the aide.

"Yes, sir," Captain Martin said, turning on a heel to leave.

LeDoux turned to DeLuca one more time.

"This is going to have to be unofficial, at least for now. I don't like abrogating the chain of command unless I have to, but I'm going to take your word that I have to."

"I appreciate it," DeLuca said. "I just want to put this to rest, if I can. Otherwise it's going to be hanging over our heads."

"I agree," LeDoux said. "I'm going to discuss it with a few people, if you don't mind. We'll be calling you for updates. Do what it takes. I'll take the heat."

"I'd settle for an air-conditioner for my tent," DeLuca

said, raising his hand to salute. "Did I ever tell you I named my son after you?"

"Your son's name is Scott," LeDoux said.

"Yeah, and you're Scottish."

"'LeDoux' is French-Canadian. I'm only one-sixteenth Scottish."

"I know, but whoever heard of a kid named 'French-Canadian'?"

The mess hall had been constructed from a pair of adjoined double-wide mobile homes that Brown & Root, a private company, had trucked up from Kuwait, with air-conditioning and seating for two hundred hungry soldiers at a time, though all too often you had to wait an hour in the blazing sun before you ate. It was better than the field kitchens where they handed you an MRE that you had to eat sitting cross-legged in the dirt, but the food was still nothing to write home about, unless you didn't like the people back home you were writing to.

The private who brought him his food was a Wisconsin farm boy from Rice Lake named James Coombs, but everyone called him Jimmy, from the 305th Military Intelligence Combat Service Support unit. He was a young man of good humor, a soldier who gave no evidence that he'd actually realized where he was or what he was doing. Today he seemed to have good news he was bursting to share.

"I did what you told me," he said, setting DeLuca's tray down in front of him.

"You stopped listening to rap music?" DeLuca asked.

"No—I got the paperwork I need to cross-train over to CI," Jimmy said excitedly. "My CO says I should have some field experience other than KP and stuff, so he's going to get me some of that, but I was thinking maybe it would help if I had a letter from you, you know, just saying I'm trustworthy and whatever."

"Just because I haven't died of food poisoning yet doesn't mean I trust you," DeLuca said. "You sure about this, Jimmy?"

"Absolutely," he said. "I only joined CSS because I was hoping someday to open a restaurant. You think if I go CI, I can be a cop later? I think that would be neat."

"That's how I did it," DeLuca said. "I'll write you a letter."

Sykes was in the team room, facing a computer monitor. CENTCOM and regular army had all the flat screens now, passing their bulky old monitors down to the Guard units, but they still worked. Sykes's eyes darted quickly from the screen to DeLuca, then back again.

"Anything?" DeLuca asked.

"Did you know the Al-Hakam BW facility tried to claim they were manufacturing chicken feed, even though the place was surrounded by barbed wire and guard towers? Why do you think that was?"

"I don't know," DeLuca said, "but I've seen some pretty vicious-looking chickens in this country. Maybe Saddam was afraid they'd revolt."

"Sort of like, 'the buuuckkk stops here'?" Sykes said. "They had clean rooms, they had fermenters, they had eighty-five hundred liters of anthrax, and they had botulinum, which makes your tongue swell up until you choke to death. Or lisp badly, I'm guessing. Nine out of ten Iraqi

POWs from the first Gulf War had been immunized against smallpox. What does that tell you?"

"That they had it in their artillery shells and were afraid of blowback on the battlefield," DeLuca guessed.

"Except that smallpox is a strategic weapon. It's not tactical. Maybe they were afraid the Iranians had it. Dumb fuckers fought the Iranians for eight years and lost nearly a million casualties on both sides and by the end, the border had changed about three feet. In Iran's favor."

"Yeah, but what a three feet it was," DeLuca said. "What about the keywords I mentioned?"

"'*Jamrat*' had sixteen hundred plus hits because it's the name of a religious festival. Also the name of a bridge that collapsed in Mecca and killed 226 pilgrims. '*Lanatullah*' mean's 'God's curse,' but with a sense of 'God's-curse-be-upon-you,' so that's a big Islamic fuck-you to the Great Satan. Nothing on '*Alf Wajeh*.' Plenty on 'Al Manal' and the 'Daura Foot and Mouth Disease Vaccine Facility,' where they did work on viral agents like hemorrhagic conjunctivitis, human rota virus, camel pox, and botulinum. Just south of the Baghdad airport. Or at least it was."

"Was?"

"We blew it to shit," Sykes said. "Or did we? Wanna hear something funny?"

"What?"

"It got all blowed up all right, but when I punched in the GPS coordinates to see exactly which sortie tagged it, I got nothing."

"Meaning?"

"Meaning either we just lost track of what we were blowing up, and that's certainly possible, or, they blew it up themselves. Though why would they do that? UNSCOM had been all over the place. They weren't blowing up anything we didn't know about already."

"Unless they were."

"Unless they were," Sykes agreed. "So when I searched SIPERNET for *'Jamrat'* plus 'Al Manal' plus *'Lanatullah,'* I got one hit. A guy named Halem Seeliyeh. Twenty-five, Ph.D. in microbiology from the University of Cairo, too young to know anything about the early programs, but he worked as a lab assistant at Al Manal. But here's the interesting thing—before that, he worked at the main BW labs at Salman Pak, where he was one of Hazem Ali's assistants. According to his intake interview, *'Jamrat'* was one of the projects he worked on. *'Lanatullah alake'* was the curse he closed his interview with."

"So where is Halem Seeliyeh?"

"Jail. Baquba," Sykes said. "Camp Warhorse."

"Yikes. That place is a dump. Go talk to him," DeLuca said. "Take Mack with you. Find out what he knows about *Jamrat.* Ask him if he saw any trucks leaving just before the war. "

"What do I use?"

"Use your natural charm," DeLuca said. "What's he being held on?"

"Nothing, anymore," Sykes said. "He's too low level to be worth anything. They were going to let him out until he started acting like a dink. Now he's just staying after school until he learns his manners."

"Tell him if he helps us, he can go home," DeLuca said. "Assuming he's just a dishwasher and not part of the management. Use your judgment."

"Take Mack where?" a female voice behind him said.

DeLuca turned to see MacKenzie, holding a folder in her arms.

"Baquba," DeLuca said. "Camp Warhorse. I'd like you and Dan to talk to a guy there. Dan'll brief you along the way."

"Sheesh," Mack said with a smile. "The guy's TL for one hour and already he's bossing everybody around. I spent the morning digging up stuff on your boy Omar."

"Sorry," DeLuca said. She sounded hurt. Unless he was wrong about that. As his reservist friend Sami had put it, "The best reason not to have women in the military is that if the average guy in the army knew how to deal with women, he wouldn't have enlisted in the first place."

"Have fun then," she said, handing him the folder. "He sounds pretty interesting."

"Can you give me a two-second briefing?"

"This guy needs more than two seconds," she told him. "Educated at Oxford, liberal, not pro U.S. but not anti either. Sunni imam but a reform Islamist. Very progressive. His family and Saddam's family have been putting each other in jail for the last hundred years, mostly because Hadid's tribal lands stood between Tikrit and Syria. Though their grandfathers were friends. For a while, anyway."

"Omar see prison?"

"Twice, but just for a week each time. My impression was that Saddam and Omar were more or less forced to deal with each other, but neither liked it much, and Saddam was too afraid of reprisals to crack down on Omar the way he did on everybody else. Ba'ath in name only. I'll tell you one thing—his people really love him. Sort of a Muslim Martin Luther King. Very charismatic. He taught a course in France and tapes of his lectures have been circulating in Iraq for years, all word of mouth, people making copies of copies of copies."

"Lectures saying what?"

"I'm not sure exactly, but my sense is, he's mostly telling Muslims to wake up and join the real world."

"Sounds like the kind of guy we want in power after we leave," DeLuca said. "Better yet, he sounds like the guy we want to shoot the guy we leave in power and take over the country after we leave."

"Good thing we're not into nation-building," Sykes said.

"Good thing."

They were interrupted when an agent from the OMT said the south gate had just radioed to say a man named Omar Hadid was asking to speak to a Mr. David.

Chapter Five

OMAR HADID WORE BLACK PANTS, A BLACK sport coat, and a white shirt, no tie, opened at the collar. He wore a full beard but kept it closely cropped, his cheeks shaved down to the jaw line. He wore his hair short as well, his hairline receding. He had dark eyebrows and even darker eyes, a penetrating gaze, a handsome man by anybody's standards, DeLuca allowed, sort of like one of the Bee Gees, only darker. The army hadn't set up actual interrogation rooms (yet), leaving THTs to improvise, talking to suspects and informants on missions inside circled Humvees, in groves of trees, or in abandoned buildings. On post, DeLuca used a room that had been a machine shed before the war. He'd found a supply of paint and some brushes and had rehabilitated the place to the point where it was about as comfortable as an underfunded American community college conference room.

Hadid regarded him in silence when he entered. DeLuca leaned against the far wall, his arms folded across his chest.

"Sheikh Omar Hadid?" DeLuca asked.

The man nodded.

"I'm just here to collect information. You can call me Mr. David if you'd like. Can I get you anything to drink?"

Hadid shook his head.

"Have you spoken with your brother?"

"I have," Omar said.

"What did he tell you?"

"He told me you would not arrest me," Hadid said. "I told him I believed you were lying."

"What happens after this depends on what happens here in this room," DeLuca said. "You're in complete control of what happens to you."

"If I do as you wish," the other man said. "But if I should choose not to, tell me—am I still in complete control? Can I leave now? Are we finished?"

"No, you can't leave now," DeLuca said.

"Then I am under arrest?"

"You're not under arrest," DeLuca said. "I asked you here to ask you questions."

"Asked me or ordered me?" Omar said. "If you want the truth from me, I suggest you begin by being truthful with me."

"Fair enough," DeLuca said. "Maybe that will save us both time. Yes, I ordered you here, and I'm assuming you have better things to do today than talk to me."

"The hospital in my town needs an emergency generator," Hadid said. "They've asked me to find one. There is no milk in the grocery stores. No one collects the garbage. The elementary school has no books because somebody stole them. All of this comes to me. You ask if I have time for you, Mr. David? You need to ask this?"

Again, DeLuca's intuition told him Omar, like Omar's brother, was someone he could work with, someone who was direct about his self-interest. Omar was obviously smarter than his brother. According to the files in DeLuca's possession, Omar had no wives or children.

"If I help you get a generator, would you talk to me?" DeLuca said.

Omar considered.

"You bribe me?" he asked.

"A bribe would benefit only you," DeLuca said. "A hospital benefits many people."

DeLuca waited.

"It's not as simple as that," Omar said at last. "If I'm not there to oversee the installation, they could steal this one just as they stole the last one."

"If you help me, I'll see to it that you're home by suppertime," DeLuca said. "And that you get what you need for the hospital. Is that a deal?"

"What is it you want?"

"I need somebody I can count on in Ad-Dujayl," he said. "I need help finding out who's shooting at us. I need help stopping the insurgency. I need to find out who is funding it, and who is arming it, and who is organizing it. I need to find the people in the Mukhaberat who put their fellow Iraqis in jail and tortured them. And I want to do it so that one day people like you don't have to worry about milk in the stores or garbage in the streets or books in the schools."

"You want a friend," Omar said.

"That's about the size of it," DeLuca said. It had been his experience that most of the sheikhs and tribal leaders in Iraq had learned over the years, many of them the hard way, that it was expedient to suck up to whoever was in power, which in Iraq meant whoever had the most guns.

That was currently the United States, but nobody knew how long the United States was going to be around. Some figured playing ball with coalition interests was the best way to secure power later. Others calculated that after the United States was gone, it would be those who hadn't played ball who would ultimately prevail over those seen as U.S. collaborators. DeLuca had a sense that Omar was neither, that his power base was secure, now and in the future, and that his personal aspirations were genuinely altruistic.

"Your army, your bombs, and your missiles have killed our children," Omar said, sounding calm and reasonable. "According to the United Nations, the embargo before the war from 1990 to 1997 resulted in more than 967,000 deaths of children from preventable infections, diarrhea, gastroenteritis, and malnutrition. So how would you feel if people from another country came over and killed your children? This is how you felt when the World Trade Center went down. Could you be friends with the men who did that?"

"Friends, no," DeLuca said. "But if I could stop the killing, I would work with them. Just as you can help stop the killing if you work with me."

Omar scoffed. "Can I? What difference can I make? What difference can you?"

"I don't know," DeLuca said. "Maybe I could make a difference to only one child. I don't have a number in my head. To me, one is enough."

Omar said nothing. DeLuca took his silence as assent.

"According to what I've read here," DeLuca said, holding up the folder MacKenzie had given him, "you were educated at Oxford?"

"Trinity College," Hadid said. "Later I studied in Paris. And two years religious study in Cairo."

DeLuca opened the folder and looked in it.

"Oxford Debate Society president," he read. "What did you debate?"

"'Resolved that the money spent on the wedding of Prince Charles and Lady Diana Spencer constitutes a squandering of resources better spent on the remedy of social ills,'" Hadid said sarcastically. "I was for the resolution."

"Did it pass?"

"Yes," Hadid said.

"There must have been a lot of royalists in the room," DeLuca said. "Is that why you were elected president? Because of your persuasiveness?"

"I suppose."

"What were your dealings with Saddam?"

"My dealings?" Omar said. "Where you come from, what are your 'dealings' with the local Mafia boss who extorts protection money from you? Saddam stayed away, as long as he got paid. I saw that he got paid. During the embargo, things came in from Syria, through Ad-Dujayl. Saddam wanted his taxes. I oversaw the collection of such 'taxes.'"

"You ever keep any for yourself?"

"For myself?" Omar said. "No. For my tribe, my city, for the villages, I kept all I could get away with."

"You were a member of the Ba'ath party?"

"They listed my name on their membership rolls," Hadid said. "It was a way to control me. A way to bind me to their party resolutions."

"You were Mukhaberat?" DeLuca asked.

"In the same way," Hadid said. "To charge me with betraying state secrets and arrest me, first they had to make a show that I had access to such secrets. One day I received a letter appointing me as deputy director in my district. I asked them, if I am the deputy director, then who am I deputy to? This, they wouldn't tell me."

"How would you describe your politics? Moderate?"

"Moderation is a matter of context," Hadid said. "The Wahabis would think me a radical revolutionary for saying women should not be veiled unless they choose to be, and that women should participate fully in society, and democracy is compatible with Islam, and cutting off a thief's hand or stoning an adulteress is un-Islamic and unacceptable. For calling them the abuses that they are, even though my proofs use sacred texts that the scholars cannot refute. Then again, I suppose to some Western minds, when I say I believe in sharia, and fasting, and the mastering of one's appetites, or when I say the United States is wrong to support Ariel Sharon because he is as much a butcher as Saddam, overseeing the slaughter of thousands at Sabra and Shatilla, then I suppose I am an Islamic extremist and perhaps even a terrorist."

"In a global context, then," DeLuca said.

"I suppose I am a moderate," Omar said. "Islamic teachings must be interpreted in light of contemporary context. I am pro-Islam. I am not anti-West. I read the *New York Times* every day online. Iraq has never been anti-West, as I'm sure you remember from the days when Saddam was one of your best allies in the Middle East."

"You think democracy is compatible with Islam?"

"Yes," Hadid said. "But not as you have installed it in Afghanistan, where in every district, the warlords run for office and the people have a choice between voting for them or being shot, and the central government can't begin to influence what goes on in the provinces. And not as you would have it in Iraq, where Kurds would only vote for Kurds, and Sunnis for Sunnis, and Shiites for Shiites, and Swamp Arabs for Swamp Arabs, and ancient conflicts drive the elections. A nation cannot be host to open dissent or to true freedom without a belief system that unifies it. In your country, it's the belief in democracy that unifies you. In the Arab world, sharia is the belief system that unifies."

"Let's talk about the WMD," DeLuca said, taking a seat and sitting across the table from Omar Hadid, who had barely stirred in his chair. "I assume you spoke with your brother about what we talked about yesterday."

"I was waiting for you to ask," Omar said.

"What did you think when he told you?"

"What did I think? I was angry at him, at first, for not telling me sooner and for letting a man like Al-Tariq stay in my home, though I understand he did not have a choice."

"Do you believe your brother?"

"Of course I do," Omar said. "Would you not believe your own brother?"

"Where do you think Al-Tariq is?"

"I don't know. I've asked to be informed if anyone sees him. I will tell you if I learn anything."

"I'd appreciate that," DeLuca said.

"We may differ on many things," Omar Hadid said. "We do not differ on Al-Tariq."

"What about the Jamrat Project? *Lanatullah? Alf Wajeh?*" Omar shook his head after each question.

"I heard of these for the first time just this morning."

"Would you let me know if you learn anything?"

Omar nodded.

"If you want to know what's going on in the Sunni Tri-angle," Hadid said, "you must know Imam Fuaad Al-Sadreddin. He will know what is going on better than I. I would write you a letter of introduction if you'd like."

Counterintelligence had been trying for months to get to Al-Sadreddin, one of the more influential Sunni clerics, but so far, he'd been unwilling to talk to anyone from the coalition.

"Why would you do that for me?" DeLuca asked.

"There are things you want from me," Omar said. "There are things I want from you. Right now, there's something we both want. My brother is not like me. Per-haps I should be more like him, more cautious. If Al-Tariq was in my house and I was there, I would kill him myself. I would find the means. Your President Bush uses the word evil with some frequency, and often incorrectly. It's a word that applies to Al-Tariq. The Koran is clear against the killing of a human being, but the text allows for the removal of evil. If you can do that, I will help you. After that, I don't know."

DeLuca looked at him a moment, then opened his sat phone.

"Where do you want the generator delivered?"

"The hospital is in Ad-Dujayl," Omar Hadid said.

DeLuca instant-dialed from his contact list. The phone rang three times before a voice answered.

"Captain Martin," he said. "This is Mr. David with a code Hazel request—I need a generator delivered to the hospital in Ad-Dujayl. With a team to install it. What do you have for me? Uh-huh. Would that be big enough to power a hospital? Uh-huh. Hang on."

He turned to Omar Hadid.

"How much fuel do you need?"

"As much as you have," Hadid said. "There are tanks in place to be filled."

"Send a tanker, too," DeLuca told the aide to LeDoux. "Tomorrow morning will be fine. Thanks much."

He hung up.

"You'll have it tomorrow," he told Hadid. "If you don't have it by noon, call the post and ask to speak to me."

Hadid nodded.

"Perhaps you should visit the hospital yourself," he said. "Room 406. He's registered under a false name. You might want to speak to him."

"Who would that be?"

"Hassan Al-Tariq," Hadid said. "Mohammed Al-Tariq's son. One of them. The other is Ibrahim."

"Why's he in the hospital?"

"He was shot," Hadid said. "By whom, I could not tell you. Or why. But the apple never falls far from the tree, as you might say."

Back in Tent City, someone with his shirt off was doing pushups in the middle of the floor. DeLuca stood in the doorway watching for a moment. Twenty quick pushups later, the man sprang to his feet, drenched in sweat, threw a rapid succession of punches and jabs at an imaginary opponent with a quick Ali-shuffle of his feet, then turned and saw DeLuca standing there.

"Sorry," he said, grabbing a nearby towel and throwing it around his neck. "Gotta catch my PT where I can. I'd use the gym but nobody told me where it is. You the TL?"

"David DeLuca," he said, offering his hand. The other man shook it, his grip firm.

"Julio Vasquez," the other man said. "I'm a bit early but we made better time than we thought. I'm your new boy."

"You a fighter?" DeLuca asked.

"Naw," Vasquez said. "I wrestled a bit in college. Freestyle. Back in the world."

"What was your record?"

"Sixty-six and one," he said, without a trace of bragging in his tone. "I lost the NCAAs in the finals. I was teaching gang bangers in a youth police league when my unit got called. LAPD."

"Boston PD," DeLuca said.

"I went to college in Boston. Where is everybody?"

"Dan Sykes and Colleen MacKenzie are at Warhorse conducting an interrogation. You'll like Sykes—he's sixth-degree black belt in karate. Maybe you could wrestle him."

"Sounds like a bad kung fu movie," Vasquez said, switching to imitate a dubbed-in voice. "My art is stronger than your Chinese boxing—but now let us fight to see who is better! Warhorse is a shit hole."

DeLuca liked him.

"You can put your stuff over there," he said, gesturing toward Doc's cot. He noticed, included among Vasquez's gear, an oversized black nylon bag. "What's that?"

"Satellite dish," Vasquez said. "You mind? In Tikrit, we could get Lakers games. My TV is tiny but the picture is good."

"Where'd you get the dish?"

"From a kid in the market," said Vasquez. "Traded him a Shaquille O'Neal jersey and some cheap bling-bling. It's okay, isn't it?"

"As long as you finish your homework," DeLuca said. Vasquez made it three Californians, all in their mid-twenties. "Welcome to the team. You might want to brush up on some of the files when you get time."

"Already started. I heard you guys were good."

"We've done okay."

"Just okay?" Vasquez said. "Man, word I got was that Mr. David took more names off the blacklist than anybody."

"Sometimes things have fallen our way," DeLuca said. "It's mostly luck."

"That's not what I heard," Vasquez said. "I heard you're the best."

"Do you blow smoke up everybody's ass, or is it just me?"

"Little of both," Vasquez said. "My *abuelo* taught me you catch more flies with honey."

"Actually, you catch more flies with shit," DeLuca said.

"What I could never figure out was why anybody would want to catch flies in the first place," Vasquez said. "I hate flies. I had enough of them growing up, man."

With his wavy dark brown hair, dark complexion, thick eyebrows, and the swarthy five-o'clock shadow of a beard, Vasquez could probably pass for Arab, DeLuca surmised, and that could be a good thing, an advantage that neither he nor Sykes nor the fair-haired MacKenzie could boast of.

"How's your Arabic?"

"Good enough to sell camels," Vasquez said. "My Spanish is better."

"How are you at waiting tables?"

"Lousy," he said. "Why?"

"Tomorrow night, CENTCOM is having a big banquet for all the top sheikhs and tribal leaders in the country. They want the wait staff to be CI."

"This is more than a hospitality gesture, I take it?" Vasquez asked.

"Fancy as it gets," DeLuca said. "You'll be wearing white gloves. And surgical gloves underneath. While everybody else is schmoozing, we're going to be collecting fingerprints and DNA off the glasses. And wearing wires to assist in any eaves that need dropping. Plus we get to eat in the kitchen."

"I come all the way to Iraq to be a waiter," Vasquez said. "My mother would be so proud."

"You go by Julio?"

"Hoolie," Vasquez said.

"Hoolie it is, then," DeLuca said.

When Sykes and MacKenzie returned, DeLuca introduced Vasquez and called for a team briefing in the OMT. Before the meeting, he introduced Vasquez to Reicken and was impressed by how quickly Hoolie greased the lieutenant colonel and ingratiated himself, using all the techniques they taught in books like *How to Win Friends and Influence People*. DeLuca had instructed him not to ask about the fourteen caramels. Vasquez recognized Reicken immediately for what he was, "a real Class-A Remfro." In soldiers' jargon, "Remfro" was a Vietnam-era term that stood for "Rear Echelon Motherfucker" and identified the guys who took all the credit without ever leaving the safety of their desks. Hoolie had spent the time waiting reading the sitrep on the raid at Ad-Dujayl and then Al-Tariq's file. DeLuca had spent the time reviewing Julio Vasquez's 201 file.

"So what have you got for me?" DeLuca said at the briefing. "Halem Seeliyeh."

"Where do you wanna start?" Dan asked.

"Anywhere," DeLuca said. "Microbiologist?"

"Not even," Sykes said. "No person by that name took a degree from the University of Cairo during the years he said he was there. Apparently he was padding his résumé. I'm thinking maybe he was just a biology major somewhere. I didn't press it. He did work for Hazem Ali at Salman Pak, mostly drive his car and take care of the chickens."

"This was at the so-called chicken-feed plant with the guard towers?"

"That was Al-Hakam, not Salman Pak," Sykes said. "But they had chickens there too."

"I was thinking maybe it was like the way they take canaries down in coal mines," MacKenzie said. "If the canary stops singing, you know you've got a leak. Maybe the chickens were there to detect BW leaks."

"Or to test them on," Dan said. "Or it was just to maintain the cover story that it was a chicken-feed operation."

"I saw a nasty cock fight in Basra," Hoolie said. "Maybe it was just a hobby."

"How many chickens?" DeLuca asked.

"How many?" Dan said. "I didn't ask. It sounded like a lot. Hundreds."

"What about Al Manal?" DeLuca asked. "The Daura Foot and Mouth Disease Facility."

"He got transferred there," Dan said. "In 1999. Right after the U.N. inspectors got thrown out. He saw a lot of construction equipment, at first, but he wasn't sure what it was for."

"What did he do there?"

"Well, from the sound of it," MacKenzie joined in, "they kept everybody pretty isolated so that whatever the process was that they were working on, the workers only knew their specific step, but not the whole thing. Seeliyeh's job was to take powder from brown bottles and add it to a growth medium in vials. He'd let the stuff sit for a few days, and then he'd add something to it and run it through a centrifuge and drain off the liquid at the top. He said he'd run that liquid through a filter, add a few drops of some other liquid they gave him, and then pass the whole batch along to the next room."

"Were there chickens at Al Manal?" Hoolie asked.

"That was Salman Pak," Dan said.

"I know there were chickens at Salman Pak," Hoolie said. "I was wondering if there were chickens at Al Manal."

"I don't know," Dan said, sounding slightly perturbed. "Foot and mouth is a cattle disease, so if that's what they were working with, I'd assume they'd keep cattle around as a cover and not chickens. It might have been part of a plan to attack our food supplies."

"Let's not assume," DeLuca said. "How long was he working there?"

"Right up to the end," MacKenzie said. "He said they

pulled everybody out and shut it down when they knew the war was coming."

"What did he wear when he worked?" DeLuca asked. "Did he wear a hot suit?"

"Nope," Dan said. "But he saw other areas where they wore them. And he said his ears kept popping when he moved from room to room sometimes. You know what that means, right?"

"Negative air pressure," DeLuca said. "It sounds like a biocontainment lab."

"Sounds like," Dan agreed.

"Did he ever see Dr. Germ, or Hazem Ali, or for that matter Mohammed Al-Tariq, hanging out in the cafeteria?"

"Negative," Dan said. "But I don't think he would have. My impression is that he was pretty far from the center of things. This was one step up from tending chickens, remember."

"Lanatullah?"

"Never heard of it," Dan said. "I mean, he knows it as a curse, but as far as he knows, that's all it is."

"So he had no idea what he was working with?"

"They didn't tell him," Dan said. "All he knew was that he was working from instructions from a book and the instructions were labeled 'protocol 16.15.' And he thinks the brown powder was something called IL-4."

"Which is?"

"IL-4 is the gene that produces interleukin-4," Dan said. "Interleukin-4 stimulates the production of antibodies to fight off infections. Which would more or less check out if they were making vaccines, the way they said they were. Biology was never one of my better subjects.

Plus if you Google 'IL-4,' you get sixteen thousand different scientific papers on it, so we might want to narrow it down some. My sense is that it's one of the more common genes used in medical research."

"Could somebody get me the name of somebody who knows about this stuff?" DeLuca asked. "Preferably somebody in country I could meet with face to face."

"I'll look into it," MacKenzie said.

"I'll see what I can find out about 'protocol 16.15,'" Dan said.

"What about when they shut it down?" DeLuca asked. "What did he remember about that?"

Sykes and MacKenzie exchanged glances, and Sykes smiled, taking a slip of paper from his shirt pocket and handing it to DeLuca, who opened it. On it, he saw two names, Faris Saad and Razdi Chellub.

"Okay," DeLuca said. "And they would be?"

"Truck drivers," Sykes said. "More specifically, the guys who moved everybody out of the lab."

"Two guys?" DeLuca said. "Moved a whole lab?"

"Probably not all at once," Dan said. "Maybe not the whole lab. Nobody's been through the debris field to figure out what the pieces are, so for all we know, the lab equipment itself is still under there."

"How did Seeliyeh know their names?"

"His boss asked him to recommend some truckers," Dan said. "'Men who could be discreet,' supposedly. One is his cousin, and the other is a friend of the cousin. I'm not sure which one owns the truck. I guess they used the truck to run the embargo."

"Addresses?"

"He hasn't seen them since the war started," Dan said. "He thinks they might be in the Hurriya district in west Baghdad."

"I can do the truckers," Hoolie said. "I'm going to need a translator, though."

"I'll introduce you to Adnan," DeLuca said, handing Vasquez the slip of paper with the truckers' names on it.

"All right if I give Seeliyeh a call myself?" Vasquez said. DeLuca saw Dan bristle a bit, Hoolie's request implying that Dan might have left something out.

"Sounds like Dan covered it," DeLuca said. "Why do you want to call him?"

"I just want to ask him about the chickens," Hoolie said. Dan rolled his eyes. "I like chickens. I used to keep them when I was fifteen."

"We don't want to know what you did with them," Dan said, "especially if there was any duct tape involved."

"Hey, *cabrone*," Hoolie says. "Everybody knows you can't duct tape a chicken. Didn't they teach you anything in that Ivy League school of yours?"

"Stanford's not in the Ivy League," Dan said.

"I know it's not," Hoolie said, smiling brightly. "I was just kidding you."

"Where did he go to college?" Dan asked, once Hoolie was out of earshot. DeLuca could have answered the question—Vasquez had gone to Harvard—but given how he preferred to portray himself as a street-smart Angeleno, DeLuca decided he'd let Vasquez tell Dan himself, if the subject ever came up again.

"Don't anybody forget the banquet tomorrow night," DeLuca said.

"Looking forward to it," MacKenzie said. "I never get tired of behaving subserviently in front of Arab men."

"Dan, I've got something else for you tonight," DeLuca said. "Mack, you help Hoolie get up to speed. Dan and Khalil and I are going to pay a sick call."

The job was locating specific Iraqis, starting with the little guys and moving up the food chain, a task complicated by the fact that there were no working telephones, no phone books where you could look somebody up, and no public records of where anybody lived, on streets that didn't have names. Occasionally you could find the local postman, who knew where people were, or seize the records in a police station, which occasionally proved useful, but lacking that, the best a team could do to collect human intelligence was to rumble into a town in four or five Humvees accompanied by tanks or Bradleys and start asking around, shouting in the middle of the marketplace, "I'm looking for Ali Baba or anybody who knows him." That was often enough. Traveling in armed convoys, it was impossible to sneak up on anybody, but at least you didn't have to honk the horn to get attention. For all the resistance to the occupation, there were still a lot of people who wanted to work with U.S. troops, to curry favor, to suck up to power, in exchange for cash or just to finger their enemies, but there were ways to work it.

From the outside, Ad-Dujayl Hospital resembled something like a California elementary school, a long, low two-story X-shaped building surrounded by date palms, with a circular driveway in the front and a large parking lot to the left of the main entrance. Inside, it hardly looked like a hospital, the floors filthy, ceiling panels missing to expose the wiring behind them, cracked plaster, flies buzzing everywhere, toilets that were simple pear-shaped holes in the concrete floor, no running water, and few medications available, few before the war due to the embargo and even fewer now that so many people needed them. He saw patients lying on dirty blood-soaked sheets, their bandages bloody and in need of changing. He heard patients moaning, and screaming babies, children with birth defects, and he saw young injured men lying on cots, surrounded by their families, waiting for haggard-looking doctors with impossible work loads to make their weary rounds.

DeLuca found the patient he was looking for in a private corner room, number 406. His sheets were clean, and he had equipment that was apparently unavailable to the other patients, including a morphine drip with a microflow regulator he could use to self-medicate. He didn't have a private nurse, but he did have a personal servant who slept on a blanket in the corner to prepare his food and bathe him.

"Hassan Al-Tariq?" DeLuca asked.

The man in the bed looked at him.

"Tell him my name is Mr. David. Tell him we know he's here under a false name because he has enemies. Tell him we can move him to a safer hospital where there are better doctors."

Khalil translated.

Hassan said nothing. His breathing was rapid and shallow, his forehead coated with a patina of sweat indicating a high fever. DeLuca noticed a doctor in a dirty white coat standing in the doorway, a confused look on his face.

"Are you his doctor?" Khalil translated. When the man said he was, DeLuca asked him, through Khalil, what

Hassan Al-Tariq's condition was. The doctor invited Khalil into the hallway, where he spoke at length, in a voice too low for the patient to hear. DeLuca took a position at the door.

"He says his blood is poisoned," Khalil said. DeLuca looked at the doctor.

"Sepsis," the doctor said, nodding. He struggled for the English word, then corrected himself. "Septicemia."

"He was shot," Khalil continued, "defending his house from looters. He has a bullet in his spine and will never walk again, but the doctor thinks it won't matter because he doesn't have what he needs to fight the poisoning. Antibiotics. If he goes into shock, he will die."

"Is he in pain?" DeLuca asked. "Can he talk?"

Khalil translated. The doctor answered.

"He is in much pain," Khalil said. "He has morphine. The doctor says they received a phone call from someone instructing them to give this man whatever he needs to not feel pain."

"A phone call?" DeLuca said. "From whom? Did he know who called?"

Khalil and the doctor spoke again.

"It was the hospital administrator who received the phone call," Khalil said, "but it was from someone he knew to be afraid of. Under Saddam."

"Daddy?" Dan said.

"Or somebody who used to work for him," DeLuca said. DeLuca wasn't sure the phone call proved anything. "Has he had any visitors?"

The doctor shook his head.

He returned to the patient. Khalil joined him.

"Do you understand English?" he asked.

Hassan Al-Tariq appeared to be more alert than before. "Fuck you," he managed to say.

DeLuca waited. When Hassan reached for the flow regulator connected to the IV drip, DeLuca grabbed it, holding them just beyond Hassan's reach.

"If you want this, you have to talk to me," he said. "I'm sure there are a lot of other patients who need this more than you do. I'll give it back to you if you help me." Khalil translated.

"*Lanatullah,*" Hassan said.

"Tell him his father wants to see him," DeLuca said. "Tell him I can take him to see his father."

The ploy seemed only to confuse the man in the bed.

"We're holding him not far from here," DeLuca said. "He's asked to see you." Khalil translated.

Hassan glared at them both.

"*Waish itgul? Abouy mat zaman,*" the son said.

"'What are you talking about—my father is deceased,'" Khalil translated.

DeLuca leaned down and put his face close to Hassan's face, holding the flow regulator in front of the sick man's eyes. He couldn't be certain, but it appeared that if Mohammed Al-Tariq were alive, Hassan was unaware of it.

"*Alf Wajeh,*" DeLuca whispered.

"*Lanatullah,*" Hassan repeated.

DeLuca decided it was time to play a hunch, something that had been in the back of his mind since speaking with Ali Hadid. If the Thousand Faces constituted a terrorist group within the United States, subdivided into autonomous cells, then somebody had to be coordinating them. There was something odd about what Ali had reported, the quote, "*Lanatullah* is in the land of the infidels." It made "*Lanatullah*" sound like the name of a person. Perhaps it was, a code name of some sort.

"*Lanatullah* can't help you," DeLuca said. "*Lanatullah* is sitting in a prison cell in Guantanamo, Cuba, right now." He held the control to Hassan Al-Tariq's pain medication behind his back, his thumb on the red button. "*Lanatullah* is telling us all kinds of things. We know about *Jamrat*. We know the names of the *Alf Wajeh*. We know about your father's involvement."

"Never," Hassan said in English. "*Lanatullah* is become death. He is the teacher and you will learn. *Rah yentagem lana. Lanatullah* cannot be contained. You do not have it." With each sentence, as Hassan spoke, DeLuca pressed the red button behind his back, delivering a series of small doses of morphine to Hassan's bloodstream, positively reinforcing the defiance as a way of getting the walls to fall and the gates to open up. As a cop, DeLuca had worked reticent gang members the same way, pretending their curses hurt his feelings or that their foul mouths offended him, until they started saying more than they meant to say simply because it made them feel powerful, and power was the ultimate narcotic. Sometimes the best way to get somebody to talk was to make sure talking felt good.

Hassan stopped.

He closed his eyes.

"What up with that?" Dan said. The doctor examined the patient.

"He sleeps," the doctor said.

"I think I mellowed his harsh," DeLuca said, dropping the flow regulator. "Let's talk in the hall."

Outside the hospital room, he turned to Khalil. "What was that he said in Arabic?"

"'He will avenge. For us,'" Khalil said.

"'For *us*'?" DeLuca asked. "Not 'for *me*'? You're sure?" Khalil nodded.

"'Become death,'" Dan said. "Why is that ringing a bell? That's not just bad grammar."

"Robert Oppenheimer," DeLuca said. "Alamagordo, New Mexico, July 16, 1945, after the first test of the A-bomb. 'I am become death, destroyer of worlds.' He was quoting Vishnu in the *Bhagavad Gita*."

"'He is the teacher and you will learn,'" Dan said. "What's that mean?"

"'*He* is the teacher,' not '*it* is the teacher,'" DeLuca said. "But then, 'you do not have *it*,' and not 'you do not have *him*.' And '*contained*'? '*Lanatullah* cannot be contained.' Not '*arrested*' or '*imprisoned*.' Contained."

"You think *Lanatullah* is a person? Or a thing?"

"Maybe both," DeLuca said.

He was considering what to do next when he saw a man at the end of the hall. The man, in blue jeans, white shirt, and jogging shoes, stopped in his tracks when he saw DeLuca and Sykes in full battle rattle.

DeLuca and the man made eye contact.

The man took off running.

DeLuca took off after him, racing at full speed, drawing his Beretta from his leg rig as he ran, which slowed him down. He turned left where the hall came to a tee. At the far end of the adjoining hall, he saw a door swing shut.

He turned, dodging an empty gurney still rolling into his path. When he looked behind him, he saw Sykes, trying to catch up. A family of three, huddled by a water cooler, cowered as he ran past.

The door led to an empty stairway. DeLuca heard nothing, flying down the stairs three at a time and hitting the landing hard enough to make his knees buckle.

Double doors opened onto a wider corridor, the walls lined with children's portraits of Saddam rendered in Crayon. Briefly, DeLuca saw the running man's white shirt veer suddenly right where the corridor ended. Another set of double doors opened onto the hospital lobby, which was crowded with groups of Iraqis huddled together, women holding children, men supporting other men, old couples with nowhere else to go. DeLuca raced toward the front door and stepped out into the night.

There, he paused, listening, catching his breath.

He heard only crickets, music playing from a car radio, the chunk-ka-chunk of a nearby oil pump and the far-off whine of a motor scooter engine. Whoever he'd been chasing had escaped, disappearing into the neighborhood. DeLuca lacked the manpower to go after him.

Sykes caught up to him, out of breath, his own automatic at the ready.

"Nothing?" he asked.

DeLuca shook his head, scanning the horizon.

"Shit," Sykes said.

DeLuca radioed the Hummer and asked the MPs if they'd seen anybody run past. They hadn't. He looked around one more time.

"You wanna tell me who that was?" Sykes asked. "Or were we just chasing him because he ran?"

"Or was he just running because we were chasing him?" DeLuca countered.

"Does this have anything to do with it?" Dan asked, taking a wanted poster with DeLuca's picture on it from his pocket. "Look, man, I got your back no matter what, you know that. I was just wondering."

"I doubt it," DeLuca said. He'd asked Reicken to keep it quiet, but a war zone was a hard place to keep anything quiet for long. "If they were trying to collect, they would have shot at me, I'd suppose."

"Then who was it?"

"I'm not 100 percent," DeLuca said, holstering his weapon, "but if I had to bet, I'd bet it was Hassan's brother Ibrahim. You see the family resemblance?"

"I saw a white shirt," Sykes said. "I never caught the face. Let me guess—he had a mustache?"

"You might want to practice looking at faces," DeLuca advised the younger man. "White shirts are all the same."

Upstairs, he instructed the doctor to contact the post when Hassan Al-Tariq awoke. He told the doctor he was a friend of Omar Hadid, and that he would appreciate it if the doctor kept track of visitors. He hoped Hadid would back him up. He had a feeling he would.

It was 2200 hours by the time he got back to Balad. He was dog-tired, but he had one more phone call to make. It was two in the afternoon back in Boston. He dialed the number he'd programmed into his phone and waited.

"Walter Ford," the voice on the other end said.

"Professor Ford," DeLuca said. "I heard you've been giving poker lessons and I was hoping I could sign up for a class."

"Hello, David," Ford said, as calmly as if he'd been expecting the call all day. "You must have been talking to

Gillian. She should know better than to go against me with a sixty-five."

DeLuca could easily picture his old friend, largely because he was as much a creature of habit as anybody he'd ever known. It was summer, so Walter would be wearing gray pants, a short-sleeved white shirt, and a red tie, held in place with a Shriners tie clip. There would be a cup of green tea in a Red Sox mug next to him, kept warm on a hotplate Walter's wife, Martha, had given him. He was as unflappable and as indefatigable as anybody DeLuca had ever known, training he claimed he'd received in Vietnam, where he'd been a marksman with Special Forces, sitting watch in the jungle for hours on end without moving a muscle, staring through a 25X scope mounted to a .50-caliber M-40A1 sniper rifle that allowed him to take out targets from nearly a mile away. During a crackdown on the Boston Mafia's Anguilo family, Ford had sat surveillance on a north-end Italian social club on Belgravia Street for as much as twelve hours a day, seven days a week, for nearly three months. His wife was thrilled when he retired to teach criminology part time at Northeastern University, in one of the best criminal justice programs in the country. His pension would have been enough to live on, but he wasn't the type to stay home baking bread.

"What are you lecturing about today?" DeLuca asked him.

"Sexual homicide, motives and motifs," Ford said. "The kids love this one. They like the story about the guy with the heads."

"Everyone likes that story," DeLuca said. "You got a minute? I know these are your office hours . . ."

"I'd rather talk to you," Ford said. "Yesterday a student asked me why they called him the Boston Strangler. Sometimes I lock the door and pretend I'm not here."

"I think I got something I could use some help with," DeLuca said. "A guy I was hoping you could find."

He filled Walter in. Walter listened. When DeLuca was finished, Walter Ford thought for a moment.

"Let me try to sum it up from my notes and you tell me if I forgot anything or if I'm leaving anything out. You got a guy named Mohammed Al-Tariq, with a Q, not a K, who everybody thought was dead, who might not be quite as dead as people think, and he's putting together a group called the Thousand Faces of Allah, or *Alf Wajeh*. A-l-f capital W-a-j-e-h. And you think the leader is a guy named Lanatullah. Capital L-a-n-a-t-u-l-l-a-h."

"Not a proper name," DeLuca said. "More like a code name."

"And you think maybe this guy is a teacher? The guy in the hospital called him a teacher?"

"He might have been speaking metaphorically," De-Luca said.

"And you think these guys may be planning some sort of large-scale attack on the United States," Walter said. "And you're calling me."

"I'm calling a lot of people," DeLuca said. "Including my brother-in-law Tom at Homeland Security, who I think you should call. He'll have an idea of what's getting batted around in the chatter. Right now it's just a rumor. I couldn't begin to list all the rumors we're chasing over here, and about half of them involve large-scale attacks on the United States."

"I can imagine," Ford said. "So this isn't a nuclear

thing, as far as you can tell? I read an article about dirty bombs that scared the crap out of me."

"Nothing is pointing that way," DeLuca said. "At least for us. My source said he thought it was biological, so that's where we're heading. But that could mean any number of things. Could be chemical. We're trying to narrow it down. And find somebody willing to flip for us."

"So I'm looking for an academic, then," Ford said. "Male, most likely. Anybody who might have written a book entitled, *'Alf Wajeh and Me—How I Became Lanatullah and Led a Biological Attack on the United States.'* That about it?"

"Yeah," DeLuca said. "You could start by searching Amazon.com."

"I'll call your brother-in-law and talk it over with him."

"Why don't you see if Sami wants to join the party," DeLuca said. "If he's free. Have you talked to him lately?"

"I talked to him this morning," Walter Ford said. "He wanted me to come with him tomorrow and cruise over to P-town to see a man about a diesel."

"How're the stripers hitting?"

"Better than the Sox."

Sami's full name was Sami Jambazian, a Lebanese-American who'd retired from the police force as soon as he got his twenty in and bought a party boat dubbed *The Lady J* that he ran out of Gloucester. He kept a harpoon on board in the belief that one day he'd come across one of the giant bluefin tuna the Japanese sushi buyers with their dockside freezer trucks were paying as much as thirty thousand dollars a fish for, but other than that, he was something of a pessimist, frequently cranky. He was tough, brave, loyal, and best of all, he was fluent in Arabic.

"I'll see what he's up to," Walter said. "It might be good for him. He says he doesn't miss the job, but I think he does."

DeLuca got two pieces of bad news the next morning.

The first was that Hassan Al-Tariq had died during the night, succumbing to septic shock. The doctor hadn't seen anyone trying to visit Hassan before he died. DeLuca told the doctor to call him if anybody inquired about the body.

The other bit of bad news came at the morning briefing. Halem Seeliyeh was dead, shot in his bed on his first night home, Vasquez had discovered. Probably by someone who wanted to keep him quiet, DeLuca guessed. No word on whether there'd been chickens at the Daura Foot and Mouth Disease Facility.

Chapter Six

THE BANQUET WAS HELD AT CJTF-7 HQ, BIAP, OR
Combined Joint Task Force Seven Headquarters, Baghdad International Airport, in a large room that had been
the Iraqi Air Force's officers' club, before CJTF-7 had
filled it with computers and flat-screen monitors, but all of
that had been removed for the feast. Two U-shaped configurations of tables faced each other, with the Americans
sitting on one side and the Iraqi bigshots on the other, the
tables bedecked with white linen tablecloths, bone china,
silver services, and fine crystal goblets. The guests were
from the DIA's "white list," men of influence in Iraq, tribal
leaders and sheikhs, religious leaders, doctors, mayors and
governors and police chiefs (along with their entourages,
aides, and servants), chauffeured to the dinner in Chinook
helicopters and driven from the landing zones in limou-
sines escorted by Humvees and Bradleys. A company of
M1 tanks surrounded the building, inside a perimeter of
concertina wire, manned by infantry and MP security
patrols, with Apache and Cobra gunships flying watch overhead. Inside, NCOs in dress uniforms with white towels
over their arms waited on the guests, refilling glasses of
chai and bottled water and soda and bringing the dishes

one at a time, eggplant and tomato dishes, raw vegetables, whole Tigris river catfish served on rice, beef Wellington, and carrot cake drizzled in a raspberry reduction.

DeLuca found Mack near the bar, waiting with a tray in her hand containing three empty wine glasses, a white apron tied around her waist.

"What's this fly doing in my soup?" he asked her.

"That's fly soup," she told him. "It's a local delicacy."

"Anything interesting?" he asked her.

"Maybe," she said. "The guy at table nine is the PUK's director for Kirkuk. He was telling the man next to him he knows who set off the bomb outside the party offices, but he told us he had no idea. Sounds like he's making plans to take care of it himself." The bomb had killed five civilians, including two children, on a day when Kurdistan Patriotic Union leader Jalal Talbani had been visiting party headquarters.

"*Rah yentagem.* Did he say who?" DeLuca asked.

"He thinks it was Ansar al-Islam," Mack said, referring to a group of militants, many of them foreigners with Al Qaeda ties, operating on the Iraq-Iran border. "But he thinks the KDP gave them directions." The KDP was the Kurdistan Democratic party, currently in a struggle with the PUK for domination of Iraq's Kurdish-dominated north.

"What's up at table ten?" DeLuca asked. "Those guys look like they're about to strangle each other."

"They might," she said. "They've been talking about horse racing. The old guy is one of the biggest breeders in Iraq and the sheikh across from him is trying to get him to admit the races were fixed under Saddam. Or something like that."

"Carry on," DeLuca said.

He extracted a bottle of tonic water from a chest full of ice and went out onto the balcony to enjoy it, leaning on the railing and watching the palm trees silhouetted against the lights of Balad in the distance. High overhead, a pair of jets streaked across the sky.

"It's not Herr Totenbrau, but it's cold," a voice behind him said. He turned to see Phil LeDoux. "Mind if I join you?"

"You don't have official duties that are more pressing?" DeLuca asked.

"I think we're making some good headway in there," the general said. "They can probably spare me for a few minutes. How's your evening been so far?"

"Pretty good," DeLuca said. "I'm working on the name of a horse in the fifth race at the Baghdad Equestrian Club. I'll give you a call if I get it. I was going to call you anyway. Things might be developing. You got a minute?"

LeDoux took two cigars from his shirt pocket and handed one to DeLuca.

"I've got as long as it takes to smoke one of these," he said, lighting his and extending his lighter to his old friend. DeLuca spat the end of the cigar off the balcony, lit his cigar, then briefed LeDoux on recent developments. He recapped his discussion with Omar Hadid and his offer to facilitate a meeting with Imam Fuaad Al-Sadreddin. DeLuca described his hospital visit, and how Mohammed Al-Tariq's oldest son had referred to *Lanatullah* using the masculine pronoun, calling him a teacher, seeking vengeance, though he didn't seem to know if his father were still alive, and finally his chase of a man he presumed to be Hassan Al-Tariq's younger brother Ibrahim.

DeLuca told LeDoux what they'd learned from the lab technician at Al Manal, and the leads they were looking into, the truck drivers they were hoping to track down, the gene IL-4, and "protocol 16.15," whatever that was.

"Unfortunately, both Hassan and Seeliyeh are dead," DeLuca finished. "Hassan more or less from natural causes, but Seeliyeh was murdered in his sleep. Which in this country almost qualifies as natural causes. I'm worried that he was killed to keep him from talking to us."

"Any other reasons why somebody might want to kill him?" LeDoux inquired.

"In Iraq?" DeLuca said. "Are you serious?"

"Forget I asked." LeDoux blew a cloud of smoke out into the night. "Is this pretty much confirming what you've been thinking?"

"A lot of it is heading that way," DeLuca said.

"What about the rest of Al-Tariq's family?" LeDoux wanted to know.

"Four wives but just the two sons," DeLuca said. "I was thinking I might want to talk to them."

"Whereabouts?"

"Unknown. But not unknowable."

The general tapped the end of his cigar on the railing, knocking the ashes off. The ashes drifted slowly to the sand below.

"Captain Martin told me today you asked for a generator," LeDoux said. "I'm afraid I might have barked at him a bit, but I told him if you asked for something, not to bother me, short of you wanting your own personal tank battalion."

"I appreciate it."

"Tell your friend Omar Hadid that I'd like to meet him," LeDoux said. "Purely on a social basis. We invited him tonight but he declined." As he spoke, a fair-haired woman in her mid-thirties came out onto the balcony alone, a wine glass filled with club soda in her right hand. She raised an eyebrow briefly at something LeDoux said, then took a position at the balcony railing far enough away to indicate she had no desire to eavesdrop.

"I'm not surprised," DeLuca said. "I'll tell him."

LeDoux crushed his cigar out in a nearby ashtray.

"You finish yours," he told his old friend. "I've got to go back in and hobnob a bit more."

DeLuca found himself at the railing, staring off at the city lights and at the stars shining in the black sky above. The night air had cooled. The woman down from him had a pale lavender shawl around her shoulders. She was wearing an off-white linen dress that was simultaneously modest and stylish, hemmed at midcalf, sleeveless with a collar that turned up against her neck. She was wearing pearls, though there was nothing old-ladyish about them. He watched as she opened her purse, removed a pack of cigarettes, then searched the rest of her purse, apparently in vain, before putting the cigarettes back. She laughed to herself as she closed the purse with a snap.

"I do have a light," he said to her. "If that's what you need."

She looked straight ahead a moment before turning to him with a polite smile.

"Thank you, but I'm all right," she said.

She was British. He felt uncomfortable, afraid he'd given her the impression he was trying to pick her up.

Apparently she felt uncomfortable too. She turned on a heel to leave.

"What was so funny?" he asked her.

She stopped.

"Woman on balcony fumbles for a match," she said, rolling her eyes. "The scenario bears a resemblance to a bad soap opera, don't you think? Sorry about that."

She moved again toward the door, then stopped, thinking. She turned again.

"If you don't mind, I really would appreciate a light," she told him. "Now that we understand each other. I really shouldn't smoke at all, but right now I think I could chew off my own arm for a puff. Pathetic, isn't it?"

He knocked the ashes off his cigar, drew on it once to fan the ember and then offered it to her. She leaned forward and lit her cigarette, closing her eyes as she did.

"If the smell of the cigar bothers you, I'd be happy to put it out," he offered.

"No no no," she said. "I rather like the smell of cigars. Perhaps not in enclosed spaces, but they remind me of weddings. Positive associations."

"They remind me of poker games," he said.

"Also positive associations, I hope," she said.

"Pretty much," he said.

"Except when you lose?" she asked.

"Even then," he said. "Nobody ever loses much."

She smiled.

"Old friends?" she asked. "Same faces for the last twenty years?"

"Yup," he said. "Though nobody has the same face they had twenty years ago."

"Sounds nice," she said.

"Why the eyebrow?" he asked. She looked puzzled. "When you walked out. The general and I were talking and I saw you raise an eyebrow. It spoke volumes."

"None of my business," she said. "I shouldn't have been listening in. Didn't intend to, really."

"But?"

"I recognized a name," she said. "When you see Omar Hadid, you must tell him that Evelyn Warner says hello." She extended her hand. DeLuca shook it. She waited a moment, then said, "Now the fact that you've got nothing on your uniform and haven't introduced yourself yet makes me think you must be CIA. Am I right? You don't have to answer that, of course, but it's all right if you do— I grew up with a father who was MI5, so I was raised to keep secrets."

"David," he said. "DeLuca. And I'm not CIA."

"Counterintelligence," she guessed next. He said nothing. "BBC, world service, in case you were wondering."

"I was," he said. "Television or radio?"

"A bit of both, actually," she said. "I've apparently turned into the go-to girl here. Old Middle East hand and all that." He'd thought she looked slightly familiar and realized where he must have seen her, a face on one of the television screens at the TOC where it was sometimes possible to learn more about what was going on by watching the cable news programs than by reading sitreps.

"I should have recognized you," he said.

"Given that I dress like this about once every two or three years, I don't see how you could," she said.

"Are you here in a work capacity?" he asked.

"I'm a guest," she said. "Of General Denby. Off-duty for a change, so feel free to speak your mind—you're off the record here, David."

He liked the way his name sounded with a British accent coloring it.

"You're on a date?" he asked. "You're off the record, too."

She laughed.

"No, not a date. Not quite. Denby's an old friend. I think I've been interviewing him since I was fresh out of university. Which was where I knew your associate, Mr. Hadid, by the way. One of the better batsmen the Trinity cricket team ever had, I should say."

"You knew him from Oxford?"

"Different colleges, but yes. We were members of some of the same clubs."

"'Resolved that the money spent on the wedding of Prince Charles and Lady Diana Spencer constitutes a squandering of resources better spent on the remedy of social ills,'" DeLuca said. "And you lost."

"Very impressive," she said, smiling. "As I recall, I argued some rubbish about the impoverished proletariat needing vicarious thrills. Did he say he won? Well, I suppose he did. He was older than me. How's he faring?"

"I gather he's doing all right, considering," DeLuca said.

"He's a good man and he's had to deal with a terrible situation for quite some time," Evelyn Warner said. "Been meaning to ring him up but haven't had the chance. Busy busy."

Something else was coming together in DeLuca's mind, something he'd read back before he'd deployed, when he'd tried to research as much about Iraq as he could. The name "Warner." Where had he heard it? Then he remembered.

"Any relation to Lady Anne Strevens-Warner?" he asked her.

She looked down, then up again.

"Guilty as charged," she said. "This is her shatoosh, actually." She spread her shawl out, then wrapped it around herself again. "A gift from old King Faisal himself. They say these are made from the belly hairs of an endangered Tibetan antelope. They say the hairs are so fine, you can tell if your shatoosh is genuine if you can pull it through a wedding band."

"Can you?" he asked.

"If I knew where my wedding ring was, I suppose I could give it a go," she said.

"You can use mine if you want."

"Oh, no fair, no fair," she said. "Men's rings don't count. Too much diameter. Has to be a woman's." She smiled again. She blinked, embarrassed. "I don't know what's wrong with me. First I ask you for a light, like some schoolgirl punting on the Cherwell, and then I manage to slip into the conversation the fact that I'm not married anymore. Let me tell you, Mr. DeLuca, I am not a flirt and I am not coy. I am simply very tired and not myself and I've had a terrible week."

"Why a terrible week?" he asked.

"Oh, that dreadful David Kelly thing," she said. "My friend Alec was the reporter. And then my mother told me Father is driving her crazy. Just retired and doesn't know what to do with himself. She's going to be smoking crack in a matter of weeks if it keeps up. But that's all right. I come from a long line of solitary women."

All DeLuca knew, and this incompletely, was that Evelyn Warner's great-grandmother, Lady Anne, had been dubbed "The Female Lawrence of Arabia" for the work she'd done in what was then Mesopotamia in the first part of the twentieth century. She'd been an explorer and an archaeologist traveling alone throughout the region at the turn of the century. It had been her maps, and more important her personal connections, that helped British colonial interests secure Iraq's oil wealth to fuel their ships during the First World War. Afterward, she was named Chief Counsel to the British High Commission for Oriental Affairs, serving as principal advisor to British-installed King Faisal I. Some called Lady Anne "The Uncrowned Queen of Iraq." She finished her years establishing what would become the Iraq Historical Museum, the same museum that was ransacked during and after the recent American bombing.

"I'm surprised, given all that she did, that your great-grandmother found the time to raise children," he said.

"Bear them, yes," Evelyn Warner said. "Raise them, no. That task fell to the governesses and private boarding schools. Another British tradition to which I am heir. Do you have any children, Mr. DeLuca?"

"One," he said. "A son. Scott."

"And where is he?"

"He's at Kirkuk," DeLuca said. "Though I can't say I've seen much of him. We've both been a bit busy."

"Now that's fascinating," she said. "Do you think I might interview the two of you? I've been thinking of doing a story on all the father-son pairings in this war. There are so many in this war. What does he do?"

"Intelligence," DeLuca said. "Image analysis." He liked this woman, but he felt that he'd disclosed more personal information than he was comfortable with. "I thought you said you weren't working tonight."

"You're right, you're absolutely right," she said. "Forget I asked. But I want you to know that if you ever want to tell your story, I can be quite useful to you. I speak fluent unaccented Arabic and I do know a great many people in addition to Omar Hadid. I treat my sources right and I keep my word."

She crushed her cigarette out in the ashtray after smoking only the first half of it and wrapped her shawl around her shoulders again.

"Ever run across a character named Mohammed Al-Tariq?" he asked. He was fishing, but he suspected he was fishing in promising waters.

"Oh, dear," she said, her voice turning serious. "Now you've put me off my party mood. What have you got to do with that hideous man?"

"I'm looking for his people," DeLuca said. "His aides. His family. I interviewed his son yesterday in a hospital."

"Hassan or Ibrahim?"

"Hassan," DeLuca said. "Unfortunately, he died last night. Septic shock."

"Good," she said. "Not unfortunate at all. Ibrahim is worse. I could tell you stories, but I suspect I don't have to."

"Unfortunate because I had some more questions to ask him," DeLuca said.

"The father is purely evil," she said. "The sons, hardly less. If the father's gone, the world is better off by half."

"What do you mean, 'if'?" DeLuca asked. "We have proof that he's dead. One hundred percent confidence. That's what the file says."

"Do you now?" she said. "Well, that's a relief. American intelligence can't be wrong ever, can it?"

"Point taken," he said. "Why doubt it, though? Suppose I'm curious."

She stared him down, trying to read his expression. She looked sad, and a bit fearful.

"You're going to think me very strange, and you don't even know me. I don't believe in ghosts, David DeLuca," she told him. "But sometimes a feeling comes over me when I walk through a cemetery. That something that wants to be laid to rest hasn't been. Maybe it's because I'm English and we have so many very old cemeteries. Yesterday I visited a mass grave site. Outside Shorish. The number of the dead was over five hundred when we left. They're still counting. And there are 263 other mass burial sites being investigated. This was Al-Tariq's work. And I felt those souls. You're probably going to think I've lost my senses, but I felt them. I couldn't help it. And they're not at rest. Not at all. They're not at rest because the man responsible has not been brought to justice. That was the feeling I got. I wouldn't pretend to have any special abilities, David. I truly don't believe in psychics. It's just a feeling I have, but yesterday it was overwhelming. That's why I was taken aback when you asked me if I knew him. If your proof is conclusive, then I want to believe it. But then I can't explain the feeling I had. Al-Tariq is evil. Personified. And the souls he killed are not at rest."

"Do you think he had weapons of mass destruction?" DeLuca asked.

"Do I think Iraq had massive stockpiles of them? No," she said. "I think your president and my prime minister quite cooked the books on that. But they had some. Do I think Mohammed Al-Tariq was trying to obtain them, for his own personal uses? I'd heard that. They used a variety of things in 1988, during the Anfal. I tried to get a camera crew in there when I heard, but I'd just started at the Beeb and I lacked the wherewithal. By the time we got there, all we found were dead birds. Thousands of them. They found traces of sarin. It seemed fairly clear though that they used different substances in different villages. Field-testing them. VX. Anthrax. And Al-Tariq controlled these things. But who am I to judge? The first country to use poison gas in Iraq was England, suppressing a Kurdish revolt in Sulaymaniyah in 1919."

"After World War I ended?"

"Yup. I've been going over this in my head since before this idiotic war began—since I realized your president has failed to grasp, as the British empire failed to grasp, the most fundamental element of the Arab mind. I've never known more loyal or more hospitable friends than the Arabs I've known, but the dark side of that is, I can't think of anyone more apt to make an enemy out of the outsider who comes uninvited. And the Arab remembers who his enemy is for a very long time. You just can't invade and befriend a country at the same time, even if you do get rid of men like Saddam or Al-Tariq. If you really didn't want to deal with terrorist threats, you might have wanted to think twice before you created a million new terrorists. And those million new terrorists, Al Qaeda or whatever they want to call themselves, are self-motivated, but they're going to need three things to be effective:

money, arms, and leadership. And that's precisely what Mohammed Al-Tariq was arranging for before the war began. Did anybody really think they didn't know how defenseless they were going to be against the initial invasion? They weren't planning for that—why try? They barely resisted. They were planning to take the blow, suffer the casualties, let the troops in, and then destroy the coalition over the next ten or fifteen years. I think Al-Tariq has been planning for years what he'd do, once Saddam was removed. The coalition could hardly have done him a bigger favor. If he's still alive . . ."

"What?" DeLuca said.

"It's something I would pray to stop, but it's not something I would know how to pray for," she said. "You don't pray to God to stop the Devil. Only men can stop the Devil."

She was quiet, gazing out at the night landscape one more time. Then she reached into her purse and withdrew a card.

"There's my sat phone number, and this is my number in London where you can leave messages," she said. "Do call if you need anything. I think Al-Tariq's family may be in Iran. Somewhere between Sanandaj and the border. That's what I've heard. Unsubstantiated. Possibly entirely erroneous. I'm working on developing contacts in that area, so I'll let you know if I'm successful. If you do get there, his first three wives are going to be too scared to talk to anybody, but the fourth one might be approachable. The others won't be."

"Why?" DeLuca said. "What did they do?"

"They bore him daughters," Warner said.

"I thought he only had the two sons."

"He does," Warner said.

DeLuca didn't have to ask what might have happened to the daughters.

He didn't know exactly how much stock he put in the concept of "woman's intuition." Probably not enough. The Englishwoman's apprehension at the burial site didn't interest him nearly as much as her expertise and the things her sources had told her. He realized he was going to need a bigger team.

He checked the battery on his sat phone. He hoped he had enough juice to make one more call before recharging. He dialed.

"Image analysis," the voice on the phone said.

"Lieutenant Scott DeLuca, please."

He waited. A moment later, his son came on the line.

"Hey, Pops," Scott said. "What are you doing at BIAP? Oh, wait—that's the big banquet thing, right? How's the food?"

"How'd you know I was at BIAP?"

"GPS on your signal," his son said.

"I didn't know you could do that," DeLuca said. "I thought I had to carry a transponder."

"We just got it in," Scott said. "Still testing it. Are you on the balcony?"

"Yes, I am. And the food is excellent," DeLuca said. "I'll save you some leftovers. I need to talk to you, if you've got time for your old man. Not on the phone. In person."

"About Mom?"

"Not your mother. Business. You free tomorrow?"

"I can make myself free. What time?"

"How 'bout lunch? I'll bring the MREs."

Chapter Seven

IN A QUIET NEIGHBORHOOD IN READING, MASS-achusetts, Bonnie DeLuca and her best friend Caroline sat in the living room, sipping white wine and watching television, the Larry King show, with the sound off.

"All right, I'll drop it," Caroline said, curling her legs up beneath her on the couch and grabbing another handful of popcorn. "I just think you should take care of yourself. I really worry about you."

"You don't have to worry about me," Bonnie said.

"Well, somebody does," Caroline said. "David certainly doesn't. I just don't understand how he could put you through this again. After you told him how hard it was the last time. I don't get it. A man who loves his wife doesn't put her through something like this."

Bonnie started to cry again.

"I pray for you both," Caroline said. "I'm not saying he's a bad guy. I'm just saying that you're not taking care of yourself, and you have to, because nobody else is going to do it for you. And if that means . . . disconnecting . . ."

Bonnie sipped her wine. She was falling into bad habits again. Tonight she was drunk, but she didn't care.

"What do you think I should do?" she asked.

"I can't tell you what to do," Caroline said. "I just want you to be happy. And I know you're not happy in this marriage. I can see it. You shouldn't have to go through this. You're a nervous wreck. You don't sleep. You're too thin . . ."

Larry King's guest was a Middle East expert named Mahmoud Jaburi. Bonnie turned the sound on.

"Larry—the United States won every battle they engaged in in Vietnam, too. Iraq is not Vietnam. The insurgents are not being backed by a neighboring power the way the North Vietnamese were backed and armed by China. Yet the insurgents have a similar sense of unity and purpose, and this sense grows stronger every day. It may be even more dangerous, in a culture where martyrdom brings with it the gift of paradise. For every Iraqi who is killed, a thousand new faces will rise up . . ."

Bonnie turned the sound off.

"I hate it when these guys speak English without an accent," Caroline said. "It's creepy. At least when they have an accent, you can tell they're foreigners."

Downtown, near the intersection of Kneeland and Tremont, the lights burned in the basement windows of an old brick building where Gillian O'Doherty regarded the patient before her. She'd arrived frozen and sealed in plastic, festooned with yellow and red biohazard warning stickers, a seven-year-old Holstein thought to have been afflicted with bovine spongiform encephalopathy, more commonly called "Mad Cow disease." The "downer" had been sent to Gillian because her laboratory, connected to Tufts University, the nation's leading college of veterinary medicine, was one of the few equipped to handle large-animal tissues under level-two biocontainment protocols. Most animal procedures were handled by the day shift, but the cow had come in with an urgent memo attached; news of the cow had leaked to the press, and the National Dairy Association was afraid the public might panic and stop buying milk, even though Mad Cow could only infect people by way of the diseased animal's sweetmeats, and not via the milk.

"Hello, Bossie," Gillian said, grabbing the animal's carcass by the horns and turning the head to improve her angle of attack. "Wouldn't it be nice if people's heads had handles on them like yours does? Make my job so much easier. One minute now. I promise you, you won't feel a thing."

She adjusted her lights, then checked the laminar flow hood above the table. The hood, the HEPA filters, the gloves, and the mask she wore over her nose and mouth were all largely superfluous, given that the only way she could really catch the disease would be to dig a spoon into the animal's brain and scoop out a mouthful and eat it, but all the same, she'd been in the business long enough to know better than to alter standard operating procedures.

From a tray, she took a scalpel and inserted it just below the animal's left supraorbital foramen, slicing in a semicircular motion above the eye itself and peeling off the animal's three eyelids. She dropped the tarsal glands and the first and second eyelids into a square stainless-steel pan but set aside the third eyelid, which contained the lymphoid tissues. It took her a few minutes to prepare a slide of the lymphoid tissue, which she then examined under an electron microscope. She was looking for PrPscs, the telltale clumps of misfolded prion proteins that would indicate transmittable spongiform encephalopathies, but also scrapie and a few other nasties.

The lymphoid tissue looked normal.

"I guess we'll have to go a bit further, love," she said. "Think happy thoughts."

She set the blade for the circular saw to make an inch-deep cut and began her first pass just behind the left horn, working her way through the lateral parietal bone, across the occipital, then the medial parietal, taking care to keep splattering to a minimum. The work beneath the horns took a bit longer. She cleared the meningeal integuments with a scalpel and lifted the skullcap. A quick glance beneath the skull told her further microscopy would not be necessary. The right hemisphere of the brain looked good, but the left hemisphere had been pushed aside. In its place, she found a rather large endogenous budding of metacestode *Coenurus cerebralis,* or tapeworm larvae, which had evidently caused acute meningoencephalitis and explained the ataxia and motor deviations reported by the farmer. *Coenurus cerebralis* was an intestinal parasite common to dogs. The cow would have ingested the eggs while grazing somewhere where an infected dog had recently defecated in the grass.

She took a sample of the larvae and sealed it up in a glass tube, to send to the National Dairy Association to reassure them.

"Well, Bossie," she said. "No wonder you were acting strange. You must have had a terrible headache."

She then regarded the carcass. She could have left it for the morning crew, but she liked to leave the lab spotless, just as she liked to arrive to see the lab in spotless condition. Using a hand saw, she removed the animal's extremities, then began to disassemble the carcass. She placed the animal parts in a large plastic bucket mounted to a rolling dolly, and when the tub was full, she pushed the cart over to the digester, the largest of its kind, big enough to dissolve a large horse, and pressed the button that hydraulically raised the stainless-steel lid. It took her seven trips, but after nearly an hour's work, she'd managed to load all the pieces into the machine. She set the timer and then pressed the button that lowered the lid. She listened as the lid sealed itself, then watched to make sure the green light indicating complete closure came on, at which point the timer began to count down from sixty minutes. Over the next hour, the animal parts would be washed in an alkaline bath at high temperature and under pressure, until every cell wall and molecular bond had been denatured, at which point the bath would be brought to a neutral pH and then the slurry would be flushed into the sewer system, safe as flushing tap water. In the morning, the lab assistants would find only a pile of bones, rendered soft enough to crush between your fingers.

She was tired. In the freezer, she saw the package her friend David DeLuca had sent her. She would have gotten to it right away if the American Dairy Association hadn't been so pissy about getting quick results. She would get to David's syringe first thing in the morning.

In his study above his garage, attached to a barn-red two-story colonial in the town of Peabody, Walter Ford sat at the antique walnut roll-top desk his wife, Martha, had bought him to celebrate his retirement from the police force, going over his lesson plans for the next week. This semester, the was teaching two graduate classes at

Northeastern University's College of Criminal Justice, one in "Research and Evaluation Methods: Surveys, Observation, Archival Data, and Procedures," another in "Statistical Analysis: Probability Distributions, Sampling, Hypothesis, Correlation, Regression, and Forecasting." It was a good fit for him, despite the fact that he sometimes clashed with a couple of the academic stars on the faculty who taught the more theoretical classes, "Justice and Society" or "The Philosophy of Violence," but who'd never actually carried a badge or walked a beat.

He'd decided to give both classes a new section that hadn't been on their syllabus at the beginning of the semester, assigning them a hands-on nuts-and-bolts sort of contemporary case survey. Their task would be to learn and list the names (and biographical material, including immigration status) of every Arab scholar or touring Muslim polemist, whether of Islamic national origin or otherwise, teaching, lecturing, or traveling within the United States in the last five years, examine their rhetoric (academic papers, essays, criticisms, class descriptions, and so forth) to arrive at their terrorist potential index (after first agreeing on a methodology and the parameters for defining that), calculate their travel and communication patterns, look for data clusters cross-referenced against intelligence chatter concerning keywords including *"Lanatullah,"* "God's Justice," *"Alf Wajeh,"* "Thousand Faces," and a number of other variants, and then make predictions about who might be doing what, when, and where. Tom Miecowski, at the New York office for Homeland Security, had given Walter the telephone number of a man in the Washington office named Katz who'd already been compiling that sort of information, though Katz still lacked the manpower to push his analysis forward. Walter had promised to share his results with Katz, who, in exchange, gave him a starter list of 643 names of Arab academics he'd come up with so far. DeLuca had also given Ford his SIPERNET password, and with it, access to the federal Secure Information Protocol database on terrorists shared by Homeland Security, the CIA, the FBI, DIA, NSA, and nine other intelligence agencies. The SIPERNET information was for Ford's eyes only, but he could use it to support or refute the things his students came up with using Google. Between SIPERNET and Google, Walter wasn't so sure that Google wasn't the more useful tool.

"How to protect and ensure the rights of the innocent?" Ford scribbled in longhand on a pad of yellow legal paper, in the section where he listed questions to raise with his students.

DeLuca had also given Ford a set of code templates that SIGINT had derived from deciphering speeches by Al Qaeda members and insurgency leaders inside Iraq. DeLuca said they'd found messages hidden inside press releases and public statements, messages often broadcast on Al Jazeera television in the Middle East. It was possible that whoever he was looking for was using the American media in a similar way. It was worth looking into, though they were going to need typed transcripts of those speeches deemed suspicious, which was going to be a lot of work.

"Freedom of speech—how it makes it easier to catch the bad guys," Ford wrote.

He had twenty-five students, thirteen in one class and twelve in the other. He anticipated a number of them were going to grumble about how boring the work that they were about to perform was.

"Impatience is the chief characteristic of the criminal mind," he wrote. *"Tedium is therefore law enforcement's best friend and surest ally. Not one out of a thousand criminals has true patience, because they invariably lack true inner peace. Tortoise vs. hare analogy: The prisons are full of hares, and the tortoise gets the doughnut."*

He turned off the light and set his reading glasses on the desk. He looked at the clock on the wall. It was twelve-thirty. He was tired.

At the door, he looked around the room one more time, then turned off the overhead light. He paused at the window on the landing. Crickets chirped loudly in the night.

In his boat *The Lady J,* docked in Gloucester harbor, Sami Jambazian tried to sleep. The air was cool, the boat barely rocking in its slip, a quiet night, save for the occasional sound of music coming from the jukebox at Jolly Roger's Tavern, whenever a drunk opened the door and stumbled out onto Harbor Street. He rarely slept on the boat, but he had a party of ten from a medical convention in Boston who wanted to hit the water at five.

The boat was a thirty-eight-foot Bruno Stillman with a ZF twin-speed transmission. He'd bought the boat used off a Portuguese captain for fifty thousand dollars, a loan he'd be paying off for some time, the way things were going, what with alimony, child support, and college tuition on top of that. He'd been thrilled when his oldest daughter Briana got into BU and figured he'd find the money somewhere to pay for it, and it had been tough, but he'd managed; now his ex-wife Caroline had called to tell him the good news—their youngest daughter, Kate, had been accepted at Amherst College, one of the most expensive schools in the country. Where was he going to come up with that kind of cash?

Tomorrow was going to be another one of those unpleasant things you do for money. Doctors weren't the easiest customers to deal with. Their checks cleared, but they tended to be obnoxious and demanding.

On such days, he wondered what he'd been thinking when he'd planned for a second career after retirement. He was only forty-two, a young man—there was still a lot of good he could do. Taking guys out fishing was okay, but he couldn't fool himself into thinking it was important.

The trip the next day went well, good weather, even seas, and hungry fish. Everybody caught enough to fill their coolers. They tipped Sami an extra hundred, which was nicer, and when Sami complained to one doctor about the high costs of health insurance and how his monthly bill was now higher than his mortgage, the doctor gave him his card and suggested they work out a barter arrangement, medical care (within limits) in exchange for fishing trips. Sami said he'd think about it.

He was cleaning up when he saw the car stop at the end of the dock, a blue sedan with the words U.S. Army in white letters on the door. A pair of neatly dressed specialists approached, saluting him as they neared.

This wasn't what he wanted to see.

His service status was IRR, for Individual Ready Reserve, which meant that he was eligible to be called to active duty for eight years after completing his voluntary service commitment. It was a mobilization tool dubbed "the backdoor draft" and something that, as far as Sami knew, hadn't been used since 1968. Technically, the army was within its rights to call him up, though Sami had long since considered himself retired. The specialists apologized and told him his country needed him, and that he had twenty-four hours to get his affairs in order before he was to report to Fort Devins, for immediate deployment to Iraq, where his orders were to report to one Sergeant David DeLuca, at the counterintelligence battalion working out of Camp Anaconda, in Balad, thirty klicks north of Baghdad.

"Motherfucker," Sami said under his breath.

Chapter Eight

DELUCA WASN'T BIG ON FLYING.

It made no sense whatsoever, he knew, but he just felt that airplanes were bad luck, or rather that if his own luck ever ran out, as one day it surely would, it was going to be on an airplane.

Helicopters were worse, and he was in one, flying north to the Air Force base at Kirkuk where SIGINT and IMINT had their headquarters. The city of Kirkuk, 255 klicks north of Baghdad and just over 200 from Balad, was too far away to risk sending a Humvee convoy, so he'd hitched a ride on a Blackhawk, one of two flying north that morning, with a full bird colonel and his aides in the second chopper, both birds skimming the ground at nearly two hundred miles an hour.

As the ground raced past, he saw the vegetable and date palm plantations of the Diyala River floodplain, the Khan Seyyid palm oasis, which the pilot gave a wide berth to, then the Delli Abbas region with orchards full of fruit trees planted in rows. He watched herds of goats and flocks of sheep scatter as the chopper roared overhead. His stomach started to lurch up and down in his gut as the

chopper hugged the terrain of the Jebel Hamrin high-
lands, with more fertile farms and plantations, then the
wadis of Salahiyeh and Aq Su. His gut turned over again
as the helicopter suddenly rose to slice between the peaks
of Neft Dagh and Ali Dagh, and then it dipped again
beyond the defile, plummeting down its steepest incline
like an out-of-control rollercoaster. He glanced below
again and saw some sort of mosque or sanctuary, four
large white domes arranged in a square configuration. He
considered asking Allah for safe passage but figured the
guy had to be pretty busy, with everything else that was
going on in that part of the world. Then he saw oil facilities, well fields, pumping stations, refineries, and tank
farms, and he knew he was getting close to Kirkuk. He
wondered how much better off Iraq would have been if it
never had any oil. First the French came for it, until they
were displaced by the Germans after Kaiser Wilhelm II
negotiated with the Ottoman Empire for the rights to
build a Berlin-to-Baghdad highway, the Germans in turn
ousted by the British, who weren't about to let Germans
either control the oil or stand between them and the shortest land route to India. As far as the Iraqis were concerned, the United States was just the latest invader to
give it a go. They were wrong, but he could see how they
felt that way.

Finally he saw, below, the post, identifiable by its
hundred-foot-tall antennae anchored with steel cables
against the desert winds, satellite dish arrays and microwave
transceivers, a cinderblock building newly constructed to
house all the electronic equipment, and a massive generator
next to it to power it all, the whole complex painted desert
tan and draped with desert camouflage netting.

Scott was waiting for him next to the LZ, standing apart from the larger contingent there to greet the full bird colonel. DeLuca hadn't seen his son since Christmas, though they'd been in the same country for months. He looked good, taller than his old man, leaner, his hair short now where it had been shoulder length in high school, but he was still the same kid DeLuca loved with all his heart. He saluted his son with as much respect as he'd ever saluted anybody.

"Hey, Pops," Scott said. "How was your flight?"

"I'm going to walk back," DeLuca said. "How are you?"

"I'm good," Scott said. "I'm swell. I'm in Kirkuk. What can I say? How's Mom?"

"Okay," DeLuca said. "I haven't called her in a while but she was good, last I checked."

"You want a quick tour?"

"Absolutely," DeLuca said. "I want to see all your toys."

The young lieutenant wore a security pass clipped to the pocket of his DCU and showed it to the guards at the door leading to a large hangar. Another sentry stood guard at the far end of the hall. Scott showed his pass again and the sentry stepped aside.

The ceiling of the hangar was made of vaulted concrete, hardened against bombardment or aerial attack. On the floor of the hangar, DeLuca saw an odd array of strange-looking winged vehicles of varying sizes, many of them being attended to by maintenance technicians. Closest at hand was a drab gray vehicle about forty feet long.

"This one of the Predators I've heard so much about?" DeLuca asked.

"This piece of shit?" Scott said, wiggling the wing. "This is an Iraqi UAV we seized when we got here. Officially a Czech Aero Vodochody L-29 'Mayo' trainer that's been modified. This one is over thirty years old."

"They had unmanned aircraft?"

"The joke around here goes that Saddam was trying to develop UAV capability because during the first Gulf War, all his live pilots got in their MIGs and flew across the border into Iran and surrendered at the first sign of trouble. Note the spray nozzles and the wing tanks."

"For?"

"Well, probably not for crop dusting," Scott said. "Chemical dispersal. We didn't find any residue so this one was never loaded, but who knows?"

Beyond the Czech vehicle was a row of four airplanes about the same size as the L-29 but clearly of a more modern design, white as snow with long narrow wings, like those on a glider, and a fuselage bearing a slight resemblance to a beluga whale, with a hump where the head would be and a single jet engine mounted atop the tail, with two fins in a vertical vee configuration.

"That's a Global Hawk," Scott said. "Fifteen million dollars each, so try not to break it. Stays in the air for over forty hours and covers up to three thousand square miles with a sixty-five-thousand-foot ceiling. Fourteen-thousand-mile range. Color nose camera, variable aperture video, variable infrared for low light and night shots, SAR cameras—synthetic aperture radar—for looking through smoke or clouds, like your NVGs but a million times more sophisticated. No offense."

"Dust storms?"

"Less effectively, but yeah," Scott said. "All real time via satellite. You've already watched the images at your ops center. They don't fly these low enough for anybody to hit them because they're so expensive. Did great work over Kosovo. We fly two and the CIA flies two from Langley. The Predators you were asking about are over here. Surveillance or UCAV capable. Unmanned Combat Aerial Vehicle. Old-time Air Force guys think an uninhabited system is cheating."

"Maybe someday we can have uninhabited offensive systems fighting uninhabited defensive systems and then we could fight whole wars where no actual living people die," DeLuca said.

"Yeah, but that would take all the fun out of it," Scott said.

DeLuca and his son walked down a line of eight smaller vehicles, each about twenty-five feet long with a wingspan only a third of the Global Hawk's. The plane looked like a very large white plastic spoon, turned upside down, giving it a bulbous nose with its fins in an inverted vee configuration and a pusher prop mounted at the tail.

"Rotax 912 piston engine," Scott explained. "Top speed is about how fast you drive on the Mass pike. Forward-looking Lynx SAR cameras for all-weather night or day surveillance, Versatron Skyball turret camera with electro-optic and infrared sensors. These are only about $4 million each, so they don't mind losing them. Let me rephrase that—they mind a great deal, but they fly them lower than the Global Hawks. Also flown remote. The cameras on this thing could read a postcard from ten thousand feet. Though if it was from you, I don't think anybody's developed a computer big enough to read your handwriting."

"Your grandmother wanted me to be a doctor," DeLuca said. "She was so disappointed."

"We can also load these up with a mission package," Scott said. "Lasers, targeting systems, Hellfires. Remember Qaed Salin Sinan al-Harethi? The Al Qaeda guy who blew up the USS *Cole*?"

"Sure."

"Got him in his car in Yemen with one of these," Scott said. "Mohammed Atef in Afghanistan, too. Those eleven-foot guys over there are AA1 Shadows, sort of mini-Predators. We've been using them a bit more lately."

"What's this?" DeLuca asked, pointing to a row of small doughnut-shaped devices, about four feet across and three feet tall, with a tripod rising from the doughnut, holding a camera. "Are these the robo-vacuum cleaners you use to keep the hangar clean?"

"You haven't seen these? They're pretty new. This is your basic MPSSMP," he said, pronouncing it "Mis-map." "Also known as AMGASS, for either 'Multi-Purpose Security and Surveillance Mission Platform' or 'Air Mobile Ground Security Surveillance System.' Sikorsky calls them 'Cyphers.' We call 'em 'Saucers.' It's a heli-copter. Vertical takeoff, lands on up to a fifteen-degree slope, runs from a laptop off Ethernet wireless, visible light video, infrared, laser range finders, sensor packages to go into an environment and check for chemical or bio-logical weapons, with long-endurance hover capabilities, and it's virtually silent. They made these to look around corners and to hover outside windows in urban terrain. They've got a much smaller version, no bigger than a dinner plate, that they made to fly into caves, I heard. I haven't seen that one yet."

"And I take it those little jobs over there aren't model airplanes you guys fly as a hobby in your off hours?" DeLuca asked.

"These," Scott said, leading his father over to a large table, "are Hawks. 'Desert Hawk' or 'FPASS' for 'Force Protection Airborne Surveillance System.' Here." He picked one up and handed it to his father. "Five pounds, one-thousand-foot ceiling, ninety minutes of flight time. All the same imaging as the others. They developed these back home at Hanscom. Also programmed with a laptop. You can't fly them remote but you can send a new flight program."

"Hand-launched?" DeLuca wondered.

"Maybe if you had an arm like Roger Clemens," Scott said. "Launched with a bungee cord. All you need are two trees, or fenceposts. They're working on a backpack version, but right now this is as portable as it gets. Good for tactical surveillance, over the next hill or into the next valley. That sort of thing."

"It's amazing how small they can make these," DeLuca said.

Scott smiled.

"You think this is small? Come with me."

He led his father to a room at the far end of the hangar, through a set of double doors and into a brightly lit workshop where, at a laboratory bench, a technician in a white lab coat was tinkering with a device about the size of a small hair dryer. Scott put out his arm and stopped his father from going any farther.

"This is as far as we can go," Scott said. "These are the

micros. DARPA is having us field-test them but they haven't really been deployed yet in any practical way."

Suddenly, the "hair dryer" the technician was working on began to buzz softly, and then it lifted two feet straight up into the air, hanging above the workbench while the technician controlled it with a joystick attached to his laptop. It looked like nothing more than a giant bug, six inches tall and three inches across. It flew toward DeLuca and stopped three feet from his face, watching him with a small camera mounted where the head might go. The technician rotated his laptop, where DeLuca saw his own face on the screen.

"Good closeup, don't you think?" the technician asked.

"Better than the picture on my driver's license," DeLuca agreed.

"I heard somebody saying in the future, the average soldier is going to have one of these, connected to a PDA," Scott said. "One can only imagine the ways the average GI is going to think of to abuse them. Women's shower rooms would be my first guess. I heard DARPA also has a flying camera no bigger than a raisin. Robofly, they're calling it."

"Maybe they can program them to fight the sandflies," DeLuca said.

"Come on," Scott said, exiting the workshop and leading his father to a connecting hallway. "Let me show you the control room. That's where we run the big boys."

DeLuca understood what his son was referring to. For all the different Unmanned Aerial Vehicles being deployed in the Iraq theater, it was still true that about 90 percent of the intelligence being used by CENTCOM was coming from satellites, and that, as much as anything else, explained how the United States had been able to overwhelm Iraq's defenses with such relative ease—combined with U.S. night vision capabilities and complete command of the skies, it had been a bit like boxing with a blind man. According to Scott, the United States had been taking the high ground over Iraq since the end of Gulf War I, launching satellite after satellite, both from Vandenberg AFB in California and from Cape Canaveral in Florida, until now over a hundred new satellites were in place, some in geosynchronous orbit twenty-two thousand to twenty-five thousand miles over the Middle East, others in elliptical or polar orbits to pass over the region twice a day in staggered rotations.

"Everything you're about to see is redundant," Scott said in the elevator. "All the systems installed here have twin processors sistered to them elsewhere, both as a backup in case something happens here and to keep things running if we want to pull out or reassign personnel. We also have a facility in Doha."

"NSA?" DeLuca asked.

"NSA, CIA, DIA," Scott said. "The National Reconnaissance Office runs the show, but the show's all over the map."

"Why put anything here at all?" DeLuca asked. "Why not just run the stuff from beach chairs in Hawaii?"

Scott smiled.

"There's talk of doing just that, next time," he told his father. "The idea that command and control needs to be in theater is under review. The old guys think you still have to get your boots on the ground. The younger guys want to put together a 100 percent wireless army where the only boots on the ground collecting intelligence are going to be CI, with complete uplinks. That's where it's headed."

"I suppose that could be an improvement," DeLuca said, "considering that right now I'm holding my team together with walkie-talkies I bought at Radio Shack."

When the elevator doors opened, what DeLuca saw made the Tactical Operations Center's "Star Wars Tent" look about as technologically advanced as the operating room in an old Frankenstein movie. It was a large, darkened room, about the size of a school gymnasium but with a much lower ceiling, and it was filled with computers and other equipment, manned by personnel who were mostly facing the far wall, where DeLuca saw three large flat-screen monitors, each the size of a multiplex movie theater screen. The center screen in the triptych was slightly larger than the other two and showed a map of the world, filled with colored blinking lights that were moving along faintly traced lines. The side screens showed video images in picture-in-picture formats, some constant, others changing every few seconds, others streaming in real time. It was something like a cable TV channel surfer's ultimate fantasy. Above it all was a banner that read "We Own the Night."

"The center screen gives us a quick visual on which spysats are coming online or going off," Scott said, "and each system has a different color. Lacrosse is blue, and Onyx blinks once a second, Indigo blinks twice, and Vega doesn't blink, so the controller knows what he's looking at without reading anything. Keyhole is red. DSP birds are green—that's Defense Support Program. They orbit at twenty-two thousand feet geo with infrared sensors to look for heat plumes to tell us whenever anybody launches a missile anywhere in the world. The DSPs are being replaced by SBIRS, Space-Based Infrared, but that program got set back a bit when the shuttle broke up over Texas. It's supposed to be up sometime next month but it's still going to take a while after that to test it. Yellow is SDS relays in high elliptical that let us relay all this data back to Washington, and elsewhere. The white lights are the DSCS birds. Defense Satellite Communications System. They handle all the tactical communications, from infantry right up to the president. And that one there," Scott said, pointing to a light on the map, "is DSCS 3-B6, which went up on March 10. That's the newest one. We have sixty-five DSCS total. We also have six Milstars that are jamproof and nuke hardened, not that we're worried about that right now, UHF follow-on milcoms, gapfillers because we're already running out of bandwidth, defense meteorological sats to give us the weather reports for Iraq . . ."

"Let me guess—hot?"

"Let me check . . . yes, hot," Scott said. "They also keep track of solar flares and sunspots, which could really screw things up. Plus about three dozen or so NAVSTAR GPS sats that tell the trucks and the Tomahawks and everybody else where to go. And we're not really keeping track of the half of it—if I wanted to show you everything in the sky, that board would look like the White House Christmas tree."

"Who are these guys on the floor?" DeLuca asked. There had to be over a hundred people in the room, most of them with their faces lit by the blue light of their computer screens.

"Mostly operations or tech support," Scott said. "Taking orders from the field and trying to fill them. Half these guys aren't even military. Subcontractors, but good people. Over there is where you get your falcon views. In the far corner where it looks like they're playing shopping mall video games, those are the UAV pilots. That panel is search and rescue . . . Which reminds me of something. Can you wait here a minute?"

DeLuca nodded. His son walked over to a desk where a pair of young technicians were working. One left the room for a moment, then reappeared and handed Scott a small box, first noting the numbers on the side and entering them into his computer. Scott took the box and returned to his father's side.

"This is for you," he said, handing his father the box. "I think I missed Father's Day, so consider this a late present."

"What is it?" DeLuca said, opening the box. Inside, pressed into a protective foam mold, he saw a small capsule, an inch long and half an inch wide, rounded at both ends, with a hole at one end, presumably to hang it from a keychain or necklace. Scott took it from the box, gave it a half-twist, and handed it back to his father.

"Now it's activated," the younger DeLuca said. "It's a transponder. I promised Mom I'd keep an eye on you. The battery's good for three months. It sends out a coded signal IDing you every ten seconds, and the frequency shifts to prevent the bad guys from getting a lock on it. They make 'em for pilots who get shot down, but I thought you might want to have one. You can also swallow it and it keeps working, but don't forget to get it on the other end. They're like a thousand dollars apiece."

"You talked to your mother?"

"She gets worried, not knowing anything," Scott said.

"I should call her," DeLuca said. "Sometimes it just makes things worse."

"Well," Scott said. "I told her you probably wouldn't want to wear it, but I promised her I'd ask."

DeLuca looked at the transponder one more time, then put it in his pocket.

"So what exactly do you do around here?"

"I run a Keyhole team," Scott said. "One of three. The one we're on overflies Baghdad at 0200 and 1500 hours. NRO has three Keyholes and three Lacrosses passing twice a day and we get about two hours' coverage per pass, so that's basically 24/7. Back in the sixties the KH-1s used to actually drop film canisters from space and the Air Force had to send PJs out of Hawaii to jump into the Pacific Ocean and retrieve them. Our bird's a KH-12 that sees one hundred miles either side of track and reads down to four inches. We knew Castro was going to need minoxodil before he did. Data stored, accessed, and analyzed in supercomputers at the Pentagon."

"You're doing good stuff, Scottie," DeLuca said. "I sort of had a favor to ask. I could run it through Uncle Phil's office if you need it to be official, but I think they'd just send you back to talk to me."

"I gathered you didn't come to see me because I forgot to bring my raincoat to school."

"I'm looking for somebody," DeLuca said. "Is there someplace we could talk?"

Scott took him to a lounge adjacent to the ops room. There was a microwave, a toaster oven with a basket of bagels next to it, jelly, peanut butter, soda machines, even a pair of treadmills and two stationary bicycles. A television in the corner played a DVD of *Singing in the Rain*, but no one was watching it. Scott got his father a cup of coffee and led him to a conference table in the corner.

"What's up?" Scott said. "Who you looking for?"

DeLuca told him his story. Al-Tariq could still be alive, and if so, it meant trouble. So far, small things, none of them conclusive, seemed to indicate that it was true. DeLuca needed to talk to the family. Scott listened closely, chewing on his pen as he did.

"So the guy in hospital," he asked, "you think it was the son . . ."

"Ibrahim."

"But you couldn't positive ID him? His picture's on file, right?"

"It is," DeLuca said. "I didn't get that good a look at him. I think it's more important right now to look for the wives. We're having pretty good luck, in general, getting wives to flip once they know they're going to be safe. Walter should teach a course—'How to Infiltrate a Chauvinist Society 101.'"

"And your source said she thought they were somewhere between Sanandaj and the border?"

"That's what she said. Is that a problem?"

"We've been watching all the roads, but the eastern border is pretty hilly. We can see wherever we want, don't get me wrong, but the birds over Baghdad are going to be looking a bit sideways if we want to see into Iran. We could go geo but those are so high you lose resolution. I'm guessing we're looking for license plates on a Mercedes caravan or something like that. We might have some unmanned stuff on file, too. You have any idea when they would have gone?"

"None," DeLuca said. "He might have gotten them out before the war or after. I thought everybody was going to Syria."

"Nine out of ten did. Maybe that's why he went the other way. Iran's been Iraq's mortal enemy since snakes walked, but if this guy had as much cash as you said he had, I'm sure he could have bought himself a few friends."

"What would it take to put together the reconnaissance?"

"Not that long to search what we've got on file," Scott said. "Longer if we have to start from zero. I might want to send a G-Hawk if I can't find anything. Depending on availability. Have you got Al-Tariq's file?"

"Not on me, but it's on SIPERNET."

"I'll call you when I find something out. I have your number."

Back in Tent City, DeLuca found Dan lying on his bunk, reading one of his Arabic books. When Dan didn't say hello when DeLuca walked in, he made little of it. It took a moment for DeLuca to realize something was wrong.

"Something eating you?" he asked.

Dan looked up from his book.

"Why did I go with Doc to talk to the mayor instead of going with you to talk to Hadid?" he asked.

"What?" DeLuca said.

Dan repeated the question.

"I don't know," DeLuca said. "You'd have to ask Doc that. It was his decision."

"He's not here," Dan said.

"So I guess we can't ask him," DeLuca said. "What's the problem? Talk to me."

"The problem is this," Dan said. He handed DeLuca a piece of paper, folded into thirds. DeLuca opened it. It was the note Doc had left him, and the words: "If Reicken hasn't told you yet, remember to *take special care of* Dan."

"In case you're worried, I wasn't going through your things. It was sitting out in the open, and Mack was buzzing around, and I was afraid she'd see the prom picture I downloaded. I picked up Doc's note by accident. I apologize for reading it."

DeLuca considered what to say.

"I think he probably wanted you with him at the interrogation because he thought the mayor would open up to you before he would to a woman."

"Bullshit," Dan said. "He kept me with him because it was the safer mission. I don't want anybody taking special care of me, David. Let me go on the record with that."

"Reicken hasn't said anything to me about it," DeLuca said. "I don't know what he said to Doc."

"But you knew," Dan said. "You knew Doc was making accommodations."

"He mentioned that Reicken had gotten the word from on high," DeLuca said. "He didn't say what he was going to do about it."

"You know why we're driving up-armored Hummers?" Dan said. "When all the other Guard and Reserve units are driving soft-tops? I called my father. He told me he'd pulled some strings and got 'em for us."

DeLuca thought that was interesting, considering how Reicken had made a point of boasting how he'd stood up for his men and put himself on the line for them when he requested armored Humvees for his CI battalion.

"Then we've all benefited from your companionship in more ways than one," DeLuca said.

"Don't bullshit me," Dan said. "If I wanted to be bull-shitted, I could have stayed home."

"I know," DeLuca said. "You're right. I won't bullshit you."

"Reicken didn't give you any special instructions?" Dan asked, almost spitting out the last two words.

"Nothing," DeLuca said. "That's the truth."

"It's just fucking insulting," he said. "If I'd heard it from somebody I didn't respect, I'd kick his ass in a New York minute. I wouldn't expect my old man to understand that, but I'd expect you to."

"I think I do."

"I was happy when I heard you were going to be the new TL," Sykes said, "but if all you're going to do is babysit me, I'll get a transfer. I love this team, but if that's the deal, I'm out of here."

"Let me tell you the truth," DeLuca said. "I wasn't sure what I was going to do about . . . special considerations. I hadn't had time to think about it. I didn't think it would be right to put someone else on the team at extra risk just to spare you, frankly, but I was also trying to think of how to spin Reicken on this, because he's such a royal ass-sucker that he'd step all over my shit and yours if I got between him and the ass he was trying to suck. So I hadn't quite decided, but now I have. You'll get the same treatment everybody else gets, but in exchange, you're going to have to promise me something."

"What?"

"You're going to have to promise me you'll watch your own ass and not take any stupid chances, because I'm thinking maybe you're the type who's going to try to do something extra, just to prove himself, now that you think we've been babying you along. That was Doc's call. This is mine. You're the same as everybody else. If you've got something to prove, it's nothing that the rest of us don't have to prove. I expect 110 percent from myself and from everybody else, so if I catch you giving 111 percent, I'm going to step you back, not because Daddy wants me to watch over you but because if one person on a team starts trying to be the hero, it puts everybody else in danger, and I'm not going to let that happen. Okay?"

"Okay," Dan said.

"Good," DeLuca said. "And as far as I'm concerned, this doesn't have to go any further than here. So I'm done with this, if you are. Did Mack see the prom picture?"

"No," Dan said. "I wonder what the story was with the geek she went with? She could have done so much better."

In the OMT, DeLuca checked his e-mail. There were two messages from his son. The first said only, "Files attached." The second one explained:

Army Knowledge Online
From: Scott.DeLuca@us.af.mil
To: MrDavid@us.army.mil

Hey Pops,
As per, had some luck. It took a while because they didn't use their own cars. I checked all the convoys and cross-border traffic in that region. Attached (separate

e-mail) find maps (NIMA, local) with coordinates and related imagery. Positive ID on three of four wives, w/ approx. 4 other males, presume bodyguards/ servants. No comsig in or out so far, which is weird. No sign Ibrahim either, but we don't have back data. Will maintain surveillance when possible and provide up-dates. Area is hot with you-name-it (Ansar Al-Islam, Mek, et al.). Tell whoever goes to bring help, and keep me posted. Scott.

The third e-mail was from his wife, who wrote:

Dear David,
This is not working. I don't want you to call me to "try to work things out" one more time. How many times can we do that? Why should either of us have to live this way? Love is not supposed to feel this bad. It just isn't. I haven't slept a whole night since you left. I haven't been happy since long before that. I'm not sure that you have either. These are just facts. I feel like I just realized them tonight, but I've also known them for a long time but I guess I've been in denial. I'm going to talk to a lawyer and figure out how to do this and where to go next. I can't live this way any longer. I deserve to be happy. You need to be free to do what you feel you need to do without someone like me holding you back, so I'm not going to do that anymore.

I'm sorry if you think doing this via e-mail is the wrong way to do it. I wanted you to know as soon as possible, but I knew I couldn't say what I needed to say if I was talking to you on the phone. Please be careful.

                                                     Bonnie

He'd heard a story, since he'd first joined the military, probably apocryphal, about a soldier on TDY who gets a package in the mail, unmarked, and in the package there's a videotape. In handwriting he doesn't recognize, it says, "Show this to all your friends." The tape is of a woman in a ski mask, having sex with a dozen or so bikers. At the end of the tape, she takes off her mask, and it's the guy's wife, who gives the camera the finger and says, "I want a divorce, asshole." It probably never happened, but DeLuca understood why guys kept telling the story. It was everyone's worst nightmare.

The e-mail from Bonnie wasn't a nightmare, or even a dream. It was altogether too real. And not entirely unexpected.

Chapter Nine

DELUCA HADN'T RIDDEN ON HORSEBACK SINCE he'd first become a cop, working out of a small adobe office in Yuma, Arizona, and occasionally joining border patrols with the infamous "Shadow Wolves," a group of Native American police officers from the Tohono O'Odham tribe, employed by the INS and the DEA to track smugglers along the Mexican border. The horse he rode east toward the Iranian border was named Shabbut, "because he smells like fish," Khalil explained. Khalil rode in front of him, following their guide, Bassam, with Adnan bringing up the rear. Since he was a teenager, Khalil had been smuggling alcohol and cigarettes across the border into Iran for his uncle, but only between Halabjah and Hawsud and never all the way to Sanandaj. Bassam was from the Koli clan, and would be able to arbitrate any encounters with members of the Imani or Sursur clans they were liable to meet along the way. He looked about fifteen. He would have to do.

The horses were Akhal-Tekes, a tough Turkish mountain breed descended from horses left behind by the Mongols in the thirteenth century, short and stocky with thick coats and stubby black manes, not much to look at, Khalil said, but they were acclimated to the elevation and could go forever on little food or water. DeLuca and his two informants had flown to Irbil, where they'd driven the Hamilton road in a vehicle provided by special ops, a beat-up white Toyota pickup truck, though the mechanic had assured them the flaws were purely cosmetic, the truck otherwise sound and sure to bring them to their destination without attracting too much attention from highwaymen, thieves, tribal rivals, insurgents, or lone gunmen. They'd been stopped twice by U.S. patrols, once in the Safin mountain village of Salaheddin and again at Spilik Pass, just beyond the ruins of Princess Zad's castle, according to Khalil, who was acting as a tour guide along the way, much to Adnan's annoyance. They'd switched to horseback in Halabjah.

"Beyond this point," the post commander there had told him, "you're on your own. Just so you know, a lot more people go into the Zagros than come out."

There'd been no point in asking Reicken for permission to go into Iran. Reicken let his THTs plan their own missions with a hands-off I-can't-get-in-trouble-if-I-don't-know-about-it attitude, anyway. DeLuca didn't mind that there were only the three of them. When he'd learned the location of Al-Tariq's family, he'd talked it over with General LeDoux, who told him that even he would have a hard time okaying a mission into Iran, which, if it failed, would compromise delicate diplomatic negotiations going on intended to coax Iran into opening up its nuclear arms program to U.N. inspectors. On the other hand, there'd already been more than a dozen successful covert insertions, using one or two people, usually special ops. To pass for a local, he'd sent Khalil to purchase the appropriate clothing, he'd let his beard grow for a few days, and he'd applied a military version of the skin-darkening "instant tanning" creams sold on the civilian market back home, a product dubbed "Goon Juice" originally developed at the army lab in Natick. He carried the magnum in a shoulder holster and the Beretta in his leg rig, but he also carried, to blend in, a Kalashnikov 5.56mm AK-101, taken from one of the weapons caches they'd recovered. He felt, nevertheless, underdressed and underarmed compared to one group they passed, a dozen men bearing Kalashnikovs, Uzis, Dragunovs, 120mm mortars, and RPGs on mules traveling in the opposite direction on the other side of a river that was at that point too deep and too wide to cross, or their passage might have been challenged. As it was, the two parties waved at each other and proceeded on their way.

"Any idea who those guys were?" DeLuca asked, once they were clear.

"Don't know," Khalil said with a shrug. "I think maybe Ansar. Maybe Talbani."

"Talbani from Afghanistan?" DeLuca asked.

"No, no—men who work for Jalal Talbani," Khalil said, laughing. Jalal Talbani was a U.S. ally, "the king of mercenaries" and the head of the Kurdish clan that controlled Sulaymaniyah. "He wants to lead independent Kurdistan," Khalil explained. "But so does Mustafa Barzani. So does Abdullah Ocalan. So do couple hundred other guys. Maybe I should do it. I think I would be good president. Do this, do that, you're fired, you go to jail, you come to my bed. How hard could it be?"

Adnan frowned. Bassam spoke no English.

They'd left Halabjah in the morning, hoping to make camp by nightfall at a place Bassam had used before. The scenery during the day ranged from appalling to breath-taking, as they followed a trail through wastelands of clear-cut forests where, without trees to prevent erosion, the hillsides had been gutted and washed away by the rains—stagnant streams silted over, one place where the runoff from a leather tannery had killed all the fish—but then the trail would traverse a series of switchbacks, climbing through scrub oak and junipers to emerge in a mountain meadow as beautiful as any DeLuca had ever seen, with fields of daffodils and gladioli. Khalil explained that Kurdistan was where such flowers had first been domesticated, and they still grew wild.

"Once there were tigers, too," he said. "The ones in the Roman Coliseum came from here. All dead now. We still have leopards and many animals. Wolf. Hyenas. Jackals. Snakes. Many many birds. If we are lucky, we'll see *halo'i homd*. Cliff eagles."

They saw villagers digging in the forests for truffles or collecting quince and hazelnuts and wild chestnuts, a staple of the poorer people's diets. The terrain grew steeper as they approached the border, headed for a little-used pass Bassam knew about. At one point they picked their way up a dry riverbed where in several places they had to dismount and lead their horses up precipitous declivities. By late afternoon, they had crossed the pass into Iran (the Kurdish map Khalil carried had no such border on it but rather marked merely an internal subdivision of a dis-putative greater Kurdistan) and descended to a high pla-teau and grasslands where shepherds tended sheep whose wool would be dyed, spun into yarn, and used to weave carpets in places like Sandar or Darsim. Snowcapped five-thousand-foot peaks rose to the north and south. At the far side of the plateau, the trail wound down into an old-growth forest of oak and chestnuts, producing a canopy overhead thick enough to block out the sun, gnarled and twisting branches that seemed interlocked, as if the forest were a single massive living organism. Squirrels chattered their warnings as the men on horseback passed.

"Bassam says many caves from here on," Khalil reported. "From before history."

"Prehistoric," DeLuca said.

"Yes," Khalil said. "Some have bones in them fifty thousand years old. I saw this once. A skeleton resting on a bed of twigs in a cave. I think somebody buried him there."

They wound along a hogback ridge, traversed a limestone scarp, and descended a series of switchbacks into a ravine that narrowed to only a few feet in places, the temperature dropping sharply between the rising walls where the sun could only shine a few minutes each day. It would have been a perfect place for an ambush. A stream formed at the base of the ravine, dropping into a doline that reminded DeLuca of the *sumideros* in Puerto Rico where he'd once trained. They turned south into a hanging valley and hugged the western wall until they mounted a short incline to a rock shelf affording a view of the valley below, the canyon wall rising a thousand feet behind them.

Bassam dismounted and directed the others to do the same and to unload the animals, then led the party to the base of the cliff and a rocky overhang that formed a smile-shaped crack in the earth, about a hundred feet across. Climbing over the bottom lip, they found a cave about fifty feet across, with a twenty-foot ceiling and a depth DeLuca couldn't estimate, because when he shone the flashlight he carried toward the rear of the cave, he saw only darkness.

They dropped their packs and bedrolls. Bassam and Khalil spoke for a few minutes, and then Khalil approached DeLuca.

"He says this is where we will stay," Khalil said. "It is safe. No one comes here so no one will bother us. We will get wood for the fire."

Enough light from the fading day filtered into the mouth of the cave to reveal a firepit and a small pile of firewood, banked against a large rock face that formed a kind of natural hearth. The temperature had dropped steadily after the sun went down, and DeLuca was glad for the wool clothing he'd found so oppressive at noon. He was hungry enough to eat his blanket, though he knew he was going to need it later. He left Adnan by the firepit and climbed back out onto the escarpment, where he dialed his sat phone. Mack answered.

"Hey, cowboy," she said. "How's it going?"

"Yippee-ti-yi-ay," he said. "What's happening there? Any luck with the truck drivers? Faris Saad and Razdi what'shisname?"

"Chellub. And some," she said. "This guy Hoolie is pretty good, by the way. Anyway, we found the sister of one of the guys but she said her brother has gone into hiding because the other guy is dead and the first guy thinks he could be next."

"He was killed?"

"I guess," Mack said. "We don't have the details yet."

"And the sister knows where her brother is?"

"She says she doesn't, but I think she does. She's going to try to find him."

"What'd you offer her?"

"We offered him protection," Mack said. "Her, we offered a microwave."

"A what?"

"Hoolie traded a guy some Tommy Hilfiger jeans for it. By the way, we hope you don't mind but Hoolie had a friend from his unit in Tikrit transferred to the team. He'll be here when you get back. Dan wants to talk to you."

"Hey, Tex," Dan said, coming on the line. "Real quick—I found a guy who could help me clear up some of the things our lab assistant pal from the Daura Foot and Mouth Disease Facility left us with. His name is Kaplan, Major, and he works right here at the CASH on post, but back home he's an infectious disease specialist at Johns Hopkins, where they do a lot of work with BWs. You're not going to like what he had to say."

"What did he have to say?"

"Well first of all, IL-4 is the gene that produces interleukin-4, which is a cytokine that stimulates the body to produce antibodies to fight off infections. We thought maybe they were working with vaccines that use interleukin-4, but then when I mentioned 'protocol 16.15,' he sort of got all pale. He went to his library and he came back with a book. *Current Protocols in Molecular Biology,* John Wiley and Sons pub., volume three, section 4."

"Which says?"

"It's directions on how to splice a gene into a poxvirus. It didn't sound that hard—he said a gifted high-school organic chemistry student could do it, and the book gives you all the instructions. It's not classified."

"So Halem Seeliyeh was doing genetic splicing?"

"One part of the process. It's not hard, but it takes a couple days. From the sound of it, they gave out different steps to different guys in different rooms so that nobody knew the full extent of what they were doing."

"And you said they were working with camel poxes at Daura?"

"They were," Dan said. "But that's also a legitimate research area. Or a cover for something illegitimate. There's a zillion kinds of poxes. The problem is, if you splice an IL-4 gene onto a poxvirus, you get a supervirus, basically. Interleukin-4 is only beneficial in controlled amounts. If you get too much, you start killing off your white blood cells."

"Like AIDS?"

"Exactly like AIDS," Dan said. "You get a nearly instantaneous AIDS-like suppression of the immune system, which renders the poxvirus vaccine-proof and makes it work a hundred times faster. They've already tested it with mouse pox. And you and I both know what poxes Iraq had in stock before the war."

Much had been made, both in Congress and in recent news stories, of failures on intelligence before the war. No one questioned whether the Hussein regime had, at one time, biological or chemical weapons. They'd already used them, during the Anfal campaign in 1988, in some of the villages DeLuca had passed through that very day. The only real question was exactly what CW and BW the Iraqis had, and how far along the research was. A number of defectors had given classified testimony in CIA briefings that Drs. Hazem Ali and Rihab Taha had been working with smallpox, probably acquired from the Russians, who were known to have produced twenty thousand tons of the stuff.

"Kaplan also thought Hoolie's instincts about the chickens were right on. You can only culture viruses in living organisms with circulatory systems. Chickens lay eggs, and eggs contain embryos. Kaplan said virologists use chicken embryos to culture viruses."

Suddenly DeLuca wasn't as hungry as he'd been before.

"Call Captain Martin at General LeDoux's office and tell him what you told me," DeLuca said. "Tell him we think we might be looking at smallpox. Keep going on the truck drivers. I'm going to be out of the office for a couple more days but we can all sit down when I get back."

"Omar Hadid called," Sykes said. "He says he can put together a meeting with you and Imam Fuaad Al-Sadreddin. That's the big Sunni kahuna, right? That could be big. By the way, where did you tell Reicken you were going?"

"Ashur," DeLuca said.

"To meet with the police chief, four o'clock, right?"

"Right."

"A car bomb blew up the Ashur police headquarters at five minutes after four today," Dan said. "Did you tell anyone you were going there except Reicken?"

"Nobody," DeLuca said.

"Well obviously there's a leak somewhere, because whoever's trying to collect the bounty knew where you were going to be."

When he returned to the fire, he saw that Khalil had caught a good-sized rabbit while he was out collecting firewood and had already skinned and skewered it to roast over the fire. Khalil reminded him a bit of Hoolie, both resourceful men of good cheer, both loose cannons, to a certain extent. Adnan was off to the side, staring out the cave entrance. Bassam had laid his blanket on the ground and set a half-dozen small tin pans before him, using them to prepare the rest of the dinner from stores in his pack.

By the light of the fire, DeLuca saw markings on the wall, a bas-relief carved into the rock itself. He shone his flashlight on it. It seemed to be a picture of some sort of horned lizard or dragon.

"Marduk," Khalil said behind him. "Babylonian sun god. He inspired Hammurabi to give his code of justice. We had laws for how to run a just government four thousand years before United States was ever a country."

"Who carved this?" DeLuca asked, running his fingers over the carving. Khalil exchanged words with Bassam.

"He says Kassitis, perhaps," Khalil said. "Persians. But not recently. Is very old."

"Ask him about the carvings over there," Adnan said with a sneer in his voice. "Then do not wonder why nobody uses this place."

DeLuca shone his flashlight in the direction Adnan had suggested. Across the cave, he saw a larger relief, a figure resembling some kind of cross between an angel and a peacock, a winged man with a fan of feathers rising behind him. DeLuca moved closer. He saw some sort of cuneiform below the carving of the angel-bird. He asked Khalil what it said.

"Y-Z-D," Khalil said. "For the Yezidis."

"Who were?"

"*Shitan* worshipers," Adnan said. "Followers of the devil."

"Direct descendants of Adam. *Zerdachis*," Khalil corrected his fellow informant. "Not *Shitan. Taus Manzuá.* The angel Lucifer who has been restored to heaven after seven thousand years. But he is redeemed, a Christian would say. For the Yezidis, Satan himself has been forgiven."

"He is lying," Adnan said. "*Shitan* is *Shitan*. The Yezidi *hashīshīyūn assassin* only say that to avoid punishment."

"He calls them dope-smoking assassins. A thousand years of massacres at the hands of Turks and Muslims gives them the right to fight back," Khalil said, turning to Adnan.

Adnan turned his back on Khalil.

"How long ago did these Yezidis live?" DeLuca asked.

"How long ago?" Khalil said, not understanding the question. "They live here now. Bassam says this is a place of worship."

DeLuca fell asleep by the fire shortly after finishing his meal, awakened sometime later by the sound of electronic beeping. When he opened one eye, he saw that Bassam was playing with his Gameboy.

The walled compound where Al-Tariq had sequestered his wives was in a resort district in the hills south of Sanandaj, where a dam created a large reservoir. Bassam had arranged for a cousin to meet them with a car and to serve as a local guide, leading them to a three-thousand-year-old castle built on a hilltop overlooking the lake below, affording surveillance of the front of the house, maybe half a mile off, and part of the courtyard.

DeLuca, using a pair of 25X binoculars, was able to observe five bodyguards patrolling the grounds. He could see vehicles coming and going, though he was too far away to see license plates. When one of the wives appeared on an upstairs balcony, minus her veil and *burqua,*

Adnan took the binoculars and was able to confirm her identity. He confirmed a second wife an hour later. The first was nearly as fat as her husband. The second had a distinctive way of smoking cigarettes, holding her cigarette in her left hand, high enough that the smoke wouldn't get in her hair.

DeLuca was trying to think of ways to talk to them, a task complicated by the fact that none would leave the house without her husband. Sanandaj was the Kurdish capital of Iran, and Al-Tariq had too many Kurdish enemies to openly move his family into the neighborhood. He'd most likely purchased the compound through a surrogate and/or under a false name, to use temporarily, until more permanent quarters could be found. DeLuca needed an Iranian collaborator, but finding one would take time.

He was still watching the house when a white SUV pulled up. He recognized the man who got out of the passenger's seat. It was Ibrahim Al-Tariq, the same man he'd chased in the hospital. He was alone. He went into the house.

DeLuca dialed a number on his sat phone. A moment later, he was speaking with his son, explaining what had just happened.

"You're sure it's him?"

"Ninety percent. You got anything up there I can use?" DeLuca asked.

"My bird's busy at the moment," Scott said. "What do you need?"

"Closeups maybe. Wait a second."

As he spoke, Ibrahim left the house and returned to the SUV. He started it, then went back inside the house.

"It looks like he's leaving," DeLuca said. "I can't follow him because I'd be the only other car on the road. Can you keep an eye on him for me and tell me where he goes?"

"The white Suburban?" Scott asked. "Got him on DSP. I can do better with a G-Hawk but it's going to take me about fifteen minutes to get one there. I'm sure I can hold him until I make the switch."

Ibrahim got into the driver's seat of the car. A bodyguard got in on the passenger's side. DeLuca watched the gates to the compound swing open as the SUV pulled out, turning on the road to Sanandaj.

The car Bassam's cousin had provided was a rather beat-up Toyota Corolla with what looked like a bullet hole in the trunk (and an exiting bullet at that), but it started and it moved, and that was all DeLuca could ask for. He took Adnan and Khalil with him. In the days before the mission, he'd constructed a cover identity as a German antiquities buyer, in the market for artifacts recently "liberated" from the various shrines and museums U.S. forces had been unable to protect from looters. Dan had found him a reference book to study, and Mack had Photoshopped him a German passport (taking the name of a real German antiquities dealer who was still in Hamburg, quite unaware that his identity was being borrowed), along with the relevant travel papers and plane tickets, but it was only superficial cover, meant to fool a few local policemen or border patrols but not something that was going to stand up to more thorough scrutiny.

They drove, leaving plenty of space between them and the car ahead.

His phone rang again.

"You might want to hold off for a second," Scott said. "He stopped to take a leak. Maybe three klicks ahead of you. Three and a half."

DeLuca directed Khalil to stop the car.

"Boxers or briefs?" DeLuca asked.

"Looks like your man goes commando," Scott said. "He's moving again. G-Hawk's in place."

The road leveled off as they approached Sanandaj, passing fields and farms, and then a tent city that had sprung up on the outskirts of town to house war refugees. Since the invasions of Afghanistan to the east and Iraq to the west, Iran had been flooded with displaced people, two and a half million Afghanis and nearly half a million Iraqis. The refugee camps sprawled to either side of the road, the Toyota's progress impeded by children playing and women pushing wheelbarrows and carts or carrying packages of bread or bags of rice in their arms, bundles marked with red crescents and red crosses. Soon, the white SUV was only fifty yards in front of them, slowly winding its way toward the center of town.

DeLuca's cell phone rang again.

"You got a visual?" Scott asked.

"Roger that," DeLuca said. "We can take it from here, but keep an eye on him in case we lose him."

"My buddy here tells me there's a nice teahouse on Ferdosi Street and a kilim dealer next to it where you can get really good deals. Mom might like one for the den."

"This isn't a shopping trip," DeLuca said.

"Just a thought," Scott said. "Nice car, by the way."

The white SUV parked on a side street adjacent to Enqelāb Square and the Hedayat Hotel, which had an outdoor patio facing the plaza, which abutted a large wall forming the northern side of the square. DeLuca watched as Ibrahim and his bodyguard sat themselves at a table on the patio. Ibrahim looked at his watch, as if he were meeting somebody, then instructed his bodyguard to wait by the car. Adnan got a good look at him and was able to make positive identification.

"You're sure he's not going to recognize you?"

"I was not around the family that much," Adnan said, referring to his bodyguarding days.

DeLuca, Khalil, and Adnan took seats at a table across the patio, where they could watch both Ibrahim Al-Tariq and the street. There was a large water fountain at the southern end of the square and in the center of the fountain, a statue of a human figure with his arm thrown up in the air in a victorious gesture. In the center of the square, there was some kind of commotion. DeLuca heard a kind of rhythmic chanting, accompanied by tambourines.

"Sufis," Adnan said.

"What are they saying?" DeLuca asked, keeping an eye on Ibrahim.

"The ninety-nine names of Allah," Adnan said.

"It puts them in a trance," Khalil said. "They sway back and forth and spin, and at the end, they eat razor blades and put needles into their eyes and livers and stab their heads with daggers."

"Is not for everyone," Adnan said. It was the first joke DeLuca had heard him make.

When the waiter came, Khalil ordered food for them in Kurdish. DeLuca saw a man approach Ibrahim's table. Ibrahim stood when the stranger approached, and then the two men sat down. The new arrival was Caucasian, about thirty-five years old, with thick glasses and a Western suit, cut poorly, or else the guy had recently lost a lot of weight. DeLuca would have given anything to know what they were talking about, but for the time being, he'd settle for knowing the name of the man Ibrahim was meeting with.

He found his phone and pressed the Select button for the Accessories menu. His battery was only half-charged. He hoped he had enough juice left. He thought he found what he was looking for on the menu, but then he lost it and couldn't figure out how to get back to it. He tried again and failed a second time.

"What is it you are doing?" Khalil asked him.

"This thing is supposed to be able to take pictures, but I can't get it to work . . ."

He fumbled with the phone another minute.

"Please," Khalil said. "Perhaps I could help you."

DeLuca handed his Kurdish friend the sat phone. After a few seconds and a beep or two, Khalil raised the phone in front of his face, pressed a button, then showed DeLuca the picture he'd taken of him.

DeLuca took a test picture of Khalil and a second one of Adnan, until he felt like he knew how the picture function worked, and then he stood and walked to a spot halfway between his table and Ibrahim's.

"Noch einmal," he called out in German. He gestured with his hands, arms extended as if he were squeezing a balloon. *"Dicht zusammen und lächeln Sie bitte. Arm in Arm."* He'd asked for one more picture, closer together and smiling, arm in arm. Adnan had evidently never put his arm around a Kurd before and wasn't keen on starting now. When they were posed, DeLuca reversed the camera and pointed it over his shoulder at the table where Ibrahim

and his guest were sitting. He checked the image, then took a second picture. The second attempt produced a good three-quarter view of Ibrahim Al-Tariq's lunch guest.

At the table, Khalil showed DeLuca how to transmit the pictures he'd just taken. He sent what he had to his brother-in-law, Tom. He sent them again, just in case something went wrong with the first transmission, along with a voice tag, saying, "Tommy—it's David. Can you help me ID this guy? I'll explain later."

When the kabobs came, Khalil and Adnan dug in. DeLuca watched Ibrahim as he ate, but only glancing his way occasionally to avoid arousing suspicion. He was drinking some sort of lemon-flavored drink when he felt a hand on his shoulder.

"Now this *is* a surprise," a woman's voice said. "I didn't expect to see you here—how are you, darling?" the woman said, sitting down in the empty chair. She wore sunglasses, and a scarf covered her head, but DeLuca recognized her immediately and was glad to see her.

"Hello, Evelyn," he said.

"This is where you say, 'Of all the gin joints in the world, why'd she have to walk into mine?'" Evelyn Warner said. "Aren't you going to introduce me to your friends?"

DeLuca obliged. She greeted each of them in their native tongues.

"You must forgive me," she said, "I feel so very foolish, but I'm afraid I've forgotten your name as well?"

"Jan Tischler," DeLuca said after blanking for a second on his cover name. "From Hamburg."

"Ah yes, of course, I'm so sorry, Mr. Tischler, so good to see you again," she said, loud enough for anyone at a nearby table to hear. "How are you? Sightseeing?"

"Business," DeLuca said. "And you?"

"Well, I'm here doing a story about the refugees, but this is my hotel," she said. "Are you staying here? It's the only one in town that takes Westerners, you know—you don't have much choice. But perhaps you're just passing through?"

"I have a couple of appointments in Kermanshah," he said.

"Kermanshah!" she exclaimed. "Lovely place. You must see the reliefs at Tāq-é Bostān. If you like hunting. Lots of naked men spearing elephants and lions and that sort of thing. Do you hunt, Mr. Tischler?"

"Sometimes," he said. "But rarely naked. I'm here currently only as a dealer of antiquities."

"Yes, that's right, we spoke of it at the party," she said, playing along. "Finding anything? Nothing without a well-documented provenance, I trust?"

"Of course not," DeLuca said. "That would be illegal."

"I was also hoping to run into an old friend of mine," she said, smiling and shaking her head when the waiter approached to ask her if she wanted anything. "Any idea where I might find the Al-Tariq estate? I heard it's around here somewhere."

DeLuca put a finger to his lips and motioned with his eyes toward the two men at the table across the patio.

"You never know," he said.

"Perhaps we could have dinner before you go," she said. "To Kermanshah. You and your friends. Somewhere where we could talk."

A roar went up from the square, where the Sufi mystics had commenced their bloodletting. A family of refugees passed in the street, all their belongings webbed to a cart pulled by a donkey.

"Self-flagellation," the Englishwoman said. "Ever a crowd pleaser."

Ibrahim and his guest shook hands as they rose from their chairs. The parting seemed amicable. The stranger walked Ibrahim to his car, then continued down the street alone, apparently without escort.

DeLuca speed-dialed his son.

"Still there?" DeLuca asked.

"You bet," Scott said.

"Follow the white SUV. I've got a new target. See you around."

He followed the stranger down Eman Khomeini Street, past a row of travel agencies, a bus company, past the Sanandaj Museum, and then around a corner toward a domed mosque with twin minarets, dodging beggars and refugees and street vendors as they went. The sound of tambourines and chanting faded behind them. He tried to fill Evelyn in as they walked.

"I'm going to have to ask you to keep this all a secret," he said. "Not for publication. Fair enough?"

"Fair enough," she said.

"Are you here alone?"

"My cameraman is with me," she said. "He's getting footage in the camp south of town. Had to register as man and wife, I'm afraid, but he's gay, so it's safer for him, too. Bit hard still for a single woman to stay alone in a hotel."

They'd turned down a small bazaar, with the sound of rap music in Arabic blasting from a boombox somewhere, when DeLuca heard tires screeching behind him. He turned quickly to see a green pickup truck approaching at high speed. He looked up the street and saw a black SUV blocking the way before them. He'd left the Kalashnikov in the trunk of the Corolla. He bent to get the Beretta from his leg rig when someone bowled him over from the side, knocking him to the ground.

Immediately, three men were upon him.

He saw two men grab Evelyn Warner and hustle her toward the van. Khalil had his arms raised over his head. Someone was pointing a gun at Adnan's head.

DeLuca threw one man off him, drove a second into a fruit stand, and had just struggled to his feet when he turned to see a third man with the butt of his rifle raised above DeLuca's head. He saw the rifle butt just before it struck him hard above his left ear.

"That didn't hurt as much as I thought it was going to," he thought.

Then everything went black.

Chapter Ten

HE WAS IN A CAR.

The car was moving at a moderate rate of speed on a dirt road.

He didn't feel the sudden lateral shifts or roller-coastering that might have told him he was on a mountain road, so his best guess was, they were more likely in a valley or on a plateau somewhere.

It sounded and felt like a large vehicle with heavy suspension and shocks that were fairly new, probably the black SUV he'd seen. It had been a four-door. He was in the far back. Someone was next to him. He heard a cough. Someone else was on the other side of him. His hands were bound behind his back with the same kind of plastic flex cuffs that U.S. forces were using in the field. His head hurt, and there was a ringing in his ear.

He heard two men conversing in the seat in front of him. One was angry. They were speaking in Arabic.

"Athun innak mukhaberat Amreekeyeh," he heard a man say. "I think you are CIA."

"I don't speak your language," he heard Evelyn say. "I work for the BBC. I'm a British citizen. My papers will tell you that. I'm a British citizen."

"CIA," the man repeated.

"I'm a reporter for the BBC," she repeated. She did not sound scared. "Do you watch Al Jazeera? I've been on Al Jazeera several times. You can call the news director there and ask him. If you take this bloody hood off, maybe somebody in your group would even recognize me. I am doing a report on the refugees. I'm trying to let the world know these people need help. If you let me go . . ."

"Shut up!" the man said. "You are CIA. You are both CIA."

"Herr Tischler is an art dealer," she said. "He is German. Germany is not an ally of the United States in this war."

"Shut up now," the man said.

The men conversed again in Arabic.

DeLuca felt behind him for anything he might be able to use to cut the flex cuffs, the edge of a seatbelt latch, perhaps.

He felt the car turn off whatever road they were on, and then the way became rougher, larger potholes and bumps, curves that threw him from side to side, things in the road that caused the vehicle to come to a sudden stop on several occasions. His best guess was that there were sheep in the road—at one point he thought he smelled some kind of manure.

The car proceeded slowly. He imagined they were in the mountains. The sunlight strobed through the fabric of his hood. Were they driving through a forest of some kind? It seemed cooler.

Then the car stopped.

DeLuca heard voices outside the car, doors opening, including the rear tailgate, and when it did, he felt a breeze. He heard the sound of a second car pulling up behind them. The men on either side of him got out of the SUV. One of them poked him hard in the ribs with the barrel of his gun. DeLuca didn't move or speak. The SUV's doors slammed shut, and he heard the muffled voices of men speaking.

He heard breathing inside the vehicle. He listened intently for another minute, until he felt certain there was only one other person in the car with him.

"Evelyn?" he whispered.

"Oh, thank God," she whispered back. "Thank God you're all right."

"Are you hurt?" he asked.

"No," she said. "I can't see you."

"I can't see either," he said. "Sit tight. We're going to be okay."

"I've been listening," she said. "They don't know I speak Arabic. One of them wants to kill us. The other wants to use us to free U.S. prisoners. And one says they should ask for money, too."

"Do you know who they are?"

Before she could answer, the doors opened again. He heard her scream as someone grabbed her and dragged her from the car. Then the tailgate opened and someone grasped him around the ankles, pulling him violently out of the car. He braced himself, landing on his back in the dirt. He went limp.

He was dragged across the ground by the feet, over a threshold and into a darkened room. The door closed behind him. He tasted blood. His own. The room smelled like goat shit. He felt with his tongue and realized a tooth had loosened. He felt something wet between his fingers, and from the pain, judged that his wrists were bleeding, too. Yet he believed all his injuries were most likely superficial.

"Herr Tischler," he heard a woman whisper urgently. "Are you there?"

He didn't answer at first, because he wasn't sure they were alone. He heard yelling outside, and a single gunshot. He listened. Nothing.

"I'm here," he said, keeping his voice low.

"Are you all right?"

"My head feels like I've been kicked by a camel," he said. "Other than that. Are you okay?"

"My right hand has fallen completely asleep," she said.

"What have they been saying?" he asked her. "Who are they?"

"I don't quite know," she said. "I don't think they're particularly good at what they do. There's quite a bit of dissension among them."

"I agree," he said. "I was afraid at first that Ibrahim had made us, but these guys have already made four mistakes. They put us together, they didn't gag us so we can talk to each other, they didn't even tie our legs, and these flex cuffs aren't meant to be used except temporarily. I'm thinking this was improvised."

"Agreed," she said. "One of the first things they did was stop to pick up a man named Hmood. I don't know his last name. The driver of our car kept asking him who he thought might be willing to pay for us. I think we're just hostages of convenience. My impression is that they grabbed us when they saw the opportunity, figuring they could trade us to somebody else who might know what to do with us."

"Can you walk?"

"I can run," she said. "I just can't see."

"Hang on," he said. "If you can. They're going to need more information before they can figure out what to do with us. I'll go first if I can and try to stop them from interrogating you, but I'm only going to get over for as long as it takes one of them to call a buddy in Hamburg to see if the real Jan Tischler is in his shop, and there are plenty of Arabs to call in Hamburg. I wouldn't count on more than twenty-four hours. Maybe not even that. I'll tell them you were trying to do a story on me after meeting me at the hotel. When I get back, I'll get the cuffs off you."

"What makes you think . . ." she began, but stopped when she heard the door open. DeLuca heard two or three men enter the room.

"I must insist on speaking with your leader," he said, mustering the best German accent he could. He tried to get to his feet. "I am a German citizen. I am a guest of the government of Iran. I have a visa."

Two men suddenly grabbed him, one on each arm, and hustled him out into daylight. He walked perhaps thirty or forty meters before entering a second building, where he was forced to sit in a chair. He felt someone tie his ankles to the legs of the chair, and then his hood was removed, another amateur mistake. There were six men in the room. Only one appeared to be over the age of twenty. The five younger men were armed with rifles, one sporting a pair of ammunition belts crossing his chest in front like some Islamic Pancho Villa, though DeLuca recognized this to be something of a fashion accessory, given that the bullets in his ammunition belts were not going to fit the gun he was carrying, an old Israeli Uzi with a stock extension. DeLuca guessed that the older man was Hmood, the one they'd stopped to get after the abduction. Hmood appeared to be in his late thirties or early forties. He wore dark sunglasses, and he was smoking a Kool cigarette.

The house appeared to be some kind of farmhouse, though the shades had been pulled, preventing DeLuca from assaying the surrounding countryside.

"Shoe ismak?" Hmood said in Arabic, repeating himself in English, walking slowly until he stood behind his prisoner. His body odor could knock a buzzard off a shit wagon, and his breath was worse than his body odor. "What is your name?"

"Meine name ist Jan Tischler," DeLuca said, laying his German accent on thick. He probably sounded like Sergeant Schultz on *Hogan's Heroes,* but what would Hmood know? "I am from Hamburg."

"I did not ask you where you are from," his interrogator said, shouting at him and slapping him across the back of his head with his hand.

"I'm sorry," DeLuca said.

"Where are you from?"

"I am from Hamburg," DeLuca said.

"Shoe btishtaghel? La min ebtishtaghel?" he said, translating, "What do you do? Who do you work for?"

"I have an art gallery," he said. "I specialize in Middle Eastern antiquities. That is why I am here."

"And who buys these things from you?" Hmood asked.

"Many people," DeLuca said. "Museums. Collectors. Japanese. Saudis. Many people."

"So you are here to assist in the looting of my country?" Hmood asked. "You are here to buy artifacts stolen from museums during the war. Is that not correct?"

"Not at all," DeLuca said. He saw the opening he was hoping for. "I had simply heard from my sources that during times of economic hardship such as these, people often seek to raise money, to feed their families, by selling heirlooms and family treasures that they might otherwise wish to hold on to. I've come simply to help those families and to make sure they get a fair price."

Hmood laughed.

"A fair price?" he said. "So you are here, out of the goodness of your heart, to help the Iraqi people. You are noble humanitarian, is that it, Herr Tischler?"

"I admit that current market forces . . ."

"Market forces!" Hmood interrupted angrily, slapping him again. "You are lying to me. You are here to take advantage. To participate in the plunder of my country. You are here to rape the Iraqi culture."

He glared at DeLuca, his nostrils flaring rhythmically, then gave a command in Arabic, and the five younger men left the room.

Once they'd gone, Hmood pulled a chair closer to DeLuca and spoke in a low voice, leaning in.

"I think, Herr Tischler, that you are an unscrupulous businessman, yes?" he said. "Perhaps the CIA pays you to tell them what you learn when you go on these buying trips . . ."

"No," DeLuca said. "I have nothing to do with them. I have nothing to do with politics. I am an art dealer."

"An art dealer," Hmood said. "And just what kind of art is it that you were hoping to find?"

DeLuca hoped he was remembering his cover story accurately. He'd done his best to memorize the fact sheets that MacKenzie had given him, and she'd done a thorough job, but he worried about slipping up.

"I want what anybody else would want," he said. "Sumerian. Elamite. Babylonian and neo-Babylonian. I have a buyer in Kuwait interested in anything from the period of al-Ma'moun the Great, anything from his House of Wisdom, but especially Arabic translations from Greek and Latin."

"And for these things, you think you can pay money and take them out of the land of their origin?" Hmood said.

"I can pay a fair price here and make my profit on the other end," DeLuca said. "Everyone is too afraid to come here at the moment. I'm the only buyer in town. I was not afraid to come. I know the Arab peoples are good businessmen, so I came."

"And look where it got you," Hmood said.

"It has allowed me to meet a man of intelligence and tact," DeLuca said, "unlike the little boys he has working for him. I think a man who can see how useful someone like myself might be, able to change artifacts into cash that might be used to buy things of greater utility. It's one thing to suddenly come into possession of a family heirloom and quite another to know how to sell it in such a way as to get the greatest value from it, and in such a way that the seller's identity might be protected. I understand of course how some of my sellers do not want their names attached to the transaction, and I can arrange for that as well."

Hmood glanced toward the door, then leaned in closer.

"Is there a particular Sumerian dynasty that you're interested in?" he asked. "Because I might know a man who might have found something from the tombs at Ur."

"The tombs at Ur?" DeLuca said. "Hmm. I would, of course, prefer first or second dynasty. I can sell third but it's usually not as valuable. And of course, if I could find someone able to give me a good supply of artifacts or references to other customers, I would include that person in the transaction and pay them a finder's fee. *Ja?* A percentage. What might the object from the tombs be—can you describe it?"

"It's a golden harp," Hmood said. "With the head of a bull, carved in gold, mounted at the front."

DeLuca had used up all the backstory Mack had supplied him with. He knew about the tombs of Ur, but he'd never heard of any golden harps. From this point on, he would have to get over with pure bullshit.

"I believe there may have been a similar item in the museum in Baghdad before the war," he said. He'd guessed correctly.

"There was," Hmood said. "Terrible thing. And this harp is so similar that I'm afraid it could be mistaken for the other. I think it must be handled just so."

"That is something I would understand completely," DeLuca said. "Bear in mind that we Germans are particularly sensitive to art objects that may change hands during times of war. Both my father and my grandfather had some experience in such areas."

"I will discuss it with my colleagues," Hmood said. "I think you could be more useful this way. They want to take you to Abu Waid and hold you for ransom. I think this could be wiser, if you can prove what you say."

"I assure you that I can," DeLuca said. "But if you do decide to discuss it with your colleagues, remember that the finder's fee is going to be a finite sum. They may wish to share in it. I also think it would be best if you did not tell the woman about our conversation. It often helps to have the assistance of a journalist in creating a provenance for such objects—a story that makes them easier to buy and sell. People see it written down and they think it must be true. I was thinking of this when I met her at the hotel. She knows nothing of my private transactions."

"She says she is BBC."

"She is," DeLuca said. "I think she could be quite useful to us, if you allow me to convince her. We might be able to tell her this was nothing more than a misunderstanding."

Hmood looked at him a moment longer, then summoned the others and directed them to take DeLuca back to where he'd been held. They put the hood back over his head, but not before he was able to peek quickly out the door. He saw a mountain in the distance. That didn't tell him much.

The first order of business was to get the hood off his head. The flex cuffs his captors had used on him were designed to serve only as a temporary restraint, made out of a double-looped strip of nylon, tougher than the plastic twist-ties used back home to close garbage bags, but that only meant it would take a bit more time to saw through them. His captors also didn't know any better than to leave two prisoners in the same room. He and Evelyn Warner could help each other.

He instructed her to kneel on the floor, then turned his back to her and worked at the hood over her head with his bound hands until he'd loosened and freed it. She then did the same for him.

"That's better, then," she whispered. "At least now we can . . . oh, dear. Are you all right? You've got blood on you," she said.

"It probably looks worse than it is. If you wouldn't mind," he said, "there's a chain around my neck. If you could loop your finger around it and pull it over my head . . ."

He felt her fingers tickling his neck.

"You're going to use your crucifix to pick the lock," she said. "The critics at the *Times* literary supplement are going to be all over that for clumsy symbolism, but whatever works."

She extracted the chain and felt the object attached to it.

"Good God—what is that? That's not a crucifix."

"That's a P-38," he told her. "It's a can-opener. Turn around and I'll cut you loose."

"Why do you have a can-opener around your neck?"

"Old soldiers' habit," he explained, using the can-opener's blade to saw at the cuffs holding her wrists. "All the old C rations came in tin cans, so every soldier before 1990 or so got a P-38. It only takes once, getting caught starving to death with a tin can full of food you can't open, before you learn to have it with you at all times. With MREs, you don't really need 'em anymore, but every once in a while, they come in handy."

"Do you think he believed your story?"

"I think he wanted to believe it," DeLuca said. "All the same, I think it would be better if we left tonight."

"You make it sound like a fait accompli," she said.

"That always sounded like some sort of fancy dessert," he said. "Like Bananas Foster or Friendly Fribbles."

"Rather you not talk about food right now," she said. "Feeling a bit peckish."

"Sorry," he said. They heard the sounds of Arab television coming from the main house. "Being a hostage has its drawbacks, but it's also a very low-carb experience. They never tell you that part."

"Are these attempts at levity for my benefit?" she asked. "Because if they are, I appreciate them. Any progress?"

"I've got a notch," he said. "That's a start."

"You're sure you're not sawing through my wrist?" she said. "Not sure I'd feel it if you were."

"Well if I do," he said, "it'll make it easier to get the cuffs off."

"Hadn't thought of that," she said. "Would you call that an off-handed remark?"

"Just off-the-cuff," he said.

"Don't make me laugh out loud, or they'll know something is up," she said. "My fiancé used to make the most inappropriate comments, just to make me look foolish when I laughed."

"He stopped?" DeLuca asked.

"No, he went right on doing it," she said. "The engagement stopped."

"Sorry to hear that," DeLuca said.

"I'm not," the Englishwoman said. "Bit of a farce, really. Known him since public school, where we made one of those desperate deals that teenagers make—if neither one of us found our true love by the time we were forty, we'd marry each other. That was the pact we'd made. Good thing we didn't follow through, all in all."

"You don't look forty," he told her.

"Oh, really?" she said. "And just how old do I look?"

Alarms went off—it was a question he knew not to answer, along with, "Do these pants make my ass look fat," and, "If you could sleep with any Hollywood actress, who would you sleep with?"

"I think I'm in quite enough trouble already," he said.

"Fair enough," she said.

"Thirty-two," he said.

"Bless you," she said. "Just a bit more than that, but no, I'm not forty. I think we jumped the gun because I was listening more to my biological clock than to my heart."

"Are the biological clocks of women in England set four hours earlier than they are in the States? Almost through," he said. "Hanging on by a thread."

"So's my love life," she said. "How about you? Are you married, Herr Tischler?"

"I was when I left Hamburg," he said. "She didn't want me to make this trip. She was afraid something bad would happen. I promised her nothing would."

"So far so good, then," Evelyn said.

"What do you know about Abu Waid?" he asked, changing the subject from one that was dangerous to one that was simply life-threatening.

"Abu Waid?" she said. "You mean Ansar al-Islam's Abu Waid?"

"That's who he's with?"

"Well, he was the number-two man in the movement until you chaps blew up the number-one man when you bombed their strongholds in Sulaymaniyah Province. Or I should say he was number three until you blew up number two, because number one is in Norway. Chap named Mullah Krekar. I interviewed him once in Oslo. Completely out of his mind and full of hate. I've heard Ansar al-Islam compared to a group of Kurdish fundamentalists similar to the Taliban, but I think they're worse. Beyond Wahabism. I read someone say they thought 10 percent of Ansar is Al Qaeda, but I think the figure is much higher. Half of them fought in Afghanistan. And now all the little splinter groups are coming back together. The Islamic Unification Front, Hamas, the Soran Forces, the Soldiers of Islam, thanks to Mullah Krekar and Abu Waid."

"How big is Ansar al-Islam?" he asked.

"I've read from five hundred to a thousand fighters," she said. "I tend to believe the higher figures. Used to occupy themselves blowing up PUK offices and massacring PUK villages, to the delight of Tehran, I should say. Anything to destabilize prospects for Kurdish independence has always been jakes by them. Most of Ansar's funding and arms have come from Iran."

"And Abu Waid is the leader?" DeLuca asked.

"I believe so," she said. "And he was Mukhaberat. You knew that, didn't you?"

"Then he's the link," DeLuca said. "With Al-Tariq. Have you ever heard of the Thousand Faces of Allah?"

"*Alf Wajeh,*" she said.

"You've heard of them?"

"Them?" she said. "The *Alf Wajeh* I know is an old poem."

"What old poem is that?"

"You probably know the biblical version," she said. "God sends the plague and the only ones left behind are the true believers. *Al-Alf Wajeh* is the Muslim version. Very ancient but basically the same myth. God delivers a plague and the only survivors are the thousand believers who go on to create a perfect world."

"Hmm," DeLuca said. "So what do you think the odds would be for some group of terrorists to come to think they're the descendants of *Al-Alf Wajeh*?"

"And therefore, invulnerable to plagues?" she asked, connecting the dots. "Not as long as one might hope. I did a story on the Lord's Resistance Army in Uganda, led by a religious fanatic chap named Joseph Kony, where thousands of village boys as young as five and six years old have been essentially abducted and trained to carry guns and magical charms and amulets, and then Kony tells them that the enemy's bullets will turn to water when they hit them. You can get impressionable people to believe a lot of things. I should guess with a group as indoctrinated as Ansar al-Islam, it wouldn't be too hard to persuade a good many that they were the *Alf Wajeh*."

DeLuca considered all the possibilities.

"So here are our options," he said. "We could let them take us to Abu Waid with the hope that he could lead us to Al-Tariq, or we could leave tonight and start over once we're back at Balad. What's your preference?"

"That first choice is truly tempting," she said, "but I think the second."

"Agreed," he said, severing the last band holding her wrists together. She tried to undo his cuffs, but her right hand was useless after so prolonged a period of constricted circulation. She swung her arm around for a few minutes until the blood returned to her hand, then helped DeLuca off with his cuffs. She wiped the blood from the side of his face and head as best she could, using the hood he'd worn, already blood-soaked.

He looked around, the only light coming from a boarded-up window next to the door. The room they were in appeared to be some sort of pen meant for animals. A quick search of the room turned up nothing he might be able to use for a weapon. He saw two bales of hay, stacked in one corner of the room.

The door opened out, but it seemed too sturdy to kick down. If he tried and failed, the others would hear.

"Any brilliant ideas?" she whispered, joining him at the window, peering out between the boards nailed there.

"I'm currently between brilliant ideas," DeLuca whispered back. "How about using your feminine wiles? Or is that a sexist thing to say?"

"I'm flattered that you think I have any," Evelyn Warner said. "Not sure 'feminine wiles' is the way to go. Not with an Arab boy. Most of them are virgins, you know. I'd probably scare him half to death if I said anything at all."

"So the 'seventy-doe-eyed-virgins-in-paradise' thing for martyrs is real?" DeLuca said.

"It's real to them," she said. "It's their best hope of ever getting laid. Thing is, the more the Arab world sinks into poverty, the fewer among them will ever have the resources to marry. Dowries and all that. My ex-fiancé used to joke that half the suicide bombers you read about are detonating from sheer horniness. Then of course, they have no actual experience with real women, but any Arab boy with Internet access can see more pornography than he'd know what to do with. The heat generated by the cognitive dissonance must be fierce."

"This kid thinks he's Pancho Villa," DeLuca said. They saw their guard, leaning against a car, with his Uzi and his crossed ammunition belts.

"The machismo is just a bluff, you know," she said. "And that's not so unlike teenage boys everywhere."

"Let's use that," DeLuca said. He looked up into the sky, which was full of stars on a moonless night. "We gotta get him to open the door. Call him over here."

He took off his boots, then stripped off his shirt and pants and used the hay to stuff his clothes until he'd made a straw dummy of himself. He tied the sleeves together with the flex cuffs he'd worn and stuffed the hood with hay as well, arranging the "body" in the corner against the wall opposite the door, his pant legs stuck into his boots. It would only fool the guard for a few seconds, but a few seconds would be all he'd need.

"I'm going to whisper in your ear and tell you what to say," he told the Englishwoman.

She called the boy over. He was hesitant, lowering his weapon suspiciously at the window as he approached.

"Tell him you don't think it's fair that he should be out here standing guard duty when the others are all inside," DeLuca whispered to Evelyn.

She complied. The boy had no response.

"Ask him if it's because he's the youngest that he has to stand guard duty," DeLuca said.

The boy replied with an angry outburst.

"He says he's not the youngest," Evelyn whispered to DeLuca. "Two are even younger than him, and they get to be inside."

"Tell him you want to trade him information for a drink of water," DeLuca said. "Nothing more than that, just a drink of water."

She did. The boy paused, then spoke.

"He wants to know what kind of information," she said.

"Information about the man you've been locked up with," DeLuca said. "A man who is not who he seems. Information that will make him an important person to the others."

She translated, then waited for an answer. Pancho Villa spoke.

"He wants to know who you are if you're not who you seem," she said.

"Not until you get some water."

She repeated it in Arabic. The boy responded angrily again.

"First information, then water," she translated.

"Tell him I work for a company that puts satellites into space, and that I told you the Americans have been bombarding Arab men with invisible energy beams that make them impotent and unable to have children. You wanted to tell him before but you had to wait until I fell asleep."

She looked at him.

"Just tell him that."

Evelyn Warner obliged.

The boy didn't answer.

"Tell him that even now, there are energy particles passing through his body that will make it impossible for him to have children, and that it's part of the American plot to take over the Arab world."

She told him.

"Ask him if he senses a tightness in his throat that makes it hard to swallow."

She translated, then conveyed the response.

"He says he does," she said.

"It's an old psychic's trick," DeLuca said. "You get somebody nervous and then you tell 'em difficulty swallowing is a sign that their dead grandmother is trying to contact them. Now tell him the stars in the sky are not all stars, and that some of them are satellites. Ask him if he sees one that looks green or red and seems to be blinking."

She translated. The boy looked heavenward, then pointed and spoke.

"Tell him you have more, but you're not going to tell him unless he gets you a drink of water. We have to get him to open the door."

She told him.

"Now go back and sit next to the dummy," DeLuca said, pressing his back against the wall next to the door. It had been a while since he'd practiced hand-to-hand combat, but he'd spent enough time training recruits in the art at Fort Huachuca and again at Fort Devin to know what do to, and he'd restrained enough freaks on crystal meth or angel dust as a cop in Boston to trust his instincts.

He heard the guard fumbling at the door latch, and then words in Arabic, shouted through the door, which he took to mean "stand back!" The door opened, and then the beam of a flashlight shone cautiously through the crack. The door opened wider, the flashlight thrust through the opening, then the barrel of the Uzi and the guard's head.

The guard leaned cautiously into the room, shining the flashlight on the Englishwoman, who'd temporarily placed her hood back over her head, and on the dummy next to her.

The boy stepped forward.

DeLuca punched him in the Adam's apple, collapsing his windpipe. To an unsuspecting victim, such a blow was instantly incapacitating, a variation on the old police choke-hold that had been banned in a number of cities for being too violent a method of restraint.

The boy went down like a sack of concrete. DeLuca caught the weapon as he fell, stripping it from his hands.

The boy could neither breathe nor call out.

DeLuca knelt on Pancho Villa's back as he searched him. He removed the ammunition belts, then felt a small lump in the boy's pocket, about the size of a pack of cigarettes.

It was his sat phone.

"You better not have made any calls," he said, completing his search while the boy gasped for air. Left in that condition, there was a good chance the boy would soon suffocate, a casualty of war, and he had no problem with that, but with the Englishwoman watching, DeLuca didn't see the need to let it go that far. He rolled the boy over, tipped his head back, opened his mouth and stuck his fingers down the boy's throat, prying his air passage open again. The boy gagged, then coughed violently, struggling to recover. DeLuca quickly gagged the boy with one of his own socks.

"Take the cuffs off the dummy, and the hood, too," he told Evelyn. She brought them to him. He bound the boy's hands behind his back, used the boy's own belt to bind his feet, then threw the hood over his head to finish the task. He handed the boy's *kaffiyeh,* ammunition belts, and weapon to the Englishwoman and asked her to put them on.

"Just walk back and forth outside while I get dressed," he said. "And before you go . . ." He hesitated.

"What?" she asked.

"Explain to him that he's going to be okay, and that I've spared his life. And that to repay me, he should go home to his mother and stop playing at war."

She knelt beside the boy a moment, then went outside to play her part.

DeLuca dressed quickly, shaking as much hay from his clothes as he could.

He joined Evelyn Warner outside. She was about the same size as Pancho Villa had been. From a distance, it would be possible to mistake her for him. DeLuca put a finger to his lips and gestured for her to follow him. Staying to the shadows, they made their way to the SUV, putting the body of the vehicle between themselves and the house. Crouching low, he opened the driver's side door. The keys were in the ignition. His Beretta was on the dash, his police special on the seat opposite the driver's.

"This just gets better and better," he told his companion, grabbing his weapons and strapping on his leg rig. The only other vehicle on the property, that he could see, was the green pickup truck he'd noticed when they'd been ambushed at the bazaar. He told Evelyn Warner to wait by the SUV.

"That Uzi's a piece of shit, but it makes a lot of noise," he told her. "If anybody comes, shoot 'em. But make sure it's not me first."

"I'll make noise," she said. "But I won't shoot anyone."

"Fair enough," he told her. "Just remember those are your rules, not theirs."

He heard music coming from the house. He smelled what he thought was incense, then realized it was curry. He couldn't see anyone when he looked in the window, but if they were eating, they were most likely seated on a rug on the floor. The music would mask the sounds he needed to make.

He crossed to the green pickup truck and gently popped the hood, lifted it, and quietly ripped out the distributor cables, flinging them as far out into the bushes as he could. He was about to move to the house when he saw something interesting in the back of the pickup, a thick yellow nylon towing cable with large metal hooks at either end. Most of the vehicles he'd seen carried such cables, in a country where sudden sandstorms could quickly bury vehicles up to their fenders in shifting sand drifts. He saw where a pole carried power and phone wires from the road to the house. He grabbed the towing cable, returned to the SUV, coiled the slack in one hand, swung the metal hook at one end of the cable in a three-foot circle, then threw the hook high in the air, draping it over the wire. When it stopped swinging, he pulled the cable back slowly until the metal hook caught the wire. He tied the other end of the towing cable to the roof rack of the SUV.

"Get in the car and stay down," he told Evelyn Warner. "I'll be right back. If you hear shooting, start the car and take off, and don't look back."

"Where are you going?" she asked. "We should go now."

"I've got two more people to find," he told her.

Khalil and Adnan had to be somewhere in the house. There were no other outbuildings to look into.

He circled the house, then crawled until he was directly beneath the side window to the main room. He chambered a round in his Beretta, then rose against the wall. The bedroom was lit by a bare bulb hanging from the ceiling.

He saw four men. Hmood sat in an easy chair before a television with the sound off, watching a soccer game. Two men sat at a card table, looking at magazines, a radio on the table next to them playing the music he'd heard. The fourth man sat at a door across the room, in a folding chair, his AK-47 propped against the wall next to him. The kitchen was empty. There were two twin mattresses on the floor to either side of the fireplace, each strewn with castoff clothing. Three other Kalashnikovs and an Iranian SIG rifle rested against the wall by the door. Hmood wore a .45 automatic in a shoulder holster. The house had three rooms, the kitchen, the main room, and the room being guarded. That had to be where Adnan and Khalil were being held.

He circled around the back of the house, until he found the back window to the bedroom. The room was dark, but even without lights, he could see a pair of legs belonging to a body on the floor, the rest of the body hidden by the bed. He couldn't see anyone else. He considered his options. If the men in the other room heard him, he would have to bolt and leave his informants behind, something he didn't want to do unless he absolutely had to.

The window swung out on hinges. He worked the left side first, moving it slowly, lest the hinges complain.

When he had both sides opened, he climbed in, taking care that nothing of his clothing caught on the sill. Inside, he crouched behind the bed, his automatic aimed at the door.

He moved to the body on the floor. It was Khalil. Adnan was nowhere to be found. Khalil's legs were bound at the ankles, tied tightly by wire, which took him longer than it should have to undo. He loosened the flex cuffs binding Khalil's wrists behind him, then rolled him over on his back. He loosened the hood and removed it. He felt the neck for a pulse.

When Khalil opened his eyes and saw who was crouched over him, he smiled. DeLuca put his hand over Khalil's mouth before Khalil could make a sound, DeLuca putting a finger to his own lips to signal the need for silence. He pointed to Khalil, then to the window. Khalil looked at the window, then at DeLuca and nodded, then raised a finger and pointed to his leg. DeLuca lifted the man's pant leg, high enough to see what Khalil was indicating, a fragment of bone sticking out from the flesh, just above the ankle.

He gave DeLuca a smile and a thumbs-up, nevertheless.

DeLuca helped him to the window, holding the smaller man beneath the armpits. He helped him raise his injured leg, lifted him, and slid him across the sill until he was able to sit upright. The young Kurd grimaced from the pain as he moved, clenching his teeth, but didn't make a sound.

The drop to the ground outside was going to hurt. DeLuca would be able to lower him most of the way, but there was no way he'd be able to cushion the blow entirely. Khalil collected himself, then gave DeLuca a thumbs-up for the second time. DeLuca helped Khalil out the window, grabbed him by the wrists, then lowered him the remaining few feet. Khalil went down and didn't move, but again, he didn't make a sound.

Once he was outside, DeLuca maneuvered Khalil into a fireman's carry and moved him to the SUV, setting him down on the ground on the far side of the vehicle. Warner joined them.

"I'll take care of the leg when we get out of here," DeLuca said. "Where's Adnan?"

"I don't know," Khalil said. "I saw him running through the bazaar. I think he may have gotten away."

"He's not in the house?"

"I don't think so," Khalil said, in obvious pain. "I did not see him."

"Then we go," DeLuca said. He gestured for Evelyn to cover the house for one more minute, then opened his sat phone. The power indicator registered that his battery was next to dead. He dialed his son's number.

"DeLuca," his son said.

"Same here," DeLuca said. "Need your help, Scooter. You got a picture?"

"Negative," his son replied. "Got your location, though. What do you need? You need an air strike? I could get something on you in three minutes."

"Negative," DeLuca said. He'd already decided he might want to keep Hmood and the others alive for questioning. "We can deal with this later. Can you jam calls coming out of here? I need a few hours."

"I can't personally," his son said. "I can get it done in five but I have to make a call."

"Make it two," DeLuca said. "I don't want anybody phoning the highway patrol. One last thing—where the fuck am I?"

He heard a beeping sound, and then his battery cut out before he could get an answer.

He helped Khalil into the backseat of the SUV, then told Evelyn to get in on the passenger side.

"If the car doesn't start, we're on foot. Khalil . . ."

"Give me the Uzi," Khalil said. "I will try to hold them back as long as I can . . ."

"And don't touch anything metal," DeLuca said. "If we're lucky, we won't electrocute ourselves."

He gave his son one more minute, keeping his eye on the house's front door, then realized he could wait no longer when he saw a figure appearing on the front steps.

"Stay down" he said, turning the key.

The SUV, a Ford Bronco, roared to life.

He threw it into drive and floored it.

The wheels spun in the dirt. He looked back as the towing cable pulled the wires down behind him. He saw sparks in the night, a bright flash, then another, and then the lights in the house went dark, his wheels throwing up a rooster tail of gravel as they spun against the road.

Shots rang out.

He ducked reflexively.

The rear window shattered. He heard more gunshots.

The car fishtailed in the gravel as they picked up speed.

They were fifty yards away, then a hundred. He saw no lights in the rearview mirror. No one was following.

Another shot broke one of the back side windows.

Then they were safe.

Ten minutes later, he realized that he was rapidly running out of gas. A bullet had evidently struck the tank.

He looked for a place to ditch the vehicle, without a light in sight and no idea where he was.

Chapter Eleven

PROFESSOR JABURI DID NOT LIKE TO WAIT, ANY more than he tolerated lateness. Two more minutes, he decided, and he would use his rental car and drive himself. He'd been in the lobby of the Palo Verde Inn for nearly five minutes beyond the appointed time before the car from the university pulled up. The professor of Islamic studies who'd been designated to serve as his host apologized, explaining that there'd been an accident in front of them that had forced them to take a detour, but Jaburi was not interested in excuses. In the car with them were two graduate students, a boy named Jonathan and a girl named Latifah, with whom he exchanged glances. They'd arranged in advance for a private meeting after his lecture, but he'd yet to meet her.

They drove down Speedway Avenue, the road as ugly as any he'd ever seen in America, lined with fast food restaurants, strip malls and strip joints, muffler shops and big box warehouses, porn shops, lawn ornament dealers and secondhand clothing stores. The American professor of Islamic studies droned on and on about how the University of Arizona had one of the highest populations of Arab students in the country due to the warm climate, blah blah blah, things any idiot tourism office guide might have been able to tell him. It took him a few minutes, once they'd arrived at the lecture hall, before he could regain his composure.

"Tonight, I will place in context for you the last thirty thousand years of human history," he began his lecture, "and I will show you exactly how it was that the Neolithic hunter-gatherers chose the Fertile Crescent of the Middle East as the place to create modern civilization as we know it, how the seeds of social evolution first took root between the Dijla and the Furat, and how civilization continues to flow from this source; in this light, the struggle today in Iraq may be seen as merely the latest expression of a process that has ebbed and flowed literally since the beginning of recorded time, in a most fortunate and unfortunate of lands, where the forces of geology, of biology, and of history have made it an arena, much like the Coliseum in ancient Rome, within which all true and false predictors of culture must eventually do battle."

He went on to limn the procession of powers and governments that invaded, occupied, and eventually left Iraq in defeat, starting with the Garden of Eden and moving quickly through the Sumerians, the Babylonians, the Assyrians, the Medes, the Persians, Alexander the Great, the Parthians, the Buwayhids, the Seljuk Turks, Genghis Khan, the Black Sheep Dynasty, the White Sheep Dynasty, the Ottomans, the British, and then the Americans. He listed the conquerors and the proxy rulers they left behind to rule in their stead, all of them eventually overthrown, assassinated, cast out, each leaving something of value behind, the Code of Hammurabi, algebra, an alphabet, and so on, and in that sense, he explained, the dialectic was a healthy one, though fraught with pain and suffering, without which there can be no growth. He spoke for two hours, citing names and dates and facts, all without notes. He closed with a note of warning, explaining that for the first time, civilization had the means with which to destroy itself many times over, weapons of mass destruction, nuclear, biological, chemical, things that were themselves an unstoppable expression of culture and, as controversial as it might sound, something to be welcomed and embraced, a culmination of thirty thousand years of human progress and something that could be predicted, prepared for, and put to use.

"The fires in the forge of change have never burned as hot," he said. "From this current conflict, a new world will emerge. A better world, in the end, a world that George Bush and the Americans will not recognize, and a world that the Iraqis will not recognize either, because this has always been the case. This has always been the historical dynamic. In great times, great changes occur, and these are indeed great times."

He took questions afterward. He'd delivered the lecture before, and inevitably, someone asked him if he were advocating the use of weapons of mass destruction. He explained, again, that he was neither advocating nor not advocating, but that their very existence signified the powerful forces of change that were afoot, and that those forces would express themselves, whether the weapons themselves were used or not.

There was the usual reception afterward, with the usual dreary assortment of fawners and sycophants, telling him things he already knew and battering him with flattery. As soon as he could excuse himself, he found his professor host and told him he wasn't feeling well, and that the girl Latifah had offered to drive him back to his hotel.

He regarded her in the car. She wore a veil and head-scarf, but the veil was pulled up only to the bottom of her chin, as was the fashion with some girls these days. She reminded him of his wife when his wife was younger, stupid and gullible and a bit frightened of him.

"I would like to see your preparations," he told her. "Primary, secondary, and tertiary targets."

She drove him first to the Tucson Convention Center, where she showed him a short alley, at the end of which were located the intake vents for the convention center's air-conditioning system. She told him the air circulated within the building every four minutes, and that she had yet to see anyone guarding the alley or the apparatus. The convention center could hold up to twenty thousand people. Next, she drove to a large hotel downtown, where she pointed out the intake vents, wide horizontal slats a mere twelve feet above the ground at the rear of the building. The hotel air-conditioning system kept the building at negative pressure, she explained, such that fresh air came in through the intake vents, moved through the hotel halls, got sucked into the rooms beneath the doors, drawn into the bathrooms, and was vented out through the bathroom exhaust fans. This was how the hotel managed to keep any smells from the rooms from entering the corridors. The air in the hotel was replaced with fresh air every five minutes. The occupancy of the hotel on an average day was about a thousand people. Her third target was the main terminal at the airport, where all the security was concentrated near the airplanes, luggage terminals, and boarding gates. The airport's air-conditioning system, she showed him, was virtually unguarded, though security officers did occasionally drive past, usually looking the other way.

"And the rest of it?" he asked her.

"I have it here," she said, gesturing toward a large straw bag in the back.

"What?" he said.

"I brought it," she said. "I thought you might want to see it."

He was furious.

He slapped her across the face with the back of his hand.

"You idiot!" he said. "You stupid stupid girl! Do you have any idea what would happen if some policeman pulled us over right now? Do you have any idea how much would be compromised? How many people are depending on us?"

He wanted to hit her again, but he was afraid the way she swerved as she drove would attract attention.

"I'm sorry," she said, crying.

He took the bag from the backseat. Inside it, he found a uniform, gray and green, and stitched above the breast pocket, the words "Carrier Air-Conditioning." He examined the uniform for a few minutes, then put it back in the bag.

"These are identical?"

"Identical," she said.

"And the IDs?"

"They are perfect."

"And your people?"

"I told them only that they have been chosen," the girl said. "And that I will contact them. They are ready."

"Have they met each other?"

"No, no," she said. "They each think they are the only one. They know nothing of each other."

"Good," he said. "At least you've gotten that right." They were at his hotel. She put the car in park and set the parking brake, turning to him, her head lowered in fear or shame. "Look at me," he commanded. "Look."

She looked up.

"Do you have a piece of paper and something to write with?" She nodded. "Get it."

She reached into the glove compartment and found a pen and a small notebook.

"Take a page out and write against the palm of your hand so you do not leave an impression on the page below." She complied. "Now write this down: 8-4-3-j-4-3-j-d-0-k-f-t-r-i-r-9-3-e-u-3-h-e-d-9-r-5-t-t-0-t-6-0-6. Show me."

She had written: 843j43jd0kftrir93eu3hed9r5tt0t606.

"Good. Three days before *'Id al-Fitr,* the last day of Ramadan, you will open an AOL e-mail account using that number as the username. This number is not written down anywhere but here. I also have it in my head. When you get home, take this piece of paper and tear it into three parts, and hide each part in a separate place. Do not put them together again until you open the account. Do not use the account. On the day of *'Id al-Fitr,* you will receive instructions as to where you can retrieve the agent. Later that same day, you will receive the signal either to go ahead and use it or to wait. Under no circumstances are you to open the bottles or break the seals on them until you receive the signal to do so. Do you have any questions?"

"No," she said.

"If you have any, you must ask them now. You will not see me again so you will not get another opportunity."

"Well . . ." she said, hesitating.

"What is it?"

"This agent that we are to use for jihad," she said. "May I know what it is? I will tell no one."

"You may tell your people when it is time," he said. "It is a biological weapon. It will not hurt you. It will only hurt the infidels. It cannot hurt *Alf Wajeh*. You must have faith."

"I have faith," she told him. He looked at her.

"But you want a scientific explanation," he said. "All right. I will tell you. It was developed by our scientists from camel pox. The blood of all Arab peoples carries a natural immunity to camel pox. This has been true for a thousand years. This is not true of the blood of infidels. So the weapon will kill only infidels. You see? Now do you have faith?"

"I do," she said.

He held his arms out to hug her. She buried her face against his chest, crying. He patted her back to soothe her.

"The world will be clean again," he told her. "As in the story of *Alf Wajeh. La ilaha ill Allah wa-Muhammad rasul Allah.*"

"*La ilaha ill Allah,*" she repeated back to him. "*Wa-Muhammad rasul Allah.*" She looked up at him, her eyes wet with tears, a beatific smile on her face, the ecstatic face of a true believer in the presence of God himself.

"*Shwaya, shwaya, ya bint Mohammed,*" he told her, "*rawgi.*" Slowly, slowly, daughter of the Prophet, be calm.

"Thank you," she said, still weeping. "Thank you."

In his room, he washed the girl's filth from his hands and turned on the television. The newsman on CNN spoke of another U.S. bombing raid in Iraq, a house in Ad-Dujayl where insurgents were believed to have been holed up, in response to a car bombing earlier in the day that had killed seven American soldiers near the front gate of the base at Balad. Such attacks were drawing away the Americans' full attention. This was good.

He turned the channel. He saw a baseball game, a soccer game, one of those "reality" shows that, when deconstructed, said more about reality as America defined it than anybody seemed to realize, a nation of whores and pimps, spreading AIDS to the rest of the world. He surfed through the pay-per-view options on the adult channels but turned the TV off. He looked at himself in the mirror, straightened his tie, and then went down to the hotel bar. He'd had trouble sleeping of late, the excitement of what he was engaged in impossible to push from his thoughts. He sat at the bar and ordered a cognac.

He'd been there a minute before he noticed the girl at the table behind him. She was one of those pink American girls, wearing a miniskirt that sparkled and a top that revealed most of her breasts. She was blond with blue eyes, perhaps a natural blond, he thought, though such women were entirely rare. Her eyes were wet, as Latifah's had been. He gathered that she had been crying. He watched as she frantically dialed number after number on her cell phone. She looked off, lost and forlorn.

"Is something wrong?" he asked her.

She looked up at him.

"I can't find my friends," she said, drunk and otherwise stupefied. "I can't find anybody. I don't know how I'm going to get back to my dorm. I don't have the money for a cab." He saw a tear roll down her cheek.

"Please," he said. "Please do not cry. I will take you home. Please. It's not a problem."

She looked up at him.

"You don't mind?" she said.

"Not at all," he said. "Not at all. If you could wait only a minute. I didn't expect to be driving, so I left my keys in my room. Can you wait? And then I will drive you."

He smiled his most avuncular smile.

"Okay," she said. "I really appreciate it."

He fingered the car keys in his pocket as he walked back to his room, where he reached into his toiletry kit and found what he was looking for, a pocket knife with a three-inch locking blade and a sturdy handle. He grabbed his hairbrush as well. In the closet, he found two plastic bags meant for guests to use to carry their dirty laundry. He stuffed them into his coat pocket. Before he left, he found the courtesy guide the hotel left for its guests and a map of Tucson. He noted where the road he was on, Palo Verde, led out of town and into the desert and a place called Mt. Lemon, where he felt certain he'd be able to find a place deserted enough to suit his purposes. His own corruption was complete, he knew, but he also knew that the purification to come would make him clean again.

The girl was waiting at the bar, looking much more cheerful than when he'd left her.

"I so much appreciate this," she told him. "Some friends of mine are having a party and I'll bet they just got hammered and forgot about me. My name is Heather."

"Heather," he said. "*Calluna vulgaris*. A beautiful name. Mine is Mahmoud."

They shook hands.

He'd nearly gotten her to his car when he heard tires screeching. A red convertible pulled up, stopping suddenly. In it were three girls, screaming through the open windows.

"Heather, we're so sorry," one called out. "Are you okay? We came to give you a ride. My cell died."

"These are my friends," Heather told Jaburi, relieved. "You guys, I was so like worried you'd forgotten me. I even had to get this old guy to give me a ride. Thank you so much, Mr. Mahmoud. I really appreciate your offer. See you later."

The blond girl drove off with her friends.

Jaburi tossed his car keys once in the air, then pocketed them and headed back to his room. As he did, he walked past a rented white Dodge Intrepid, where Walter Ford sat, watching him.

The section Walter had assigned his students had gone well, both in his Research and Evaluation Methods class and in his Statistical Analysis class. Some students had grumbled that it seemed like a lot of busywork for nothing, but that was exactly the point. Others found exactly what he was trying to teach them, that the powerful new search and evaluation tools available to modern law enforcement were revolutionizing police work, and if it often seemed true that old forms of tedium were merely being replaced with new ones, in the end, it was worth it—that the value of patience had gone up, not down, with the advance of technologies.

They'd started from the list DeLuca's brother-in-law, Tom, at Homeland Security had obtained for them and added another 531 names to it. They'd identified the top one hundred academics in order of frequent flier miles racked up. His students formed two-man teams and divided the subjects between them. They'd developed parameters for measuring an individual's political leanings, using profiling guidelines developed by Homeland Security. When he brought in a political science professor from MIT who'd done a statistical analysis of revolutionary movements throughout history that proved, with an 89 percent degree of accuracy, that most radical social movements were led by men (or women) who'd been the youngest-born in their families, each team ranked their suspects in order of birth order and concentrated on the top two. When a religion professor spoke to his classes and said that the most radical believers were often converts or prodigal sons returned to the fold, the teams looked for academics whose views weren't simply extreme or overpolitical but had changed in the last ten years. Academic writings, papers, and books were collected and assembled, scanned and entered as text files.

Ford's interest was piqued, however, one night when one of his more gifted students, a boy named Eli, told him he'd found something interesting, a man named Mahmoud Jaburi, a highly respected professor emeritus at Princeton, currently on sabbatical. He'd been born in America, the son of an imam and Islamic scholar who'd taught at Yale until he was recalled to Baghdad to head a mosque there. The Jaburis constituted the largest of the Euphrates tribes, and the surname was the name most frequently cited when Eli ran a check of prisoners currently being held by coalition forces in Iraq. What excited Eli was genealogical research he'd done, revealing that not only was Professor Mahmoud Jaburi the twelfth of twelve sons, but his father, the imam, was thirteenth of thirteen, and his grandfather was ninth of nine. Further research indicated that while Mahmoud Jaburi's writings were extremely liberal-minded when he was a younger man, and quite brilliant (his IQ was reported to approach 200, with a virtually photographic memory), his views had shifted 180 degrees upon the death of his father to become radically conservative.

It got Walter Ford curious, so he'd isolated Jaburi's travel patterns and asked Tom to run a correlation for terrorist chatter. In each city where Jaburi visited, in the days after, terrorist chatter increased. The statistical probability that it would increase consistently after each and every visit was low, yet correlation did not imply causality. Jaburi was a popular, charismatic man, with several websites dedicated to him. Transcripts of his speeches were disseminated through such websites, posted by ardent followers who taped his speeches and preserved them in cyberspace. It wasn't until Ford broke down Jaburi's transcribed speeches that he became truly suspicious. Jaburi had used the phrase "thousand faces" more than twenty times in the last year, never in the context of explicitly identifying a terrorist group by that name, but in a more general sense. Perhaps it was just a phrase he liked, Ford thought. Or was it something in his subconscious slipping out?

Jaburi was charismatic. He was familiar with America and American customs, and he spoke English without an accent. He was trusted by the U.S. government and had often sat on government panels in the past. He was wealthy enough to travel freely, though he had a wife and two young children, rendering him less suspicious than a single man traveling alone. He had contacts and connections all over the country. And everywhere he went, the chatter increased. And in the last year or two, his message had become increasingly apocalyptic and full of doom.

That was enough for Ford to want to see him in person.

He'd flown to Tucson, using frequent flyer miles, and attended the lecture. He'd been enormously impressed by the man's breadth of knowledge and faculty for recall, as if he had a million facts and names at his fingertips. He'd seen Jaburi get into the car with a young Arab girl after the reception. He'd followed as they drove past the convention center, past a large hotel and then the airport. It didn't seem like a typical city tour. And then, much to his surprise, he'd seen the older man raise his hand and strike the girl, an arm flying across the front seat, clearly silhouetted in the rear window by the lights of an approaching car, even though he'd been of the impression that Jaburi and the girl had never met before.

He watched Jaburi meet the blond girl in the bar, and he watched as the blond girl got into the red sports car and drove off with her friends.

Perhaps it was nothing, but Walter Ford had a feeling that the blond girl had been very lucky. He took the digital voice recorder he carried with him at all times and made a note to call Eli in the morning and ask him if he wanted to do any work for extra credit, cross-checking Jaburi's travel patterns against sex crimes in the FBI register.

DeLuca was happy to observe that his gas gauge was no longer dropping. They were somewhere in high country. They kept going. They crossed a ridge, the road traversing a basin and range topography, negotiated a pair of switchbacks and descended to a primitive caravansary that looked more like a cemetery than a town. DeLuca saw no electric lights, only a single kerosene lantern in the center of town, tended by an old man who looked at them, expressionless, as they approached. DeLuca stopped the car, and Evelyn Warner asked the old man if he could tell them where they might find a doctor. He pointed down the road.

"He says next village," she told DeLuca. He looked at the gas gauge.

"Did he say how far?"

"Half a day," she said. "But that's by camel."

They crossed a vast rock-strewn pediment, circled a volcanic crag, and climbed for another thirty minutes to a high pass. DeLuca had hoped, crossing the pass, to see the lights of a city below, but he saw only darkness. Soon enough, the empty gas gauge warning light lit up. They were still in the middle of nowhere. DeLuca always assumed you had another gallon of gas before you were really out, but he'd never tested that assumption. Evelyn thought that was something he ought to know, as a former police officer.

"I don't recall telling you I used to be a cop," he said, glancing over his shoulder to the backseat, where Khalil had either fallen asleep or passed out.

"I'm a reporter," she told him. "I often research the people I meet. Did you know that someone put a bounty on your head?"

"I'd heard," he said. "Ten thousand dollars. It's nice to know what you're worth."

"I heard fifteen," she said.

"It's gone up, then," he told her.

He saw a light in the distance, and then a town, not much bigger than the last one, with a few houses that had two stories, but again no trees. There seemed to be some kind of central village square, where they saw a dry fountain, a donkey, and a car, an old Trabant. At the far corner of the square, he saw a light above a door where he recognized the Arabic word for "police." He wasn't sure he wanted to talk to the police, or answer any questions. It had to be well after midnight. No one was about.

Then he saw, down a side street, what he was looking for, a sign hanging from a pole and, on the sign, a physician's caduceus, along with another symbol in Arabic that he didn't recognize. With the engine off, the town was dead silent.

"You might want to keep the engine on," the Englishwoman said.

"I might want to," he agreed, "but we just ran out."

The doctor was a young man, a Kurd, reed thin, with a close-cropped beard. His wife came to the door as well, tying off her bathrobe, an apprehensive expression on her face.

They brought Khalil in, laying him flat on the doctor's examination table, and then the doctor suggested DeLuca roll the vehicle into an empty garage across the street, where he would deal with it in the morning. Ansar al-Islam controlled the village, he warned, though the people were PUK sympathizers and by and large supported coalition efforts in Iraq. The doctor was the only person in the village, other than the police, who had electricity twenty-four hours a day. The others in the village were only allowed it for four hours in the morning and four hours in the evening, at least until the hydroelectric project to the north of town was completed. The village was called Hukt. They were about five miles east of the Iraq border and twenty from Sulaymaniyeh. When DeLuca asked him if he could get any gasoline, the doctor shook his head. Getting gas could take days.

"There is a bus to the border," the doctor said. "Once you are there, I think you could cross. I will take care of your friend."

The next morning, the bus dropped them off at a refugee camp a short distance from the boundary dividing Iran and Iraq. There had to be somewhere between five and ten thousand people in the camp. DeLuca saw displaced people with thousand-yard stares on their faces, mothers giving their children crackers for supper, a woman with a teenage boy so sick he could hardly move, another boy using the branch of a tree for a crutch, his leg red and inflamed. In the distance, a fight broke out in the men's section of the camp, where he was told by a Swiss aid worker that recruiters for Ansar al-Islam and Al Qaeda were at work, urging young men to join them and fight the good fight. In the women's section, he saw four men from a white Isuzu van, examining the women closely, and occasionally, they'd tell a girl to stand up and turn around. Evelyn identified them as slave traders, telling girls they could get them work as domestic servants in rich Saudi or Kuwaiti households, and then they'd take them to brothels in Turkey instead. The camp was a scene of anguish, and fear, and most of all, chaos.

It wasn't hard to slip back across the border into Iraq.

Two miles down the road, they found an American patrol and surrendered to them. Lacking identification, it took a few phone calls before the patrol released them.

Chapter Twelve

DELUCA WAS OUTRAGED WHEN HE HEARD THE news. While he had been in Iran, a second raid had been conducted at the home of Omar Hadid. This time, the mission had ended badly. They'd received a tip that the home was housing armed insurgents, a tip that was confirmed by aerial surveillance. The day before, a car bomb on the road leading to the base had pulled up next to a Humvee full of infantrymen before exploding, killing six Americans and leaving the rest of their battalion hungry for revenge. A convoy was sent, Humvees, Bradleys, and, this time, four Abrams A-1 tanks. As DeLuca understood it, the convoy was again fired upon from the house, this time by rocket-propelled grenades. The tanks opened fire, and the house was quickly reduced to a pile of rubble and ash. When the smoke cleared, they found twelve bodies, two women and ten men, including that of Ali Hadid. The two women were his wives. Kamel Hadid had been seriously injured and taken to the hospital. Omar, who'd not been present at the time of the raid, had been located and arrested. He was being held at Camp Anaconda, pending interrogation.

Reicken had ordered the raid. DeLuca had half a mind to walk into his office and dump his desk on top of him, but unfortunately, Specialist Washington told him the lieutenant colonel was going to be working in the Green Zone for a few days.

DeLuca gave orders to have Omar Hadid brought to him.

When he walked into Tent City, his friend Sami was waiting for him, looking like somebody had just beat him to a free parking spot in Kenmore Square before a Red Sox game. Next to him, DeLuca saw, was a German shepherd, who looked on, curious.

"How was your flight?" he asked. "What's with the dog?"

"It's not my dog," Sami said.

"Okay," DeLuca said. "Flight good?"

Sami glared at him.

"Food okay?"

Sami glared at him.

"I imagine you're curious to know why I've invited you here today . . ."

"*Invited?*" Sami spat. "You think I'm here because I was fucking *invited*? I'm thinking of putting my fucking boat up for sale because my daughter . . ." DeLuca let his old friend vent for another few minutes. He knew that beneath Sami's gruff exterior, there was a gruff interior, but inside that, he had a heart of—well, his heart was gruff, too, but somewhere in there was the most loyal friend a man could ever hope for, and DeLuca had asked for him because he needed a loyal friend, and one who spoke fluent Arabic. Sami was finishing up. ". . . eight weeks, just to get reimbursed for the fucking airline ticket. If ever."

"You done?" DeLuca asked.

"I'm just getting started," his friend said. "But fill me in and maybe I'll tell you the rest of it later. If I'm still here."

DeLuca briefed his friend as completely as he could, taking him from the initial raid on Omar Hadid's house right up to what he knew about the second raid. Sami listened closely. DeLuca had always been surprised at the kind of close attention Sami was able to pay and the things he was able to notice and remember. Sami was highly intuitive. When he was done, he asked Sami if he had any questions.

"So you want to pull in this Al-Tariq guy, or do you want to let him swim a little bit while you get his people?"

"Pull him in," DeLuca said. "Maybe if we take him out, somebody else will step up, but we think they're more likely to scatter."

"So what's my role?" Sami Jambazian asked.

"What I need from you," DeLuca said, "is to hang around here and figure out who's been tipping people off about me."

"You're talking about the ransom. I mean bounty. Whatever."

"Yeah," DeLuca said. "I'm not worried, personally, but it's already compromising operations. So far I'm guessing it's just some asshole who wants the money, but if Al-Tariq's alive, then I could see how the guy might turn into Al-Tariq's eyes and ears around here and maybe do more damage than just clipping me."

Sami thought a moment. When he dangled his hand over the edge of his folding chair, the dog nuzzled it, looking for attention. Sami scratched the dog behind the ear.

"And you think the car bomb in—what was the name of the town?"

"Ashur."

"You think that was for you?"

"Maybe," he said. "It could be a coincidence."

"So how do you want me to play it?"

"Up to you," DeLuca said.

"Hmm," Sami said, thinking again. "Maybe I'm a disgruntled Arab-American . . ."

"And/or a devout Muslim," DeLuca said.

"Shit," Sami said. "I haven't read the Koran since I was fifteen. Okay. My parents would love this. Anyway, something like that."

"You could pretend you're in some sort of financial difficulty," DeLuca said.

"I could *pretend* that," Sami said. "Let me just take a second and figure out what that might feel like. Okay, got it. So what's my job? What's my unit?"

"Whatever you think would help," DeLuca said. "CI can wear any uniform we want when we work a case, or if you want, you can go sterile and nobody knows your rank, name, or unit. Or you can be a civilian. Whatever you see fit."

"Can I be a general?"

"You could," DeLuca said. "Though I don't know if anybody's going to believe a general is going to do a hit on a sergeant for fifteen thousand dollars."

"Shit. Good point," Sami said. He thought some more. "I'm thinking I'm just a lousy weekend warrior with maxed-out credit cards and a bitch for a wife back home who wants more alimony. Where's a place I could work where I'd meet everybody?"

"Mess hall," DeLuca said. "I know a kid in CSS who'd be dying to help you. I'll take you to meet him. His name is Jimmy."

Vasquez entered and interrupted them. DeLuca made the introductions.

"I don't know who the dog is," DeLuca said. "He seems to be visiting us."

"That's Smoky, man," said Vasquez. "I worked with him in Tikrit and had him transferred. They were going to get rid of him and loan him to the South Koreans, but those people eat dogs, man. I had to rescue him."

"He's military police?"

"Fully trained," Vasquez said. "He's good on checkpoints but not much use for guard duty. That's what they were saying, anyway. Doesn't have a mean bone in him."

"What *does* he do, then?" DeLuca asked.

"Sniffs bombs," Vasquez said. "Other stuff. Whatever you want him to. You just hold something under his nose and tell him to go find more and he does."

"Does he crap inside tents?"

"Don't we all?" Vasquez said, grinning. "By the way— your guy is waiting for you."

Omar Hadid had been held for two days, but he looked like he'd been in longer. His clothes were rumpled and his eyes were bloodshot. He had a bruise on his temple. He regarded DeLuca with a blank expression. DeLuca sat opposite him.

"How've you been treated?" DeLuca asked. "Can I get you anything?"

Omar didn't answer. DeLuca considered what he had to offer. The question was how to win back Omar's trust. He thought he'd give sincerity a try.

"If you're straight with me, I can have you on your way home within the hour," he told the Iraqi. Omar stared at him again.

"Why should I believe you?" he asked.

"I'm sorry about your brother," DeLuca said. "I really am. I was hoping he could talk to my friend, General Le-Doux. The general who wants to meet you. Your brother was essential to what I'm working on right now. I was out of the country when the raid happened. If I'd have been here, I would have stopped it."

"You say," Hadid replied.

"I'm truly sorry," DeLuca said. "How's Kamel?"

"I'm told that if he lives, he will be paralyzed," Omar said flatly. "They think his neck may be broken. Among other injuries."

"Where is he?"

"He's in the hospital, in Ad-Dujayl."

"He should be at the CASH here," DeLuca said. "The Combat and Support Hospital. Some of the best doctors in America are working here."

"Thank you, no," Omar said.

"Omar, it's a better hospital. No offense, but I was in yours. Until a little while ago, yours didn't even have electricity. I know you don't want him to die."

"At least he will die in an Iraqi hospital," Omar said.

"If you think that's going to prove a point, somebody would have to be paying attention," DeLuca said, "and the only one who is is me, and I already take your point."

If DeLuca wanted to reestablish a cooperative relationship, he'd be foolish to try to force Omar to compromise first. He had to show him the way.

"I'm going to make a phone call," DeLuca said, taking his sat phone from his pocket. "You can stop me at any point in this call. When I'm done, you can go back to your cell if you want, or we can stay and talk." He dialed. He waited. "Captain Martin," he said, "this is Mr. David. I have a code Hazel request. I have a boy with a serious neck injury. His name is Kamel Hadid, and he's in the hospital in Ad-Dujayl. He's . . ." He turned to Omar. "How old is he?"

"He is twelve," Hadid said. That was younger than Ali had told DeLuca before, but no matter.

"He's twelve years old. I want you to find the best neurosurgeon in theater and fly him to the hospital. Hang on a second." He turned to Omar again. "Has Kamel had X-rays?"

Omar shook his head.

"He's going to need X-rays, too. You'll need portable equipment because the hospital doesn't have any. Upon the surgeon's recommendation, if the boy can be moved, once he's stable, I want him medevaced to Balad and put on the first plane you can arrange. I want him flown to Logan Airport in Boston, and I want the plane met by an ambulance. I want the ambulance to take him to Boston's Brigham and Women's Hospital. ASAP. Call me when you set it up."

He turned off his phone.

Omar Hadid seemed unmoved.

"Now please bring my brother back to me," he said. "And then bring his wives back to him. Can you do that, Mr. David?"

"I cannot," he said. "I can't change the past. I can only change the future. As can you, if you work with me. But I understand your grief. If you'd rather be alone with your grief, I'll have you escorted back to your cell. If you'd prefer to work toward changing the future, I'll send you wherever you want to go."

DeLuca rose from his chair. He turned and walked away. He was in the corridor when a guard caught up to him and told him Hadid wanted to speak with him again.

Hadid hadn't moved from his chair.

"What is it you want?" he asked.

"Just the truth," DeLuca said. "Same deal as before. Were you housing insurgents?"

"Was I?" Omar said. "No. But I've been living in my office, since the war began. My brother lived at my house. He called me and told me men had come and he could not make them leave. He was afraid that they would kill him if he looked like he was a collaborator, but he was afraid he would be killed by Americans if he let them stay."

"Who were they?" DeLuca asked. "Were they working with Al-Tariq?"

Omar shook his head.

"They were nobodies," he said. "Common criminals. One said he was in contact with Abu Musab al-Zarqawi, but my brother said he thought this man was a liar who was trying to make himself seem important. My brother was not a strong man, Mr. David. This is why they knew they could use him this way. My brother called me and asked me to come over and make them leave. When I got to the house, it was gone."

"They fired on the convoy and the convoy responded," DeLuca said. "This is within the rules of engagement."

"Perhaps they should have just let your tanks drive up and kill them," Omar said.

"You fire on us, we're going to fire back," DeLuca said.

"All right," Omar said. "But what happens when both sides take this position? Who fired first in this war? These men in my house—in the name of defending one's country, even thieves and drug runners may have a holy cause."

"I'll leave it to wiser men than myself to sort out what's holy and what isn't," DeLuca said. "My focus is on what's evil. Holy men can choose their own paths toward faith, but evil men are all the same. You know who I'm looking for. If Mohammed Al-Tariq is still alive, I have to find him before he can accomplish more evil. And I can't find him without help. This is your country. Do you want men like Al-Tariq left free, or do you want them stopped? Because I can stop him if I can find him, but I can't find him without you. It's that simple."

Omar considered his options, his arms folded across his chest, his head tilted to one side. Finally he leaned forward, placing his hands palms down on the table.

"I am free to leave?" he asked.

"You're free to leave," DeLuca said.

"I will make arrangements," Omar said. "Meet me at the gate tomorrow at noon. I will have a car. You may bring a translator, but you must not bring an armed convoy. I will personally guarantee your safety. Imam Al-Sadreddin will speak with us only if you come to him this way."

*   *   *

DeLuca spent the afternoon doing Reicken's paperwork, reading the reports Dan Sykes and MacKenzie and Vasquez had left him, researching interleukin-4, and skimming the chapter from *Current Protocols in Molecular Biology*, volume three, section 4, that Dan had photocopied for him, though it was slow going, too much scientific terminology to make it a quick read.

He sent Gillian O'Doherty an e-mail that read:

Gillian,
Any news for me, re the syringes? Sorry if you tried to call—spent the last four days in Iran having guns pointed at my head. There are probably bars in the Combat Zone in Boston where that sort of thing goes on all the time, but it was somewhat novel to me. Let me know as soon as you know anything—the game is afoot.

D.D.

He sent another to his wife that read:

Bonnie,
I'm sorry to get your latest message and sorrier still that it's taken me this long to respond. I was on a mission that I can't really talk about here, but it took me out of the country for a few days and took a few twists and turns that could not have been anticipated. Also, FYI, my phone died, and I was out of touch with everybody, not just you.

I thought we had an understanding that you weren't going to do anything until I got back? I thought we had a deal, that whatever was going on between us was going to be put on hold until then. Am I wrong about that, or is that an accurate assessment of how we'd left things?

I know this is not what you want to hear, but what I'm doing right now is important and needs my full attention. I can't tell you what that is, however. I do understand how this might drive you crazy. It requires considerable faith, on your part. Maybe you're right—maybe that's too much to ask. Maybe it's easier for me to put everything on hold (and impossible for you) because every minute of my day is filled to overflowing with things to do to keep me distracted and preoccupied. I would like nothing more than to be able to come home to you and have nothing but a solid month of unbroken days to spend talking to you and holding you in my arms and making love to you and getting to know you again. That's the worst part of this, the way it makes us strangers to each other, again and again.

Maybe that's what you can't stand. I don't know, right now, how to avoid it. Please don't do anything until I get back and have a chance to make it right to you.

                                                    Love, David

P.S. I'm sending a kid named Kamel Hadid to Brigham and Women's Hospital for treatment. He's lost his family and I promised his uncle that I had people in Boston who would look in on him once in a while. Is that something you could do? Let me know if it isn't and I'll make other arrangements.

MacKenzie, Sykes, and Vasquez brought in Faris Saad that evening. They'd found him through his sister and promised him U.S. government protection. He'd been hiding in a small village in the desert, a hundred miles west of Baghdad, when they picked him up. Dan asked DeLuca if he wanted to lead the interrogation, but DeLuca deferred to the team, though he called in Sami Jambazian to act as translator.

Faris was, understandably, a nervous little man, constantly twitching and looking over his shoulder. Vasquez assured him that he was perfectly safe.

"We want to know about a load you picked up from the Daura Foot and Mouth Disease Facility in Al Manal." Sami translated the questions and answers, sitting at the end of the table. Saad chain-smoked cigarettes as he spoke.

"I do this once. In March. Before the bombing started."

"And you were alone? Or with somebody?"

"With my friend Razdi. Razdi Chellub."

"You'd driven with Razdi before?"

"Yes," Saad said.

"What did you pick up?" MacKenzie asked him. "Do you remember what it was?"

"I don't know," the trucker said. "Boxes."

"Boxes. What size boxes? Big enough to hold shoes, or big enough to hold air-conditioners?"

"Air-conditioners," he said. "Not so big, but big."

"How many?"

"Four or five, I think."

"What was in the boxes?"

"I don't know."

"What did you think was in the boxes? What did they tell you it was?"

"I don't know. Food, I think."

"Food?" Mack said. "Did you lift them? How heavy were they?"

"Yes. They were heavy."

"So you thought they were full of food, but heavy, like canned goods, not bread?"

"Heavy. I don't know what. Like a case of wine."

"Did they make a sound when you lifted them? Did anything inside rattle?"

"I don't remember. I think no."

"But you can't be sure?"

"No. I was scared. Because of the men. Two men came with us. With guns. They were there when the trucks were loaded and unloaded."

"Who were they?"

"I don't know. I think Mukhaberat."

"Did they say they were Mukhaberat?"

"They did not have to."

"What did they do?"

"They told us not to stop ever. They spoke to the people when we crossed the border. And when we got to Beirut, they put the boxes inside other boxes."

"Where in Beirut did you take them?"

"To the shipping company. By the docks."

"What was the name of the shipping company?"

"Moushabeck Shipping Ltd.," the trucker said. "In the Hamra. Where the Corniche ends."

"And these men, from the Mukhaberat—they took the boxes from Al Manal and put them inside other boxes?"

"Yes."

"Were these other boxes marked?"

"Yes," he said. "In English."

"Do you remember what it said?"

"No," he said. "Razdi said it was food."

"The boxes they put the boxes into? The boxes the shipment went inside of, these boxes were labeled as food?"

"I think. Some kind of importer of food, I think. Razdi knew. This is what he said to me. Razdi could read English. A little."

"But Razdi is dead."

"They killed him. They will kill me, too. He told me to hide, as soon as we got back."

"These men, the men with guns, they didn't return with you?"

"They wanted to, but Razdi did not wait for them. He knew."

DeLuca turned to Sami.

"What do you think? What's your bullshit detector saying?"

"This guy's being straight with us. He's scared shitless. I've got family in Beirut. My cousin Yusef is a cop there. I can ask him to look into it."

"Do that," DeLuca said. "What does he need from us?"

"He said all he wants is enough money to get to Syria. He has family in Damascus."

"How much does he need?"

Sami asked him.

"He says he needs a hundred dollars," Sami said.

"Give him a thousand, and give his sister five hundred for helping us," DeLuca said. "Tomorrow you and I are going to talk to a holy man."

Imam Fuaad Al-Sadreddin had been, by some accounts, the second-most-powerful man in the Sunni Triangle, after Saddam himself. Saddam's government had been largely secular, Baghdad a city of nightclubs and bars where alcohol flowed freely and women could walk the streets unveiled if they chose to. To a certain extent, the war with Iran was an armed confrontation between strict and loose Islamists, with the forces commanded by the radical Ayatollah Khomeini waging a holy war against the infidel Iraqis. Sadreddin had formed a partnership with Saddam, as he had to do, but it had been an uneasy partnership. Saddam knew Sadreddin could turn the Sunnis against him, and Sadreddin knew Saddam could turn his army against him. Each had spies inside the other's houses.

Omar arrived at a gate outside the mosque, where he spoke with an armed guard, then turned through the gates and down a drive to the mosque, which was guarded by at least a hundred heavily armed men sporting AK-47s and assorted small arms. The mosque was impressive, about a thousand years old, with golden onion domes and six-story minarets, decorated with brightly colored tiles of gold, red, blue, and black, with armed guards manning the balconies. The prayer hall inside was large enough to hold five hundred prayer rugs side by side, Omar said. Brightly colored murals on the walls of the *liwan* depicted ancient Islamic tales.

Sadreddin was seated on the floor, at the head of a massive rug woven in intricate patterns of black and red and gold. He was dressed in a black robe, his head bound in a black turban. Despite his age (he was nearly eighty), his hair and beard remained a dark black, such that he'd earned the nickname the Black Monk among certain members of the intelligence community who'd been trying to contact him. DeLuca was the first Westerner he'd met with.

DeLuca, Sami, and Omar Hadid sat opposite the imam, who did not offer food, as had every other Iraqi DeLuca had ever met formally. Omar had told him not to expect the kind of hospitality he'd been shown elsewhere. Sadreddin believed the United States occupiers were true infidels, enemies of his faith and of everything he stood for. He was only meeting DeLuca, Omar said, as a personal favor.

Omar spoke for a few minutes. Sami didn't bother trying to translate, indicating to DeLuca by facial expression and gesture that Omar was saying all the right things. Sadreddin's bodyguard was a former Iraqi Olympic wrestling champion named Goliath, Omar had explained, who'd never lost a match and had therefore escaped the wrath of Saddam's son Uday, who'd made it a practice to torture Iraq's international athletes when they didn't perform well. Goliath was about six foot eight, DeLuca guessed, and maybe 350 pounds of solid muscle, with a heavy beard, cut close, and no discernible neck.

When Omar was done speaking, Sadreddin stared at DeLuca, who hadn't felt such a stare since Sister Michaeletta caught him spitting on her jade plant. Then Sadreddin spoke. Sami translated.

"I will have Sunnis sitting on the command council," Sadreddin said. "I will give you the names. They will represent us in the interim government, and in what will follow. The Sunni people will not be ruled by Shiites."

"He doesn't beat around the bush, does he?" DeLuca said to Sami. "Tell him I will take the list of names to my friend General Phillip LeDoux, who has the ear of Paul Bremer." Sami translated. The imam spoke.

"He wants a guarantee," Sami said.

DeLuca considered lying as one option, but thought of Sister Michaeletta, who had taught him that lying only got your knuckles rapped with a metal ruler. Sadreddin didn't look like he had a metal ruler on him, but you couldn't be too careful.

"I can't make such guarantees," DeLuca said. "Anyone who tells you they could would be lying to you. I did not come here to lie to you. I came to seek your help finding Mohammed Al-Tariq. If you help me, I guarantee I will make certain that General LeDoux and Mr. Bremer are aware of your concerns. They're both of the belief that all the peoples of Iraq must be represented on the governing councils, and that such ruling bodies must not be used to exact revenge or redress ancient grievances. I'm also certain that once General LeDoux receives the list of names I will give him, he will want to meet with you to discuss those names, once he has had time to look at them."

The Black Monk was expressionless. DeLuca was glad he wouldn't want to play poker with this guy.

"Al-Tariq is dead," the imam said. "Your own people have said so."

"I believe my own people could be wrong," he said. "We are currently reexamining the proof that led us to believe he was dead. Meanwhile, I've received indications that he is not. If you could use your contacts and connections to confirm his status, one way or the other, it will help me know what to do next."

The imam whispered something to Goliath, who helped the older man to his feet and escorted him from the room.

"Was it something I said?" DeLuca muttered beneath his breath.

Goliath returned.

"My English is not so good. I say this in Arabic," he announced, then spoke for several minutes before leaving them alone. DeLuca looked at Sami.

"That was interesting," Sami said.

"What did he say?" DeLuca asked.

"He said the imam once had a mentor whom he revered and respected," Omar Hadid said. "A very scholarly, learned man who'd talked a bit too openly about how they needed to replace Saddam with someone more religiously inclined. I knew him. Al-Tariq tried to have the man put in prison, but his followers surrounded him and protected him, so instead, Al-Tariq sent an emissary, another imam from a mosque in Baghdad, as his delegate, and then behind closed doors, the man Saddam sent assassinated Sadreddin's mentor by slitting his throat. This is why Saddredin has agreed to help you."

"Goliath said he'd be in touch, possibly later today," Sami added.

"What was the name of the assassin?" DeLuca asked.

"Jaburi," Sami said. "Imam Razul al-Jaburi. Mean anything to you?"

"Not personally," DeLuca said. "Could be worth looking up when we get back. Does the name mean anything to you?" DeLuca asked Omar.

"I know the name," Omar said. "It's a common one."

When he got back to the OMT and searched the SIPERNET database, he learned that Imam Razul al-Jaburi had died of cancer years ago, but that his two oldest sons (he'd had twelve) had been named in the Deck of Cards. His other sons included lawyers, bankers, the youngest a respected academic. All in all, the Jaburi tribe seemed like a lot of bad apples, in a very large orchard.

He checked his e-mail one last time before going to bed. There was no response from his wife. There was, however, a response from Gillian O'Doherty, who wrote:

Dear D,
Sorry for the delay. Had a mad cow on my table the other day, not as mad as they thought, it turned out, but no doubt good and pissed off after I was through with her.

Had a chance to run the syringes and compare to the Al-Tariq file. Interesting results. The DNA is a positive match. There is no doubt. The FBI could ballpark the samples only within the month, but I can confirm that the DNA on the needles is probably less than a month old. This would indicate that the user was your man. However, the fingerprints on the syringes do not match the fingerprints in the file. This is also definite, or as definite as one could ever be.

What do you want me to do next?

Gillian

DeLuca hopped a Blackhawk the next morning and flew to BIAF. All physical evidence involving tissue samples or biological materials was kept at CJTF-7's CASH facility, in a freezer room that had been part of the airport's cold storage. The guard at the door scrutinized his B&C before letting him pass. Mohammed Al-Tariq's file contained reports and photographs, all of which had been scanned and placed in the digital files DeLuca had already read. The pictures of the dead Al-Tariq matched pictures taken of him when he was alive. The pictures from the recovery scene were, to say the least, grisly.

DeLuca was more interested in the tissue samples, and specifically, an item that had been labeled Exhibit 4a/ 1054, one that had caught his eye when he saw it on the evidence list. The heavy glass jar, about the size of a large container of pasta sauce, was filled to the top with formaldehyde, and in the formaldehyde floated a human hand, yellow and bloated, the tissue ripped at the wrist, the hand otherwise surprisingly undamaged.

He ordered the hand to be prepared for shipping and gave the sergeant in charge of the evidence room Gillian O'Doherty's address, advising him to mark the package URGENT.

He wrote Gillian a note out in longhand to go along with the package. His note read:

Gillian,
You're going to think this is crazy, but tell me if the prints you get off this match the prints on the syringes. No, I haven't lost my mind. Yet. But I'm getting there. Rapidly.
David

Chapter Thirteen

DELUCA WAS ON HIS BUNK, READING REPORTS, when a runner said a man named Goliath was at the gate, refusing to speak to anybody but Mr. David.

"Who's Goliath?" Hoolie asked from where he sat cross-legged on the plank floor, brushing Smoky for fleas.

"Sadreddin's bodyguard," DeLuca said. "Used to be an Olympic wrestler. Heavyweight."

"Goliath Bakub?" Hoolie said. "*The* Goliath?"

"You've heard of him?"

"Only since high school," Vasquez said. "You ever heard of the Persian Pretzel Hold? He invented it."

"This is going to be bullshit," Sykes said.

"Hey, *cabrone*—why are you so down on me, man?" Vasquez said. "I'm not shitting you. He had this hold, man, only one guy ever got out of it and beat him. Guy named Kelsey, in the World Games, down in Brazil. You can call him and ask him if you don't believe me."

"Oh yeah?" Dan said. "So how did he beat him?"

"I asked him that once," Vasquez said. "Ol' Goliath, man, he got Kelsey in his Pretzel Hold, and I said to Kelsey, 'How'd you escape that hold, man?' And Kelsey said, 'There I was, in the Persian Pretzel Hold, and I thought I was doomed, but then I opened my eyes and I saw that right in front of me, two inches from my face, was a pair of testicles, so I figured, what did I have to lose? So I bit 'em. Man, you'd be surprised at what you can do when you bite yourself in the balls, man.'"

Hoolie had a belly laugh at Dan's expense for about three seconds, and then Dan launched himself through the air, landing on Vasquez in midchuckle. The dog cowered behind the water cooler barking while Vasquez and Sykes wrestled. Mack rolled her eyes and went back to reading a six-month-old edition of *Vogue*.

DeLuca was happy to see his team members getting along so well.

Goliath was waiting outside the gate, leaning against the side of a black Cadillac. When DeLuca reached him, he took a map from his briefcase and spread it out on the trunk of his car. The map gave a topographical view of a mountain rising sharply out of the western desert, and at the foot of it, the town of Sinjar, about 160 kilometers west of Mosul, near the border with Syria.

"Sinjar Jebel," Goliath said, pointing to the forty-five-hundred-foot mountain peak in the upper left corner of the map. He moved his massive finger to the town. "Sinjar. Is Yezidi place. He is here." He pointed to an area on the map, making a small circle. "This valley. Ibrahim, yes. His father, sometimes mostly. His men, yes."

DeLuca studied the map for a moment. The road was narrow, with high country to either side. An armored column would be sitting ducks, assuming they could even navigate the switchbacks. The road led to a high valley, following contours that grew closer and closer together, and then the road disappeared into what the map symbol indicated was a tunnel, the sort of choke point that was easily defended and nearly impossible to pass. DeLuca knew there were bunker buster bombs that could be used to open tunnels and clear out caves, even tactical nukes suitable for the task, but if the tunnel went in deep enough, not even tacticals could solve the problem. The area Goliath had indicated was beyond the tunnel, surrounded by mountains on all sides.

"Can I keep this?" he asked. Goliath nodded. DeLuca told Goliath he'd be in touch.

"I will go with you," Goliath said.

"Thanks for the offer, but that may not be necessary . . ."

"I will go with you," Goliath repeated, leaning over DeLuca until he blotted out the sun. "Imam Sadreddin insists. I will go."

"That will be fine, then," DeLuca said. "Happy to have you along."

Goliath got in his car and drove off.

"Maybe we can find you a Humvee to snack on along the way," DeLuca added.

DeLuca called for a meeting with General LeDoux the next day, after forwarding the general a one-page synopsis of the situation and the Air Force's most current aerials of the region. Phillip was accompanied by Captain Martin, as well as by a senior master sergeant named Johnson who told DeLuca his friends called him Preacher. LeDoux had said only that Johnson would probably be able to help them, and DeLuca took his old friend at his word, without knowing exactly what or who Johnson was attached to. They met in a room in the building adjacent to the TOC, where Scott, who'd joined them for the briefing, was able to plug in his laptop and connect it to a digital projector to make a PowerPoint presentation.

"We've been looking at the Sinjar Jebel range for a long time," Scottie said. "Basically for as long as the no-fly zone was being enforced, and Sinjar is well within the zone. In 1997, we had an antiaircraft battery light up their radars here and here, and in 1999 we had one here," he indicated, using his finger to tap the wall where the image was being projected, "but that's it, and nothing in the valley the imam has indicated for us. But that doesn't necessarily mean anything—this part of Iraq has been a hideout for political and religious dissidents since the Medes, basically. Sinjar itself was originally a Roman fortress."

"Three thousand feet?" Johnson asked. He spoke with a heavy southern accent; perhaps that was why he was called Preacher, for his evangelical intonations.

"About that," Scott said. "The area indicated, the Zinab valley, is as inaccessible as any you're going to find in Iraq. The roads are basically goat trails, and there are caves everywhere. The tunnel the road into Zinab uses probably started as a natural cave that got excavated. It's a half-mile long and goes straight through the mountain. Any tank or Bradley that got disabled inside would jam up the works, but as best we can tell, they're not going to get that far anyway because it just doesn't look wide enough. Foot access is pretty much the road, too. Tenth Mountain could probably rope in over the ridges, but not easily or quickly, and they probably couldn't take much with them."

"Choppers?" Johnson asked.

"Not good," LeDoux said. "Lieutenant?"

"The general's right," Scott said. "We don't think we've failed to get triple-A flashes because they're not there. This picture here," he said, moving the PowerPoint ahead a slide, "is of an energy signature typical of the newest SAMs, which we know Saddam was buying after he kicked the inspectors out, when he pretty much knew we were coming. We took out a couple dozen in Baghdad, so we can confirm the signatures. In Zinab, we've got energy signatures here, here, here, and here. And they're pretty tucked away, probably in caves, which is going to make it really difficult to knock them down. And the topography forms a kind of natural bowl, so any helicopters trying to fly in will come in below the SAMs. It would be a bit like shooting fish in a barrel. Iraqi triple-A is about as incompetent as it gets, but even they could cause us problems with these conditions. Plus the winds. It's not somewhere where I'd want to fly a helicopter."

"There are others kinds of air support we could throw in," LeDoux said, "but we're trying to contain rather than disperse, right, David?"

"If there's biologicals there, yeah, containment—good idea," DeLuca said. "My main problem is, I need Ibrahim, or Al-Tariq if he's there, alive. There's something going on, and they know what it is."

"We've been having a really close look in the last twenty-four hours," Scott continued, moving to the next slide, "and here's what we've found. This building here, the white square there, was originally a monastery built during the Crusades and dedicated to Saint George, but it was more of a fortress than a monastery. A French knight named Robert de Boissy held out for sixty days there against Saladin, who eventually starved him out and chopped his head off. Anyway, the walls are six feet thick, which makes it impossible for us to jam any electronics inside. And we have reason to believe they've got significant electronics, because they're running generators 24/7. UAV intel suggests somewhere between eight and twelve people. And these," he said, zooming in, "are munitions casings. Whoever's in there is armed to the fucking teeth. Pardon my French, General."

"I speak French, too," LeDoux said, turning to Preacher Johnson. "I'm thinking HAHO or HALO. What's your opinion?"

"I'd have to check with meteorology, but off the top of my head I think HAHO is out. My boys are the best but nobody can fly square chutes into mountain terrain at night where there's wind like what I imagine we're going to find here. Especially if it's too windy for choppers. HAHO could scatter people half the way to Turkey. I think we're looking at a HALO jump." He turned to DeLuca. "You okay with that?"

DeLuca had to pause a moment. HALO stood for High Altitude Low Opening, a method of insertion for parachute troops that involved jumping out of an airplane from six miles up, dropping at speeds approaching two hundred miles an hour and waiting until the last moment to open your chute, as low as two thousand feet. It was a way to quickly insert men into an area undetected, as opposed to the alternative, a High Altitude High Opening jump, where jumpers opened their chutes as high as thirty thousand feet and then steered them like kites, riding the winds and following a navigator while traveling as far as a hundred miles across the landscape below. Veteran paratroopers called HALO jumps the ultimate thrill ride.

"Sounds good," he said. "When?"

"Dad . . ." Scott said, but DeLuca silenced him with a glance. Not even Phillip knew about his fear of flying. It was a nonstarter. You did what you had to. This was too important, and since he was the only one who'd seen Ibrahim Al-Tariq in person, he had to go.

"It'll take us twenty-four to pick the LZ and get our shit together and check the weather reports," Johnson said, "but we've got no moon for the next two days. I like my missions like I like my humor—the darker the better. You've jumped HALO before?"

"A hundred times," DeLuca lied. "You?"

"Sergeant Johnson is a TL with Task Force 21," LeDoux said. "I'm sure you've heard of them. They have a lot of skill sets, but they also play old time hockey. This is too strong for MPs or Fourth Cav. You'll be in good hands. Co-NCOICs, of course. You want somebody from your team?"

"One guy, I think," DeLuca said. His son looked concerned. "Don't worry about it," DeLuca said. "Any idiot can fall out of an airplane."

"Preacher Johnson is the best," LeDoux confided to DeLuca when the master sergeant had departed. "He was jumping round chutes into typhoons over North Vietnam when you and I were hanging out at the mall. He could still carry you over a mountain on his shoulders if you break your leg."

"Vietnam?" DeLuca said. "How old is he?"

"We think he's in his late fifties," LeDoux said. "Somebody deleted his birthday from all of his records. Probably him. And nobody has the balls to ask him. He doesn't want to be forced to retire."

"You're a general," DeLuca said. "Why don't you ask him how old he is?"

"I may be a general, but I'm not crazy."

DeLuca had indeed heard of TF-21, a task force so named because it supposedly comprised the top twenty-one Special Forces operatives chosen from Army Rangers, Delta Force, Navy SEALS, Green Berets, Air Force PJs—they were the best at what they did, everybody said, though no one knew exactly what they did. They'd been on the ground in Iraq for weeks before the war, dressed as Iraqis, marking GPS positions, collecting DNA, and gathering evidence before it was destroyed, and they'd been on the ground tagging targets with lasers to help guide the JDAMS, cruise missiles, and smart bombs as they fell. It had been TF-21 intelligence that had led to the decision to bomb the palace where Saddam and his sons were thought to have been hiding, two days before the planned opening of the air campaign. They had no base, never stayed in one place for very long, and generally kept to the sidelines, staying clear of publicity and embedded reporters. DeLuca was looking forward to meeting them.

He tried to convince himself that he was also looking forward to jumping out of an airplane from six miles up, but he wasn't having much luck.

Reicken was angry when he found out he'd been excluded from planning the mission. It was the second time in as many weeks—he'd been angry the first time when he learned DeLuca had gone to Iran without telling him. He hit the ceiling a third time when DeLuca told him he'd chosen Dan Sykes to go with him on the jump. He explained, as patiently as he could, that it wasn't a mission for Mack, and that between Dan and Hoolie, Vasquez had two weeks of jump school, whereas Dan had been a member of a jump club in California since he was sixteen.

Dan had arranged for a training jump with a helicopter pilot he knew. Practicing a HALO jump wasn't possible after Reicken decided commissioning a C-130 for the job would have been a bit extravagant. Instead, they were to take a Blackhawk up to twelve thousand feet and jump from there. Sami walked him to the chopper, where Dan and the jumpmaster he'd booked were waiting for the pilot and the flight engineer to finish their preflight protocols.

"So how you doing with this jump stuff?" Sami said.

"I'm doing," DeLuca said. "Why do you ask?"

"Just wondering," Sami said. "Me, I gave this shit up a long time ago. Why jump out of a perfectly good airplane, right? I mean, I did my training but that was enough, you know?"

"Do you have a point?" DeLuca asked. "Or are you just trying to get on my last nerve?"

"Dave," Sami said. "Scott told me you don't like to fly."

DeLuca stopped in his tracks.

"He shouldn't have said anything," he said. "It's nothing. It's a minor discomfort."

"He said on a rough flight when he was younger, you started barking like a dog," Sami said.

"One little yip doesn't mean you're barking like a dog," DeLuca replied, walking more quickly now. "People yip. So what?"

"When's the last time you jumped, then?" Sami asked.

"I had to stay current when I was an instructor at Devin," DeLuca said.

"I looked at your records," Sami said. "You had three training jumps, and before each one, you reported in sick. I don't think you've jumped since Benning."

"Look—I don't want to talk about it," DeLuca told his friend. "If you want to do something useful . . . go check the parachutes or something."

The jumpmaster, a Sergeant Green, gave DeLuca and Dan a brief rundown of all the things they'd have to remember.

"You'll be flying the latest MT-1X ram air chutes, double-layered squares with 375 square feet of rip-stop desert camo nylon, with an open nose that inflates to present a profile something like the wing of an airplane. Without any brakes, you'll be flying forward at approximately thirty miles an hour. That means if you get a ground wind of thirty miles an hour, if you don't land into the wind, you'll hit the ground at sixty. We got very little wind today and there's a windsock next to the LZ for us to watch, and I'll guide you in, but be aware of that. On the mission, you won't have a windsock, so listen to the nav. He'll give you the vector. Release your chute immediately upon landing, unless you want to be dragged across the desert. You control your flight with your toggles. Toggle left to turn left, toggle right to turn right, both at once to brake your forward speed. Half-toggle, quarter-toggle, half-brake, full—we'll have a chance to practice these things a bit. This is important—when you're landing, you want to slow down as much as possible. Flare too late and you hit hard and break a leg. Flare too soon and you stall your chute, and you're just as dead if you frap from a hundred feet as from ten thousand. You pull your chute by grabbing your D-ring, which is located here on your right chest strap, grab it and then throw a jab with your right hand. You should feel a tug. If you don't, it might mean your chute's trapped in the vacuum that forms directly above your back in free fall, so just bring an arm in and roll a bit to free it. If it malfunctions, which with these chutes happens once every two hundred jumps or so, or if you get a partial, pull your cutaway before deploying your reserve. You do not want to have your reserve chute get tangled with your main. Before you pull your main, wave your arms to signal anybody above you that you're deploying and check over your shoulder and below—we don't want people free falling through each other's chutes. Worst-case scenario and you're in a death spiral on your main with one side tangled, you'll have knives to cut your lines, but you only have about twenty or thirty seconds. I'll be on radio telling you what to do every step of the way, and I want you to listen to me but think for yourselves, too.

"Now, during free fall, you will become a human missile. Terminal velocity is going to be 125 miles per hour. If you find yourself in an uncontrolled tumble, simply spread out your arms and legs and arch your back as much as possible and you'll come out of it. You will feel a sense of euphoria, like you're floating on air, because you are floating on air. You may subconsciously wish to prolong this experience—you must maintain awareness. Guys have frapped, believe it or not, because they simply forget to open their chutes. I knew a photographer once whose job it was to take pictures of tourists on their first jumps, and he'd jumped twenty-five times in one day, and on his twenty-sixth and last jump of the day, he exited the plane and grabbed his camera but forgot to put on his parachute. Keep that sort of thing to a minimum. Maintain awareness. If you should drop below a thousand feet, it's too late—it would take superhuman strength to brake your chute before you hit the ground . . ."

Sergeant Green continued. DeLuca was pretty sure complacency and euphoria weren't going to be a problem, but he listened intently all the same.

Dan looked like a kid in a candy store, shifting his weight from side to side with his hands clasped behind his back as he took instructions. DeLuca saw Sami eyeballing the helicopter, chatting with the flight engineer and the pilot, then crouching low to examine the parachutes where they lay on the tarmac. Sami turned each one over, feeling inside them briefly, then returned to the flight engineer to ask him something. DeLuca saw a concerned expression on his friend's face as he approached, asking to speak in private with Sergeant Green. Sergeant Green followed him to the parachutes and examined them a second time. He spoke to Sami, who then went to where DeLuca and Dan were standing.

"Let's get some coffee, okay?" Sami said.

"What's up?" Dan said, grabbing Sami by the arm. "We're delayed?"

"There's not going to be time for a practice jump," Sami said.

"Because?" DeLuca asked. He knew Sami would give it to him straight.

"Because the chutes have been tampered with," Sami said. "Somebody cut the lines. Reserves, too. The sergeant says they're going to have to repack all the chutes before anybody can fly again. The FE gave me a description of the guy who delivered them, so I'm going to look into that. You arranged this through Reicken's office?" he asked of Dan, who nodded. "Who did you talk to?"

"His secretary," Dan said. "Washington."

"So nobody else knew you were going to pull a training jump?"

"I don't know," Dan said. "I don't think so. I mean, the flight crew knew, but . . ."

DeLuca came quickly to the same conclusion Sami had.

"Whoever it is is getting his information from Reicken's office," Sami said. "That's where the leak is. You wanna call off the mission?"

DeLuca considered what the truck driver who'd dropped off his load at Moushabeck Shipping Ltd. in Beirut had told them. Something deadly had been shipped. There was no telling, yet, where it might have ended up, but there was a high degree of probability that it was in the United States already.

"No," he said. "But let's make sure we double-check the parachutes we use on the mission."

Chapter Fourteen

HE GOT A MESSAGE FROM PREACHER JOHNSON that the mission was a go and scheduled for 0200 hours that night. He tried to catch a nap but wasn't able to sleep, so he hit the "gym," which was nothing more than a large tent full of free weights not far from the showers, hoping a light workout might tone his muscles up a bit for the job ahead and occupy his thoughts for a time. When he found himself setting personal bests in both the bench and overhead presses, he realized how much nervous energy he was expending and decided to cut back and save some of it for later. He was starting his last set when Mack interrupted him.

"You've got visitors. Front gate. Your boys are back."

Adnan and Khalil were waiting for him at the front gate. Khalil had a walking cast on one leg, and limped accordingly. Adnan looked no worse for wear.

"It's good to see you, Mr. David," Adnan said. "I wasn't sure that I would when we were separated in Sanandaj."

Adnan explained that he'd avoided capture by diving into a stall at the bazaar where the merchant, a soap dealer, hid him. Later, Adnan tried to find out who'd taken DeLuca and the others and where they'd gone. Asking around led him to a man who claimed to be a member of Ansar Al-Islam. He wanted to know why Adnan was asking so many questions. Adnan lied and said he was looking to join a group, to do something, to defend his homeland. He was taken, blindfolded, to a village outside of Sulaymaniyah where he was beaten during his questioning. He recognized the voice of one of his questioners to be that of Abu Waid, the former Mukhaberat chief and a lieutenant of Al-Tariq.

"How did you know it was Abu Waid?" DeLuca asked him.

Adnan didn't seem to want to answer at first.

"I knew him. From before," he said.

The fact that Adnan had escaped capture when the rest of them hadn't had made DeLuca suspicious, thinking it possible that Adnan had set them up. His story made sense. Yet DeLuca also knew there was something Adnan wasn't telling him. "You want to tell me how you knew him? That seems a bit unlikely for a lowly Republican Guardsman."

Adnan looked at Khalil, then back at DeLuca.

"This Kurd," he said. "I thought he had sold you to them. I thought he had sold me as well. I was raised to never trust a Kurd. But the man who hid me told me Khalil was hurt, trying to stop a man who had come after me. And then Khalil tells me how after you had escaped, you came and rescued him, when you did not have to. I think other men would have left him to die."

Adnan looked at his feet, then sideways at Khalil before lifting his head again.

"I was not just Republican Guardsman," Adnan admitted. "I was Mukhaberat. As I told you before. Each unit of the Guard contained at least one agent, to make reports if any soldiers appeared to be disloyal. During the war in Kuwait, I was given a rifle and told to shoot any man who ran away from that stupid war. Men who had fought for eight years against Iran. Men with families. I could not kill my friends, just because they wish to lay down their weapons, after so many years, rather than fight the United States, who we could never defeat. So I went with them when they surrendered, and I hoped my family had gotten out. But they did not. This is how I knew Abu Waid. He was my commanding officer. And he remembered me."

"So what did you tell him?" DeLuca wanted to know.

"He wanted to kill me," Adnan said. "For being a collaborator. I convinced him I was only doing it so that I could obtain information about the Americans, to give to mujahadeen, for the jihad."

"Did he believe you?" DeLuca said.

"He wanted him to prove it," Khalil interjected. "Adnan has asked me what I thought he should do. I said I thought you would know."

"Abu Waid wants information," Adnan said. "Something he can use against the Americans. I must prove to him that I can be useful as a spy. This was how a man could move up in Mukhaberat, by betraying somebody, to show your loyalty. I think he wants me to give up someone important. To take hostage. I don't know what to do."

DeLuca thought a minute. Betraying somebody to prove your loyalty seemed a bit Orwellian. Could he trust Adnan? Was he telling the truth?

"Do you think Abu Waid will take you in if you help him?" DeLuca said. "Did he say anything about who he was reporting to? Where his money was coming from?"

"He did not say," Adnan said. "But I believe it is Al-Tariq. I heard them talk about someone they called 'The Fat Man.'"

DeLuca considered.

"We can give you something," he told his informant. "Miss Colleen will let you know. Come back tomorrow and she'll brief you. Mr. Hoolie will be with her. Okay?"

"Thank you," Adnan said. "I am sorry."

"Don't be," DeLuca said. "If we can get you next to Al-Tariq, it might work out for all of us."

He talked to Phil LeDoux about an idea he had, then called Mack and Vasquez in for a meeting. DeLuca explained that General LeDoux's office was going to call and give them the location of Counterintelligence Headquarters, which they were to pass along to Adnan, to give to Abu Waid. Such information would undoubtedly invite an attack, DeLuca said, but the information had to be significant. He asked them if they had any questions.

"Just one," Vasquez said. "I didn't know there was a CI headquarters."

MacKenzie looked at him.

"Oh," he said. "I get it."

"You sure you went to Harvard?" DeLuca asked him. "There's a building on the edge of the post that's been empty since we got here because it's too vulnerable to rocket and mortar attack. It's up to you guys to figure out how to make it look occupied. Timers on the lights, some fake antennae and dishes on the roof, maybe a couple of cars parked outside. Something tempting to blow up."

"Like Macaulay Culkin in *Home Alone*," Hoolie said.

"Yeah," DeLuca said to Vasquez. "Just like Macaulay Culkin in *Home Alone*."

*   *   *

Omar Hadid called him at his private number an hour later. He'd spoken to a mother. She said her son had disappeared, six months ago, Omar said. At first she thought he was dead, or that the Americans had put him in prison, until she got a message from one of his friends, saying her son had been sent to America, chosen because he spoke English and because of his profession.

"What did he do?" DeLuca asked.

"He repairs air-conditioners," Omar said.

"I appreciate your help," DeLuca told him.

"One other thing," Omar said. "I've been told that when my brother was killed, he was trying to surrender. That he had a white flag. Have you heard this?"

"I haven't," DeLuca said. "I'll have someone look into it."

Sami's cousin in Beirut had looked at the records for Moushabeck Shipping Ltd. On March 18, the day before the bombing of Baghdad began, a shipment had arrived on a truck driven by two men, Faris Saad and Razdi Chellub, who signed off on the delivery invoice. All the other records of what they'd delivered and what ships might have carried the cargo had been mysteriously deleted from the company computers. Four ships left Beirut that week headed for the United States, two flagged out of Liberia, one out of Malaysia, and the fourth sailing registered as a Mauritanian vessel, the four ships headed for, respectively, Duluth, Mobile, Galveston, and Boston. Sami handed DeLuca a list of the names of the ships, including the S.A. *White Crescent,* which had arrived in Boston, after making various stops, on the third of May.

DeLuca called LeDoux back. LeDoux had bad news. The Pentagon wasn't willing to put the name of Mohammed Al-Tariq back on the most wanted list, the evidence that he was dead still too compelling to warrant a change of status. LeDoux had a sense that something like terror fatigue was setting in. "We used to have just Hamas and Hezbollah and the Taliban and Al Qaeda," LeDoux said. "Now we have the Sons of Islam, Abu Musab al-Zarqawi, Mohktadi al-Sadr, Harith al-Dhari, the Association of Muslim Scholars, Jund al-Islam, Ansar al-Islam, Attawhid wal Jihad, the fedayeen, the Kata'ib al-Jihad al-Islamiyah . . . Throw in a new name like *Alf Wajeh* or the Thousand Faces of Islam and people roll their eyes and say, 'Hey, call me back when they blow something up.' Plus I think we're getting resistance from the CIA. They've got nothing, so they're not going to credit the humint from a little THT of ex-cops and unseasoned Guardsmen fresh out of college. Plus—and you're going to hate this—apparently they talked to Reicken, and he said he wasn't putting much stock in what you were bringing him."

"He said that?" DeLuca asked.

LeDoux could hardly go against the Pentagon, but at the same time, he was scheduled to fly to Washington to meet with the secretary of defense and to testify before the Armed Forces Committee, where he would take it up again if the opportunity presented itself, and if it didn't, he'd create the opportunity. DeLuca understood what LeDoux was saying. It was the kind of thing that could be a career ender. The army liked people who played ball and didn't rock the boat, a fact that was true at any level and even truer at the highest levels. LeDoux had been told, once, to drop it. The Pentagon didn't like to tell people twice what to do. Phillip LeDoux was putting himself on the line for him.

"In the meantime," he told DeLuca, "have fun tonight. I know guys who've been dying their whole lives to get a HALO jump in under combat conditions. Just remember what we used to say in Germany . . ."

"'If you can't get out of it, get into it,'" DeLuca said.

He e-mailed his brother-in-law, Tom, Walter Ford, and Gillian O'Doherty, advising them of everything he'd learned, and to be particularly alert to anything unusual that might involve Boston Harbor or dockworkers, and in particular the ship S.A. *White Crescent*. Gillian was at her desk when she got the e-mail. She was able to instant message him back.

GODoherty: Hello David. What are you up to tonight?

MrDavid: Nothing much. You got my e-mail?

GODoherty: I did. I can't think of anything that came in involving seamen or dockworkers off the top of my head, but I'll check my files. I have something of a backlog, I'm afraid. I was hoping to catch up before they tear the building down and we have to move everything, but I don't think that's going to happen. Speaking of which, I've been wringing the hand you sent me.

MrDavid: And?

GODoherty: Hard to explain or understand, actually. Here's the problem. The DNA from the hand you sent me matches the DNA from the syringe and the DNA from Mr. Al-Tariq's CID file. So the hand is/was his, and the syringe was one he used.

MrDavid: Perhaps I'm being dense here, but, uh, how could a severed hand use a syringe? The syringes were ones he'd used before he was killed. Is that what you're saying?

GODoherty: No. You say he was killed on March 19, correct? That was when his house was bombed?

MrDavid: Correct.

GODoherty: I rechecked my previous data. The DNA on the syringes was not old enough to have been sampled prior to March 19. But that's not the curious part.

MrDavid: It's not?

GODoherty: No. Do you remember me telling you the fingerprints on the syringe matched the fingerprints in the file?

MrDavid: Yes.

GODoherty: Well, the prints on the syringe don't match the prints on the hand you sent me.

MrDavid: But the DNA does.

GODoherty: Yes.

MrDavid: How certain are you?

GODoherty: Positive. In both cases.

MrDavid: Does that mean someone else injected him? I'm confused.

GODoherty: So was I, so I reran the syringe. Originally I took the DNA sample from a dried blood cell I found on the needle, but this time I took a second sample from a skin cell I found on the plunger of the syringe. The plunger sample matched the needle sample. He injected himself.

MrDavid: And the syringe DNA matches the file DNA?

GODoherty: And it matches with the hand DNA. But the fingerprints don't match. And the fingerprints on the hand don't match the fingerprint samples your undercover special ops people collected from Al-Tariq before the war.

MrDavid: But the hand is his?

GODoherty: Not necessarily.

MrDavid: I thought you said the hand's DNA matched everything else.

GODoherty: It does. But the fingerprints on it are different.

MrDavid: ?????

GODoherty: I ran more tests on the hand. This is not Al-Tariq's hand. Al-Tariq was diabetic. This is not the hand of a diabetic person.

MrDavid: How do you know?

GODoherty: There are tests.

MrDavid: Maybe he wasn't diabetic in his hand. Is that a stupid question?

GODoherty: Yes, it is.

MrDavid: I have a feeling you know the answer to this and you're not telling me.

GODoherty: I might. The file you sent me said Al-Tariq was diabetic but it didn't say if it was Type 1 or Type 2. Type 1 is childhood onset and Type 2 is adult onset. To contract Type 1, you need to have a genetic mutation known as SUMO-4. He was obese, correct?

MrDavid: Correct.

GODoherty: Then he probably had Type 2, which starts when you eat all the time and your pancreas is constantly releasing insulin into the bloodstream, until you become hyperinsulinemic. Type 2 can be controlled through diet and exercise, but it doesn't sound like our man was the sort of person to watch his diet or work out. Type 1 is genetic. Type 2 isn't.

The hand you sent me was not part of the remains of Mohammed Al-Tariq. It wasn't the hand of a diabetic. It doesn't even have enough adipose tissues to be the hand of an obese person.

MrDavid: But it has his DNA.

GODoherty: Yes.

MrDavid: How is this possible?

GODoherty: The only way I know how would be if Al-Tariq had an identical twin. Twins have the same DNA but different fingerprints. A twin wouldn't necessarily be diabetic, if we're talking about Type 2. Though some say obesity is genetic. Neither sample contains the SUMO-4 variation. The file you sent me doesn't have Al-Tariq's birth records or say anything about a twin brother, so there's not much I can do about it from here.

MrDavid: That would explain how we could have "positive proof" that he's dead, and yet he could still be alive. Like Saddam with all his body doubles. Only better.

GODoherty: Sort of. I think it might have been an intentional deception. The hand you sent me was wearing Al-Tariq's ring, but the ring didn't fit and there were no sloughed skin cells beneath the ring. I think the ring was added later. Plus it was missing the stone, whatever that means.

MrDavid: We can probably find out if he had a twin. Good work.

GODoherty: Is there anything else I could do for you, David?

MrDavid: Just what I said before. We think they may have used a container ship to ship whatever it is they're hoping to use. I gave Walter and Tom the names of the ships that left Beirut that week. Right now we're thinking it's something biological. Plague, smallpox, hemorrhagic fevers, etc. Maybe somebody got contaminated somewhere along the way.

GODoherty: I think we'd have heard about it by now. I'll look into it. Anything else?

MrDavid: Maybe one thing.

GODoherty: What is it?

MrDavid: Could you check in with Bonnie?

GODoherty: I'd be happy to. What do you want me to say?

MrDavid: I wish I knew. Just talk to her. Sometimes I think she thinks I'm just over here drinking beer and eating pretzels.

Gillian had an appointment with her oncologist, so she wrote herself a Post-it note and stuck it to her computer monitor to remind herself to search her files for anybody who worked on the docks who might have taken ill or died in the last few months. She seemed to remember a burn victim, but that obviously had nothing to do with international terrorism. It was still worth a look.

Before she left for her doctor's appointment, she called Bonnie DeLuca and left a message on her answering machine—would she like to get together later, maybe for dinner, to keep an old woman company?

Bonnie heard the tail end of the message as she rushed in the door, but by the time she managed to return the call, Gillian O'Doherty had stepped out. She'd just come from Brigham and Women's Hospital, where a young man named Kamel Hadid had undergone spinal surgery. She'd managed to find a translator from the Boston College Foreign Languages department to help explain to Kamel what was happening to him, and she'd brought him a portable CD player and some CDs she'd gotten from the Boston Public Library of classical piano music after learning that Kamel was a budding pianist. The doctors said his prognosis was guarded but optimistic. The nerve damage was not as severe as had been previously estimated, and he'd already recovered a slight amount of sensation in his toes, indicating that he might not be paralyzed, as had first been thought.

He was a sweet kid. Visiting him had made her feel better. Maybe that could be a part of the solution to her problem, she thought. Maybe the problem was that she had a lot of love to give and no one now to give it to— maybe if she gave it to somebody else, she'd feel better. That didn't mean having an affair, but maybe if she took care of other people and did something that made her feel useful, she'd be happier. She'd been a year short of finishing her nursing degree when she'd met David DeLuca. Perhaps, once she'd found an apartment, she'd go back and finish her degree . . .

Mahmoud Jaburi's morning lecture nearly filled the University of Minnesota's Northrup Auditorium, where he spoke on the subject of Globalism, Islam, and the Passion of al-Hallaj, the "Keeper of Consciences" and an ancient Muslim mystic and martyr who was becoming something of a cult figure in contemporary Iraq. Born in 858, al-Hallaj had memorized the Koran by the time he was twelve and fasted in silence for an entire year before his first trip to

Mecca; he'd been imprisoned in Baghdad by the Caliph al-Muktadir in 911 for plotting to overthrow the established order, giving of his own blood and flesh in the name of Allah with his death by dismemberment and decapitation in 922, the pieces of his body burned and tossed into the Tigris. Jaburi explained how today, teenage suicide bombers visited his cenotaph in Baghdad, citing him as their patron saint.

"A spiritual awakening is afoot in Iraq, it is alive, and it's growing, spreading from the fertile fields of the Dijla and the Furat, in English the Tigris and Euphrates, like a holy virus that will infect and purify other Islamic countries. The U.S. invasion of Iraq is converting Iraq, the most secular of Islamic lands, into the sacred land it was originally meant to be. To the pious in Iraq, the United States has done them a favor by removing Saddam, who was an obstacle to creating a pure Islamic state. The Koran teaches that before this can happen, the infidels must be removed, not just from Iraq but from the face of the planet. This is what jihad means, to these young people who pray to al-Hallaj and seek to follow in his footsteps. Hoping to plant the seeds of democracy, the United States has, quite inadvertently, unified an Islamic brotherhood that will rise in rebellion to establish a true Islamic theocracy. It is an idea that cannot be contained or controlled."

After the lecture, he was taken for a tour of the Mall of America by a graduate student named Rajan. They rode the Ferris wheel in Camp Snoopy, ate in the fast food court, and played with blocks in Lego Land, where Jaburi bought a large set of Legos. He bought a Minnesota Timberwolves jersey in a store, from the boys' section, and in a fancy women's clothing store, he bought an elegant silk headscarf. His last stop was a sporting goods store. When he was done, Rajan drove him very slowly around the mall three times.

Walter Ford, who was following them in a rental car, thought that was odd.

From the Mall of America, they drove a short way on 494 and exited at the Minneapolis–St. Paul International Airport. On the top level of the parking garage, both men got out of the car to look over the edge at the airfields below. From the airport, they took 35W downtown to the Fifth Avenue exit, took Sixth to Kirby Puckett Place, and circled the Hubert H. Humphrey Metrodome, stopping the car, but not getting out, near intake vents drawing air to keep the sports arena's inflatable roof aloft. Finally, the student drove the professor back to his hotel, stopping short of the foyer to show Jaburi something he had in the trunk, a navy blue and lime green Federal Express cap that the professor briefly examined.

Jaburi dined alone in the hotel restaurant and retired to his room early, earlier than Walter Ford expected him to return, forcing Walter to dive quickly under the bed so as not to be caught going through Jaburi's things. He'd found nothing of interest, Jaburi's briefcase full of scholarly books and academic Islamic studies journals. There was nothing remarkable about the purchases he'd made either, save one, a receipt for a handgun, a Colt automatic he'd bought with a credit card, to be sent to his home in Maryland after Minnesota's required waiting period.

Lying on the bed, Mahmoud Jaburi made a phone call, which Ford, lying directly beneath him on the floor, was able to record, using his digital voice recorder. *"Marhaba*

Aafia. Aini? Inshalla kulish tamam? Asgher? Nesreen?"
The conversation went on for about half an hour, during
which time Jaburi's voice seemed to rise in anger occasionally. He went into the bathroom after he hung up the
phone. Walter Ford considered making his escape. Yet it
had been Jaburi's pattern to go to the hotel bar before bed-
time, where he would try to pick up women. Ford decided
to wait. Perhaps Jaburi would do the same thing tonight.

Jaburi returned to the bed, turned on the television,
and watched CNN for about an hour, focusing on news
from the Middle East. Jaburi occasionally spoke to the
television, and Ford didn't think he needed a translator to
guess what he was saying, cursing and arguing with the
commentators. Jaburi channel surfed until he paused at
a movie, something starring Sandra Bullock and Harry
Connick, Jr., but apparently he didn't like Sandra Bullock
any more than he liked the news, muttering to himself and
calling her, in English, a whore. Finally, Jaburi shut the
television off and read for a while. Before he went to bed,
he got down on his knees, facing Mecca, and uttered a
prayer, which the retired policeman also recorded. From
where he knelt, Jaburi might have noticed a man lying
under his bed if he'd glanced in that direction, the bed-
spread pulled partially back on the bed, but he did not, rising to his feet and returning to the bathroom one last time
to urinate and brush his teeth.

Walter Ford waited until he heard Jaburi snoring
loudly, then slowly slid out from under the bed on the side
opposite where Jaburi lay, tiptoeing across the thick shag
carpeting toward the door. He knew now that Mahmoud
Jaburi was part of some kind of plot. How sinister it was,
he couldn't be sure, but the fact that he liked to drive

around large public buildings looked like he was planning something major. Ford paused, thinking. The man was asleep, vulnerable. Ford could end it, here and now, with a single bullet, fired through a pillow. It was only a fleeting thought, but it invoked the philosophical argument he sometimes raised in class—if you could travel back in time, to 1936 or so, and shoot Hitler, would you? Most college kids argued that it would be wrong. Most men over sixty didn't have a problem with it.

Before he left, Ford stepped into the bathroom and drew a handful of hairs from Jaburi's hairbrush. It might not be a bad idea, he thought, to have Gillian O'Doherty run Jaburi's DNA and get it on file, just in case they ever needed it later.

When he got back to his motel, he called the only Arab-speaking person he knew, other than Sami—Sami's sister Riva—and played her the telephone conversation he'd recorded. The telephone conversation was a man calling his wife, Aafia, the two of them talking about their kids, Asgher and Nesreen, what the son wanted for his birthday, how they were watching too much television. The male voice said that to celebrate the end of Ramadan, he wanted to take his family sailing, and he asked her to make the arrangements to have their summer place on Cape Cod cleaned and prepared for their arrival.

The prayer was also of the standard variety, the *Al Fateha,* then the *Rukéteen,* with a few added words that sounded a bit egomaniacal, the prayer of a man who clearly saw himself as an agent of Allah, if not Mohammmad's equal, judging from the very personal way Jaburi spoke to his God, highly unusual for a Muslim. She said one line disturbed her, or rather, confused her, a part of his prayer where he asked Allah to give him the strength of al-Hallaj. Ford explained that al-Hallaj had been the subject of his lecture earlier that day.

"Well, I'm like the last person to argue with a Muslim scholar," she said, "but from what little I can remember of my religious education, al-Hallaj was crazy. Or that's what I was taught, anyway. He kept asking people to kill him. Something like that. It was years ago. I could be wrong."

DeLuca ran into Colonel Reicken after dinner. Reicken said he wanted to wish DeLuca luck, and added that he'd had an idea.

"When you get back," he said, "I'd like to sit down with you and your friend General LeDoux. Nothing formal, just a chance to debrief and get to know each other. Maybe dinner in the officers' mess. When you get back. No hurry. Say, listen—do you know a sergeant named Jambazian from Support Services? He's been asking a lot of questions about you. I know you were concerned about that bounty thing, and I hear he's Arab-American. I'd keep an eye on him if I were you."

"Thanks, sir," DeLuca said. "I'll bear that in mind."

"I put in a follow-up call on the evidence we sent to Gillem, by the way. I told them to expedite. They thought they could have something for us in two or three weeks."

"That's great, sir," DeLuca said. "You're the best."

He needed to find MacKenzie to tell her to start looking into whether Mohammed Al-Tariq had a twin. She wasn't in her quarters, so he sought her at the Balad Ladies' Club, an empty Iraqi Air Force storage shed some of the women in the battalion had made into their own gathering place, complete with curtains on the windows. For all the good work that men and women in the battalion were doing side by side every day, everyone agreed it was a good idea to give the women a place to socialize or piss and moan or whatever they did there. When DeLuca rounded the weather station, he found a group of women sitting at a card table, playing poker outside the BLC by the light of a single candle. Joan VanDamm was among them, rising from her seat when she saw DeLuca coming.

"Hey, Sarge," she said, smiling. "You looking to lose some money? We have a seat open if you want to sit in."

"Not tonight," he said. "I'm looking for Mack, and I'm in a bit of a hurry . . ."

"I heard," VanDamm said. "My husband said only an insane person would jump HALO into the mountains at night. He used to be a Ranger."

"He could be right," DeLuca said, realizing his nervous energy showed. "Is she in?" VanDamm put her hand on his arm, then pointed to a towel hanging on the doorknob. DeLuca was puzzled.

"Someone left a towel on the doorknob? What? She's in the showers?"

"You've obviously never lived in a women's dorm," VanDamm said. "The towel means she's indisposed."

"She's not feeling well?"

Three of the women at the poker table giggled.

"She's got company," VanDamm said quietly.

"Company," DeLuca repeated, and then, in a rush, he got it. He felt as if, all in an instant, a giant billboard had sprung from his head with flashing lights saying, I'M AN IDIOT, in letters twenty feet high.

He understood better when, half an hour later, Dan Sykes came back to Tent City looking oddly invigorated and refreshed. When DeLuca asked him where he'd been, he said he'd been with MacKenzie.

"Doing what?" DeLuca asked.

"What are you—my dad?" Dan said.

"No, I'm not your dad, but I am team leader," DeLuca said. "I went to find Mack and they told me she had company."

"We had some things that needed taking care of," Dan said. "Personal things. As I understood it, we were both on personal time. If you needed something . . ."

"I didn't need anything," DeLuca said. "I mean, I did—it looks like Al-Tariq might have an identical twin that we didn't know about. I need Mack to look into it while we're gone. So you and Mack hooked up, then?"

Dan stared at him.

"I have no intention of talking about my private life like I'm some jackass frat boy," Dan said. "What's it to you?"

"It's nothing personal," DeLuca said, "but it is business. You tell her you have a fiancée?"

"No," Dan said. "Why? Do you want me to? I thought what happens on TDY stays on TDY. That was my understanding."

"What goes on between you and your fiancée is your business," DeLuca said, "but if you fuck up the chemistry of this team by screwing over one of your fellow team members, then that becomes my business. A team works when the partners feel equal and take care of each other impartially. If two people get involved, that impartiality goes right down the toilet. Get it? That's why they have rules against fraternization in the services."

"Mack and I can keep our personal and our professional lives separate," Dan said. "That's between me and her. And for the record, we talked about it and we agreed that if it starts to get in the way of business, it's over. I needed to release a little tension. I think we both did. That's all it was."

"That's all it was," DeLuca said. "Now who's thinking like a frat boy?"

"Point taken. Briefing's at 2200 hours, right?" Dan said, looking at his watch. "I'll meet you there. I want to grab a shower first."

DeLuca spent the time breathing slowly, visualizing what he was going to need to do, resting his eyes and breathing, slowly, quieting his heart.

He sat up.

When he dialed Bonnie's number on his sat phone, he got a busy signal.

It was time to go.

He dialed one more time.

Busy.

It was time to go.

Chapter Fifteen

TF-21 ARRIVED AT THE TOC AT THE SAME TIME as DeLuca, racing to a dramatic stop in a pair of black SUVs with tinted windows. They looked more like a rock and roll band than a military unit, six men in all, led by Preacher Johnson, the only clean-shaven one in the group, the others sporting beards ranging in length from Ulysses S. Grant to ZZ Top. A Humvee arrived at the same time from the front gate, disgorging a massive figure dressed head to toe in black sweat pants and sweatshirt. For all the liabilities Goliath posed as an untrained amateur, it had been determined that it was more important to curry favor with Imam Fuaad Sadreddin than it was to worry about what could happen to Goliath—he could take his chances along with the rest of them.

DeLuca introduced Goliath as his translator.

Preacher Johnson stood in front of a six-foot-square plasma screen in the briefing room. The C-130's flight crew sat to one side, a second flight crew opposite them whom DeLuca took to be the extraction team. DeLuca was surprised, and more than a little pleased, to see Scott there, accompanying his boss from Image Analysis, a captain whom DeLuca knew only as Jefferson.

"I just wanted to tag along," Scott said. "Hope you don't mind."

"I don't mind," DeLuca told his son.

Johnson laid out the basics. The mountain stronghold was in a former monastery with walls too thick to breach with explosives at close quarters. Elevation, 3,550 feet, ground temperature due to be somewhere around fifty degrees. In addition to the main building, there was a wing of what looked to be living quarters and some kind of barn or large shed where they presumed vehicles were stored. Close surveillance by satellites and UAVs over the previous twenty-four hours suggested the building was occupied by approximately ten men. There was a garbage dump outside the back door to the main building, suggesting that door led to a kitchen area—a pair of black bears had been observed rummaging in the garbage.

"So anybody sees any black bears, tell Goliath here and he can pick 'em up and throw 'em in the bushes," Johnson said. "Now, no offense to all present, but for a number of reasons, we don't use our names when we go on missions. I will introduce my men only as Sergeants Blue, Red, Purple, Yellow, and Pink. Anybody who wants to make a joke about Sergeant Pink, you may make it now."

No one spoke.

"My men will have chemlights on the backs of their Kevlars until we land, glowing in their designated colors, so you will know who's who in the air. The rest of you will wear the standard green. Everybody's got GPS transponders, too." Johnson went from man to man, handing out two-foot lengths of plastic tubing, chemlights like the kind little kids sported at a Fourth of July fireworks displays. "These light up in the infrared spectrum, visible only to someone wearing night vision goggles. That's to keep us from shooting each other once we're on the ground, because the enemy won't have these. You wear them around your neck. The navigator is the first man in and he'll paint the LZ with infrared, but remember to disengage your NVGs before you flare because you're not going to get any depth perception if you try to land with them on. The LZ is a field north of the monastery. As of two weeks ago, they were grazing sheep there."

"Kept for romantic purposes, I'm guessing," Sergeant Blue said, interrupting. The others laughed. Somebody made a bleating sound.

"Anyway," Johnson continued, "they were grazing sheep, so it's unlikely it's mined. Chances are much better that some motherfucker is going to be shooting us out of the sky. Pink is navigator. Blue is two in the stack, Yellow is three. You pull at 2,000 feet. Sergeants DeLuca, Sykes, and Mr. . . ."

"Bakub," Goliath said.

"DeLuca, Sykes, Bakub, and the rest of us pull at three thousand, and because we have some newcomers, I'm going to assign escorts to make sure you get on the ground in one piece. Red is with Sykes, Purple is with Man Mountain Mike, and I'll take Sergeant DeLuca down. We are your personal saviors, so pay attention to us. We're going to need separation when we pull, but we'll help you maintain your intervals. Sergeant DeLuca and I are co-NCOICs on this, by the way. Now there's a slight complication. We have a new moon, which is in our favor, and we're going to be jumping into a cloud deck, so we're going to have all the darkness we could hope for. However, that cloud deck is right about 13,000 feet . . ."

"Question," DeLuca said. "Is that 13,000 above sea level, or 13,000 above the 3,500 feet we're landing at?"

"That's sea level," Preacher Johnson said. "Excellent question. Your altimeters are calibrated to zero out at sea level. The LZ is 3,500 feet so you're going to pull at 6,500. Don't wait until your altimeter says 3,000 or you're going to frap. We don't have Combat Control on this to give us the local barometrics so we're not recalibrating. The tricky part tonight is going to be that your altimeters only go up to 13,000 feet, and because of the new Soviet triple-A, we're going to be jumping from 39,000 feet. With luck, they'll think we're just a commercial passenger jet at that altitude. Triple-A can't shoot down anything higher than 35,000 feet. However, what that means is that your altimeters are going to circle their orbits three times. Three. We're starting at 39,000 feet, so you're going to zero out at 26,000 feet, and then the needle keeps going, so you'll zero out again at 13,000 feet, at which point your altimeter is going to be counting down to zero, and from above, a cloud deck looks just like the earth, so every bone is your body and every cell in your brain is going to be telling you you're about to frap. If you pull early, there's no telling where you're going to end up. You'll be wearing a full Gore-Tex jumpsuit and a Mister Puffy, but you're still going to get wet. The temperature at 39,000 is going to be somewhere between fifty and sixty below zero, with the wind chill pushing that closer to eighty below, so be glad you're staying dry until then. My guys, no funny stuff inside the clouds . . ."

"How thick are the clouds?" Dan asked.

"Hard to say," Johnson said. "We think somewhere

between 500 and 1,000 feet, but if conditions change, they might extend all the way to the ground."

"What happens if they do?" DeLuca asked.

"You're going to have to pull at 6,500, whether you're in the clouds or not," Johnson said. "The odds are, you'll be clear by then, but we won't know until we go. Flying your chutes inside of cloud cover is going to be . . . interesting. We train to land using GPS systems only, but if we lose sight of you in the clouds, you're on your own, at least until you hit the ground and we hook up again. Watch your altimeters, slow down as much as you can when they hit 3,600, keep your knees bent and look for dirt. You will land eventually. That's rule number one of parachuting—you must land on the ground the same number of times as you jump out of an airplane. Now I'm going to turn the podium over to Sergeant DeLuca and have him tell you all what it is we're looking for."

DeLuca felt slightly weak in the knees, thinking about what Johnson had just said. He drew a deep breath.

"What we want," he began, "is to take everybody we find in for questioning. The best information we have is that the monastery is where we're going to find a man named Mohammed Al-Tariq, the former head of Saddam's secret police. His son will be there as well. Al-Tariq was responsible for using BW and CW during the Anfal campaign that followed the Iran-Iraq War. We believe he may have built his own private laboratory at a place called Al Manal, disguised as something called the Daura Foot and Mouth Disease facility. I could speculate on what we think he produced there, and the intel is good, but nothing's confirmed yet, so I'm going to hold off. It doesn't matter—he's got something nasty, and he's planning to bring it."

"Excuse me," Sergeant Red said, "but it matters a whole fucking lot if we're jumping into it. We've got testing equipment and chem suits if we need 'em, but nobody said we were jumping into BW."

"What up, dawg—you've had your rabies shots," Sergeant Yellow said.

"We're not dealing with BW," DeLuca said. "Not here, anyway. As far as we can tell, it left Iraq on trucks when the bombing started and got into Syria somehow and got put on ships in Lebanon. The shipments are relevant only because of what it means to our mission. If the WMD are deployed and dispersed, then there has to be some sort of central command and control. The organization that's being put together to deliver the attack is something called *Alf Wajeh*, or the Thousand Faces of Allah. I doubt they have a thousand agents in the field—we all know how these terrorist organizations inflate their own numbers to make themselves scarier. Our operating theory is that this network is going to be centralized and controlled by Al-Tariq, the same way that Al Qaeda was or is centralized in Bin Laden. The monastery could be the headquarters, so we're looking for communications equipment, computers, laptops, Palm Pilots, or PDAs, anything that might be used to store the information needed to coordinate a large network or to facilitate communications."

"First thing we take out are the roof dishes," Johnson said. "The area is too remote for land lines, but they've got all sorts of stuff on the roof, hidden under tarps, so we haven't seen them until now, but they're there."

"What we don't want," DeLuca continued, "is for the alarm to sound and for somebody inside to send the go-signal to deploy the WMD. That's why we can't fly in a thousand guys and blast the crap out of everything, because that would give them time, and it would also destroy the information we need."

"We have hunter-killer UAVs in the air, once the shit hits the fan, but the mission is to get in before they throw down," Johnson said. "And then we shoot the pistols from their hands just like the Cisco Kid. Sergeant DeLuca is right about taking prisoners if possible, but the ROE is shoot to kill. Use your discretion."

"They don't know we're coming," DeLuca concluded, "but they probably know we're aware of them."

"That why they put a bounty on your ass?" Sergeant Pink asked.

DeLuca shrugged.

"Maybe," he said. "But if anybody here needs a quick fifteen thousand, you'd be much smarter taking out a home equity loan, with the interest rates they're offering these days."

"Twenty-five," Sergeant Blue said. "It's gone up."

Sergeant Pink whistled.

"That's a new bass boat, where I come from."

"That's as much as your sister could make in a year, blowing sailors, where you come from," Sergeant Purple told him.

Scott walked his father to the plane, apologizing and explaining that he had to catch a ride back to his unit with Captain Jefferson. He wanted a moment to speak with his father in private.

"So, Pops," Scott said, eyeballing the C-130 that waited for them on the tarmac, dark save for a faint glow from the green and blue lights of the cockpit control panels, the only colors that wouldn't wash out the night vision goggles worn by the pilots. "You remember that time when I was going to Boy Scout camp, when I was twelve, and I was all freaked out about bears, so you gave me Grandpa's World War II medal for bravery and told me it would give me courage? You said it was magic."

"I remember that," DeLuca said.

"Well, I know how much you looked up to Grandpa, even though you didn't always see eye to eye," Scott said, taking from his neck a thin gold chain and on it, a hexagonal brass medallion with a war eagle in the middle. "So I thought I'd loan it to you. You can give it back to me the next time I see you."

DeLuca held the medallion in the palm of his hand and looked at it for a moment, then put his head through the chain and tucked the medal inside his T-shirt, next to his P-38.

"Thanks," he said.

Suiting up for the mission made him feel like he was preparing for a moon landing. They dressed out of the back of one of the SUVs, changing into what Sergeant Blue told him was an ECW or Extreme Cold Weather system. The first layer was expedition-weight polypropylene long underwear, complete with a fleece balaclava over his head; over that, woodlands green camo pants and black fleece zip-up turtleneck top, and over that, the "Mister Puffy suit," comprising a down-filled jacket and down-filled overalls. The outer layer was a Gore-Tex jumpsuit, loose-fitting on everyone except Goliath (who could barely squeeze into the largest set of clothing Preacher Johnson could find), completed by insulated Gore-Tex boots, polar-fleece mittens and Gore-Tex mitten shells. Over their faces, they wore MBU-12/P pressure demand oxygen masks, a soft rubber faceplate bonded to a hard plastic shell with a built-in microphone for radio communication, and over that, an insulated jump helmet with built-in speakers. The masks were connected to 106-cubic-inch portable bailout oxygen bottles, carried in a pouch and worn on the left side, the right side reserved for weapons.

As for weapons, DeLuca wasn't sure he'd ever seen, in all his years in the military, as small a group carrying so much armament. Apparently the men of TF-21 were free to choose whatever weapons they wanted to carry, regardless of nation of origin. Sergeant Blue favored a pair of AK-47s, arguing that if he ever ran out of ammunition, most of the time he'd be able to borrow more from the enemy. Pink bore an Italian Beretta AR-70, a Mac5 machine pistol, and an old-fashioned sawed-off Italian shotgun. Red had an Austrian Steyr AUG and an M-12. Yellow favored a brace of Striker 12 Street Sweepers capable of firing a dozen 12-gauge shotgun shells in as many seconds. Purple wore a set of Tec-9s and an Israeli Galil that had been fitted with a grenade launcher. Preacher Johnson carried a Street Sweeper, a Colt AR-15, an M-10, and a Tec-9, making DeLuca feel positively naked with his Beretta and his Smith and Wesson. He was given his choice and asked to select from an array of weapons, choosing an M-12 for its compact size and because he'd fired one before. Dan chose an army-issue Colt AR-70. Goliath picked up a Kalashnikov and field-stripped it in five seconds, putting it back together again and grabbing a handful of clips like he was grabbing French fries at McDonald's. In addition to assault rifles, Sergeants Pink, Blue, and Yellow were filling packs with C4 plastic explosives, 80mm backpack mortars, silencers, claymores, and MREs, the packs to be worn between their legs and lowered to the ground on tethers just before landing.

Sergeant Blue handed DeLuca a roll of duct tape and instructed him to tape over the barrel and sights of his weapons. "In case you get dirt in 'em when you land," he explained. "Or if they get tangled in your lines. Tape the triggers, too, so you don't accidentally blow your leg off. Makes it much harder to land."

The C-130 took off at about 0100 hours. They sat in metal seats, facing each other along opposite sides of the fuselage, the plane empty and cavernous, except for them, buckled in with five-point harnesses, their faceplates attached to the central oxygen console, from which they'd prebreathed pure oxygen in advance of takeoff. They'd continue to breathe pure oxygen until they reached the target, at which point they'd switch over to their portable systems, which contained about thirty minutes of oxygen, more than enough to get them safely on the ground. Because the cabin wasn't pressurized, DeLuca felt his ears repeatedly pop and unpop as they flew. The only light was dim and red. Occasionally a man would flip his NVGs down to test the batteries and settings. Sergeant Yellow, who seemed to be the coolest cucumber among the bunch, kicked his head back and slept, while Preacher Johnson next to him used his NVGs to read a book. When DeLuca flipped his goggles down to see what book it was, he saw that it was a Bible.

No one spoke, each man left to his own thoughts.

When they got a signal that they were thirty minutes from target, DeLuca heard Johnson's voice in his intercom.

"Let us pray," Johnson said, speaking slowly and calmly. "Dear Lord, we want to start by acknowledging the separation of church and state, and this being a U.S. military mission, please consider this prayer as entirely unofficial and of a personal nature. We are mindful, as well, of your commandment, 'Thou shalt not kill,' but see ourselves as your agents executing the enforcement of that commandment, for we are tasked tonight to stop a bunch of motherfuckers who would certainly kill a whole lot of innocent people if they could, and thus we ask your forgiveness and hope that you might grant us the wisdom and courage to carry out our mission and kill these motherfuckers before they kill us, thy will be done. And lest anybody think this is some bullshit my-God-is-bigger-than-your-God holy crusade sort of nonsense, we recognize that you and Allah probably play handball together every day and that Jesus and Mohammad are like the Babe Ruth/Lou Gehrig combo on your heavenly team, and that it's not our place to decide who's got you on whose side and who doesn't, because we know you hate this whole fucking mess as much as we do. If you can, please give Mr. David and myself, we of a slightly advanced age, the fortitude to show these flatbellies how it's done. Grant our leaders the wisdom and the courage to know what's right, and lead us safely back home to our loved ones, who clearly don't deserve the shit they have to take from us or the worries we put them through. And if one of us should fall tonight, please let him into Heaven, where we promise we'll do a better job than we've done here, because these are good men, Lord, they're good men in a bad place, doing a job that has to be done, so that other people can live their lives in peace, or in service to you, if that's what they want to do, because we know that the death that comes to us tonight means the end of life to some but the beginnings of better lives to others. So make us quick. Make us strong. Make us smart. Make us brave. Make us tough. Make us cruel, and let us all come home again together. Amen."

"Amen," DeLuca said.

Fifteen minutes before they reached their targets, he saw the jumpmaster stand by the jump door and point a finger at the ceiling as the ramp lowered. The sky was full of stars. Preacher Johnson gave him a thorough going over, fastened a green Cyalume chemlight to the back of his helmet and cracked it until it glowed, detached his oxygen mask from the central console and reattached it to his portable system, checked to make sure it was working properly, and then gave him a thumbs-up.

"You're good," he told DeLuca. "I guarantee you I'm going to get you down. Okay? I guarantee it."

"Alive?" DeLuca said.

Johnson just winked at him, strapping an eight-foot length of bungee cord to DeLuca's right arm, just above the elbow. "This is so I don't lose you. I'll cut you free just before it's time to deploy. Just watch the others and do what they do."

The jumpmaster pointed all five fingers toward the ceiling, and then he straightened his arm to point out the door.

Sergeant Pink went first, followed by Blue, and then Yellow, the three men stepping backward off the ramp to let the force of the air streaming below hit them on their chests. Purple went next, tethered to Goliath, then Dan and Sergeant Red, and then, before he knew quite what was happening to him, DeLuca backed off the ramp with Preacher Johnson next to him, flying out into the sky.

It took him about ten seconds to reach terminal velocity, at which time he experienced an adrenaline rush unlike anything he'd ever known before.

"Arch, DeLuca," he heard Johnson's voice in his headset. "Arms out, legs apart. You're doing great. Try to relax. Pink, Blue, form up and maintain intervals. Sergeant DeLuca, I'm going to turn you a bit so that we can see each other, all right?"

DeLuca felt a gentle tug on his arm. The earth below seemed black and featureless, not a light to be seen, until he remembered that he was looking at the top of a vast cloud cover. He looked at his altimeter. It read five thousand feet. The clouds looked as flat as the desert. He checked his altimeter. It read zero.

"Cloud deck is thirteen thousand more, right?" he asked.

"Correct. Sergeant Pink," Johnson said calmly, "why don't you go on ahead and tell us when you're through, okay?"

"Roger that," Pink said. DeLuca watched as Sergeant Pink brought his hands in to his side and dove headfirst, accelerating as he reduced his wind resistance.

"Two thousand above deck and falling," Johnson said. "Maintain awareness. Keep your intervals. Sergeant DeLuca, prepare to get hit in the face with an ice-cold hose."

The cloud deck approached rapidly. For a second, DeLuca imagined that it was the ground, that he would die, that this was it, his life was over, a good life all in all, no regrets . . .

"Pink in," he heard.

"Blue in."

"Yellow in."

Then he hit.

Nothing had ever felt as bracing. In the darkness, he could see nothing. He felt a gentle tug on his arm. "That's me, Sarge," Johnson said in a soothing voice. "I'm right here. I'm not going to let you go."

DeLuca heard a ringing sound. He heard it again. An alarm? Had something gone wrong?

"Sergeant DeLuca," Johnson said. "When we get down, would you kindly remember to turn off your cell phone? Thank you."

DeLuca knew, without having to check, who had called—Bonnie had an absolute God-given knack for always calling at the worst possible moments.

Then he was out of the clouds. It was dark below.

"TLs out," Johnson reported. "Newbies, watch your wrists. When you see your altimeters flashing, pull your D-rings and check for deployment. Mr. David, you're going to be on your own but I'll be right above you, giving you directions. We'll count down from ten. I'll pull at five and you pull at zero, please. From . . . ten, nine, eight . . ."

When he got to zero, DeLuca grabbed his D-ring and shot his right arm forward.

He felt his body flip as his chute deployed.

"You'll want to toggle about three-quarters right and rejoin us," Johnson instructed him. He found his toggles and pulled down on the right one. "Careful not to spiral. Let up. Okay. Steady. Come on back to me. Good."

"Pink is good," DeLuca heard in his headset.

"Blue good."

"Yellow good."

"Red good."

"TLs are good."

There was a pause.

"Sergeant Purple," Johnson said. "Sergeant Purple," he repeated. "Report, please. Has anybody seen Sergeant Purple or Mr. Bakub?"

"Negative, Blue."

"Negative, Pink—vectoring right."

"Keep your intervals," Johnson said. "Stack looks good. Mr. David, toggle right just a tad. There you go."

"Smoke deployed," the navigator said. "Wind speed three knots blowing due east. Setting up right."

DeLuca understood what was going on. Something had gone wrong with Goliath and Sergeant Purple, but no one was talking about it.

Then his headset crackled.

"Purple is good," a voice said. "Sorry to worry you. Jabba the Hutt had a problem with his main so I had to cut him free. He's on his reserve . . . somewhere."

"Somewhere?" Johnson asked.

"Lost him," Sergeant Purple said. "I was at eight hundred when I pulled." DeLuca remembered his instructor telling him it would take superhuman strength to brake a chute that opens below one thousand feet.

"Mr. David," Johnson said, "you're a bit wide, so let's spiral at half-toggle right and bring you back into the wind. A little more. A little more. Looking good. Hold it. Do you see the ground? Three-quarters. Okay, slow but steady, a little more . . . now full brakes."

DeLuca pulled his toggles all the way down, his arms straight and pressed against his sides, his knees bent. He hit the ground softly and ran three or four steps forward before stopping. He cut his chute loose and saw it collapse behind him.

The group gathered where a small clump of scrub oaks formed a small copse at the north end of the field. The night was as dark as they could hope. There was no sign of Goliath.

"Don't worry, Purple," Johnson said. "By this time next week, he'll be back sitting on his mama's lap. Meanwhile, everybody pay up."

As the team stripped off its jumpsuits and insulation layers, each TF-21 member approached Johnson and handed him two hundred-dollar bills.

"We like to pay our bets before the mission starts, in case we have next-of-kin issues," Johnson explained to DeLuca.

"What was the bet?"

"A hundred that I couldn't get you down in one piece, and then when they met you, we made it double or nothing you'd stick the landing."

They were crouched low, removing the duct tape from their weapons and rechecking their equipment while Johnson downloaded the latest falcon view to his PDA. Imagery indicated two guards on the roof and one in the courtyard, where the generator was located. DeLuca and Johnson studied the photograph.

"There's no backup generator?" DeLuca asked.

"Not one that's running," Johnson said. "They might have backup."

The plan they'd discussed during the briefing looked solid. Sergeants Blue and Pink were to scale the roof, take out the guards and the communications equipment. From the roof, they'd have command of the courtyard below. Sergeants Red and Yellow would enter through the kitchen and clear the living quarters before proceeding to the main sanctuary. Purple and Sykes would secure the barn, entering from the north side and working through to the courtyard doors opposite, where they would take out the guard in the courtyard and the generator next to him. DeLuca and Johnson had the main gate, guarded by decorative barbicans and spanned by a pair of thick wooden doors that were currently open. The monastery had been built on a promontory, with two of the main building's outer baileys flush to the cliff walls, an overhang to the east, and a steep, nearly vertical two-hundred-foot drop to the south—no wonder Saladin hadn't had much luck assailing the fortifications.

"Crack your necklaces, boys," Johnson said. "Stay tight."

They moved stealthily down the tree line where the woods dropped off along the mountain's eastern slope. They came to a barbed-wire gate, and beyond it a lower field. A wide lane opened up at the southwest corner of the lower field, leading to the barn.

They stayed off the road, picking their way through dwarf pine and scrub oak until they reached the crest of a small rise, affording them a view of the buildings about a hundred yards below. Sighting through the NVG-assisted scope on his Steyr, Sergeant Red offered to pick off the guards on the roof, an idea that had some merit but one

DeLuca had to veto—it would give the others too much warning. Sergeant Blue proposed a complete stealth attack, taking out the guards in silence and then whoever was asleep downstairs, but there was too much risk involved. Instead, a little more "shock and awe" was called for, an attack that created chaos and confusion and one that DeLuca hoped would be over quickly. Johnson sent Blue, Pink, Red, and Yellow off to circle left, while the rest of the team crossed the road one at a time on DeLuca's signal.

"Let me know when you're in position," Johnson said.

"How many Hellfires have we got again?" DeLuca asked him.

"Six," Johnson said. "And a couple Warthogs that can be here in ten minutes. All you gotta do is ask."

"You guys willing to cue this to the Hellfires? I'm thinking one on the generator and two on the roof. It means we're going to have to be sitting pretty close."

"We can paint the generator with infrared, but I don't know about the roof," Johnson said. "That's the problem with lasers. They tend to go in a straight line." He surveyed the surrounding hillsides. "I could send someone up the mountain, but that's going to take time and he might be too far away. Aw, what the fuck—they gotta have the damn coordinates zeroed in by now."

He instructed his men to advance to their positions and wait for the rocket attack before beginning the assault, then called the flight office in Kirkuk controlling the Predators and told them what he wanted.

DeLuca and Johnson crouched along a ravine, moving west to approach the front gates, stopping in a wooded gully, and crawling on their stomachs to the crest of a rise, from where the gates lay directly in front of them, about sixty yards off, the last forty open ground. The fact that the gates were open suggested they certainly weren't expecting company.

"Blue Team in position," he heard on his headset.

"Red team, too," a second voice said.

Then a dog started barking.

"Aw shit," Johnson said. "Why didn't we figure that? They got sheep, they got sheepdogs. Any time you're ready, Kirkuk."

DeLuca hoped that the dog barking in the night was a commonplace occurrence, but he feared the opposite, and that inside the monastery, men were waking up and reaching in the darkness for their weapons.

Then there was no more darkness, the air split by a spectacular blast as a Hellfire missile screamed down from above and detonated in the courtyard. A moment later, two more blasts shook the ground, missiles striking the communication equipment on the roof and sending fragments over DeLuca's head.

"Go go go!" Johnson radioed to his men.

DeLuca and Johnson ran to the gates, where a large fire burned in the courtyard, flames rising above the casements, smoke filling the air.

Dan and Sergeant Purple rushed the shed, firing as they went to clear the way, the building smelling of straw and sheep shit and chemicals. They raced past a pair of vehicles, then took cover as someone fired on them from the courtyard door. They fired back and the figure fell.

DeLuca saw flashes in the cloister windows opposite the gates, where he and Johnson took cover at opposing gatehouses. The power was out. So far so good. He flipped his NVGs down as three more explosions shook the roof, probably grenades from Sergeants Blue and Pink.

Two men ran into the courtyard from the main building and were cut down in a hail of fire as Purple opened up with his Tec-9 and Johnson engaged with his Street Sweeper, catching the enemy in a withering crossfire. When DeLuca saw a man running from the colonnade to the main portal, he pointed his machine pistol at him, the weapon roared in his grip, and the running man fell.

"Red—are you good?" Johnson called out when he saw a particularly large fireball roll from the far windows of the cloister.

"Good good good," Red shouted back. "We're clear here."

"Move on the main. The main!" Johnson told them. "Blue, Pink—where are you?"

Someone fired from one of the windows of the main building, a staccato roar from what DeLuca guessed was a large-caliber machine gun.

"On the roof—clear here."

"Can you get down?"

"Repeat?"

"Can you get in? Trap door, staircase, something."

"Staircase. Taking fire."

DeLuca crossed into the courtyard and took cover behind what appeared to be an old well. He saw the double lancet windows flash twice, Sergeant Blue dropping grenades down the staircase, and ducked as the glass blew out. They'd tried to get intel on the Monastery of Saint George (a set of thousand-year-old blueprints would have been nice) but could collect only general information, that similar abbeys of the era featured simple living quarters or cells, a building for the animals and the equipment they used, a place where food could be prepared or stored or consumed, and a larger sanctuary for group worship, with perhaps an office attached and a place for the abbot to reside—that was where DeLuca expected to find Al-Tariq.

Someone fired out the window again.

He ducked his head and ran for the central portal, slamming into the wall with his back and pausing to catch his breath.

Johnson slammed into the wall next to him.

"You're faster than you look," Johnson said.

"Only when I'm getting shot at," DeLuca said.

"Blue, ready?" Johnson said.

"Blue ready," Blue replied. "I left Pink on the roof."

"I've got the can-opener," Purple said, raising his grenade launcher.

"We're in the foyer," Red called in. "The sacristy. Whatever it's called."

"Eyes, boys. Don't shoot anybody with a necklace on," Johnson reminded everyone. DeLuca ducked reflexively as something in the barn exploded, probably some kind of gasoline storage tank. "On three. One, two . . ."

Purple blew the doors in with his grenade launcher.

They rushed the main building, firing into it as they went. DeLuca saw Dan take a window. He dove and rolled through the door as someone fired from the chancel rail. Yellow fired back, and the man was dead. A second man fired from the transept. Preacher Johnson returned fire with his Tec-9, shattering tile and glass, a chandelier dropping to the floor as the man died.

When someone scrambled for the door, DeLuca turned with his machine gun, squeezing the trigger, only to find his clip was empty. He drew his .38 and followed the figure out the door. The man shot twice as DeLuca ducked back, then kept running, firing his AK-47 a third time behind him before being clotheslined fiercely by a giant figure in the courtyard. It was Goliath. The giant wrapped his right arm around the man's neck and dropped to the ground, snapping the man's spine. DeLuca helped Goliath to his feet, whereupon he noticed the big man was limping.

"You all right?" he asked.

"I flew into the mountain," Goliath said, dusting himself off. "I lost my rifle."

"Poor mountain," DeLuca said. "Take his."

He returned to the sanctuary, where he saw, in his NVGs, six men with glowing rings around their necks, but nothing more, no one moving, and three bodies on the floor, none of them large enough to be Al-Tariq, unless he'd lost a lot of weight since the war began. Johnson shone a flashlight on their faces.

"He's not here," DeLuca said.

"We got two in the cloisters," Red said. "Two on the roof and two in the courtyard. That's nine. Isn't that everybody?"

"That was approximate," Johnson said. "Is there a basement? Anything down below?"

"It's clear," Yellow said. "Just a wine cellar. Completely empty."

"The roof is clear," Pink said, descending a corner staircase. "What have we got?"

"We got nine," Johnson said. "You see anything?"

"Just King Kong Bundy," Pink said, referring to Goliath, who stood in the doorway.

DeLuca felt his heart pounding. He heard sheep bleating, a dog still barking, a fire burning in the courtyard where the generator had been, and then the quiet was shattered as a white Toyota pickup truck sped from the barn, a .50-caliber machine gun mounted in the back spitting fire at them as the vehicle made for the front gate. DeLuca dove out the door and hit the floor, firing from between the balustrades of the arcade railing. Johnson and Blue managed to get off a few bursts as well, but then the truck was gone, bouncing down the hill and toward the woods below.

"There's another car in the barn," Dan called out.

The keys were in it, a soft-topped Humvee DeLuca suspected had been stolen or otherwise appropriated from coalition forces.

Sergeant Blue drove. DeLuca rode shotgun, literally, for the first time in his life, borrowing the 12-gauge Striker from Sergeant Yellow. Johnson was in the back. Dan was in the gunner's sling, though without a gun mounted for him to use. DeLuca handed him his M-12 and two fresh clips.

The road dropped precipitously, a winding gravel lane that was rutted and grooved where the runoff had eroded deep cuts in the surface. Humvees were built for neither speed nor comfort, but they were built for stability, and Blue drove like he'd been running moonshine on West Virginia back roads since he was twelve, running without headlights and using his NVGs to see. The taillights of the pickup truck appeared and disappeared up ahead as the road hugged the curves of the mountain, the truck perhaps a quarter mile off, but it soon became apparent that the Hummer was gaining.

"TF-21," DeLuca heard in his headset. "This is Kirkuk. Do you need assistance?"

"Negative, negative," Johnson shouted. "Lead vehicle is hostile. Trail vehicle is friendly."

"We know," the voice said. "We've got your GPS. Would you like us to take out the lead?"

"Negative," DeLuca said. "We need it intact. Can you slow 'em down a bit?"

"We can try," the voice came back.

The pickup was no more than a quarter mile ahead when a Hellfire missile struck the mountainside in front of it. DeLuca saw the brakes of the truck light up, but then the vehicle sped forward. He saw as well an explosion on a distant peak, telling him the A10 "Warthogs" were engaged, now that the Iraqi antiaircraft batteries had turned on their radars.

"Get me closer," Dan shouted.

"He's got a fifty-cal," Blue shouted back. "We don't want to get too close."

The road was rough enough that it was pointless for either side to try to fire off rounds on the fly. DeLuca was more afraid of the lead vehicle dropping off a passenger, some guy behind a rock with an RPG leveled and steadily aimed at them. At the same time, he felt the adrenaline rush of battle, the head-to-toe electric charge that made him believe he could drive through anything, the feeling that had always pushed men in armed conflict to do very brave or very stupid things, often in the same day. "It's a good thing war is so terrible," Robert E. Lee once said, "elsewise we should grow too fond of it."

A bump sent the Humvee flying, and then a large pothole rattled his teeth, centrifugal force flinging him against the door. Sergeant Blue hit the gas, gravel flying up behind them in a rooster tail. They caught a glimpse of the pickup truck again, ahead and below, curving around a rock face, and then another Hellfire struck, throwing a ball of flame in the air and scattering rocks, but the truck pressed on, disappearing around the stone face of the mountain.

"That's it for us," the voice from Kirkuk said. "We've got one more in the chamber but we thought we'd save it in case you need a kill on the other side."

"Other side of what?" Johnson asked, but then the answer to his question became evident as the Toyota disappeared into the mouth of a large tunnel, its lights dipping out of sight. Sergeant Blue slowed.

"What do we do?" he asked excitedly. "We got 'em, right? Let's just sit on it. Pin 'em down on both ends and wait for support. They can't go anywhere, right?"

"Negative," DeLuca said. "We don't know the interior topography. If it's a cave system, there could be other exits. Go go!"

Sergeant Blue sped up again, barreling into the tunnel barely under control. Once inside, the rock walls closed in, and it felt like they were going much faster than they were as the air turned colder. DeLuca flipped down his NVGs and looked at the speedometer. They were going thirty miles an hour, then thirty-five, forty . . . The tunnel bent to the left, then appeared to straighten a ways, the Toyota nowhere in sight ahead of them. Forty-five miles an hour . . .

DeLuca noticed that the bulletproof windshield of the Humvee was cracked, the fissure emanating from a pock mark the size of a half-dollar where a fifty-caliber shell had evidently ricocheted off the glass directly in front of him. A bit too close for comfort, he thought.

Then the Humvee took a hard left and slammed full speed into the back of the white Toyota truck, which had been left there to block the way.

DeLuca, as was his habit, wasn't wearing his seatbelt, better to be able to make a quick exit, he'd always felt. And so he did, flying headfirst through the windshield.

And then everything went black.

Chapter Sixteen

CIA AGENT ANDREW TIMMONS WAS AT A WHITE
House dinner, seated across from the director himself
(a sure sign that his career was moving forward), listening to the president address the assembled Arabists and
Islamic scholars (Mahmoud Jaburi was among them),
when his assistant approached the table and whispered in
his ear.

Timmons excused himself, saying he had something
he needed to take care of. He grabbed an umbrella, then
followed his assistant through the Rose Garden and
across the White House lawn in the rain to the west gate.
He crossed Pennsylvania Avenue in light traffic and went
to a black sedan, where his assistant opened the back door
for him, and he got in, handing his umbrella to the assistant, who waited outside the car.

He regarded the man next to him in the backseat.

"It's Detective Ford, isn't it?" he said, offering the man
his hand. "Agent Andrew Timmons, CIA."

"Pleased to meet you," Walter Ford said, feeling a bit
rumpled and crusty, next to the tuxedo-clad man from
Central Intelligence. "Boston PD retired."

"Yes, retired," Timmons said, smiling. "My friends

here tell me you've been following Professor Mahmoud Jaburi. Is that right?"

"Yes, sir, that's right," Ford said.

"You followed him here tonight, I gather. May I ask why?"

"Just curious, I guess," Ford said. "I didn't know where he was going when we left the hotel."

"And why are you curious, may I ask?" Timmons said. "You teach at Northeastern, is that right?"

"That's right," Ford said. "CJC Research and Evaluation and Statistical Analysis. Half-time."

"I see," Timmons said. "Karl Levitov over there is a friend of mine. Is he still teaching the section on terrorism?"

"I believe he is," Ford said. "I don't know a lot of people in the department."

"And you're teaching Research and Evaluation and Statistical Analysis. Was that how you became interested in Professor Jaburi?"

"Actually, it was," Ford said.

"How so?"

"Well," Ford said, "I was showing my classes how to do a profile, so we used the parameters we drew up, stuff like birth order and political leanings and stuff like that, and started, you know, cross-referencing—stuff I'm sure you guys do all the time. And this guy's name just sort of jumped out, so I thought I'd have a look."

"You just thought you'd have a look," Timmons said.

"Yup," Walter said.

"So you flew to Tucson and . . ." He had to consult the notes his assistant had handed him. "Minneapolis. Was this at your own expense? Motels, car rentals, meals . . ."

"My wife and I have a lot of frequent flyer miles stored up," Ford said. "And I have friends in Tucson who bought a little house out toward Gates Pass. They put me up, so it didn't cost that much."

"Can we cut to the chase?" Timmons said. "Professional courtesy and all that? Because if you try to tell me you've been doing all this at your own expense as part of an academic project or whatever, we're going to have a problem. If you'll be honest with me, I'll be honest with you. Fair enough?"

"Fair enough," Ford said.

"So who are you working for?"

"I don't think I can tell you that," Ford said. "What I could do is ask him if he minds if I tell you, and if he says it's okay, then I'd be happy to tell you."

"And this person," Timmons said. "Can you at least tell me what agency or department he works for?"

"No, sir," Ford said. "Not unless he tells me I can."

"We can find these things out, you know," Timmons said. "You not telling me now isn't going to really do anything except delay the process and annoy me."

"Oh, I know," Ford said, "and I gotta apologize for that, but I'm sure you can see that from where I stand, it's just best if I'm not the one you hear it from."

"I can't see that, really," Timmons said. "It would stand you in considerably good stead, in fact, if I did hear it from you. I'm sure you know all the ways we could fuck you up if we wanted to. I'm not trying to threaten you, Detective Ford, but I wanted to make sure you understand how the game is played."

"Like I said," Ford told him, "I'd like to help you, but I

can't. I get the idea you want me to stop what I'm doing, but I don't know why. Maybe if I knew that . . ."

"Fair enough," Timmons said. "You understand the powers I have, under the Patriot Act, I trust? If I learn that this goes anywhere beyond this car, you will have seriously compromised your retirement years. So we're clear on that?"

Ford nodded.

"All right," Timmons said. "I'll be as brief as I can. Professor Jaburi is a CIA asset. He's been an asset for a long time. And it's vital that we continue to have access to him as a resource. I think that's probably all you need to know."

"It certainly is," Ford said. "It explains a lot, actually. I had no idea. You guys work at a whole different level than I do. I know that."

"I'm going to be generous and assume whoever you're working for didn't know that either," Timmons said. "So I want you to tell him. And then have him contact me. My assistant will tell you how you can get hold of me."

As Timmons reentered the White House gate, his assistant was forced to trot to keep up with him.

"So who do you think?" the assistant asked. "FBI?"

"Who else?" Timmons said. "They've been dying to take Jaburi away from me for years."

"I don't quite see what a moron like this Walter Ford character is going to be able to do," the assistant said.

"Don't buy the bumbling Columbo bit for one second," Timmons said. "I want his phones and his files. Credit cards. Video rentals, library books, whatever. Keystroke his e-mail to me, too. Get me what you can on his wife, kids, whatever we can use. And cancel his frequent flyer miles."

In his car, Walter Ford looked at the card Agent Timmons's assistant had handed him. He'd seen Timmons meeting with Jaburi earlier that morning, but he couldn't tell what part of the government he might be working for. He'd figured the best way to find that out would be to stake out the White House and see who knocked on his window. He hadn't a doubt in his mind that Jaburi was dirty. Anybody who thought Sandra Bullock was a whore had to be certifiably insane, at the very least. Sandra Bullock was America's sweetheart.

He was worried about his friend David as well, and wondered why he'd never responded to his last e-mail.

DeLuca heard a voice say, "David. Dave. Dave De-Luca . . ."

He opened his eyes again and saw the face of Preacher Johnson, or rather, half the face. The other half was covered in bandages. Johnson's right arm was in a sling as well.

"They told me you were coming back to us," Johnson said.

"Back from where?" DeLuca asked, trying to think. "What happened to you?"

"Same thing happened to you," Johnson said. "You're in the CASH. I was your roommate, until an hour ago."

The Combat and Support Hospital was like any other fully equipped medical facility, with one significant exception: It was inflatable, a portable field hospital made of double-shelled airtight green nylon tubing, walls and ceilings held erect by a pair of large air compressor units, with sterile operating rooms, an emergency room, recovery rooms, hallways, a phenomenal piece of engineering, DeLuca had always thought, though being inside one felt like being inside a maze. It had made him feel slightly claustrophobic before, but now he just felt cold from the air-conditioning. He felt pain in his head and neck, the pain filtering through a medicated haze.

"You leaving me?" DeLuca said.

"Have to," Johnson said. "They got me a cubicle in Doha while the arm heals. Caught some glass in the face, too. They said I was going to be ugly—I said, 'What do you mean, *going* to be?'"

DeLuca had his first memory of the accident, the white truck suddenly appearing to block the tunnel.

"They said you went through the windshield. Them's bulletproof, you know."

"It had a crack in it," DeLuca recalled. "How's Dan?"

"Well, that's a funny thing," Preacher Johnson said. "Lord must have had other plans for him. He popped out of that sling and shot right over the truck. He got throwed quite a ways but he came out without a scratch."

"Sergeant Blue?" DeLuca asked.

Johnson shook his head.

"Lord had plans for him that couldn't wait," Johnson said. "Dwayne Sullivan, from Bethlehem, Pennsylvania."

"He was a good man. How about Al-Tariq?"

"Your son was right," Johnson said. "That goddamn mountain was laced with caves. Like a sponge. We had the exit covered but they never came out. Probably crawled out some rathole somewheres."

"Shit," DeLuca said. "What'd they find at the monastery?"

"CID is still processing," Johnson said. "They got the son's fingerprints. That's all I know."

"Intel?" DeLuca asked. "Computers?"

"Just a couple power supplies without the laptops attached," Johnson said. "I'm kicking myself for not disabling the vehicles. I let you down."

"You didn't," DeLuca said. "Can I ask you a question? I'm going to need an honest answer." Johnson nodded. "Is there some reason why I can't move my legs or my arms? I keep trying but I'm not getting any response."

"Well, they got you immobilized so you don't fuck your back up any more than it already is," Johnson said. "I guess you got some disk problems, but they're not going to know how serious it is until you wake up, which you should in a few days. This is just a dream, right now."

"Really?"

"Naw, I'm just shitting you," Johnson said with a smile. "You need anything before I go? Want me to turn the TV sound back on?"

"Sure," DeLuca said. "I'm sorry about Sullivan."

"Yes, sir," Johnson said. "I am, too. I'll see you around. You'll like the night nurse—the day guy's nothing to write a book about but the night nurse has a set of cannons coulda turned the tide at Gettysburg."

DeLuca listened to CNN for a while with his eyes closed, catching up on the sports scores and the Hollywood gossip. He opened his eyes when the anchor cycled back to the day's top story: 128 passengers on United Flight 1230 from Manila to San Francisco had been hospitalized with a mysterious illness, with twelve deaths already reported in Seattle, San Francisco, Los Angeles, Denver, and Tucson. Stricken passengers and those they'd come in contact with had been quarantined. Homeland Security had declared a red alert and canceled all flights in or out of the United States, pending further investigation. Al Qaeda was taking credit for the outbreak. The U.S. economy had taken a hundred-billion-dollar hit in the last twenty-four hours, the report said, as people avoided shopping malls, baseball stadiums, or any public buildings where large numbers of people could gather . . .

Had Al-Tariq launched the attack, knowing he was being pursued and fearing he'd be caught before he could give the go signal?

"I'd have knocked, but there's nothing to knock on," a voice said. He turned to see his old friend Sami parting the Velcroed slit that served as a doorway.

"Hey, Sami," DeLuca said. "You see the news?"

"I saw it," Sami said. "You think this is it?"

"I don't know," DeLuca said. "Why is Al Qaeda taking credit? If you're martyring yourself in the name of Allah, you'd think you'd at least want to make sure they get your name right. I don't think *Alf Wajeh* and Al Qaeda are the same thing."

"Jesus—don't you ever stop? You're off the clock, David. How you feeling?"

"I'm fine," DeLuca said. "I gotta call Phillip. Is my phone here somewhere?"

"Just take it easy," Jambazian said. "You can tell him when you see him. He's been checking in. Right now, your job is to get better."

"How long have I been here?" DeLuca asked.

"Three days," Sami said.

"Can you do me a favor and find a doctor named Kaplan? Dan said he works here." If the attack was under way, there was no time to lose, and if it wasn't, there was still no time to lose.

"By the way, we got the guy who was ratting you out. Arab-American named Richard Yaakub," Sami said. "Kid from Chicago who grew up in Baghdad. Did you know you're up to twenty-five thousand dollars? Anyway, this guy Yaakub seemed to know about the bounty, so I said you were doing this dangerous mission, near Zurbatiyeh, and it's called Operation Thighmaster, for no reason except that I needed a word that's not going to come up in conversation, so I tell Yaakub, and only Yaakub, and then I call SIGINT and said call me if the word 'thighmaster' comes up in any of their intercepts. Sure enough, half-hour later, from a pay phone right on the base, Yaakub is calling his buddies, talking about Operation Thighmaster, and then they see all these groups near Zurbatiyeh going underground and whatever. So we pop him and search his stuff and what do you think we find? A fucking baby monitor. Hooked up to a voice-activated cassette recorder, in case he missed anything while he was out. So we toss Reicken's office and find the sending unit behind a panel in the drop ceiling. Low tech as it gets."

"In that case, I got some good news and some bad news," DeLuca said.

"Which is?"

"I'm going to send you home," DeLuca told him.

"No way," Sami said. "I'm staying until this thing is finished."

"You did your part," DeLuca said. "You can help Walter. I can get you on an Air Force flight if they don't let you fly commercial."

"What's the bad news?" Sami asked.

"Your unit is scheduled for deployment in January," DeLuca said. "You'll rotate home early with time served taken off the back end. Sorry about that. That information isn't for public consumption just now, but it will be soon enough. Go home and catch some fish. Go get that giant bluefin you've been talking about."

"Did I tell you I saw him?" Sami said. "Gigantic sonofabitch, thirty-thousand-dollar fish easy. We were two miles into restricted waters, but he can't hide there forever."

"You get him, Ahab," DeLuca said. "You could tell somebody on your way out that I think whatever they're giving me for the pain is wearing off."

On the television, a spokesman for the administration was talking about proposed federal legislation, the Project BioShield Act, committing $5.6 billion through the year 2013 to defend the nation against biowarfare. That included a $22.1-million-dollar grant to Colorado State University to build a 33,850-square-foot level 3 biosafety laboratory and $900 million to purchase 60 million doses of a new smallpox vaccine, Modified Vaccinia Ankarta or MVA, from the Acambic Corporation, a British biotech firm with U.S. offices in Cambridge, Massachusetts. Homeland Security secretary Tom Ridge came on to say an effort was being made to coordinate responses to bioterrorism among the departments of Homeland Security, Health and Human Services, Department of Defense, and the National Institutes of Health, focusing on early warning systems, decontamination systems, and improved distribution of antibiotics and vaccines.

"In Iraq," the newscaster concluded, "one of Saddam Hussein's former scientists, Alaa Al-Saeed, told David Kay's Survey Group that Saddam had extensive biological weapons programs, paying their research scientists as much as eight thousand dollars a month. Earlier this year, Danish troops discovered about one hundred 120mm shells containing a blistering agent, possibly mustard gas, near Qurnah, 250 miles southeast of Baghdad . . ."

He was interrupted by a male nurse, a lieutenant with the name "Growhowski" stitched above his left breast, who told him the pain was a good sign—it meant his nerves were coming back online. He said the doctor would be with him shortly.

DeLuca smiled to see his next visitors.

Dan had a bandage on his cheek where he'd been cut but looked otherwise hale and healthy beneath his San Francisco Giants cap. Mack was in fatigues and a T-shirt. Hoolie'd brought Smoky with him. They gave him a gift they hoped would cheer him up, a red and white bumper sticker that had originally read NO WAR IN IRAQ, which someone had taken a scissors and altered, inverting a letter to make it read NOMAR IN IRAQ.

"How's your head?" Mack said. "They're not made for breaking bulletproof windshields, you know."

"Now you tell me," he said. "How're your people back home? They watching the news?"

"My mom's a little freaked," Vasquez said. "She's a bit of a germ freak."

"Do you think Flight 1230 and *Alf Wajeh* are connected?" Dan asked.

"I don't know," DeLuca said. "My gut tells me they're not. You don't need a thousand guys to attack one airplane."

They filled DeLuca in on the progress they'd made since the Sinjar Jebel raid. Vasquez had been pressing Lebanese National Telephone to release the phone records of conversations between the Daura Foot and Mouth Disease facility and Moushabeck Shipping Ltd. The ship manifests for the four ships that sailed that week were due to arrive any day. MacKenzie had tracked down one of Al-Tariq's former bodyguards, who had no idea whether Al-Tariq was alive or dead, but he did vaguely recall some sort of family secret that nobody was allowed to speak of. She'd located the hospital where Al-Tariq was born, but his birth records had been destroyed.

"In the bombing?" DeLuca asked.

"I don't think so," Mack said. "I think they were destroyed a long long time ago. But get this—there was only one obstetrician at the hospital at the time, and he's still alive. I'm going to talk to him in the next few days to see if he remembers anything. I'd be surprised if he did, but it's a lead."

"Good work," DeLuca said.

"I talked to CID," Dan said. "They said Ibrahim's fingerprints were all over the monastery, but not the old man's. No syringes, nothing. They're still running the DNA but they don't expect much. But guess who else they think was there? Probably in the truck we were chasing?"

"Who?"

"Abu Musab al-Zarqawi," Dan said, referring to the Jordanian militant believed to be the top Al Qaeda representative in Iraq and the man in charge of the most active and dangerous of all of the insurgent groups. "The twenty-five-million-dollar man. Not that I need the money, but that would have been sweet."

"What was Zarqawi doing there?" DeLuca asked.

"Who the fuck knows?" Dan said. "Maybe *Alf Wajeh* and Al Qaeda are playing on the same team after all."

"That's not what I wanted to hear," DeLuca said.

Mack looked concerned. DeLuca saw the expression on her face.

"What?" he asked.

"We have more bad news. We were thinking we'd wait until you were feeling better. Jimmy. The cook. IED," Vasquez said, the acronym standing for Improvised Explosive Device, a generic term to describe the roadside bombs left to explode in the hands of whoever came across them. "They left it under a dog, man. The dog had a broken leg, they broke his leg, and when Jimmy went to help it, they blew it up with a garage-door opener."

DeLuca took the news hard. He remembered a really nice kid, with a sort of doomed feeling about him, a kid who was too good to be true, too optimistic and unjaded to last very long, in a war that swallowed the innocent whole.

"What about the other thing?" DeLuca said. "For Abu Waid?"

"Adnan says it's scheduled for tomorrow morning," Dan said. "Car bombing at 'Counterintelligence Headquarters' in Baghdad. We expect sixteen wounded and eight dead. We're going to leak a couple of fake bios with fake relatives back home for the reporters to talk to, and we got two guys who're going to dress up in bandages and fake blood and whatever for the cameras. Adnan says the people he's been talking to are quite pleased. We told him you'd probably want to debrief him, as soon as you were feeling better."

"Good work," DeLuca said.

They made their goodbyes and exited, promising to keep him posted, and then MacKenzie came back with one more thing she felt she needed to say.

"We wanted to be up front about this," she told him, "but Dan and I wanted you to know that we . . . seem to be getting involved. Romantically. This is strictly off-duty, but we thought you should hear it from us. Scuttle-butt being what it is."

"Just be careful," DeLuca said. Had Dan told her about his fiancée? It was none of his business.

"We are," she said. "It's not even . . . I mean, it is what it is. But it's probably nothing more than that. I mean, who knows, right?"

"Who knows?" DeLuca agreed.

DeLuca's doctor arrived a few minutes later. Scottie was with him. The doctor, a Captain Thomas, asked Scott to wait outside a moment while he examined his patient. He adjusted the steel brace that stabilized DeLuca's head, checked the IV drips (currently Percocet and a muscle relaxant), and he prodded DeLuca in various parts of his body, his toes, hands, thighs, asking him if he felt any-thing, and each time DeLuca was happy to report that he did. He could bend his hands at the wrist but was having trouble raising his arms or lifting his legs, movement that would come with time, the doctor assured him.

"What's your pain level? Scale of one to ten?" Captain Thomas asked him.

"I don't know," DeLuca said. "Up and down. Between five and nine, maybe. What's going on in my neck?"

"You had a concussion. Are you having any memory problems?"

"I can still remember my first wife," DeLuca said.

"When you get better, we'll hit you on the head again and see if we can take care of that," Dr. Thomas said. He told DeLuca he had swelling in his second, third, and fourth cervical vertebrae, and that was pressing on a nerve or two. When the swelling went down, they'd be able to tell if there were any ruptured disks or permanent nerve damage.

"So it's like whiplash or something?" he asked.

"Yup," the doctor said. "Weapons-grade whiplash. Oh yeah—you took a round in the side, but we sewed that up for you."

"I got shot?" DeLuca said.

"Right below your flak jacket," Dr. Thomas said. He handed DeLuca a patient-controlled flow regulator, similar to the one that had been hooked up to Hassan Al-Tariq. "This will let you control your own pain meds. Click click, but don't get carried away. Have you ever been addicted to anything?"

"Just doughnuts," DeLuca said. "But I'm Atkins now."

"I'll send in your son."

Scott was carrying something in his hand, a three-day-old copy of the *Boston Globe,* but it was the real thing, not a printout off the Internet. He said he thought his father might want to read it, whenever he was feeling better.

"I brought your phone, too," he said, setting it on the stand next to the bed. "In case maybe you wanted to call home."

"Have you talked to your mother?" DeLuca asked.

"Not about you," Scott said. "But about this flight out of Manila, yeah. She's pretty casual about it, I think, but she's seen orange and red alerts come and go. She says Kamel is doing really well. She sees him pretty much every day. He's not walking yet but she thinks he will be pretty soon."

"I'll call Omar and tell him," DeLuca said. "I'll call your mother, too."

"Speaking of Omar," Scott said, "I have something for you. They're investigating the raid on his house. Couple soldiers complained to their chaplain that they were ordered to fire on a white flag. The chaplain convinced them to go to their company commander, and now they're being court-martialed for the shooting. JAG asked IMINT if we had any pictures."

He reached into his briefcase and took out a sleeve of photographs, which he showed to his father, one by one. In the pictures, DeLuca could clearly see the Hadid house, and the garden where Specialist Ciccarelli had fallen, and in the driveway, Ali Hadid waving a white flag, and in the next picture, Hadid bloodied on the ground.

"Reicken is saying he wants to make sure those responsible are brought to account, but you know what that means." It had been DeLuca's experience that whenever a commander facing an investigation said he wanted to make sure those responsible were "brought to account," what he meant was, he was going to stop the buck before it got to him. Scapegoating was the military's dirty secret, except that it happened so often that it was hardly a secret anymore.

"Hmm," DeLuca said. "Do they think they can tie it to Reicken?"

"The captain on the ground says he called the post," Scott said. "Reicken says he wasn't informed."

"These are for me?" DeLuca asked. His son nodded.

"I was wondering what else you thought I should do with them," Scott said.

"Send copies to Captain Martin in General LeDoux's office, and we'll strategize from there," DeLuca said.

"I got something else you're not going to like," Scott said. "Last night, Delta Force kicked in a house we've been watching near Biyara, which was Ansar al-Islam before the war and probably still is. The town is half sheep and sweat-shops with little girls tying knots in rugs, and then there's one house using enough electricity to light up Fenway Park. They got away, but they left their toys behind. They had G5s and scanners and 2,400-dpi laser color printers and exotic papers with watermarks and buried ultraviolet security threads and the whole nine yards, and on the one hard drive they didn't erase completely, we found templates for false identification papers. All kinds. Passports, driver's licenses, business cards, security passes, corporate IDs, the works. Judging from the equipment and the software they had, the IDs they were generating were probably first rate. Good enough to fool the people taking IDs at airports, anyway."

"No master list of false identities, I suppose? That would be too much to ask, wouldn't it?"

"It would," Scott said.

"Any sense of how long they'd been operating?"

"Six months," Scott said. "Maybe longer."

"Ties to *Alf Wajeh*?"

"The car Ibrahim Al-Tariq was driving in Sanandaj was also photographed at the house in Biyara. But that just connects the car—not necessarily him."

"But probably him."

"Probably him."

DeLuca wondered why there were no photographs of Mohammed Al-Tariq himself. How could he stay hidden for so long? It felt like he was chasing a phantom, sometimes. Maybe everything was still the way it looked before—Al-Tariq was dead, and there was no plot, no Thousand Faces of Allah, no *Lanatullah*.

"Knock knock," he heard a voice at the door say. He turned to see a tall man in DCUs, over which he wore a white doctor's coat, and he had a stethoscope hanging around his neck. He was in his fifties, balding, and he wore black-rimmed glasses. "I'm Major Kaplan. I was told you wanted to see me."

"I'll leave you alone, then," Scott said, rising to go.

"Stay, stay," DeLuca said. "Major, this is my son, Lieutenant Scott DeLuca, just visiting his old man. Down from Kirkuk."

"Lieutenant," Kaplan said, shaking Scott's hand rather than saluting. "Your dad is one tough old bird, but you probably already knew that. Not many guys who go through the windshield of a Humvee live to tell about it."

"It had a crack in it," DeLuca said.

"What was it you wanted to see me about?"

"Have you got a few minutes to answer some questions?" DeLuca asked. "I know you're busy." Kaplan shrugged. "Have you been watching the news? This flight out of the Philippines?"

"I haven't been watching the news, but I've been briefed," Kaplan said. "What about it?"

"Is it what they're saying it is? Bioterrorism?"

"No, it's not," Kaplan said. "It's bird flu. Same thing that came out of Hong Kong four months ago and Beijing seven months ago."

"You're sure about that?"

"Positive," Kaplan said. "I think twenty or thirty people have already fully recovered. Don't get me wrong, this thing kills people, but it's not BW."

"Why aren't they saying so?" DeLuca asked.

"Politics," Kaplan said. "That's a personal opinion, not a medical one. They had guard units taking over airports and government troops assuming the role of law enforcement, so I think they have to keep the scare going for a few more days to justify that. Which, in my opinion, is utterly immoral, because the next time when we really do need to sound the alert, people are going to think it's just another false alarm. But don't get me started."

"You worked out of Johns Hopkins, stateside, right?" DeLuca asked. Kaplan nodded. "My agent Dan told me. He talked to you a while back, about interleukin-4 and the *Current Protocols in Molecular Biology* stuff. He said you were part of a program, studying bioterrorism."

"I worked closely with Don Henderson at the School of Public Health," Kaplan said. "And then the Johns Hopkins Center for Civilian Biodefense Studies. We did a lot of BW event planning. I was also a consultant to UNSCOM, until Saddam kicked us out in 1997."

"So you're aware of who we're looking for and what we're dealing with," DeLuca said, "from what Dan told you?"

"I'm aware," Kaplan said. "It's been a topic of discussion among myself and some of my colleagues."

"And you think it's smallpox?"

"I don't see what else it could be," Kaplan said.

"They were working on camel pox at Al Manal," DeLuca said.

"That's just a proxy," Kaplan said. "You work on something that won't kill you, until you get the procedures down, and then you move them over to something more lethal. And smallpox is about as lethal as it gets. There've been estimates that D. A. Henderson's work toward eradication has saved as many as fifty million lives, not that the Nobel people seem to care. I've heard it referred to as the 'Demon in the Freezer.'"

"And we know he had this?" DeLuca asked. "Is this what Rihab Taha and Hazem Ali and the others were working with?"

"The answer is probably," Kaplan said. "Based on what Hussein Kamel told us when he defected and what UNSCOM turned up before Saddam stopped the inspections, we *know* he had 8,500 liters of anthrax, 20,000 liters of botulinum, 2,200 liters of aflatoxin, plus ricin, mycotoxins, hemorrhagic conjunctivitis virus, rotavirus, and smallpox. Plus a variety of delivery systems. Though smallpox has its own built-in delivery system. It's one of the world's most infectious agents. It just keeps on coming. I just read a statement from a guy at Los Alamos who said he thought a smallpox attack could be controlled by early detection and targeted vaccinations. I read that and thought—what planet is this guy living on?"

"So what would happen?" DeLuca asked. "Suppose somebody sets off a smallpox bomb somewhere . . ."

"It doesn't have to be a bomb," Kaplan said. "Let me walk you through it, because these are exactly the studies we did at Johns Hopkins, in a variety of scenarios, most recently one called 'Dark Winter' that we ran at Andrews Air Force Base in 2001. We crunched the numbers in all kinds of ways and we kept coming up with the same results."

"Okay," DeLuca said. "I'm listening."

"So, suppose somebody gets hold of a research sample of variola major. Just basic plain old variola major, last seen on this earth in 1977 in Yugoslavia, but kept since then in cryogenic suspension inside isolation chambers inside maximum security laboratories at the CDC in Atlanta and at the Russian State Centre for Research of Virology and Biotechnology in Koltsovo, Novosibirsk. We know the Russians had twenty thousand tons of smallpox in stock at one point, and considering you don't need more than an amount equal to the amount of ink in an average fountain pen to start your own epidemic, let's just assume it's fair to say nobody is going to be able to account for all those twenty thousand tons of smallpox. Somebody could easily have gotten some and sold it to somebody else."

DeLuca thought of the Russian-looking man Ibrahim Al-Tariq had been having lunch with in Sanandaj.

"Remember, too," Kaplan continued, "we live in a world where nobody under twenty-five years of age has been vaccinated for smallpox, and anyone over twenty-five would have very little residual immunity. The United States has 250 million people and an extremely sophisticated medical infrastructure, and we still have only enough vaccine to vaccinate between six and seven million people. Globally there's maybe one dose of vaccine in existence for every twelve million people. And some of that is too old to use."

"I heard on the news this morning they're going to spend $900 million to buy 60 million doses of something called MVA . . ."

"Modified Vaccinia Ankarta," Kaplan said. "But it takes ten to fifteen years to bring a drug to market. Buy stock in Acambic Corporation, or Bavarian Nordic, out of Denmark. I'd bet you Cheney did."

"So we have ineffective vaccines?" Scott asked.

"Let's even suppose stocks are effective," Kaplan said. "During the last known smallpox outbreak, in Yugoslavia, each of the first generation of victims infected about thirteen other people before they themselves were diagnosed. It took twelve to fourteen days before they became febrile. So, suppose an ordinary smallpox virus was released in the U.S. by terrorists, say in a large hotel with a thousand guests. They aerosol it into the ventilation system somehow. Now thirteen thousand second-generation carriers are created over an incubation period of the next twelve days. Though in some cases, the disease takes a form they call black pox, which kills in three to five days. So for twelve days, suppose a quarter to a third of those one thousand first-generation carriers drives or flies to other cities. The first infected person walks into a hospital or health clinic within three or four days, say, the rest straggling in later. Nobody expects smallpox anymore, so the first diagnosis might be chicken pox. Blood tests on the first patient are ordered, though until pustules form, there's little cause for alarm. Once the pustules form, infectious disease specialists are called in. Smallpox is diagnosed. The hospital immediately quarantines the patient in a negative-pressure room with HEPA air filters and vaccinates the patient and anyone on the staff who might have been exposed. City and state health commissioners are contacted, the state medical examiner, the police, the FBI, who then try to discover and track down anybody the patient might have come in contact with. There's an attempt to suppress news coverage of the outbreak, but then another case turns up, and another, and another. Perhaps they're all taken to the same hospital, which would then have to be quarantined and cordoned off by police to make sure nobody tries to leave. The whole hospital. But the odds are, all the patients aren't going to go to the same hospital. Multiple hospitals would eventually have to be quarantined.

"Okay? So now the Centers for Disease Control and Prevention gets involved, along with Health and Human Services and the National Security Council. The news media have to be informed. They're asked not to sensationalize the story, but Fox News runs one of their 'fair and balanced' stories about how the end of the world is approaching, and the *New York Post* headline says, WE'RE ALL GOING TO DIE in hundred-point type. The president gives a news conference, saying all that could be done is being done. It's not enough. Supplies of vaccine in the infected city would be used up within the week. And remember, it's in more than one city. Health workers take care of themselves and their families first. Cops enforcing the law raid clinics and put doses in their pockets because nobody wants their kids to die this way. The CDC arranges for shipments from emergency reserves. Other cities refuse to give up their supplies as the federal system begins to crumble. Health-care responders, police, firefighters, and hospital staffers are vaccinated, but that just angers the ordinary citizens unable to acquire the vaccine.

Within ten days, all quarantine facilities in the contamination zone are full to capacity as the number of victims exceeds isolation capabilities. Maybe healthcare workers improvise by converting armories or convention centers into quarantine facilities. Somebody's got to stand watch, to make sure the quarantines aren't violated. That means troops.

"The news starts reporting on plague riots in other cities where uninfected people clamor in protest, pleading to be vaccinated. Ambulance drivers, police, and healthcare workers refuse to respond to reported cases. All transportation stops to prevent the spread. Airports shut down. Roadblocks go up. Chaos ensues. There's looting, and there's widespread panic as infected people who don't know yet that they're infected get in their cars, hoping to escape the contagion. Schools are quarantined and parents are told to stay away, but parents aren't going to stay away—they're going to go get their kids. The disease spreads. Entire cities have to be cordoned off, with soldiers shooting any citizens who refuse to obey orders or try to escape. Assuming the rate of infection remains constant, with each original victim passing the disease along to another thirteen people, after two or three generations, there will simply not be enough vaccine left, even if it could be distributed and administered, and no way to contain the epidemic, other than to isolate the city, using military power if necessary, and nothing else to do but to allow the disease to run its course through the remaining population."

"Jesus," Scott said.

"Wait till I get to the scary part. That's with plain old variola major," Kaplan said. "In best case, you get a million dead and the plague is contained within six to eight weeks. In a worst case, you get a couple hundred million dead and you never really get containment. It just kills everybody it can kill and runs out of fresh meat. And then it spreads globally. Okay? But suppose we're talking about a new virus, a 'DB' or 'Doomsday Bug.' Weaponized smallpox. With variola major, you can actually save somebody's life if you vaccinate them in three to five days. You can take the same virus and bioengineer it to be 100 percent fatal, 100 percent contagious, and resistant to any known vaccines—in other words, a virus that would, if released into the general public, effectively kill 100 percent of the population. I've also heard the term 'EWA' for 'End of the World Agent.' In DOD circles, the Doomsday Bug is considered a weapon that hasn't been worth developing because it's just too horrible to ever actually use. Who'd use a weapon that would destroy the user as well as the intended victim? You'd have to be crazy or suicidal. Gee—know anybody in this part of the world fitting that description?"

"And this kind of bioengineering—this is something you think the Iraqis were capable of? Gene splicing and all that?"

"Gene splicing's not that hard. All you need's the raw materials, the Wiley book, and a few quiet moments."

"So how would you create a Doomsday Bug?" Scott asked.

"Interleukin-4 is a good start," Kaplan said. "That makes it resistant to vaccines. You can speed it up, so that it's all black pox, and make it all kill in two or three days, which lowers the amount of time between generations, so there's less time for a carrier to pass the disease along, but that's easy to counter if you make it even more contagious, which you might be able to do by making it smaller. Every strand of DNA has hundreds of thousands of genes they call G-DNA or Garbage DNA. Trim away the garbage and you get a lean, mean killing machine. Variola major is transmitted fomitically—fomites are substances that absorb and transport germ particles. In this case, body fluids. The virus lives in the back of the patient's throat and is transferred every time the person exhales or coughs or sneezes. But if you want to make it truly airborne, just make it smaller, and it starts to live on the wind. It rises from the dead bodies as they bleed out and lose fluids. As a bomb, you could mix weaponized smallpox with some sort of evaporant, maybe a light oil, and fill up a water balloon and throw it into a crowd. So do I think the Iraqis could have this? They certainly could, no question."

"UNSCOM never found anything?" Scott wanted to know.

"I think we were getting close when we got kicked out," Kaplan said. "Saddam couldn't develop his nukes because the Israelis and the United States kept blowing up his reactors and missile factories. Some of us figured he probably said the hell with it, I'll build something they can't find or blow up. We were bombing Iraq on a weekly basis throughout most of the nineties, but he wasn't just fighting us—he had seventy-five million people next door in Iran who hated his guts and wanted to come rescue their oppressed Shiite brethren. And Iran had Scuds, and a nuclear program that nobody was bombing—yet—so he needed something to threaten them with, to keep them on their side of the mountains. Plus, I don't think he even really knew exactly what his own people were doing. He was so paranoid, moving from palace to palace, that he kept himself isolated from what was going on inside his own research programs. His own sons had militias and weapon stockpiles that Daddy didn't know about."

"And Mohammed Al-Tariq?"

"Top of the list," Kaplan said. "I warned you about getting me started, didn't I?"

"You warned me," DeLuca said. Kaplan took off his glasses and cleaned them on his coat sleeve, examining them for spots in the fluorescent lights overhead. "Have you heard the story of the *Alf Wajeh*? I only have it secondhand, but as I understand it, it's more or less the Muslim version of the story of the plague in the Bible. The plague comes and only the faithful, the one thousand, survive. There's some evidence that that story might be back in play."

"Meaning?"

"We're anticipating multiple attacks. Possibly in the hundreds."

"My God," Kaplan said.

The three men were silent. Between the three of them, there was little else that could be said.

"Have a nice day," the doctor said at last, smiling a bitter, angry smile. He took a card from his pocket and gave it to DeLuca, adding, "Keep me posted. I'll e-mail you if I think of anything else."

He left DeLuca alone with his son.

"I was scared when we couldn't get a read from your transponder at Sinjar Jebel," Scott said. "When you went into the tunnel. But I'm more scared now."

"Where is it, by the way? My transponder?"

"It's on your bedstand," Scott said. "That's how I found your room. This place is like a maze."

"Then lock onto my signal, Scottie," DeLuca said. "Because as long as I'm alive, this isn't going to happen."

"You still think you're Superman?" Scottie asked.

"And Batman, too," DeLuca said.

"Whatever happens, we go down swinging, right, Pops?"

"Right," DeLuca said.

"Will you call Mom?"

"I'll call her. I don't know what I'll say, but I'll call her."

"Why do you always think you have to know what you're going to say before you call?" Scott said. "Just call."

The phone rang back in Massachusetts six times before Bonnie answered. He realized his biggest fear was that she wouldn't answer, which would mean she was out, which could mean she was sleeping with somebody else . . . It was a crazy insane jealous idea, but it was also the number-one reason why soldiers were hesitant to call home. Bonnie sounded groggy when she answered.

"Hello?" she said.

"It's me," he said. "I'm sorry to wake you up."

"It's five in the morning."

"I know. That's why I said I'm sorry to wake you up."

"Are you okay?"

"I'm fine. Everything's fine. I got a mild case of whiplash when my Hummer hit a . . . goat. How about you?"

"I'm tired. I had a hard time getting to sleep. I have been for a while."

"I'm sorry."

"Yeah, well . . ."

"Bonnie, I'm sorry about everything."

"I know you are."

"I can't really explain."

"I know you can't. Gillian dropped by and tried to tell me how important the work you're doing is."

"It is."

"I'm not arguing with you. I'm sure it is. I just don't really care anymore."

He didn't know what to say.

"Bonnie . . ."

"It doesn't matter. It's just not what I want. This is not what I want. Lying in bed talking to you at five in the morning from five thousand miles away is not what I want. And this isn't going to change."

"It's going to change. As soon as . . ."

"As soon as what? As soon as the world is a safe place to live again? When is that going to be, David? Tell me so I can mark that on my calendar."

He endured another long silence.

"I tried to call you the other night," his wife said.

"That wasn't a good time."

"Well it's never a good time, is it?"

"No, but that was really not a good time. I should have shut my phone off . . ."

"Shut it off," she said. "I'm not calling again. I'm through. I quit. I can't do it anymore. I just don't have anything left for you. And don't say you're sorry again."

"This Flight 1230 stuff," he told her. "It's nothing to worry about. It's not an attack. It's just the Asian flu."

"I know. It was on the news before I went to bed."

"I thought maybe you'd be worried."

"I wasn't. By the way, your young friend Kamel took six steps today. It's going to be a long road, but they think he's going to regain full use."

"That's good news. I'll tell his uncle. But Bonnie?"

"What?"

"Just don't have him over to the house. Okay? I'm probably just being paranoid, but it would be better if the people he's related to didn't know my last name or where I live."

"Well, you're too late. I had him over last night, for dinner. In his wheelchair. With Caroline and her daughter. I thought it would be good for him to meet somebody close to his own age."

"Okay then," DeLuca said. "I just didn't want to have to worry about your safety."

"Oh didn't you?" she said, laughing. "*You* didn't want to worry about *my* safety? Gee, I *wonder* what *that* might feel like . . ."

"Bonnie," he began. He wanted to tell her to get a smallpox vaccination, but he knew he couldn't say even that much.

"Look—do you have any better idea of when you'll be coming home? I found an apartment but I don't want to move in and then have to carry both the rent and the mortgage."

"I don't know," he said. "I can't tell you when I might be home. I saw Scott tonight, by the way."

"How is he?"

"He's great. You'd be proud of the work he's doing."

"Look, David, the paperwork will be waiting for you, okay? I'm assuming you'll want to use your friend Don as your lawyer. Is that right? Because if it is, I could get things started from here."

"Bonnie, we said we weren't going to talk about this until I get back . . ."

"Yeah, but when will that be, David? Enough, okay? Enough. Enough. All right? Enough."

The phone went dead.

He decided now would be a good time to up the dosage of his painkillers. He tapped the red button four times. The pain in his neck went away. The pain in his heart did not.

When he woke up again, he felt a warm hand on top of his own. He opened his eyes and saw a welcome face.

"Hello, Evelyn," he said. He was still feeling the effects of the drugs, feeling slightly woozy and carefree, the ache in his neck a dull throb now. "How are you?"

"I'm well," she said. "The issue is, how are you? I was talking to your friend Preacher Johnson. He gave me quite a scare. He said they didn't know if you'd be . . ."

"Paralyzed?" DeLuca said. "If you see him again, tell him I'm going to do the cha cha on his grave. It's just a couple of swollen disks. They say."

"I'm so glad," she said. "I never quite knew what it was like to share a foxhole with somebody, but it's true what they say, isn't it?"

"About what?"

"About sharing a foxhole."

"What do they say?"

"Well, I don't know, but they must say something. At any rate, I'm delighted to see you. You're not an easy person to track down, even when you're unconscious. I had to call old Denby and ask him a favor, and he called your friend General LeDoux, who told me to talk to your Colonel Reicken. He's quite an idiot, isn't he?"

"Lieutenant colonel," DeLuca corrected her.

"Not anymore," Warner told him. "He was just promoted to full bird."

"What?" DeLuca said. "Why?"

"Oh, God knows why," she said. "I think much of the credit goes to you—you chaps have been doing so well that the man in charge gets the bump for a job well done. Isn't that how it goes?"

"That's how it goes," DeLuca said. He made a decision. It was his job with CI to investigate malfeasance or corruption within the ranks, internal crimes ranging from theft to treason, and things like troops opening fire on men who were waving white flags.

"Evelyn," he said, "you can protect your sources, right? If I were to tell you something in confidence—give you information—can you promise me it won't get back to me?"

"For you, darling, I'd go straight to prison," she said. "Particularly if I knew you'd come visit me there. Though that might look a bit suspicious. What is it?"

He handed her the photographs Scott had given him and explained what they were and how they'd been taken.

"You can't print those or they're going to know what office they came out of," he said, "but here's what you can do. Find a prisoner named Richard Yaakub, an Arab-American, probably still here on the base, unless he's been transferred, and ask him if he has anything on tape regarding the raid, because he bugged Reicken's office with a baby monitor hooked up to a voice-activated tape deck, so it's possible. The odds are, you're not going to get the tapes, so when you don't, go to the JAG office and tell them about the tapes, because I'll bet you they don't know about them, and then leak them the photographs somehow, without them knowing it's you? Can you do that?"

"Oh love, this is exactly what I can do," she said. "You don't like this fellow very much, do you?"

"I'm not doing it because I don't like him," DeLuca said. "I'm doing it because he's killing people unnecessarily, and making it harder for the rest of us to do our jobs. I just don't want to be connected because I don't want whoever they send in to replace him to think he has to kick my ass for taking Reicken down. I have enough people who want to kick my ass as it is."

"They've got to get through me first," she said. "I think I'm one of your biggest fans. Though your teammates sure think highly of you. They can't believe you'd regain consciousness in a hospital bed and two minutes later you're back at work."

"I think pretty highly of them," DeLuca said. "Besides, work takes my mind off my other sorrows."

"If you have sorrows bigger than the ones I'm already aware of, I think I'd rather not know about them," Warner said. When they heard a disturbance in the hallway, she lowered her voice. "It's a bit past visiting hours, I'm afraid. I was really just going to leave you a cheery note because I thought you'd be asleep."

"What time is it?"

"It's after eleven," she said.

"That's past curfew," he said. "How are you going to get back to your hotel?"

"Thought I'd find a place here somewhere," she said. "I think I've slept in more folding chairs in the last few months than I care to remember."

"You could have the Preacher's bunk if you want it," DeLuca said. "Just pull the covers over your head if anybody comes in. And pray nobody gets hurt tonight and they need the bed."

"I pray that all the time anyway," she said. "It's truly tempting. I can't remember the last time I slept anywhere where the air-conditioning actually worked."

Just then they were interrupted by the night nurse, a woman with the moniker WHEELER on her nametag. She did indeed have, as Preacher Johnson had put it, "cannons that could have turned the tide at Gettysburg." When she leaned over DeLuca to adjust his IV drip, his face was buried in the shadow of her colossal bosom. She asked him how he was doing, took his vitals, then shot Evelyn Warner a look before exiting and said, "It's after visiting hours."

"There goes my sleepover," Warner said, once she was gone.

"Stay," he bade her. "Stay anyway."

"Well, it's not like we haven't slept together before, is it?" she said. "It's always an adventure with you, isn't it? Considering you're temporarily quadriplegic, I'm certain you'll be a perfect gentleman. Not that that's what I want. You get a bit weary of perfect gentlemen after a while. A nice imperfect gentleman, that would be nice."

"Well I don't want to brag," DeLuca said, "but I'm about as imperfect as anybody you'd ever care to meet."

She pushed the second bed closer to his. He felt in an unusually mixed and confusing mood. His conversation with Bonnie had left him with only one conclusion, that his marriage was over, and there was nothing he could do about it. The sight of Evelyn Warner had made him purely happy, her bright wit, her good cheer, and her beautiful face just the thing he needed, right then.

She secured the Velcro holding the door shut, turned out the lights, and lay down on the bed next to his, covering herself with the blanket. He heard her shoes fall to the floor. The CASH was not a private place, even with the doors shut, with walls of nylon and air, and sounds filtering through the walls of people talking and electronic equipment beeping. Other times, when the air-conditioning kicked in, the sound of air rushing through the nylon ducts nearly drowned out conversation, bathing the whole place in a wash of white noise.

"David?" she asked him.

"Yeah?"

"Nothing," she said. "I just think you're a really good man and I wondered if you knew that. If anybody had told you lately."

"Not lately," he said. He wanted to tell her about his marriage, but he didn't want to be one of those guys who whined, saying, "My wife just doesn't understand me . . ." Then he realized that wasn't it. He didn't want to bring Bonnie up because she didn't belong in his life anymore. She'd asked, quite clearly, to be let go of, and he would honor her request, and not think of her again, at least not tonight. "Thank you for saying that. Even if I know it's not true."

"It is true," she said. "And don't give me that imperfect crap again. You are a good man, and I know 'em when I see 'em. You remind me of my father."

"Is that good?" DeLuca asked.

"It's always good when a woman tells a man he reminds her of her father, but it's never good for a man to tell a woman she reminds him of his mother. Which I don't, I hope."

"You don't," he said.

"Am I right? Let me guess. Big Italian family, warm and loving, blue-collar father, mother saying *'Mangia, mangia'* all the time and whacking you with a twisted-up dishtowel whenever you snuck a cookie before dinner."

"Not even close," DeLuca said. "Small and bitter. And white-collar. One sister, Elaine. My father worked way too hard for Nationwide Insurance, and my mother couldn't cook for shit. Everything was frozen and then boiled. And nobody talked. Code of silence. *Omerta.* You probably heard of it."

"And nobody in the Mafia?" she asked.

"Nobody," DeLuca said. "Though I've got a cousin in Brooklyn who's been trying to get in since high school. How about you? What did your father do?"

"Guess."

"Well," DeLuca said. "Let me try. Owned a publishing company, member of Parliament, Lord of Banbury. Your older brother Nyles runs the publishing company now and your younger brother Harry plays in a rock and roll band. Your mother is Lady Banbury. She was a commoner when your father met her and she doesn't feel like she fits in with the peerage, but she's a terrific horsewoman and an accomplished poet. And she's very proud of you."

"I don't know if I should feel flattered or invaded," she said. "You looked me up."

"I'm counterintelligence," DeLuca said. "That's what we do. But that doesn't mean I know you."

"No, you don't," she said. "But you could, if you wanted to."

They'd been lowering their voices ever since they'd started talking with the lights out, her lips close to his ear. He couldn't turn his head, but he liked knowing she was there, that close to him. She put her arm across his chest, propping her head up on her other arm so that she could look at him, half on her bed and half on his now.

"You're quite good-looking, too, you know," she said. "So many of these soldier boys become harsh-looking. Or sad. Or full of themselves. But I have a feeling you look like you always do. I don't know why I think that. I could be wrong. I was so sorry when I read about your sister, David. That must have crushed you."

"Did I tell you about Elaine?"

"No you didn't," she said, "but you're not the only person who knows how to look someone up. I couldn't imagine what it must have felt like, when it happened. Nine-eleven. It must have felt like the world was ending."

"I guess it did," DeLuca said. "One kind of world, anyway. I wish I could turn my head so I could look at you."

"I'm right here," she said, sitting up and leaning over him, her face eight inches from his. She regarded him a moment, smiling, and then she kissed him, as gently and as sweetly as he'd ever been kissed, her lips gently caressing his, her tongue softly probing his mouth, brushing against his teeth . . .

And then she lay back on her bed.

"I'm going to have to stop now, while I still can," she whispered, out of breath. "I think one second more and I would become utterly abandoned, which is something I want to experience with you, David DeLuca, but perhaps some other time when you're not in traction. And lest you think I have some sort of fatal attraction to men with bullet wounds, this is something I've thought since the first time I met you."

"But . . ."

"Shh," she said, pressing a finger gently to his lips. "More to come. Plenty of time. Sleep sleep. I'm right here if you need anything."

He woke the next morning to the sound of Evelyn Warner talking sotto voce on her sat phone. The television was on, the volume down low, barely audible. On the screen, a picture of a building in Baghdad, the front of the building collapsed, the rest of it smoking. A crawl at the bottom of the screen said, "Car bomb explodes at U.S. Counterintelligence Headquarters in Baghdad." Evelyn looked horrified when she realized DeLuca had seen the screen.

"Oh, my God," she said. "I'm so sorry. I have to go. This happened just this morning."

On the television, a picture of one fictitious Sergeant Alvin King, 1974–2004.

"My cameraman is waiting for me. I can come back. Are you okay? I'm so sorry. I know these were the people you worked with. This is very confusing to me. I have one source saying how terrible it is and another saying he didn't know anything about any counterintelligence headquarters . . ."

DeLuca hated what he had to do next.

"Nobody did," he said. "That was the point. I knew Al King." A second picture showed a Lieutenant Ray Shuman. "I knew him too. What are they saying? How many?"

"Eight dead, twelve wounded," she said. "I'm trying to figure out where they're taking them. I have to go. I'm so sorry."

"I'll be all right," he said. He hated this, hated it, but the press had to be convinced that the attack was real. It was his best, and perhaps his last, chance at getting close to Mohammed Al-Tariq. He didn't have a choice in the matter.

"I'll come back," she said. "Your man Vasquez was by this morning and he left you this," she said, opening the laptop computer that rested on DeLuca's bedstand. "It's all hooked up. I wish I could stay. I have to go. My cameraman is waiting."

"I understand," DeLuca said, wondering if she'd ever speak to him again, once she uncovered the ruse, as he was certain she would. "Go. I'll catch up with you later."

Chapter Seventeen

GILLIAN O'DOHERTY WAS WORKING LATE (HER fifth late night in a row), listening to baseball on the radio. She liked the background noise, the murmur of the crowd, the distant vendors shouting out "Peanuts! Popcorn!" She rarely paid attention to who was winning, or even playing. Tonight the Sox were playing in Oakland, and it looked like extra innings.

She'd spent the afternoon processing Walter Ford's request to give him a DNA analysis of a suspect he identified as M.J. Probably not Michael Jackson, she presumed, filling out the paperwork the FBI lab in D.C. was going to need to do the workup. He'd sent her a hairbrush.

She'd come back after a late supper to search her database, in response to the e-mail from David DeLuca that directed her to look into anything mysterious or unusual that might have occurred involving dockworkers or the shipping industry. She'd come up with four recent deaths that might have warranted further study. The first was a young man named Murphy, an airport water-taxi captain who'd been stabbed in a bar in Charlestown, but reading the case more closely, he was just a poor kid who insulted another man's motorcycle and ended up with severed right subclavian and common carotid arteries, bleeding out in the parking lot. The second was a Ukrainian sailor named Alexiev with a blood alcohol level that had been three times the legal limit, who'd fallen off his ship and died when he struck his head on a forklift below, crushing the right parietal bone all the way to the sagittal suture. The third case was a union official who'd been shot in his car, a single bullet from a .22-caliber automatic, the bullet entering the occipital bone at the mid-left-lambdoidal suture and exiting the skull just below the left lacrimal. The officers working the case were looking at it as a mob hit. A test of the hair stuck to the bullet suggested the union official had a cocaine problem, which might have had something to do with why he'd been shot, but it hardly added up to an international conspiracy.

The fourth case was a dockworker named Anthony Fusaro, a burn victim who'd died in a fire in his North End triple-decker. According to the report, he'd been drinking in bed (a bottle of alcohol was found nearby), probably fell asleep smoking a cigarette (a lighter was found next to the bed), and perished in the ensuing conflagration. She had a tissue sample in the freezer to test for the presence of drugs or disease, but it hadn't seemed terribly important, and no next of kin had been clamoring for answers, so she'd let it slide while she pursued more pressing matters.

She took the sample from the freezer and set it in a petri dish to thaw. It had the familiar yet odd smell of charred human flesh, like roast mutton but slightly more chemical. The sample had been taken from the vastus lateralis, according to the tag. The rest of the body had been bagged and cremated when no one claimed it, but she was sure she had enough tissue to work with.

"Pleased to meet you, Anthony," she said, holding the sample up to the light. From the sounds coming from the radio, somebody had hit a home run. "Let's see how you're doing tonight."

She washed her hands with betadine, donned latex gloves and a surgical mask, following universal precautions, turned on all the laminar flow units in the lab, and then set about preparing a 1:800 dilution of the subject's serum. Using a pipette, she transferred the diluted serum to a rack of test tubes containing antigen/antibody complexes. It would take about an hour to create titers. Beyond the usual infectious agents, she tested from a kit that had been supplied to her office by the Centers for Disease Control, containing the more exotic agents likely to be involved in biological attacks, including anthrax, botulinum, aflatoxin, ricin, mycotoxins, hemorrhagic conjunctivitis, rotavirus, and smallpox. Any infectious bug would have to follow Koch's postulates to be proven—she had to be able to isolate it, propagate it outside the host, and cause the same disease by returning it to a similar host.

While she waited, she examined the tissue itself for cutaneous affects, first with the naked eye, then with a 10X magnifying glass, and finally with a stereo microscope. She perceived, in the burned flesh, what appeared to be an array of abutting rings, approximate circles individually uneven and erosely bordered but evenly distributed. She was surprised at how easily the epidermis separated between the spinosum and basale stratum, with charring on the base membrane and again between the dermis and the subcutaneous musculature, as if the skin had come loose before the fire started. She'd hypothesized that the rings were the result of droplets of fire retardant falling on the smoldering flesh, but a closer look under the microscope suggested a varying density to the carbon residue, as if the skin had been scarred or pocked before burning.

When she returned to the rack of test tubes, she saw that every antigen/antibody complex assayed had come back negative except one.

Her heart jumped in her chest.

Anthony Fusaro had died of smallpox.

Proving Koch's third postulate was beyond her capabilities, given that the smallpox virus had no reservoir other than human, no intermediate species to jump to between primary hosts, which had, in part, been why it had been possible to eradicate it in the general population. Had there been a secondary host, for example mice or rats, eradication would have been much more difficult.

Quickly, she resealed and sterilized the petri dish containing the tissue sample, double-bagged it, then placed it back in the freezer after affixing a biohazard warning sticker to the outside of the label, upon which she'd written "variola major." She considered calling the Centers for Disease Control immediately, but it was approaching three o'clock in the morning, so she held off. As a precaution, she cracked open an NBC (nuclear/biological/chemical) quick-response kit developed by the CDC for distribution through the Strategic National Stockpile Program, found a dose of smallpox vaccine, and inoculated herself. It probably wasn't necessary, and even if it were, she could have waited until the Public Health Office opened in the morning to get a smallpox vaccination, but why bother other people when she could take care of it herself?

The chempack also contained a Centers for Disease Control reference CD, so she popped it the drive of her desktop and opened the smallpox file. She skimmed the historical information, the story of colonial Lord Jeffrey Amherst killing the local Native American tribes by giving them virus-saturated blankets, and she scanned the story of D. A. Henderson's work to eradicate the disease, clicking her way to the electron microscopy itself, where she called up a picture of the virus variola major. Then, using her own electron microscope, she compared what she had in her lab with what she found on the CD, expecting final confirmation.

Instead, she observed that the virus under her microscope was different from the organism pictured on the CD. For one thing, the virus in her lab was much smaller, about seven microns across. For another, it had a different shape, a bend where variola major was straight. She copied and saved to disk the digital images she was observing. She saw where the new virus had formed endosomes on the surface proteins of the host cells, and where the viral proteins had formed fusion loops and then trimmers to catapult the virus into the cell's nucleus, where it would redirect the host cell's DNA to make copies of the virus rather than of itself.

Then, she saw something she'd never seen before, or rather, she'd seen it, but she'd only seen it in time-lapse microscopy. This was happening in real time, viral particles penetrating host cell membranes and commandeering the host cells' DNA at speeds she didn't quite believe were possible. She could actually watch it as it occurred.

Poor Anthony Fusaro had never stood a chance.

Perhaps to reassure herself, she found the syringe she'd used to vaccinate herself and injected a drop of vaccine onto the slide under her microscope's lens, hoping to document the process whereby the vaccine killed the virus.

But an odd thing happened.

Rather than witnessing the destruction of the virus, she watched as the virus ripped through the vaccine, using it as a kind of energy source. The result, in the human body, would be to turn the body's immune system (the lymphocytes, antigens, T-cells, and phagocytes) against itself, something like the way AIDS worked, but at a vastly accelerated rate. She directed the computer to record her images at set intervals to document the rate of viral reproduction, fascinated and unable to take her eyes from the scope.

And then, a thought occurred to her. She sat up in her chair, thinking a moment, then found a fresh syringe and extracted a sample of her own blood. She prepared a slide, and then examined it.

The same virus that had killed Anthony Fusaro was now replicating rapidly in her own blood, coursing through her body. By now, it was no doubt everywhere inside of her.

"Oh, my," she exclaimed. "Well. I guess that proves Koch's third postulate, doesn't it?"

And then she set about her business, opening a new file and typing as fast as she could, because she knew she didn't have much time, and that the morning shift would be arriving in only a few short hours.

When DeLuca was finally able to log on to his computer and check his e-mail, he read only the relevant messages.

The CID lab at Fort Gillem regretted to inform him there'd been a delay in processing the syringe he'd sent them, but that he could expect a response in another four to six weeks. Scottie e-mailed him to say he'd forwarded the photographs they'd discussed to Captain Martin c/o General LeDoux's office, with a brief query added at the end: "How'd the talk with Mom go?"

He read with interest a report from Walter Ford on one Professor Mahmoud Jaburi describing Jaburi's activities and Ford's suspicions. He said Gillian O'Doherty was processing the man's DNA, which Ford intended to use to cross-reference against other crimes in the cities where he'd visited.

Needless to say, I CCed Tommy at HS in case he wanted to go through channels there, but I was also thinking of talking to our friend Mike O'Leary at the FBI. He's been promoted since we worked the Angiulo thing but I've stayed in touch and had him come talk to my classes. He can back me up but he could also take the ball and run with it if I get benched for some reason. What do you think?

Just when you say to yourself you're too old for this shit, there's more shit.

Yours,
Walter

DeLuca wrote his friend back saying he thought it would be a good idea to contact O'Leary, and that he probably carried enough weight to run interference against Timmons for him if he needed it, but also to give Tom a chance. He finished by adding:

I'm too old for this shit, too, but fortunately, the shit is aging at the same rate. No rest for the weary. Who did you see a few years ago when you had that back problem? I might need to consult with somebody when I get home.

                                                  David

The last e-mail he opened was from Gillian. She wrote:

Dearest David,
I wish I had better news for you, and I suppose in a way I do, because I have achieved some positive and reliable results, but I fear I've discovered something I wish wasn't true.

Attached to this letter, you will find the report I've been working on for the last few hours. I've sent copies to you, to Walter, to Tom, to the Boston police, to the Centers for Disease Control, to the FBI, to the Public Health office, and a couple other places (a printed-out sterilized hard copy is also in my safe), but let me put it in a nutshell for you.

When you asked about dockworkers, I checked my files and found a man named Anthony Fusaro who'd died in a fire. When I ran my tests, I discovered that Mr. Fusaro had an **extremely virulent form of weaponized smallpox** that would have killed him if the fire didn't. It is, I believe, quite different from ordinary smallpox and much deadlier, smaller, more infectious and vaccine-resistant. I don't know how Mr. Fusaro might have contracted this illness, but I imagine Walter and our friends on the force will be able to track that down. The fact that Fusaro died in a fire is fortunate. I think whatever fomites might have existed in his house would have been destroyed by the heat. None of the EMTs who handled the body were affected. I believe the virus was stopped there, except for that which existed in his blood, where it persisted, in those parts of his body that weren't burned all the way through.

Unfortunately, in the course of doing my work, I seem to have contracted the disease myself, even though I followed the safety protocols, as I usually do. My mask only filters out particles larger than twenty microns, and these things are about seven, so I may have inhaled the viral particles. The fact that these viral particles can be spread through mere evaporation is alarming, to say the least.

We may be lucky, in one sense. Because of the "Mad Cow" scare and because the prions that cause BSE are such tiny buggers, the HEPA filters in our laminar flow units were upgraded a year ago to two microns. That means, I believe, that the air is safe and that no viral particles have escaped my laboratory, which is not quite airtight but which is kept at negative pressure all the same. The new lab they're building will be even better, they tell me.

However, midway through my examination, I realized, much to my chagrin, that the agents I'm working with should really only be handled in a level four biosafety laboratory, and mine is only level two. "May be safe" isn't good enough. I'm sure that if I gave you time, you'd arrive at the same conclusions I've arrived at, but for the sake of brevity, I'll spell it out for you, so you can see my logic:

1. If this agent is easily transmitted, and is extremely dangerous; and
2. If this lab is contaminated and must therefore be decontaminated; and
3. If I too am contaminated; and
4. If I leave this room, I will quite likely spread this disease; and
5. If I could seal off this room somehow and allow the illness to run its course, nevertheless, whoever examines my body will themselves become contaminated;
6. Then I have no choice but to destroy myself in such a way as to avoid leaving a body, while at the same time destroying this laboratory.

And there you have it. Bit of a pickle.

The building is scheduled to be torn down in a few months anyway, and no one else is working in the building at this hour. I've scrubbed everything I could think of with betadine. I've also gathered together fire accelerants and materials, and I've rigged a timer that should work. I've left instructions that the building is to be thoroughly incinerated before anybody goes in to look for me.

These instructions MUST be followed.

By then I will, however, be gone. I need to explain this last bit, because it might create an unnecessary amount of ambiguity if I don't. Because fire obviously didn't quite complete the job with Mr. Fusaro, at least not until he was ultimately cremated, I fear I cannot consign myself to the flames and hope for better results, plus I quite don't like the idea at all. However, happily, we have a device here that's designed to dispose of large animal carcasses (lucky we're connected to Tufts). All that's left are the bones, which crumble like soft chalk. These may be interred as per instructions I left with my attorney when I was diagnosed with cancer a year ago. That, FYI, is no longer in remission. I was running out of time as it was.

So please, David, do not worry about me. I believe I've taken every precaution now that I could take. The digester works on a timer, and the lid self-seals, so all I have to do is set the thing and get in. We are occasionally called up to euthanize animals, so I've prepared a lethal dose of pentabarbitol to use, once I'm inside. I'll be dead within two or three seconds of injecting myself.

You will find Mr. Fusaro's tissue sample in my safe, which is fireproof, as well as a sample of my own blood. It's possible that a vaccine can be made from them, otherwise I would have destroyed these too. I've taken care to secure the samples, and they're clearly labeled. You will also find the Scotch I was hoping to drink with you. Please pass it around at the next poker game and pour a shot over my grave if you get the chance.

I am quite at peace with all this, David. I look forward to being reunited with my Robert. I've been a good Catholic all my life, and I believe in the promise of eternal life, and if that should prove not to be the case, I'm going to come back and strangle a few priests I could name. It would have been nice to fill an inside straight against you all one more time, but I'm old and enough is enough. I've had a wonderful life and you've all been a huge part of it.

I do fear for what could be a rather serious public health crisis, regarding this virus I've got. It worries me that there could be more of the virus from wherever Anthony Fusaro got it, and that it could get out into the population. I've never seen anything quite like it, in all my years of medical science. But it gives me some sense of peace to know that good men like you are fighting to prevent this. If my death can aid the fight, it will not have been in vain.

Be well, David, and say goodbye to the others for me, and share this letter with them if you see fit. Goodbye, and love.

Gillian

The e-mail had been sent seven hours earlier. When DeLuca finally got Walter Ford on the phone, Ford told him the building had burned completely to the ground, and that Gillian's bones had been found inside the digester, along with seven partially dissolved buttons, the rubber soles of her jogging shoes, a syringe containing traces of pentabarbitol, her rosary beads, a string of pearls, and an empty picture frame.

The safe had been sealed in plastic and sent to the Centers for Disease Control in Atlanta.

Chapter Eighteen

COLONEL STANLEY REICKEN, WHO HAD BEEN denying that his men ever fired on Iraqi insurgents in the middle of surrendering ("While I'm certain my men are innocent of these charges, at the same time, we want to get to the bottom of this as soon as possible, in order that . . ."), first learned of the photographs when he saw them on Al Jazeera television, at which time he told reporters they were fabrications, adding, "It's simple to doctor photographs using computers these days—our people in counterintelligence do it all the time." DeLuca would have slapped himself in the forehead if he hadn't thought he'd pass out from the pain.

When the various experts began to authenticate the photographs, stating that they were images from the United States' own satellites, Reicken called for an investigation into leaks coming out of the IMINT office, only to learn that the photographs had been made public by the judge advocate's office, whereupon Reicken changed his tune and said that while he had no personal knowledge of the events transpiring at the house of Omar Hadid, it was his responsibility as commanding officer to make sure those who did know were held to account, no matter how high the rank.

Later that evening, Al Jazeera broadcast a tape recording, purported to be Reicken's voice, saying, "I don't give a shit what he's waving in the air—I want the house taken down, do you understand, Captain?" Reicken denied that it was his voice, adding that it was as easy to edit and doctor a tape recording, taking words out of context, as it was to doctor a photograph, and who could believe anything they saw or heard on Al Jazeera anyway?

DeLuca had been working hard to get better ever since he'd read Gillian's e-mail. He would grieve for her later, he decided, but for now, she was the inspiration he needed to get back on his feet and do whatever he could to give her death meaning. Thanks to her, the thing was real now. Nobody could dismiss what he was telling them or ignore him or write him off as some inexperienced Guardsman. The CIA had to listen now. CENTCOM had to listen. The Pentagon and the White House had to listen.

He was on his feet when LeDoux found him. He'd ditched his hospital johnny and was having some trouble getting his pants on when LeDoux walked in on him. He knew someone important was coming down the hall by the number of "Attention!"s and "As you were"s he heard.

"What are you doing out of bed?" Phillip asked.

"Mooning you, apparently," he said.

"Get back in bed, and that's an order," LeDoux said. "Your doctor told me it would be two or three weeks before you'd be walking."

"He told me that, too," DeLuca said. "Phil, there's no time. After we fucked up at Sinjar Jebel, Al-Tariq has gotta be moving up his deadline . . ."

"Sit! And don't make me talk to you like you're a goddamn guard dog. All right?"

"I'm really much better," DeLuca said, sitting gingerly in the chair and grimacing slightly when he tweaked his neck. "Not quite at full speed, but it's not a big deal."

"I'll let the doctors tell me how big a deal it is," LeDoux said. "I suggest you do the same. Your friend Evelyn called me for a quote about Reicken."

"What'd you say?"

"I said we were taking care of it. I didn't tell you this but we were already looking at him for how he was handing out no-bid contracts to Halliburton for work at Anaconda, and elsewhere. He's not the only one doing it, but it looks like there may be some quid pro quo involved."

"Kickbacks?"

"Something similar," LeDoux said. "It's being handled. How did she get those tapes? What was this guy's name? The one who made them?"

"Yaakub," DeLuca said. "Richard Yaakub."

"Friend of yours?"

"Not exactly," DeLuca said. "I guess Evelyn's powers of persuasion were better than his interrogators'. Can we talk about something that's actually important?"

"I'm sorry about your friend Gillian."

"She was brilliant," DeLuca said. "In thirty years, I don't think I ever once bluffed her off a hand. She beat me like a redheaded stepchild. So what's happening?"

"Well," LeDoux said, "thanks to her, I think we're going to get the support we need. Don't expect to see any of this in the papers, but things are moving. The people who matter are on this. What's the word on Al-Tariq?"

"Still working," DeLuca said. "We think the CI HQ thing is working, but it might take time. They want more from him. My boy Adnan lost his family—you don't get more motivated than that. I'm meeting with him day after tomorrow."

"You think he's up to it?"

"He was undercover with the Republican Guard for years," DeLuca said. "He thought we didn't know. He knows the tricks. We make him an asset to them and they're not going to look too closely at the rest of it. They might be paranoid, but in the end, everybody sees what they want to see. I don't have to tell you that."

"CI's just a state of mind, right?" LeDoux said.

"He'll come through," DeLuca said. "He knows we're in a hurry, but I don't want to force it and tip his hand."

"Speaking of force," LeDoux said, "we're looking at another option. We're going back to Sanandaj. In numbers, this time. With permission from the Iranian government, by the way—they don't like these guys any more than we do, but don't be surprised when they bitch about the violation of their sovereign territories and the whole nine yards. We need family members to talk to us. Right now, it could be our best shot."

"Not a problem," DeLuca said. "Now that I'm a HALO expert."

"David," LeDoux said, "that's not how we're going, but more to the point, I'm sorry, but you're not part of this. You're not even supposed to be sitting in that chair, goddamn it."

"You're going to need somebody who's been there before . . ."

"That's not as high a priority as . . ."

"You can't hospitalize someone against their will. Everyone has the right to refuse treatment."

"Maybe in a civilian hospital, *Sergeant* DeLuca," LeDoux said. "I'm not going to jeopardize the mission as a favor to you. Fair enough? Healthy, you're the first guy I want, but injured, you're a liability. I know that's harsh. I'm sorry."

At that moment, Captain Thomas appeared in the doorway with DeLuca's chart under his arm. The doctor snapped to attention and saluted when he realized there was a general present.

"Doctor?" DeLuca said. "Just tell me something—what would I need to do to get out of here? You've got stronger painkillers than this, right?"

Dr. Thomas looked at DeLuca, then at the general, wary of coming between them in a dispute.

"Lift your arms as high as you can," Thomas said. DeLuca complied. He wasn't quite ready to do the wave yet, but he could get his hands up even with his ears. "Rotate your head as far as you can," the doctor told him. "First to the right. Then left." If he moved slowly, DeLuca could move his head with about 50 percent of the flexibility he'd had before.

"So?" DeLuca asked. Thomas put his hand on the back of DeLuca's neck and pressed.

"The swelling is down, but it's not gone. I could prescribe pills that will take the pain away completely," Thomas said.

"But?" LeDoux said.

"But," Thomas said, "you don't necessarily want to be pain-free. People with back or neck injuries take pills that take the pain away and then they do more than they should, because they're not feeling anything, and they reinjure themselves. You could be fine, or you could hurt yourself and be looking at anything from bed rest for a few months to being in a wheelchair for the rest of your life."

"Well then it's a no-brainer," DeLuca said. "I go. Write the prescription."

"Stop," Phillip LeDoux said. He paused. DeLuca waited, knowing he'd pled his case and would have to abide by whatever LeDoux said. LeDoux knew it, too. "The mission is in three days. At which time we'll review. In the meantime, David, you do what you can to rehab. And then we'll talk. I meant what I said."

LeDoux moved toward the door, then stopped.

"By the way—I got Sadreddin's people on the governing council. Took a bit of doing. All but one. The rest checked out."

"I appreciate it," DeLuca said. "It's going to pay off. How about Omar Hadid?"

"Not this round," LeDoux said. "He's second generation. I had a long meeting with him. I was impressed. I'd hate to play cards with that guy."

"I have to call him," DeLuca said. "His nephew's doing great, by the way."

"That's good to know," LeDoux said. "He'll be happy to hear it."

The general saluted them both, turned on a heel, and left, his departure accompanied by the same "Attention"s and "As you were"s that had attended his arrival.

DeLuca addressed the doctor.

"So can I go now?" he said. "Where do I get the drugs?"

"I at least want you to meet with a physical therapist to show you some exercises to help with your flexibility," Dr. Thomas said.

"Deal," DeLuca said.

DeLuca spent another day in the CASH and then checked himself out. He hated nothing more than wasting time. Given the scenario Kaplan had painted for him, that was truer now than ever before.

MacKenzie was in the team room. She looked surprised to see him.

"What are you doing here?" she said.

"I was bored," DeLuca said. He wore a foam collar around his neck that made him feel utterly dorky. Dr. Thomas had suggested a firmer plastic neck brace. The foam collar had been a compromise. DeLuca figured he'd wear it while he slept.

"You okay?" she said. "You need a back rub or something?"

"*Muy bueno.* Maybe later," he said. "I just came from the physical therapist and I need to sit down."

He grabbed one of the desk chairs and rolled his way over to her. He'd decided to take his pills in half-doses, to keep the pain level high enough to avoid being oblivious of it, but low enough to function. For now, it lent a certain stiffness to his bearing, and probably looked worse than it was.

"What have you got for me? Where're Dan and Hoolie?"

"Waiting at the gate for Adnan and Khalil," she said. "I think Adnan has something for us. He and Khalil are becoming quite a pair. It's nice to see they don't hate each other's guts anymore."

"There's hope," DeLuca said.

"How were you planning on getting together with them?" she asked. "The CASH was off-limits. And now you're here . . ."

"That's a good point," he said, thinking. "I don't want them to know I'm not 100 percent. Maybe the Oasis," he said, referring to a spot in the middle of Camp Anaconda where a half-dozen hammocks had been strung between palm trees in a small grove that afforded the only natural shade on the base. There were lawn chairs, a card table, and a barbecue grill, too, an idyllic scene, if it weren't for the occasional random mortar round that passed over-head.

"I'll go make sure it's available," she said. "So do you want the good news or the weird news, or the weird weird news first?" she asked.

"Good, then weird," he said. "Then I'll see if I'm still in the mood for the weird weird."

"Good news—remember I said I had the name of the only obstetrician working in the hospital where Al-Tariq was born?" she said.

"Where his birth records were missing?"

"Yeah, but it had to be this guy. Ahmed Shahab was his name. Still is his name."

"You got him?"

"We got him," Mack said, swelling with pride. "Dan and me. He's in a nursing home in Kut. He's eighty-three years old. So Dan and Hoolie and Smoky and I went and talked to him."

"And?"

"He remembers the birth," she said. "He said he delivered a lot of babies but this was the only one where there were men with guns waiting outside the delivery room. Al-Tariq's family was powerful in that region—I guess the expectant poppa was expecting trouble, too. Anyway, Shahab was working under duress. And something happened all right."

"Twins?"

"Yup," she said. "The first baby, Mohammed, came out just fine, but the second, Dawud, was not okay. He was alive, but he was blue, with an umbilical cord wrapped around his neck. The doctor said Mohammed tried to strangle his brother in the womb. At any rate, infant Dawud spent too much time deprived of oxygen for Dr. Shahab to do anything about it. That meant an IQ of somewhere between sixty and eighty. Retarded, or whatever the politically correct term is for it." She took a long pull on her water bottle. "Now you want the weird news?"

"Okay," DeLuca said.

"So Dr. Shahab was Al-Tariq's pediatrician, too," Mack said. "He said this was something he knew he could never tell anybody, but now that the regime has fallen, he can talk. So when Al-Tariq is fourteen years old, he comes into the doctor's office and the doctor diagnoses him with syphilis. How do you get syphilis when you're fourteen?"

"Any number of ways," DeLuca said. "Not all of them voluntary."

"Father wheels the kid right out of the office and they never talk about it again."

"They didn't treat it?"

"No telling," she said. "Shahab was afraid to bring it up again, and then they changed doctors."

MacKenzie took another draw on her water bottle.

"Still want the weird weird?"

"Sure."

"So Jaburi grew up in the United States, right?"

"Until his family moved back when he was fourteen," DeLuca said. "The father had a mosque in D.C."

"Well, close," Mack said. "Jaburi's family went back when Jaburi was fourteen, yeah, but his father sent young Mahmoud home two years earlier, when he was twelve, to begin his religious studies. So guess what old family friend the twelve-year-old Mahmoud stayed with?"

"Who?"

"Mohammed Al-Tariq and his family. Al-Tariq's father and the Imam Jaburi were tight. Mahmoud Jaburi and Mohammed Al-Tariq were like stepbrothers."

"Interesting," DeLuca said. "Good work."

"When you're feeling better," Colleen said, "would you tell me about your friend Gillian? She sounds like a remarkable person."

"I'll do that," DeLuca said. "How are you and Dan . . . doing?"

"Good," she said. "Did you know he's engaged?"

DeLuca wasn't sure what to say.

"I knew that," he said.

"Thanks for not telling me."

"How did you find out?"

"Have a look," she said, taking the mouse to her computer, logging on to the Internet and clicking on a web page she'd bookmarked, a website dedicated to the forthcoming nuptials of Sergeant Danforth L. Sykes, Jr., and one Sidney A. Prescott, with a picture of the two of them smiling brightly and toasting each other with tilted champagne flutes. The exact date of the wedding wasn't set, pending Sergeant Sykes's return from the war in Iraq. "Don't tell him. Apparently his bride-to-be is planning this as a surprise."

"This is how you found out?" DeLuca asked.

"Dan told me, but this is how I found out—I already knew." She spun around in her chair and looked at him. "I was just Googling him to pay him back after he showed me how he found my prom picture. Plus I found sixty thousand hits for Dan Sykes Senior—did you know Dan's father is a senator?"

"I knew that, too," DeLuca said. "He asked me not to tell anybody. He didn't want any special treatment."

They were interrupted when the phone rang: an MP, telling them there'd been an incident at the south gate. Someone named Khalil Al-Penjwin had been apprehended trying to sneak a bomb onto the base.

Mack drove. This time, DeLuca remembered to fasten his seatbelt. The gate was a hardened shed between the inbound and outbound lanes, ringed in concertina wire, where vehicles were forced to zigzag between pairs of thick iron rods set into the roadway, leaving no way for a speeding vehicle to crash through the barricade. Outside the gate, there was a truck, manned by MPs, where Iraqis could exchange weapons for cash.

Three MPs with rifles surrounded Khalil, who lay spread-eagled on the ground, face down, and one had his foot on the young Kurd's neck. Hoolie was holding

Smoky back as the German shepherd continued to bark at the man on the ground. Nearby, two MPs knelt on the ground, searching through the backpack that Khalil always carried, strewing the contents in the sand before them. Khalil was shouting something in Arabic. Dan was with Adnan and another MP, who held Adnan firmly by the arm.

DeLuca asked what was going on.

"Smoky started barking," Dan said. "Right when these guys pulled in."

DeLuca saw a beat-up black Mercedes parked outside the gate, a car that Khalil sometimes drove.

He crossed to where Hoolie was trying to restrain the dog. Vasquez told him they were about to bring Adnan and Khalil across when Smoky went ballistic and started barking. The MPs immediately searched the two Iraqis and found a quarter-pound of C4 plastique, attached to a detonating device devised from a car door opener. The MPs had been unable to find the sending unit that could have triggered the bomb. They'd disarmed the bomb as soon as they found it.

"They didn't search his bag before they let him in?" DeLuca asked.

"I guess we vouched for them," said Vasquez. "We said we were expecting them."

"You guess?" DeLuca said. There was no need to criticize. He knew Julio was aware of what he'd done wrong.

He crossed to Khalil.

"For you—I bring it for you, Mr. David. Tell them. I'm your friend. I bring it for you. To show you."

"Let him up but hold on to him," DeLuca told the MPs, then went to see the IED they'd found in his pack. The chunk of C4 was slightly smaller than a cigarette pack. The door opener was something you could buy from any auto parts supply house, attached to a common nine-volt battery.

"What do you mean, this was for me?" he asked, returning to where the MPs held the smaller man. "You still hoping to collect the reward? Khalil?"

Khalil was terrified. DeLuca told Hoolie to take Smoky away.

"No no no, Mr. David—a boy gave it to me. I swear I swear. He found it on his uncle's table. In his house. He was afraid."

"A boy said, 'Here, take this bomb and bring it to the Americans'? With a remote detonator on it? And you put it in your backpack, without knowing where the remote was? Whoever had it could have blown you up any time they wanted to. That's just too stupid for words."

"I don't know. I am sorry. I thought I would show you. Maybe you could find who has done this."

DeLuca crossed to Adnan.

"Did you know anything about this?" he asked.

"No, I did not," Adnan said calmly. "He picked me up half an hour ago. This is first time I see this."

DeLuca looked back to Khalil, then gestured for the guards to release him.

"You know what I think?" he said to Dan. "I think he's telling the truth. It really is too stupid a story, so it has to be true. Khalil's too smart to try something like this. But he is naïve. Load 'em up and bring 'em to the Oasis."

"Whussup with that?" MacKenzie asked DeLuca when he got back in the Humvee.

"He was just bringing me a present," DeLuca told her, climbing into the vehicle.

"You're looking pretty spry," she said.

"Adrenaline," he told her. "Best painkiller in the world."

At the Oasis, DeLuca eased himself into a lawn chair, just as Dan and Hoolie arrived with the informants. The slightest sliver of a moon hung in the sky. It would be gone soon, and when it reappeared, Ramadan would be over and a night of celebration would ensue, with much feasting and revelry. While DeLuca and the others got comfortable, Mack and Dan went to the mess hall and returned with a cooler full of soda, hamburgers, hot dogs, and potato chips. Khalil decided he'd try a hot dog, even though it contained pork. Adnan stuck to beef. They ate in a circle. Khalil described a wedding feast he'd attended as a child that had lasted for days. Adnan was more reticent, but that was nothing new. DeLuca could see, on Adnan's face, the times he was reminded of the family he'd lost. DeLuca thought of Bonnie, wondering if he'd truly lost her, and then he thought of Evelyn and wished he could see her again, somewhere far from Humvees and Bradleys and young men risking and losing their lives.

"So Adnan, my friend," DeLuca said, as the chit-chat dwindled and Hoolie lit a small fire, using the grill as a fire pit and igniting scrap lumber from a pile nearby, "tell me—what have you been up to?"

The night was supremely quiet, stars twinkling against a black canvas. DeLuca wondered how many of them were satellites.

"Mukhaberat," Adnan said at last. "I think it still operates. The man I spoke with, after the bombing . . . I am sorry you lost your friends."

"We gave you the location because we thought we could protect it," DeLuca said. "We miscalculated. It's not your fault."

"The man said he wanted me to meet someone, so he took me. I was blindfolded, so I don't know where, but he took me to Abu Waid."

"And they mentioned Al-Tariq."

Adnan shook his head firmly.

"They said I am not to mention this. Not to ask. I deal only with Abu Waid. If I ask who is above me or who is below me, they will kill me, they said. So that no one can betray the others. So I don't know."

"What does Waid think?"

"I don't know," Adnan said. "He wanted to know if anybody suspected I was the one who gave the information about the building. I said no, I was certain that no one did. He knew about that man, the one who was giving information . . . the American."

"Richard Yaakub?"

"Yes," Adnan said, "so I told him Yaakub was the one who was suspected, not me."

"That's good," DeLuca said.

"He told me he had a special thing for me to do," Adnan said. "I don't know what. He wants to meet again tomorrow. I think this thing will happen soon. Whatever attack they are planning."

"How soon?" DeLuca wanted to know.

"I don't know, but they were saying, '*Id Mubaraq.*' When they would greet each other, '*Id Mubaraq.*'"

"Which means?" DeLuca asked.

"'Blessed *Id,*' or 'Happy *Id,*'" Khalil said. "It is how

Arab people greet each other on *'Id al-Fitr*. The last day of Ramadan."

"When was the last day of Ramadan? I thought it was still going on?"

"It is," Adnan said. "So why do these men say *'Id Mubaraq'*? I don't understand."

"Because that's the day," DeLuca said. "That's the day they're planning to attack."

"People say 'Merry Christmas' for weeks before it's actually Christmas," Dan said.

"Yeah, but they don't say 'Happy Birthday' before it's your birthday. Or 'Happy New Year's' before it's New Year's Eve," Vasquez said.

DeLuca looked up at the sliver of the moon and asked, "When is it, exactly?"

"Two days," Khalil said.

"Do you agree?" DeLuca said, turning to Adnan. "Was that what you thought?"

"I think this could be," Adnan said. "They gave me this and said to drink it. They told me that those who drink it will be well and have no reason to be afraid."

He handed DeLuca a small glass vial of a pale green liquid. DeLuca held it up and looked at it against the illumination from a distant floodlight. It was clear, with a slight brown or greenish tint.

"You mind if I have somebody look at this?" he said. Adnan shrugged. DeLuca called Hoolie over and handed him the vial, pulling him down to whisper directly into his ear. "Get this to Dr. Kaplan at the CASH immediately. If he's not there, find him. Tell him I think it could be the vaccine we're looking for. I don't care if he's in the middle of open-heart surgery—tell him to drop what he's doing and have this tested. He'll know how important this is. I want to be notified as soon as he learns anything."

Hoolie took a Humvee and drove off.

"Khalil has told me you wanted to know about Al-Tariq's family," Adnan said. "That you wondered if he had a twin brother. I think this could be so. I met a man once who worked in the household, a servant. He said he used to take food to a room, upstairs, where the door was never opened. He would take the food and slide it under the door. But he never saw who ate it. He believed it was a person, someone *mutakhalef . . .*"

"Retarded," Khalil translated.

"*Mu'aq,* yes," Adnan said.

"That is very interesting," DeLuca said. It corroborated what Dr. Shahab had reported, the mentally retarded sibling, apparently kept in a room in the attic. A twin would be the perfect body double. What interested him more was this—he'd asked Khalil about Al-Tariq's family, but he never asked anything about a twin brother.

So where had Adnan come up with that?

"Did you hear anybody talking about *Alf Wajeh*?" DeLuca asked. "Or maybe al-Hallaj?"

"No," Adnan said. "I think tomorrow I will know if I am one of them. They are still suspicious, a little, but I think they will accept me."

"Let's hope," DeLuca said.

Something else about the last day of Ramadan rang a bell, but he couldn't remember what it was. He went to the team room, after the others had gone to bed, logged on and searched his files for the word "Ramadan." He found it in an e-mail Walter Ford had sent him, a report containing a translation of a telephone call between Mahmoud Jaburi and his wife. Jaburi had said he would take his family sailing to celebrate the end of Ramadan. The safest place to be, once the plague hit, would be an island. Was that what Jaburi was doing? Was he moving his family to a safe place?

He e-mailed Ford and conveyed his suspicions, telling him they were thinking the attack could be planned for the last day of Ramadan, two days hence, and to follow up on the possibility that Jaburi was going sailing.

Not sure what island—Martha's Vineyard? Nantucket? Something off the coast of Maine, like Monhegan? I could be wrong, but look into it. Find the boat.

David

While he was online, he received an e-mail from his brother-in-law, Tom, from his office at Homeland Security.

David,
I'm so sorry to hear about Gillian. Words fail me. Again. Her work was flawless. We're on it. Expect potential vaccine in two to three months.

We also have a match on the face you sent me, the guy your boy Ibrahim was meeting with in Sanandaj. He is a former employee of the Biopreparat facility in Novisibirsk named Sergei Antonov, Russian/Muslim from Tajikistan, home town a few miles from the border with Pakistan. Believed to have worked with BW. Fired for spending too much time on the job praying. We might be looking at a disgruntled-former-employee/

religious-zealot combo situation. Antonov last reported
in London. Will ask MI6 to pick him up.

    The kids want to know when their uncle Dave is
coming home. I suppose you're wondering the same
thing.

Tommy

He was about to log off when he saw the flag go up
immediately on his e-mail box. He'd received a reply
from Walter Ford, who'd written:

David,
I'm drumming my fingers over this one, but I gotta tell
you, Jaburi's not the guy. I had a talk with some people
in Washington, and anyway, to make a long story short,
I was wrong about Jaburi, so I'm off the job. Sammy
and I are going fishing on the Cape. A little vacation
would feel good, right now. You should call Sammy one
of these days. Sorry I couldn't be more helpful.

Walter

DeLuca read the e-mail twice to make sure he understood it. Walter was trying to tell him someone, probably
the "people in Washington," was watching his e-mail, so
that he could no longer talk freely. He knew by the reference to "drumming my fingers" that Walter meant the
opposite of what he was saying, because drumming his
fingers was his poker tell, the thing he sometimes did,
without knowing it, when he was bluffing. "I gotta tell
you . . ." meant "I'm being forced to say this," again probably by "people in Washington." The reference to going

on vacation and fishing was wrong, too. Walter Ford hated fishing, nor had Ford taken a vacation in forty years. "You should call Sammy" suggested he suspected his phones were being tapped, and that if he wanted to communicate, he should do so through their mutual friend, and he'd probably misspelled Sami's name on purpose. The specificity of mentioning the Cape probably meant they really were going to the Cape.

A quick call to Sami confirmed his interpretation.

"I don't know what he's up to, but he told me to get my boat ready because he was going to take me up on that offer to go fishing," Sami said.

"Didn't you tell him he was the last guy you'd ever want to take fishing?" DeLuca said.

"Exactly," Sami said. "This guy Timmons sounds greasy to me. Instead of saying, 'Don't worry about it, we got it covered,' he starts waving his dick in the air."

"I wish I could say you got nothing to worry about," DeLuca said. "I got a few friends in high places, but not that many and not that high."

"Don't worry about it," Sami said. "We're big boys."

"Yeah, but they're bigger," DeLuca said.

Walter Ford was in his office when he received the report on Mahmoud Jaburi's DNA. The report consisted of pages of numerical sequences in rows and columns that meant little to Ford, but the statistical analysis of those numbers was revealing. The results of the lab report had been broken down into seven files, with the note added: "Presume sample 1 is Mahmoud Jaburi. Cannot identify the other six."

Other six?

"Where did you get this sample from?" O'Leary asked Ford. He'd driven to the local Stop and Shop to use the pay phone to call his friend at the FBI.

"A hairbrush," Ford told him.

"From where—the locker room at the YMCA? This thing had seven different people on it. Who lets seven other people use their hairbrush? I'll get back to you," O'Leary said.

"It's better if I call you," Ford said. "How long do you think it might take?"

"Couple hours," O'Leary said.

Ford knew only that Jaburi would be on Cape Cod, at the end of Ramadan. "On Cape Cod" needed some narrowing down. He asked for volunteers among his students to help him search property titles on the Cape. Nothing came up using the name "Jaburi." His best student, Eli, suggested calling every house-cleaning service in the phone book, since Jaburi had asked his wife to arrange for having their summer place cleaned. When a Yellow Pages survey failed to produce results, Eli and his girlfriend and a couple of friends spent a Saturday visiting every village and laundromat bulletin board from Buzzard's Bay to P-town, writing down the numbers of private entrepreneurs who'd put up signs advertising cleaning services. Sure enough, Eli eventually found a woman from Senegal who'd put up a sign in a laundromat in North Eastham. She said she'd received a call from a woman named Aafia Jaburi, who'd asked her to prepare a home in Wellfleet, on Nauset Road. She told Eli the address, after he promised to keep her name out of it, since she was technically an illegal immigrant working for cash only.

A call to the harbormaster in Wellfleet confirmed that a forty-four-foot sailboat, *Aafia's Ark,* was registered to one Mahmoud Jaburi, who had a year-round slippage rented in Wellfleet Harbor. He also had private slippage at his home out on Indian Neck, across the harbor from the downtown area.

"Why two slips?" Walter asked him.

"I guess he keeps one in town for when he wants to sail across the bay instead of drive," the harbormaster said. "Maybe he just wants a place to show off his boat—it's a beautiful boat. Cherubini ketch, bronze hardware, teak decks, gorgeous brightwork. He's a good guy. Solid tax-payer."

"Yeah?" Ford asked. "How so? The 'good guy' thing?"

"Just in general," the harbormaster said. "Tips the kids at the fuel dock. Files float plans when he's going to be gone for a while so we can rent his slip out to the week-enders. That sort of thing."

"Uh-huh," Ford said. "He file one recently?"

"Let me look," the harbormaster said. Ford could hear him shuffling through a sheaf of papers. His hunch was that if Jaburi made a practice of filing float plans, he wouldn't vary his routine now, lest that raise suspicions. He was right.

"Yup," the harbormaster said. "He left this morning. Due back . . . that's funny."

"What's funny?" Walter said. "Funny ha-ha or funny peculiar?"

"Funny peculiar," the harbormaster said. "It's just that he left the return date open. Maybe he didn't know and he was going to call it in later."

"He say where he was going?"

"Well," the harbormaster said, sounding puzzled. "Nowhere around here, I can tell you that. Just the coordinates—39.70 north and 44.28 east. That's about due east from here, but . . . Jesus, 44 east is halfway around the world. He must have meant west, which is . . . hang on . . . halfway to the Azores. That can't be right. Huh."

"Because why?"

"Well, that boat's not weighted for open ocean," the harbormaster said. "Last I heard, anyway. Sailing to the Azores is not exactly a family outing."

"Just out of curiosity, where exactly is the first place you said, whatever it was?" Walter asked.

"Let me get my atlas," the harbormaster said. Ford heard a further shuffling of papers, pages turning. It took the harbormaster a few minutes before he came back on the line.

"Well," he said, laughing. "Either the guy is making a joke or he thinks the world is ending."

"Why do you say that?"

"Because 39.70 north and 44.28 east are the latitude and longitude for Mount Ararat."

"Thanks for your help," Ford said.

He called Sami, who said he could have his boat ready in fifteen minutes. With traffic, it was four hours to Wellfleet by car or two by boat, and Walter didn't think he had that much time to spare.

Sami ran flat out, glad that he'd gone ahead and had a new diesel engine put in before he'd deployed to Iraq. He'd figured he'd find a way to pay for it when he got back. The new engine was a 635 HP Cummins electronic diesel with less than two hundred hours on it, still in its first service interval and under warranty. The new engine's 635 horsepower drove *The Lady J* as fast as any in the sports-fishing charter fleet, while its large beam made it a well-behaved vessel even in heavy seas. All the same, Walter found the four- to six-foot swells of Cape Cod Bay to be nauseating, the problem only slightly ameliorated by the Dramamine patches Sami kept on board for his seasick customers.

They passed the P-town ferry where it turned toward Wood End Light and steered a course to the southeast, rounded Chequesett Point and headed north into Wellfleet Harbor. Walter had used Sami's cell phone to call the local sheriff, who met them on the dock, which would have been difficult to find from the sea without his assistance. He told them Jaburi's summer house was all closed up.

"No sign of anybody around," he said.

"Did you look inside?" Ford asked.

"We'd need a search warrant for that," the sheriff said.

"Of course we would," Ford said. "Unless we thought someone inside might be injured."

"That would, of course, be the exception," the sheriff agreed.

"Somebody hurt so bad that they're unable to call for help," Sami said.

"You guys have reason to think that might be the case?"

"Well, I don't hear anything," Sami said.

"Neither do I," Ford said.

"We'd better have a look inside, then," the sheriff said.

The house was a red cedar-sided cottage with white trim, with cedar shakes on the roof, a deck, and a manicured lawn where the dune grasses and beach plums left off, with beds of tiger lilies bobbing in the wind. They looked in vain for a spare key, then broke a pane in the door to the kitchen and let themselves in. Everything inside was tidy, the beds made, nothing in the refrigerator that looked like it was going to spoil or go bad soon. The trash outside the kitchen door contained the shuckings from sweet corn and lobster shells that stank as only lobster shells could. It looked like the Jaburi family had had one last shore dinner.

Upstairs, on a shelf above the bathroom sink, Ford found four small vials of a clear, slightly brown liquid. He put them in a ziplocked evidence bag, put that bag in another bag, put those two in a third, wrapped a large pillow around the vials and tied the pillow tight with a pair of shoelaces he took from shoes in the closet, inserted the pillow inside four sealed garbage bags and placed the entire package inside a garbage can, which he sealed with duct tape. He wasn't sure, of course, what could be in the vials, but he had an idea that it could be something very bad.

Sami had searched the car in the driveway, a new-model Cadillac that was clean, save for two pieces of evidence. The first was a small strip of paper, about six centimeters long and a centimeter wide, perforated at one edge with holes punched every half inch or so, which he found beneath the accelerator, as if it had been stuck to the bottom of the driver's shoe. Walter said it looked, to him, like the end strip from a Federal Express shipping invoice. The second piece of evidence he'd found was the plastic case for a .38-caliber Colt automatic, which Sami had found under the driver's seat. Empty.

Walter and Sami stood on the deck, where they were joined by the sheriff. The sun was setting in the west, the sky a riot of reds, oranges, and pinks blazing on the horizon. A dozen seagulls had landed on the lawn, which Sami said meant bad weather was coming.

"Look," Ford said to the sheriff, a man named Svoboda. "I appreciate your help here, but given that I don't have any jurisdiction, I'm going to need a little more help, I'm afraid."

"Just tell me what you need," the sheriff said.

"First," Ford said, "we're going to need the phone records of all calls going in or out of here for the last month or so at least."

"Not a problem," the sheriff said.

"Second," Ford said, "I don't want to worry you, but you're going to have to call your wife and tell her you're not coming home. I gotta go inside and make some calls, but before I do, I'm really sorry, but we're all quarantined. Nobody leaves until we get the all-clear, but I'm sure that we will, so as I said, don't worry about it. There's beers in the fridge if anybody wants one. I'll be out after I make my calls."

Inside the house, he called the New York Homeland Security office, where he informed Tom Miecowski of what he'd learned and what he'd been up to. He called the Centers for Disease Control and explained the situation, that he might have exposed himself to a biological warfare weapon, and he gave them the location where they could find him. He gave the same information to the Boston FBI office, and the Massachusetts Department of Public Health. Then he called David DeLuca, reaching his voice mail, and told him if it was at all possible, that maybe he could have Scottie send one of his satellites over that part of the Atlantic Ocean to help look for a

forty-four-foot sailboat named *Aafia's Ark,* make Cherubini, color white, two masts, main and mizzen, three sails
including the jib, teak decks, and bronze metal stuff, if
that helped, currently within one day's sail from Wellfleet, Massachusetts, somewhere out there in the big blue
ocean, but maybe Scottie could help narrow it down a bit.
Finally, he called his wife, Martha, and told her not to
wait up for him because he wasn't going to be able to
make it home tonight. After he hung up, he uttered a brief
prayer, hoping he'd be well enough to see her one last
time before the disease took him, if that was what fate had
in store for him.

Before he made any of these calls, he'd dialed *69 on
Jaburi's phone. The last call Jaburi had received came
from a number in Virginia, at 703-482-0623. When Ford
dialed it, a receptionist answered with the words, "Central
Intelligence Agency, may I help you?"

DeLuca slept fitfully and woke when he felt someone
gently jostling him. He opened his eyes and saw Dan
standing next to him.

"Hey, Chief," Dan said. "I woulda let you sleep but you
said you wanted to hear as soon as we heard from
Kaplan."

DeLuca sat up, surprised to discover, after a few
moments, that his neck actually felt better. He looked at
his watch. It was 0900 hours. He couldn't remember the
last time he'd slept that long. He looked at his sat phone
and realized it had come unplugged from its recharger
while he slept. He cursed, plugging it back in. Goddamn
technology. He'd missed three calls while he slept. Before

he checked his messages, he read the note that Dan had brought him. It was from Kaplan. The note said:

Mr. David. Sorry. Your "vaccine" sample is nothing more than green tea. They say it's good for you, but it's not going to stop a plague, I'm afraid. Keep me informed.

Kaplan

It made sense. If Al-Tariq were supplying a thousand agents with what they understood to be a deadly toxin, then the more people involved, the greater the odds that one of them was going to lose his or her courage. Give them what they think is an antidote, tell them they're not going to be hurt, and they're going to feel invulnerable.

"By the way," Dan said. "FYI, you know how I said I was getting out, as soon as my two years are up?"

"Yeah?" DeLuca said.

"Well, that's changed," Dan said. "I'm reenlisting."

"May I ask why?" DeLuca asked.

"The way I see it," Sykes said, "I can do more good here than I could anywhere else. For now, anyway."

"That's how I saw it, too," DeLuca said.

"My old man's gonna shit the bed when I tell him."

"How about your fiancée—what's she going to say?"

"I already told her," he said. "She dumped me."

"I'm sorry," DeLuca said.

"I was, too, at first," Dan said. "But then I thought, what kind of person would break up with somebody because they're doing what they love? Not to mention something that's really important. What kind of love is that? How small can you be?"

"I know what you mean," DeLuca said. "But it's not small. It's just big in a different context."

The first missed call was from Walter Ford, who told him Jaburi was on a sailboat somewhere within one day's sail of Wellfleet, Cape Cod. Walter wondered if they could get any help finding the boat with some of those satellites the army had up there.

When DeLuca called Sami's number, an FBI agent named Peterson answered the phone, explaining that Mr. Jambazian was unavailable. DeLuca identified himself and told Peterson Ford and Jambazian were working for him. Peterson said Ford, Jambazian, and a local sheriff named Svoboda had been quarantined in a mobile CDC decontamination and isolation unit while tests were being conducted. DeLuca was horrified—what had he exposed his friends to?

"They seem healthy, but we're going to have to wait and see," Peterson continued. Peterson's superior, a doctor named Colonel Seligson, told DeLuca they'd found four small sealed vials in the bathroom of Jaburi's house.

"About the size of a tube of Chapstick?" DeLuca said. "Clear brownish-green liquid? Black screw on cap?" Seligson said yes to all three questions. "It's tea. Check to see if it's green tea. It's a placebo. Jaburi didn't bother with it because he knows it doesn't work. Tell Walter to call me when he's out of quarantine. And tell him I'm calling Scott now."

Scott agreed to talk to his superiors at Image Intelligence immediately about Walter's request. It was only a question of what satellites were available and how long it would take to reposition them. There were G-Hawks in Washington, D.C., and a few down in Florida, but they weren't designed to get anywhere quickly.

The second call in DeLuca's voice mailbox was from Evelyn.

"Hello, David, Warner here in sunny Basra, checking in. How are you? I hope you're well. I'm quite looking forward to seeing you again. I know you're busy, but if you could find the time, could you call me and help me with a story I'm doing on that terrible bombing at CI headquarters. I don't think you chaps have gotten anywhere near your due, so, I thought I might write obituaries for your friends, if that's possible. I think the world should know what they did and what they died for—you chaps really are the only ones actually winning hearts and minds, as far as I can see, and I'm not just blowing smoke up your arse saying that. Know you're busy, but call me when you get a chance. You have my number."

DeLuca felt bad, but there was no way around it. Someday, the story would come out, but until then, he had to let her swing in the wind.

The last call in his mailbox was from Adnan, who wanted DeLuca to call him immediately. He left a number. He had something urgent to discuss.

"I told him who you are and what you have done," Adnan said.

"You told who?"

"Abu Waid," Adnan said. "He wants to meet with you. Just you. Not with a convoy to come to him. The others would know he is doing this and they would kill him. I can take you to him, though. I told him I could do this."

"Why does he want to meet with me?"

"He will give Al-Tariq to you," Adnan said. "He said he would do this. He knows that Al-Tariq is crazy. So he will give him to you, to stop this thing. We must move quickly."

"What does he want in return?" DeLuca asked.

"He wants to be governor of Irbil. I told him you were the one who got Imam Sadreddin's men on the governing council. I told him you were a powerful man in the occupation. Can you do this?"

"Of course I can do this," DeLuca lied. "That's the deal? Al-Tariq in exchange for the governorship of Irbil? Tell him I will meet with him. And that I would like it to be soon. Today."

"I will tell him," Adnan said.

At sea, 150 miles east of Cape Cod, Mahmoud Jaburi stood the night watch. It was a calm evening, and there was little to attend to, the boat adrift, with a mild breeze blowing down from the north, suggesting that the first storm of autumn was approaching. There were things he needed to do to get ready, so he placed a bookmark in the book he was reading (*Moby Dick*, for the third time) and moved to the barbecue grill at the taffrail. There, he removed twenty-four receipts from his briefcase, Federal Express "sender's copy" invoices, which he placed in the grill. He turned on the propane, pressed the ignition button, and burned the receipts.

He watched the flames. When the flames died, he dumped the ashes in the Atlantic, and then the only light onboard was the glow from the old-fashioned brass oil lantern he used to read by, and not another light or human

being in sight, in any direction. This was what he liked
about the sea, what Melville and Captain Ahab seemed to
understand, the way the sea returned man to his original
world, where he could be alone and face to face with God
in the most intimate of ways. The only evil at sea was the
evil you brought with you in your heart (Ishmael understood this), but at sea, where there were no temptations,
that evil had no power.

He looked at his compass to locate where Mecca was,
said one last evening prayer, then went below, to where
his family slept. They'd had a great day, even managed
to chase a whale for a few leagues before the beast sub-
merged and lost them. His children looked so peaceful.
He went to the galley, where he'd left the gun he'd bought,
then returned to the cabin where his children were. Using
a pillow for a silencer, he put the barrel of the gun to his
son Asgher's temple and pulled the trigger. When nothing
happened, he chided himself for failing to chamber a
round, did so, then fired a shell into his son's brain. He
quickly did the same to his daughter, Nesreen. The noise
woke Aafia up, causing her to come running. He let her
see what had happened, because she needed to understand, then fired a bullet into the back of her head.

He could not explain to them the suffering they were
avoiding, but he would do so when he met them again in
Paradise, and they would thank him.

Few people truly understood how large the ocean was,
and how much of the world was covered by water, and
how hard it was to search for something on the sea, even
something as large as a forty-four-foot sailboat, even with
the latest satellite technology. Scott DeLuca had been

watching his screen for over an hour, patched into an old NSA Lacrosse bird that, for the last fifteen years, had been tasked to watch for Soviet nuclear submarine traffic. All the registered ships in the North Atlantic quadrant could be accounted for, a fleet of purse seiners out of Gloucester, the Coast Guard cutter *Cuttyhunk* on its regular patrol, a number of private boats, but nothing remarkable. Then he saw something of possible interest, a sudden flare of light and heat in an otherwise cool, dark sea, in the approximate area where Ford had asked him to look. Scott marked the spot, to have a closer look at first light, and then, on a hunch, called the Pentagon to ask them to launch a G-Hawk to make a flyover. It would take a few hours for the UAV to arrive on scene, but it could be worth it.

Chapter Nineteen

DELUCA'S FIRST MISTAKE WAS THAT HE DE-
cided not to swallow his transponder, as he had before his
mission to Iran. He decided not to because of the difficulty he'd had recovering the device on the "back end" of
the trip, something he didn't particularly care to repeat.
Or perhaps that was just part of a bigger, more general-
ized mistake, the mistake of letting his guard down, perhaps because Richard Yaakub had been apprehended, or
because he was just getting sloppy.

He'd met Adnan and Khalil at the south gate at
1600 hours. Vasquez was with him, as was Smoky,
brought along to sniff for bombs or biological weapons.
DeLuca told Adnan he'd speak with Abu Waid alone, and
without a convoy, but he wasn't going to travel completely without backup. Dan thought he should have been
the one going with his team leader, by virtue of seniority,
until DeLuca told him he needed Dan to drive the trail
vehicle, out of sight and beyond the horizon, following
directions from Scottie, who would be monitoring his
father's position.

Khalil's car was a 1983 Mercedes, the upholstery on
the dashboard long ago shredded by the desert heat.

Adnan was in the passenger seat. They headed west from Balad on Highway 1, crossed the Tigris, and drove out of the valley so fertile it had spawned civilization itself, and after a while, into a desert so flat and barren that civilization had yet to find a place to take root. Waid had wanted to meet in the desert, out in the open, where it would be quickly evident if anyone were following them. Dan would have to leave a twenty-mile gap between them, lest his dust be visible to anybody with binoculars. They were to travel west until they saw a man dressed in red with a camel. The man would tell them which way to turn, and then they would see another man, ten miles down from the first. The second man would give them further directions, and that way would bring them to Abu Waid.

"There will be a sandstorm today," Khalil said confidently.

"That's not what our weather birds told me this morning," DeLuca said.

"Arabs don't need those things, boss," he said, pointing to his nose. "We can tell by the smell of sunrise."

"Don't listen," Adnan said. "He's a mountain Kurd who thinks he's desert Arab."

The sun was fierce. DeLuca wanted to look behind him, though he knew Mack and Dan would be far back. A pair of Predators circled overhead, at Phil LeDoux's insistence, both of them hunter-killers armed with Hellfire missiles. DeLuca hoped the technology supporting him turned the odds in his favor, but you couldn't count on technology, any more than you could count on the kindness of strangers. You could only count on yourself, and your team.

They raced past the empty oilfields, driving west toward the Syrian border, across a vast salt flat where the

windblown dust obscured the road. DeLuca grew apprehensive. They should have seen the first man with the
camel by now, he thought. Vasquez looked uneasy as
well, fingering the safety on his rifle, the younger man in
battle gear while DeLuca traveled sterile and unarmed.
He wasn't agoraphobic, but there was something about
such wide-open spaces that left him disoriented, without a
tree or hill or distant mountain anywhere to let him reset
his internal compass. He looked at his watch. It was too
early for the sun to be going down, and yet the light
seemed to be giving out.

Then he saw it, a wall of dust rising in the west, where
the winds generated by the Jebel Ansariya range crossed
the inland steppes to stir the dust from the Syrian desert
and carry it eastward, a vague dimness that would progress
from a flesh-colored sky to one of orange, then sepia, then
dark brown and then perhaps one as dark as night, though
it was still midday.

Khalil stopped the car.

"Something wrong?" DeLuca asked him.

"Don't worry, boss," Khalil said. "I have desert air filters. I think we are almost there."

"Yes?" Adnan said.

"Yes," Khalil said, wheeling about and throwing his
arm over the seat to point a .45 automatic in DeLuca's
face. Adnan pointed a similar gun at Vasquez, who raised
his hands in the air. "Put your hands behind your head—
now!" Khalil commanded.

"You, keep your hands on your head!" Adnan ordered
Vasquez. The dog, who'd been lying on the seat between
DeLuca and Vasquez, sat up. "Keep him quiet or I kill
him now!" Vasquez held Smoky's mouth shut with one

hand as Khalil got out of the car and opened DeLuca's door.

"Wait just a . . ."

"Shut up," Khalil commanded, hitting DeLuca on the side of the head with the barrel of his gun. "Shut up! Put your hands at your neck." He quickly searched DeLuca, removing the transponder from his breast pocket. "This is how you think they will find you—let's see how they find you in our desert now," Khalil said, and with that, he flung the transponder into the darkening sky. DeLuca could feel the dust filling his throat and lungs. "Watch him, Adnan," Khalil said, shutting DeLuca's door and circling behind the car to open Vasquez's door and pull him violently from the seat, throwing him to the ground. He took Hoolie's weapon from him and commanded him to get to his feet, slamming the butt of the rifle into the small of Hoolie's back, causing him to stumble. DeLuca watched as Khalil marched Vasquez into the desert, the two figures obscured by the sandstorm until they were silhouettes in a shapeless sea of orange. He saw Vasquez kneel on the ground. He saw Khalil move around behind him, and he saw him fire. Vasquez fell. Khalil stood over him, firing six more times before he stopped.

Khalil returned to the car and handed the rifle to Adnan. Then he went to the trunk and found a pillowcase, which he put over DeLuca's head, binding his hands behind him with a roll of duct tape.

DeLuca felt the car start again.

The two men in the front seat conversed in Arabic.

"Do you think he can breathe?"

"He can breathe."

"There was no reward for the other one?"

"Nothing."

"Perhaps we should have brought him with us."

"Let the sand fleas feed on his corpse. You said the Fat One only wanted this one."

"Yes."

"Then be happy. We turn him over and we are finished with this business. Tak beer."

"Praise Allah. La ilaha ill Allah wa-Muhammad rasul Allah," Adnan muttered, sounding like he wasn't completely convinced.

DeLuca understood because his Arabic was better than his German, a fact he revealed to no one, since it was almost always to his advantage to have people think he didn't know what they were saying. He spoke Arabic with an American accent, he knew, but his comprehension was good. Not even Sami knew.

He rode for another hour. His luck could hardly have been worse. Surveillance satellites and UAV cameras could penetrate fog and clouds, but they couldn't penetrate sand. Without his transponder, there was no way anybody would be able to follow the car. Sandstorms could last for days.

The car stopped.

Men yelling.

"That's him?"

"That's him. The famous Mr. David."

"He doesn't look so tough."

"Enough! Let us by."

He was pulled from the car. A man held him by the right arm, another by the left. He was brought into some sort of building with a squeaky iron door, through another door, and down a fight of stairs. He heard men calling in the distance in front of him.

"Tell them Adnan is here and he's brought the man with him."

"Where? I want to see him."

He was led down several more flights of stairs—he counted seven sets of sixteen, which put him, by his blind reckoning, well underground—through a door and into a space where the voices echoed to suggest a large cavern or cave. He guessed he was in some sort of mine, though there was no musty smell, the air dry as could be.

Finally he was led down a corridor and turned roughly into a smaller room, where he was forced to sit in a chair, his hands retaped to the back of the chair, his legs to the chair's front legs. Khalil had taken his pain pills from his pocket. He was thinking he could use one about now.

He sat in the dark, he couldn't be sure for how long. Perhaps it was an hour. Perhaps it was two. He heard a hissing sound, coming from what he thought could be a ventilation system. He heard a distant mechanical throbbing. Generators? Water pumps? Air-conditioners? Occasionally he heard the murmur of faroff voices, though never anything distinct or clear. He thought he smelled gasoline, or perhaps motor oil.

The door opened. The footsteps of two men. Three? They seemed to be building something, or setting something up.

"Hand me that. Not that one—that one."

"This one?"

"Yes. Where did you put it?"

"I didn't have it."

"I told you to bring it."
"It was just here."
"This will have to do . . ."
"Is that it?"
"I think it's ready."
"We should test it . . ."
"Which is the one. That one?"
"I think . . ."
"You think?"
"It's not mine. I've never used one like this."

He heard the crackling of plastic wrap. Someone opening a pack of cigarettes? Was he going to be burned?

Ten or fifteen minutes later, a group of men returned. Someone shuffled around him, circling him, dragging his feet, a different-sounding walk from the others, like an old man taking short old man steps, breathing heavily through his nose.

"Take it off," he heard a voice say.

Someone jerked his head back suddenly by pulling on the hood over his head. Pain shot down his neck and across the top of his skull, but he couldn't let them know how much it hurt. The hood came off.

The room was dark, until the light from a video camera shone in his face. Then a black and white television came on, the TV sitting on the table next to the camera. DeLuca saw a picture of himself on the monitor, a trickle of blood still on his cheek from where Khalil had hit him.

"Do you know who I am?" a voice behind the camera said.

"Mohammed Al-Tariq," DeLuca said.

"I am his brother, Dawud," the voice said. "Mohammed is dead."

"Dawud is dead," DeLuca said. "We found his body on the roof, where you put it."

"It was Mohammed's body that you found," the voice said.

"Mohammed has diabetes," DeLuca said. "The body did not. And you have ketones on your breath." He'd once teasingly called his sister Elaine "Juicy-Fruit breath."

There was a silence.

"What is your name?"

"You know who I am," DeLuca said.

"I do," Al-Tariq said. He came forward until his face was side-lit by the light from the camcorder. He looked thinner than he had in the pictures from his file, but the man who stood before DeLuca was still pushing three hundred pounds. He'd grown a beard as well, black with a lot of gray in it. He walked with a cane, and had an oxygen tube held in place beneath his nose by an elastic strap that went around the back of his head, the tube attached to a portable bottle that hung from his shoulder by a sling. His eyes bulged, suggesting a thyroid condition, and one of them didn't seem to focus where the other one did, the left one staring at DeLuca, the right one looking slightly over his shoulder. *"Start the tape,"* Al-Tariq said in Arabic to someone behind him. "Just tell me one thing I don't know, Mr. DeLuca—does your wife, Bonnie, have a VCR?"

DeLuca didn't answer.

He heard voices whispering in the darkness behind the camera.

"It's not working."

"What do you mean, it's not working? I can see his picture on the monitor."

"Yes, that, but the tape is the wrong kind. The tape itself."

"What do you mean, the wrong kind?"

"These tapes don't work in this camera. I told you that."

"You did not."

"I did too. This is not my fault."

"Do they work in the old camera?"

"Yes."

"Well then get the old camera."

"Yes, but that one, the batteries are not charged."

"Then charge them."

"I don't know where the adapter is."

"Well look for it. It's here somewhere."

DeLuca said nothing. He'd been told, before the war ever started, to expect to see such videos, and that similar tapes had circulated among various terrorist organizations for years.

"Why did you come here?" Al-Tariq asked.

"I had an appointment with Abu Waid," DeLuca said. "He said he was willing to betray you, in exchange for being appointed to a government position in Irbil."

"Abu Waid said this?"

"That's what I was told." His hope was to sow a modicum of dissent behind enemy lines, so to speak, but it was a hope that was immediately dashed.

"Abu Waid," Al-Tariq said, "is this true? Do you want to be mayor of Irbil?"

"Governor," a voice in the darkness said, laughing. *"Ibrahim can be mayor."*

"Shut up!" Al-Tariq barked.

The room was hushed.

"The videotape is not working," a timid voice said.

"Why not?" Al-Tariq demanded to know.

"There's a problem. We need to use the old camera. Abdullah is looking for it now."

Al-Tariq breathed angrily through his nose, then left the room.

DeLuca waited in silence, aware that there were still three or four men in the room behind the camera's light.

"Did you know that the vaccine he gave you, to take and to give to your wives and families, won't work? It's not going to protect you, or your children. It's tea. That's all," DeLuca said. "Taste it. There is no vaccine."

"He's lying."

"Shut up!" someone told him, and then a rifle butt slammed into his ribs. Perhaps a seed had been planted after all. The blow knocked the wind out of him momentarily.

Then Al-Tariq stormed back into the room, his *dishdasha* swishing against his cane, which he raised above his head and brought down swiftly against the side of DeLuca's neck, but a glancing blow that DeLuca took more on the shoulder than the neck. He gritted his teeth, though he was beyond pain now, the anger he felt inside huge but cold. His ear felt like it was on fire, glowing red hot, and he felt a trickle of blood flowing down his neck and into his collar.

"You killed my son, my Hassan," Al-Tariq said.

"Hassan was killed by looters," DeLuca said. "By Iraqis. He died from his injuries in the hospital."

"You killed him," Al-Tariq said, more dispassionately now. "So this is what will happen to you. *Do it. Show him.*"

He realized what it was that had smelled like gasoline when a chainsaw started up, somewhere behind the camera. He braced himself, but at the same time, he heard a loud yelp as two men entered, carrying Smoky in their arms, one at his front quarters, the other at the rear. They pressed the dog down on the table, the dog fighting with all his strength to escape their grasp, until a third man joined in to hold him still, and then the man with the chainsaw brought the blade down just above the animal's collar, pressing into the beast's neck until the air filled with flying fur and flesh and blood, the creature shrieking with fear and pain.

But then it was over as the head came loose. The two men holding down what remained threw the carcass in the corner, as the head rolled over on its side. Al-Tariq picked it up by one ear and set it in DeLuca's lap, prying the eyelids open so that the head was staring up at DeLuca, Smoky's tongue lolling grotesquely to one side, no longer attached at the back.

"You Americans enjoy having these things in your laps, so I will give you a companion," Al-Tariq said. He tapped the skull twice with his cane as the blood, still warm, trickled down DeLuca's legs, the gray matter from his brainpan spilling as well. "Good doggy. Isn't that what you say? I want you to think about this, David DeLuca. When I come back, you will tell me everything you can tell me about how much you and your government know about me. If you do not, your wife will receive a tape in the mail and she will see this happen to you. If you help me, I will shoot you once and that will be enough. The choice is yours."

"Guard him. Leave the door open so that you can hear him. I want the old camera set up. Where did Jamal go?

Somebody find him and bring him to me," Al-Tariq said, his voice growing fainter as the distance between them grew.

DeLuca tried not to look at the dog's head. Perhaps there was no distinction to be drawn between necessary and unnecessary cruelty, and yet during his entire career, first as a counterintelligence agent, then as a police officer, and again as CI, he'd drawn such lines, the difference between a Mafia hit that killed a hit man in a barber chair and one that killed the barber, too. Unlike some cops, he still believed there were people who were innocent. Animals, too.

He felt an anger and a sense of resolve growing inside him, the Italian kind, cold and controlled for now, but only until the time was right to turn it loose. He slowed his breathing, trying to clear his thoughts. Was the sandstorm still blowing? Had anybody seen the car? Could anybody see it now, where it was parked?

He was staring at the door when he heard a soft buzzing sound, nearly undetectable, a fly, he thought, and then he saw it land on the table in front of the television monitor. He wondered if the smell of Smoky's blood had attracted it, though it was a strange-looking bug, more like a June bug than a common housefly. It took off again, rising vertically from the table and hovering in front of the camcorder before turning, moving forward until it hung in the air a foot in front of DeLuca's face, its wings flapping invisibly. In the center of the bug was a small red light, about the size of the head of a pin. DeLuca recalled Scott telling him about the Robofly, the tiny raisin-sized UAV that DARPA had been developing, but he hadn't thought it was ready for deployment. The red light blinked in a dot-dash/

dash-dash-dash/dash-dot-dash pattern, repeated it a second time, then dropped to the floor. It took DeLuca a while to remember his Morse code: "A-OK."

He heard voices.

The voices grew louder, a man calling out in Arabic.

He saw Khalil, standing in the open doorway.

"He's still alive," Khalil said.

"Not for much longer," the guard replied.

"Can I talk to him?"

"Mohammed said . . ."

"I brought him in," Khalil said. *"I was made to stand by his side while he killed Arabs. I think I should be allowed to speak to him."*

Khalil and the guard entered the room. The young Kurd approached him, turning to see the picture on the television monitor. He looked at the head in DeLuca's lap. He left DeLuca's field of vision, then returned, holding a baseball bat in his hands.

"What is this?" he said. *"Is this an American baseball bat?"*

"Yes," the guard said. *"Louisville Slugger."*

"How do you use it? Like this?"

"Yes, I think so."

"Where did you get it?"

"We got it on e-Bay," the guard said. Khalil gave the bat a test swing. *"You know that you cannot hurt him. Mohammed would be angry."*

"I won't hurt him, I promise," Khalil said, waving the bat in front of DeLuca's face to menace him.

"This man said the vaccine they gave us will not work," the guard said. *"Do you think that's true?"*

"I don't know," Khalil said, lifting the bat over his right shoulder, striking a batting pose, *"but I don't think you have to worry about it."*

"Why not?"

Khalil swung the bat back, then brought it forward, striking the guard hard across the bridge of his nose and dropping him where he stood with a skull-shattering blow. DeLuca knew, from the sound of bone splintering, that he was dead before he hit the ground.

"That's why not," Khalil said in unaccented English.

"You look like you used to play ball," DeLuca said.

"I was a walk-on my sophomore year at Vandy but it took up too much of my time," Khalil said.

Khalil's real name was Sergeant Dennis Zoulalian, an Armenian-American from Dallas, originally. He'd been DeLuca's best student at Fort Huachuca, graduating at the top of his class and still in possession of many of the CI school records, fastest lock picked, most pushups, fastest time in the two-mile run, and so on, but his most phenomenal skill had been his ability to pick up languages. He was one of those genetically gifted linguists who could pick up a new language like Tagalog or Czech and be speaking it fluently and without an accent six months later. He'd been deep undercover in Kurdistan since 1999, building a contact base while lying low, his swarthy good looks and his innate charm making him a natural candidate for undercover work. DeLuca had chosen him to work Adnan, but only DeLuca had known "Khalil's" true identity. The other members of his team thought he was who he said he was, a young, happy-go-lucky, entrepreneurial Kurd looking to make a buck.

"What'd you say to Vasquez?" DeLuca asked while Zoulalian worked to free his arms and legs of the duct tape that held him.

"I told him to count to a hundred," Dennis said. "Fucking sandstorm. Their plan was to pop you into a second car at one of the checkpoints but leave your transponder in the first car, so that Mack and Danny and the others would follow the wrong vehicle. When the storm blew up, they told us to drive straight in. I drove as slow as I could, but the goddamn storm wouldn't quit."

"Has it yet?"

"I don't know. I haven't been up top since we came in."

"Where are we?"

"Ar Rutbah Salt Works," Zoulalian said. "Eighty klicks north of Ar Rutbah and about twenty to Syria. UNSCOM was here twice but they didn't find anything because Saddam's guys only told them about the upper level of the tunnel system. Call me crazy, but if I was searching an enemy country for WMD, I don't think I'd use the maps the enemy gave me. But that's just me. From the looks of it, Al-Tariq has been setting this place up since Gulf One. Only his top guys knew about it. I couldn't get a handle on him either, until Adnan sold you out."

"That wasn't as hard as we thought it was going to be, was it?" DeLuca said, standing and rubbing his wrists where the duct tape had pulled off the hairs on his arms. He took a few steps to stretch his legs, first gently setting Smoky's head down next to the body in position where it belonged. "I gotta say I was sort of wondering where you were. That could have been me if the camcorder was working."

"Not to worry," Zoulalian said, kneeling and searching the fallen guard for weapons or anything else they could use, handing the AK-47 he'd carried to DeLuca. "I fucked up the tapes, just in case. The spare camera, too. Besides, I was watching the whole thing on Fly-o-Vision." He picked up the Robofly and put it in his pocket. "They're rechargeable. Sends the picture wireless to my PDA."

He reached into the bag he carried and handed DeLuca his transponder, his satellite phone, and his Smith and Wesson.

"I couldn't find your Beretta," he said.

"This'll do," DeLuca said, putting his gun in his pants pocket.

"I brought these, too," Dennis said, handing DeLuca his pain pills. "Sorry about the whack on the head, but . . . you know."

"I know," DeLuca said, pocketing the pills. "Maybe later." He checked the battery power on his phone. "What the fuck was up with trying to bring a bomb in at the gate? Were you trying to convince Adnan you were with him?"

"That's the way I played it," Zoulalian said, "but honestly, I have no idea how that got there. Somebody planted it on me."

"Adnan?"

"No way," Zoulalian said. "But believe it or not, there's a lot of other guys out there who don't like me."

"I'm sure they would if they got to know you," DeLuca said.

"So what's the plan?" Zoulalian said. "I was hoping you had one."

"What are we looking at?"

"Twelve guys, or thirteen, counting Adnan, or actually twelve again, subtracting this guy. One guy's upstairs at the door at all times, and one guy walks the perimeter, but the rest are down here. There's an elevator but it only works with a key. Fat boy couldn't get in and out without it so I'm guessing he keeps the key. Him, Ibrahim, and Abu Waid are the top three. The others are just flunkies. The elevator opens at the bottom on a big main room with a bunch of computers and a kitchen and a TV connected to a satellite dish up top. There's a room for living quarters off the main room. They got a bunch of small arms and a couple RPGs but that's about it, as far as I can tell."

"Desktops or laptops?"

"Both. Al-Tariq only uses a laptop."

"Then that's the one we want. Communications?"

"Some kind of land line, I think, but I couldn't spot anything driving in, due to the storm. It'd be underground anyway, if you were thinking of cutting the lines. We could find it, but it would take time. Needless to say, we're too deep for the sat phone or the transponder."

"Could we cut the power?"

"Maybe, but we'd lose the lights," Zoulalian said. "The salt mines go on for miles. Big enough for two trucks to pass each other, but it's a total maze. I'd hate to be stuck in there without lights. Not with Injun Joe on the loose."

"Any BW or WMD?"

"Wish I knew," Zoulalian said. "Hate to guess wrong."

"What have we got going for us?" DeLuca asked.

"Other than our enormous American penises?" Zoulalian said. "Just what we've got on us. Your .357 and an M-12 I had in the car. I have another M-11 in the car, but that's still up top. And his AK."

He gestured toward the dead man at the bottom of the stairs.

"I think I'd better use one of my life lines to phone a friend. Right now I'm thinking we go up to the surface, order pizza, and then come back down and kill everybody and get the laptop. Something like that. Unless you have a better idea."

"Not at the moment," Zoulalian said.

The corridor was lit by a string of bare bulbs, one every thirty feet or so. At the end of the corridor, DeLuca saw a half-opened door, bright lights shining through the aperture, throwing a ray down on the concrete floor. Zoulalian covered him as he stepped quietly in the opposite direction, turning left up a flight of stairs and through a door, holding it open for his teammate and letting him pass through it before closing it quietly.

It seemed like their boots were loud as thunder against the metal stairs, but they didn't have the luxury of taking their time. The trouble would start as soon as someone discovered DeLuca was missing from the chair where he'd been bound. They'd locked the door, but that wouldn't buy them more than a few seconds.

At the third landing, they passed through another set of doors to where an iron catwalk, fifty feet above the floor, carried them across the original salt pit, now roofed over with corrugated tin hung across a latticework of steel rafters, joists, tie beams, posts, and struts stitched together with wire cables, though many of them were sprung or rusted through. At the far end of the pit, the catwalk turned right where a set of eight thick cables pulled the elevator up a pair of guide rails along the wall, in lieu of an actual elevator shaft. A series of rungs bolted to the wall next to the rails served as a kind of service ladder. Where the catwalk turned right, two flights of open stairs led to a door in the opposite wall and, beyond that, four more flights rising to one final door and the surface. A guard was posted outside that final door. The final set of stairs was the deepest of all, with twenty steps from landing to landing. DeLuca and Zoulalian paused at the bottom.

"Trade me your rifle," Zoulalian said quietly in Arabic. *"Time for Khalil."*

He called out to the top of the stairs.

"Abdullah! Are you there?"

The door at the top of the stairs opened. DeLuca stayed out of sight.

"What?" The man at the top called out. *"Who is it?"*

"It's Khalil, Abdullah—how are you, my friend?" he said, walking slowly up the stairs as he spoke.

"Abdullah comes next. I'm Zafir."

"I'm sorry, Zafir. We're looking for Jamal."

"I've already told them—if Jamal was here, I would know it."

"So you haven't seen him, then?"

"No, I haven't seen him. I don't know why . . ."

The guard was quieted in midsentence when Khalil grabbed him by the rifle and threw him violently down the steps. He made less noise than DeLuca thought he would as he fell. DeLuca had drawn his .357 in case a final shot was required. It was unnecessary. He knew by the angle of the head when the body landed that the man was dead.

The temperature rose fifteen degrees as DeLuca walked the last twenty steps to the surface. Beyond the door was a shipping office, long since abandoned, with a brace of elevator doors next to a dysfunctional water fountain. He went to the window. The night sky was ridiculous with stars, the dust storm long past. On the horizon, he saw the slender sliver of the new moon, signaling the end of Ramadan.

"Where's the guard on the perimeter?" DeLuca asked, speaking in Arabic in case the man was somehow within earshot.

"I don't know," Zoulalian said. *"There's a big storage dome in that direction and machine shops and garages and whatever—he could be anywhere."*

"Keep your eyes open. What time is it?" DeLuca asked.

"No idea," Zoulalian said.

DeLuca looked at the screen on his sat phone. It was twenty minutes before midnight, or 3:40 back home.

"Where's the car?"

"In the loading dock. They made me park it where our birds couldn't see it."

"Get the M-11," he whispered in English. "We might need it."

While Sergeant Zoulalian ran to the Mercedes, DeLuca stepped carefully outside and knelt by a stone wall, where he hoped the reception would be better. Speaking low, he dialed his son's number, because he wasn't quite sure whom to call first.

Scott sounded out of breath when he answered.

"I just got your signal back. Where've you been?"

"Little busy," DeLuca said. "Sorry I lost you. I need support."

"It's closer than you think," Scott said. "Get out of there ASAP. The strike is coming down in fifteen."

"What? Say again."

"Twenty-three fifty-five hundred hours, nonnegotiable," Scott said. "CENTCOM made the call when they lost your signal. LeDoux talked them into waiting until midnight, but they couldn't budge past that. They're going to take Al-Tariq out before he sends the go."

"How did they know where to hit if you lost me?"

"We bugged the car."

"Scottie, this is nuts," DeLuca said. "We need the names. You can't . . . Tell them to abort."

"Personally, I agree, but CENTCOM says right now, stopping the go is the priority. *'Id al-Fitr* starts at midnight. They think they can get the names later."

"Negative," DeLuca said. "Abort. Without the names, you got a thousand free agents."

"Can't be done," Scott said. "The B-2s left Missouri six hours ago. I'd never get the call in in time. Just get out of there. I'm ordering you, Sergeant."

"Nice try, Lieutenant," DeLuca said. He knew if they'd scrambled B-2s out of Whiteman AFB in Missouri, it meant they were sending large ordnance, precision-guided "smart bombs" and bunker busters at least. Even tactical nukes. Using first-strike nukes had long been deemed unthinkable, but using tacticals on remote desert outposts where the collateral damage would be zero was less unthinkable than it was considering some other targets.

"Dad . . ."

"Tell the pilots to zero on my transponder—I'll leave it on the roof to mark. They've got to put it down the elevator shaft. I'm going back in for the names."

He threw his transponder on the flat roof of the shed that housed the elevator's hoist mechanism, told Zoulalian to leave the car running, and explained that he was going back for the laptop. Zoulalian handed him the machine pistol.

"Not by yourself, you're not."

"I'll explain on the way down," DeLuca said as he raced for the staircase. "This place is going to light up pretty good in a few minutes."

They'd only gotten as far as the office when the doors to the supply room kicked out and they heard a woman's voice shout, "Freeze, motherfuckers—throw down your weapons!"

DeLuca stopped in his tracks, raising his arms above his head.

"I didn't know you had such a potty mouth, Colleen," he said. Mack lowered her weapon, as did Sykes and Vasquez, who stood to either side of her.

"We'd just taken out the guard when we heard voices," she said. She looked at "Khalil."

"It's all right—he's with us," DeLuca said.

"We were looking for a way down," Dan said, gesturing toward Vasquez. "We found this guy in the middle of nowhere after the storm cleared."

"I appreciate the help," DeLuca said. "Follow me. Eyes on."

They took the steps two at a time. DeLuca led the way, followed by Sykes, Vasquez, MacKenzie, and Khalil.

He kicked through the doors and led his team out onto the catwalk, pausing by the elevator rails and gazing into the shaft below where the cables ran down into a hole in the floor of the salt pit. He'd heard pilots brag that the telemetry on their smart bombs was good enough to hit a medium-sized pizza from twenty thousand feet. He hoped they were right, because anything but a direct hit wasn't going to cut it. The elevator wasn't moving. That was good.

He'd taken three steps onto the catwalk when he heard shouts down below, then gunfire.

That was bad.

DeLuca made it across just as three men burst through the doors below and onto the landing, the first looking up and firing on them. There was nowhere to take cover, the treads of the catwalk open iron grates. Mack, Dan, and Hoolie returned fire as Khalil retreated toward the elevator shaft, a position from which he'd have a better angle. A second guard took up a position beside the first, firing toward DeLuca, who was closest, his location protected by the metal stairs, the guard's rounds ricocheting wildly off the iron and throwing sparks into the chasm below. DeLuca fired a burst from his M-11, grabbing a guywire with his left hand and leaning out to get a better angle, the machine pistol kicking violently in his right arm, one of his rounds knocking a guard from the landing. A second man fell as the third burst through the door with a shout, leveling a shoulder-fired RPG at Khalil and firing. The detonation of the grenade briefly lit the abyss, affording DeLuca a glimpse of the debris below, like a massive flashbulb going off, but the grenade missed its target, allowing Khalil to return fire with one of the AK-47s taken from the dead guards, joined by fire from Dan and Hoolie. MacKenzie raced ahead to catch up with DeLuca at the stairs. The man with the RPG fell over the railing, dead, and then the room was quiet, the air filled with smoke and smelling of cordite.

"Khalil—are you all right?"

"I'm good, Mr. David," Zoulalian called back.

"Let's go!"

"You go ahead," Zoulalian shouted. "The walkway is gone. There's a gap. In the catwalk. Maybe fifteen feet. From the grenade. You go—I'll find another way."

DeLuca raced ahead, stepped over the bodies clogging the lower landing, and bolted the first set of stairs, then the second, his team close behind him. At the third, he heard footsteps below, but he didn't have time to be cautious, so he pressed ahead, spraying the hall in front of him with bullets as he emptied the M-11 to clear the way. He heard gunfire coming up from below at the last turn of the stairs. He dove low onto the landing, firing with his Smith and Wesson .357 as a man beneath him tried to duck for cover, but the man was too late, falling face down as DeLuca fired two more rounds into him to make sure. He stopped to pick up the man's weapon, a Tec-9, to replace the M-11 now that it was empty. Mack, Sykes, and Vasquez paused next to him.

"Down these stairs, turn right and right again, then a long, straight hallway," DeLuca said, trying to catch his breath. "I guess we fight our way down it."

"Me first," Hoolie said, showing him that he had a grenade in each hand.

"Go go," DeLuca said. "We'll make noise."

Where the corridor turned a corner toward the main room, they stopped, DeLuca knocking out the light bulb overhead with the barrel of the AK-47 he carried. Someone fired a burst of machine-gun fire at them from the door of the room where he'd been held. He gestured to Hoolie to show him where the room could be located.

"You're low, I'm high—don't stand up until I stop firing. Mack, you cross, Dan, stay here until we go but hold your fire. On three. One, two, three."

He stood up, firing his Tec-9 toward the door, making sure, as best he could, that his rounds carried high along the ceiling. Hoolie scrambled to the door, dove to the floor sliding headfirst, and threw a grenade into the room. It exploded a moment later, the blast throwing debris out the opened door. He got to his feet and entered the room, where DeLuca and the others joined him a second later. The explosion had ripped the camcorder from its power supply and knocked over the tripod upon which it was mounted, but the light was still working on battery power, throwing enough illumination across the floor to reveal the body of the man who'd shot at them and, beyond them, the body of the German shepherd.

"Aw Jesus," Vasquez said, panting, exhausted, his gaze fixed on Smoky's lifeless corpse. "What was he doing in here?"

"You didn't do it," DeLuca said softly. "He was already gone. Come on. Moving out. How many grenades you got?"

"Just two," Vasquez said.

"One on the door and one inside," he told Vasquez. "Let's go."

They worked their way quickly down the hall, room by room, until they heard a sudden burst of fire coming from inside the main room that sent them scrambling for cover. A second exchange of gunfire told them a struggle of some kind was going on inside the room but not directed at them. DeLuca led the others to the door, where he peered through the crack. He saw Adnan rise to his feet and fire in the direction of the elevator, then duck again behind an overturned table.

"Now!" DeLuca said, shouldering the door open and rolling once, then firing at a man he recognized as Abu Waid, who took cover behind a pair of large metal filing cabinets. Waid fired back, forcing Mack, Sykes, and Vasquez into the hall. When DeLuca stood to take him out, he thought at first that his gun had jammed, only to realize his clip was empty.

He reached for his .357, as Waid raised his rifle, pointing it straight at DeLuca's heart and smiling.

The elevator doors behind him opened.

Abu Waid turned, squeezing off several rounds before Khalil cut the man in half with a burst from his M-12.

A door at the opposite end of the room opened.

DeLuca recognized Ibrahim Al-Tariq as he bolted through it.

DeLuca squeezed off three shots from his .357 but missed.

Sykes ran to give chase.

"Don't shoot!" Adnan said, rising to his feet, his rifle leveled at Mohammed Al-Tariq, who lay wounded on the floor, next to a table where DeLuca saw a laptop computer. Al-Tariq was bleeding from where he'd been shot in the leg. Adnan had shot him.

"What's through here?" Dan Sykes asked, standing at the door where Ibrahim Al-Tariq had fled.

"The salt mines," Khalil said.

"Let him go," DeLuca commanded. He turned to Adnan.

"Lower your rifle," DeLuca commanded.

"No," Adnan said.

"Lower it!"

"No!" Adnan said, in a voice filled with an anguish that came from deep inside him. "He killed my family. He killed my wife. He killed my son, and my daughter. He tortured them. He made my wife watch while he tortured her children. It should have been me, but he killed them, and it was my fault. So now I will kill him."

"Adnan . . ."

"I'm sorry," Adnan said. "The only way I could get to him was to give them you. I'm sorry, but it was the only way. I didn't do it for the money."

"We know," DeLuca said. "That's why we picked you. We knew what you would do."

Developing human intelligence was a murky business. You had to move into communities where a hundred people had a hundred different reasons to do a hundred different things. The trick was finding someone with the strongest motivation to do the same thing you wanted to do. He'd searched his files, before ever leaving Kuwait, looking for someone he could use to take apart the Mukhaberat. He'd rejected a huge number of candidates before coming across the file for Adnan bin Saddem, a man whose family had been slaughtered by the head of the Mukhaberat. DeLuca had been improvising at first, feeling his way, trying to work his informant the way he'd worked the gang bangers back home, subtly reminding him of what he hated and who he loved and what he could do to help. When he'd learned that Al-Tariq himself might still be alive, what he wanted came more into focus. They knew Adnan was bright, and filled with a thirst for revenge, and that he could go places they couldn't go, so they'd used him, the way a hunter uses a bird dog to run ahead and flush the game. When Adnan started making his own play, saying he'd heard someone mention the possibility that Al-Tariq had a brother, DeLuca and the others had gone along with him, to see where he might lead them, and as they'd hoped, he'd led them to Al-Tariq himself.

"Do you mind if I have a look?" he asked Adnan, who continued to point his weapon at Al-Tariq. Adnan shook his head.

DeLuca crossed to Al-Tariq's laptop, where he saw a screen filled with Arabic script. He called Zoulalian over and asked him to translate. Zoulalian read the words on the screen.

"You have mail waiting to be sent . . ." he read. "It says 'send now,' 'review mail,' or 'send later . . .'"

"Click on 'review mail.'" Zoulalian did so. "What does it say?"

"Praise Allah," Zoulalian read. "Proceed to your assigned targets immediately. God is with us. Have faith, for you are the chosen one thousand."

"Delete that," DeLuca said, "and write, 'Stand down and await further instructions,' and then hit send. But copy the block of addresses first. And put it on a floppy."

"David," Sykes said from the opposite doorway. "You gotta see this."

DeLuca crossed the room, stepping over the bodies of two guards whom Adnan had apparently killed when he'd first begun his assault on the men who'd killed his family, and joined Sykes. Beyond the door, where the maze of tunnels composing the salt mines began, he saw rack after rack of shelves, and on the shelves, large glass jars filled with human body parts preserved in formaldehyde. The rumors about Al-Tariq were true.

DeLuca pulled the door shut.

"Ibrahim . . ." Sykes said.

"He's not going anywhere," DeLuca said. He looked at the screen on his sat phone. It was eleven-fifty-one.

"We gotta go, people!" he called out, just as an explosion up on the surface shook the earth and made the lights flicker. Somebody had arrived early. "Adnan—leave him. Khalil . . ."

"Laptop's in my bag," Zoulalian said, frisbeeing DeLuca the diskette. DeLuca caught it and tucked it in his shirt pocket.

"Adnan," DeLuca repeated, as another explosion shook the room, plaster dust trickling down from the ceiling. The lights flickered again. He really didn't want the power to go out.

"Go," Adnan said. "I will stay. *La ilaha ill Allah wa-Muhammad rasul Allah.*"

"*La ilaha ill Allah wa-Muhammad rasul Allah,*" De-Luca replied.

The elevator was inoperable, but given that any number of JDAMs, JSOWs, and "Daisy Cutters" were about to rain down on them in general and the elevator shaft in particular any minute now, the elevator wasn't DeLuca's first choice of transportation anyway.

They took the hall and the stairs in leaps and bounds, with Sykes in the front and DeLuca bringing up the rear. The catwalk over the salt pit swayed with each detonation up above, the air thick with dust that made the dim lights even dimmer. They were forced to stop at the end of the catwalk where the RPG fired earlier had left a fifteen-foot gap. Disconnected, the end of the catwalk rolled from side to side beneath their weight, unstable now. A single bomb dropped through the roof covering the pit would kill them all.

"Back up—back up," Dan Sykes shouted, stripping off his battle gear and dropping his weapons to the floor below. "There's an aluminum ladder on the far wall . . ."

"What are you doing?" Vasquez asked him.

"I used to do the long jump in high school."

"So did I. What was your best jump?"

"Seventeen-five."

"Go for it—mine was sixteen-eight."

Sykes backed up thirty feet as the others cleared the way for him, then raced the length of the catwalk as it wavered from side to side, throwing his body out across the void. He landed hard against the tangled metal of the opposing span, pulled himself up, and ran for the aluminum ladder. He returned, extended the ladder to twenty feet and lowered it across the gap, where Vasquez caught the other end.

"Go go go!" DeLuca shouted, holding the end in place as Khalil shimmied his way across on all fours. Once on the other side, he helped Sykes secure the far end.

"Mack, you're next," DeLuca said.

An explosion topside rocked the roof. The lights blinked off for a few seconds, then came back on.

"Now, MacKenzie!" She dropped her weapons, then crawled hesitantly out onto the ladder, which twisted and bowed beneath her weight. She was halfway across when the lights went out, and this time, they didn't come back on, pitching the room into total darkness, to where DeLuca couldn't see his hand in front of his face. "It doesn't matter, Colleen—just feel your way. Stay low and centered. Tell me when you're across."

It seemed like an eternity, but then he heard Sykes call out, "We got her."

"You're next," DeLuca told Vasquez.

"Why don't . . ."

"Now!" he growled.

He waited, holding his end of the ladder as steady as he could, the catwalk still swaying in the darkness, creating an odd sensation, because he couldn't see anything, but he could still feel it moving.

"I'm good," Vasquez shouted back.

"Hang on," DeLuca said, taking the belt from his pants and tying his end of the ladder to the catwalk as tightly as was possible, which wasn't very tight at all. He reached blindly out into the darkness in front of him, feeling for the first rung, then the second, then the third, keeping the side rails of the ladder between his legs and pulling himself forward with his arms.

Six rungs.

Seven.

How much farther?

Then the ladder twisted beneath him, skewing sideways toward vertical. He fell off to the left, hanging on to the side rail of the ladder with both hands.

"DeLuca!"

"I'm still on," he called back, kicking his leg up, trying to find something to throw it over, but there was nothing there. He tried again.

An explosion rocked the room, causing him to lose his grip with his right hand. He felt his left hand slipping.

He kicked again.

Nothing.

He reached up with his right hand.

Nothing. Where the fuck was it? Where was the god-damn ladder?

He felt the fingers on his left hand peeling away as another explosion shook him.

He couldn't hold on any longer.

He let go.

Someone grabbed him by the left wrist, pulling him up. He reached for whoever it was with his right hand. His rescuer grabbed him by the right wrist.

"I got you," Sykes said.

DeLuca felt himself being pulled bodily onto the far end of the catwalk.

"I don't know how you saw me . . ." he began.

"NVGs," Dan said. "Everybody hold hands and follow me."

He led them to the end of the catwalk, then right and through the far doors, where they scrambled up the stairs as Sykes called out directions.

"I don't understand why they haven't blown this place up yet," MacKenzie said.

"They soften the target first," Vasquez said as they raced up the stairs. DeLuca vaguely understood the procedure, attacking a hard target first with GPS-guided JSOW five-hundred-pound penetrating warheads, then a couple of two-thousand-pound Mark 84s JDAMs, and then a GBU 28 "Bunker Buster" or two, five-thousand-pound laser-guided bombs that were twenty-five feet long. That was what they'd used on Mohammed Al-Tariq's home the first time they'd attacked him from the air. It felt like they were being a bit more thorough this time.

They reached the office. One of the walls had been blown out, the roof hanging low enough that they had to duck to pass beneath it.

"This way," Zoulalian said, racing toward the car. The others followed, the way lit now by the stars above and by a number of fires burning in the various outbuildings. DeLuca thought at first that it was a miracle that the car was untouched, until he remembered how accurate the precision-guided munitions being used were. Perhaps they'd spared the vehicle intentionally.

On the other hand, it was possible that they intended to blow it to pieces if they saw it move.

He hit redial on his sat phone and threw it onto the back dashboard of the car, all five of them piling in as fast as they could, the car spraying gravel behind it as they sped away, Zoulalian at the wheel.

They'd reached the front gate of the salt works when a tremendous explosion launched the old Mercedes four feet straight up in the air. DeLuca felt the air rush from his lungs at the concussion. They landed with a crash, the car bottoming out, but they kept going, managing to put another forty or fifty yards behind them before a second massive explosion rocked the vehicle a second time, sending it fishtailing in the sand as Zoulalian struggled to regain control.

"Bunker-busters," somebody shouted.

"I got a 130 directly above us," Sykes called out, staring up in the sky with his night vision goggles. "I've got a parachute."

They all knew what that meant. C-130s were used to drop the largest nonnuclear bomb in the Air Force's arsenal, the BLU-82 or "Big Blue," also called a "Daisy Cutter." The "Daisy Cutter" had been originally developed during the Vietnam War as a device used to clear landing zones for helicopters, the shock wave blowing down everything that was more than half an inch high for hundred of yards in all directions. BLU-82s were considerably larger than the weapons used during the Vietnam War, massive fifteen-thousand-pound devices packed with 12,600 pounds of GSX gas slurry explosive, used to clear minefields, wipe out tank divisions, or delete entire building complexes from the face of the earth. They were also called "vacuum bombs" for the way they sucked all the air out of the sky. Too large to fit through the bomb-bay doors on any of the Air Force's conventional bombers, Daisy Cutters were dropped from C-130s by parachutes attached to static lines, and if DeLuca remembered correctly, it took about thirty seconds from the time they left the plane to the time they went off, about twenty or thirty feet above the ground.

Zoulalian's foot pressed the accelerator to the floor, but the car was old, the road slushy with dust and sand, and it was impossible to go fast enough.

From nowhere, a set of headlights appeared. DeLuca saw a Bradley M3A3 fighting vehicle approaching them at top speed. Both vehicles slammed on their brakes and came to a stop, facing each other.

A man ran from the back of the Bradley, waving his arms to hurry them into the armored vehicle. It was Preacher Johnson. As they scrambled in on top of each other, Johnson handed them oxygen bottles.

"Seatbelts if you can, and if you can't, hang on to something!" Johnson shouted as the massive vehicle spun 180 degrees on a tread and roared away, its six-hundred-horsepower Cummins VTA-903T diesel engine at full capacity. A second later, the inside of the Bradley was lit by a flash of light through the rear portholes. DeLuca struggled with his five-point harness, hearing it click just as the shock wave hit them.

The thirty-four-ton Bradley was lifted off the ground by the blast, as easily as a spring breeze might blow an empty French fries bag across a McDonald's parking lot, tumbling three times end over end in one direction, then barrel-rolling four times in the opposite direction as air rushed in to fill the vacuum created by the blast before the vehicle came to a stop upside down.

All was quiet, save for a soft hissing sound.

"Is anybody hurt?" he heard Johnson call out. "Report, please. Anybody dead, speak up now. Check your buddies. Who we got? Y'all sing out now."

"MacKenzie, okay," DeLuca heard Mack report, coughing from the dust.

"Vasquez okay."

"Sykes good."

"Khalil okay."

"Sergeant Pink okay."

"Sergeant Green fucking all right. Hoo yah."

"Mr. David?" Preacher Johnson asked. "Are you still with us?"

"I'm thinking," DeLuca said. "Just gimme a minute."

A minute later, they were standing on the desert floor, looking up at the stars, and at the salt works in the distance, where a carpet bombing from what Vasquez guessed were vintage B-52s launched from the Air Force base on Diego Garcia, in the Indian Ocean, were dropping wave after wave of firebombs, probably five-hundred-pound MY-77 Mod 4s, Vasquez suspected, and no one had the strength to argue with him. Preacher Johnson guessed they were making sure that any escaped viruses were thoroughly incinerated. Al-Tariq was gone. So was Adnan. There was no need to look for bodies.

DeLuca reached into his shirt pocket and removed the floppy disk. It was undamaged. Zoulalian reported that the laptop computer Al-Tariq had been using was intact as well.

DeLuca reached into his pants pocket and found the plastic bottle of pain pills that Sergeant Zoulalian had been kind enough to bring him, but he was discouraged to discover that at some point during the previous skirmish, a bullet had shattered the medicine bottle, blowing a hole in his pants as well. He reached in again and dug deep until, at the very bottom of his pocket, he found a single capsule.

"Anybody got any water?" he asked. "I think I'm going to have a headache."

Chapter Twenty

WALTER FORD WAS ON THE PHONE WITH A doctor from the CDC, describing in greater detail what he'd done and found, when he saw an FBI helicopter disappear behind the trees, about a quarter-mile off. Ten minutes later, a man in an orange moon suit walked up the driveway toward the house, carrying a large suitcase in one hand and his oxygen supply in the other. The man identified himself as Agent Peterson, an FBI epidemiologist. He said not to be alarmed, but he was there to sweep the house for any signs of biological or chemical toxins. He opened his suitcase and took from it an electronic sniffer that collected potentially dangerous chemical elements, spores, bacteria, or viral particles, broke them down into their molecular building blocks, gave each molecular building block an electrical charge so that it could be read, and then compared that recombined signature against those stored in its onboard computer. The first pass of the house showed everything to be clean, Peterson said, as had a pass over the garbage can where Ford had put the vials he'd found. However, Peterson apologized, as an extra precaution, the three men in the house would have to be transferred to a quarantine unit for testing and observation while the house, boathouse, and car were sealed and pumped full of bleach to kill any residual agents the sensors might have failed to detect.

Agent Peterson spent the next hour securing the vials for testing. Out the window, Ford saw two other moon-suited members of the FBI epidemiology team going over the boathouse. As darkness fell, a truck arrived, a semi pulling a shiny steel trailer with a pair of tinted windows toward the front. There was a door in the back of the trailer, with steps that folded down, leading up to a decontamination chamber. A hatch on the other side of the decontamination room opened onto a mobile level four medical laboratory that formed the midsection of the trailer, and beyond that, a third door led to an isolation room, where Ford, Jambazian, and Chief Svoboda were escorted, changing into white overalls while their clothes were sterilized. They met a man who identified himself as a Colonel Roger Seligson, with the CDC, who'd flown up from Washington in a military jet that landed at Otis AFB, Cape Cod. From there he'd taken a Coast Guard helicopter to the site. He had three assistants with him, and said more people would be arriving throughout the night, some coming all the way from Atlanta. He explained the tests they were going to have to do and said he was afraid it could be a while before anybody could be given a clean bill of health.

Walter said he understood. He asked, via the intercom, if he could plug in his computer and hook it up to the Internet while he waited. Colonel Seligson thought that could be arranged. He stood outside the lab window and gave the men in the isolation chamber two thumbs-up.

Walter Ford logged on. He wanted to make sure all the concerned parties were kept informed of what was happening. He got a piece of good news from Tom at Homeland Security, who told him CDC scientists in Atlanta, working on the blood sample Gillian had left for them, and on the tissue sample from Anthony Fusaro, the dockworker, had discovered that the virus was unable to survive above temperatures of 180–85 degrees, a discovery made by looking more closely at Fusaro's charred flesh, where particles of the variola-modified virus were broken down and denatured in the outer, more charred portions of the tissue but remained virulent in the more protected internal tissues.

It's not much but it's something. Now all we gotta do is hope for a 180-degree heat wave.

                                                          Tom

Walter forwarded the information to DeLuca. Seligson told him that DeLuca had been right about the clear brown-green fluid in the vials, which tests had shown to be green tea and nothing more.

He also forwarded DeLuca an e-mail he'd received from O'Leary at the FBI. Of the six individuals other than Jaburi represented by the DNA found on Jaburi's hairbrush, four had been identified as young women who'd been sexual homicide victims, and their bodies had been arranged and posed (a practice not uncommon among serial killers), their hair neatly brushed. They were still trying to identify the other two samples.

It was approaching dawn when Seligson finally told the men in quarantine he had some good news for them.

His team had been running antibody/antigen challenges all night, and all of them had proven negative, as had comparisons of workups done on the blood of Gillian O'Doherty. "Two more to go, and if those are negative, you'll be cleared for release."

In the meantime, Scott DeLuca had e-mailed to say they'd located and identified the *Aafia's Ark* from UAV photographs. The sailboat's position, N42° 59′ and W63° 29′, was roughly 230 miles east of Cape Cod, not far from the fishing grounds of Georges Bank, which had been cleared of all traffic. The sailboat was being monitored via radar by the 280-foot Coast Guard cutter *Cuttyhunk,* and by the USS *Livingston,* a 400-foot Navy Landing Ship Transport that had taken up position beyond the horizon, awaiting instructions. The intelligence community wanted to take Jaburi alive for questioning, while the Navy simply wanted to blow him out of the water and go have breakfast. Scott had sent Ford a set of digital photographs of the boat and told him if he wanted to, he could go to an IMINT website and use the password Scott gave him to watch the UAV imagery in real time. When Ford clicked over and logged on, he saw a revolving sequence of images, the boat from a distance, the boat closer in, closer still, and then the image zoomed back out to a plot of the ocean sector with the participating boats marked, the Coast Guard cutter, the LST, and closer in, a pair of fifteen-foot Navy CRRC "rubber ducks" from the *Livingston* carrying SEAL teams, circling Jaburi where he slept.

Ford forwarded the information he had to DeLuca, then left a note for his wife, who would be waking up about now. Sami had been right about the weather. Dawn had broken overcast and gray over the Cape, with a storm moving up from the south along the Atlantic coast, possibly the first Nor'easter of the season.

> Mornin', Martha my dear. Sorry I couldn't make it home last night. I gotta take a little trip with Sami this morning when we're through with the paperwork here, but I'll call you when we get back within range. All is well. Don't forget to give Kirby his flea medicine.
>
> Walter

At the TOC, David DeLuca was feeling better, with a bag of ice around his neck, a change of clothes, and a cup of army coffee in his hand. The show tonight on the TOC's plasma screens would be the apprehension of Mahmoud Jaburi. DeLuca hadn't realized how hungry he was until he'd boarded the Osprey for the trip home, when the flight engineer offered him an MRE like a stewardess passing out peanuts, and he consumed it without complaint, his body craving nourishment.

Mack brought him a plate of food from the mess hall to supplement the MRE, adding, "Don't get used to this—I'm not your waitress, but tonight I'm going to make an exception." It was good to hear she was back to her sassy self. He'd slept for perhaps forty-five minutes on the return trip to Balad, and felt slightly less blurred and ragged. Mack was bruised, her left eye black and blue and bloodshot where something, she still didn't know what, struck her, she didn't know when, in addition to a sprained left wrist. Hoolie had cracked a rib. Dan Sykes had a ruptured kidney and a collapsed lung from where he'd landed on a piece of jagged metal when he'd long-jumped the gap in the catwalk, and had been taken to the CASH for treatment. Preacher Johnson hadn't a scratch. Dr. Thomas wanted DeLuca to get X-rays and wear a neck brace, but DeLuca told him it would have to wait.

"If I were you, I think I'd be in tremendous pain," Dr. Thomas had said.

"If I were you," DeLuca said, "I'd stay you."

Phillip LeDoux had joined them in the ops room, as had a full bird colonel named Eagan from IMINT (Scott at his side) and an Admiral Bishop from the Navy, now that it was involved. Kaplan was there to provide expertise on the science side. A team of techies was already working on Al-Tariq's computer files, networked to an NSA lab back in Virginia where the government mainframes were pulling apart the *Alf Wajeh* data as fast as they could. LeDoux was at a corner table, consulting with Generals Abizaid and Sanchez, who'd flown in to consult, more brass at the TOC tonight than a marching band. Captain Martin told DeLuca the Pentagon and the head of Homeland Security wanted to go to Code Red again, but they were getting resistance from the White House and the secretary of defense, who said he didn't want to sound too many alarms. The argument for keeping Jaburi alive was that he had all the names of *Alf Wajeh* in his head and might be persuaded to part with them. The argument for blowing him out of the water was that he might have some alternative means of triggering the attack, even though his SSB had been jammed as soon as the boat was located, which prevented him from sending or receiving e-mail.

When DeLuca read the e-mail from Walter Ford, he called Dr. Kaplan over and asked him to look at it. Kaplan had worked with Seligson and knew him well. He said, reading, that the virus denatured at 180 degrees sounded about right. They'd found several JPEGs on Al-Tariq's laptop of the bottles of "olive oil" that had been used to transport the smallpox virus, so they knew what to look for. The question was, even with an NSA mainframe crunching the data and tracking down the members of *Alf Wajeh,* how would they find them all in time? There were twenty-four names in the send block, indicating twenty-four terrorist cells—even if there were ten members in each cell, a high estimate, it was still far fewer terrorists than the "thousand faces" that *Alf Wajeh* had claimed. It was still more than enough to get the job done.

DeLuca asked Captain Martin to tell Phillip he needed to talk to him. Martin came back and told DeLuca to join LeDoux at the table. DeLuca asked if Kaplan could join them. He'd seen General Sanchez in person once, but he'd only seen Abizaid on television.

"This is Sergeant David DeLuca, the top CI guy on this," LeDoux said. "And Dr. Kaplan. You had an idea, Dave?"

At the door to the TOC, DeLuca saw Captain Martin restraining Colonel Reicken, who apparently was insisting on joining the briefing. He made eye contact with Reicken, who looked utterly apoplectic at the thought that one of his sergeants could meet with the top brass and he couldn't.

"Just one," DeLuca said. "The doctor here can explain the science to you, but my thinking is, we have all these people, the *Alf Wajeh,* out there waiting for instructions, right? Right now, they're waiting. They know that it's supposed to be tonight. And it's *'Id al-Fitr* here, but it's eight hours different back in the States, so we have essentially eight hours of time lag to work with, before they see the moon or whatever. They're not suspicious, yet, but they will be if too much time passes and they don't hear anything. So, if we have all the addresses, even if we don't know who these guys are, we could still send them all instructions, only we make 'em our instructions. I wrote down what I think we should say to them. We'd probably want an Arab linguist to get the phrasing exactly right."

He handed General Abizaid a piece of paper, on which he'd written:

Praise Allah [etc.] Dear holy warriors [etc.], the time has come tonight for us to begin. Follow these instructions as you prepare for the jihad. To activate your weapons, place the bottles that have been sent to you in your microwave ovens. Do not open the bottle. Heat it on high for five minutes. Wait ten minutes and repeat, then wait for further instructions. If you don't have a microwave, submerge bottle in boiling water for ten minutes and repeat. Under no circumstances are you to open the bottles before you do this, or the agent will not work. God is great [blah blah blah].

"There's twenty-four names in the send block," DeLuca said. "I don't see how we're going to successfully bust 240 terrorists, plus or minus, without one or two getting away. This way, if we deactivate the virus while we have 'em all rounded up in one place, so to speak, we can take our time picking 'em up."

"Maybe we could add a line, something like, 'Reply to this e-mail when you're ready and give me your location so that you can be contacted,'" LeDoux suggested.

"What if this stuff boils over inside the microwave?" Abazaid said. "Won't that release the virus?"

"If it gets hot enough to boil over, it'll be dead," Kaplan said. "It only takes a few seconds, and it's going to take more than that for the solution to go from 180 degrees to 220."

"The point is," DeLuca said, "they're all out there, waiting to hear from headquarters, and the longer we wait, the more likely it is that word is going to get out about what happened at the salt works. Once that happens, and they all start to think they're on their own . . ." He didn't have to finish the thought. "I'm thinking we need to do something now. Sirs."

General Sanchez smiled.

"We'll discuss, Sergeant," he said, saluting DeLuca. "Doctor. Thank you."

DeLuca saluted back.

By the time Sami Jambazian was able to put Race Point and the P-town light astern, heading out into the open sea, it was past noon and raining, with following seas rolling in three- to four-foot swells. The weather was expected to remain steady, according to the latest reports. Sami watched his compass and his GPS receiver to stay on course, heading for the coordinates where the *Aafia's Ark* had last been seen. Walter had given Tom Sami's marine fax number, and Tom had promised to keep them up to date on what was happening.

As *The Lady J* approached within twelve miles of Mahmoud Jaburi's sailboat, Walter received a fax from Tom telling him the *Cuttyhunk* and the *Livingston* were closing in on Jaburi, making an upwind approach, given

that airborne biological agents were potentially aboard.
Sami throttled forward to make his best speed, about
thirty knots, the V-shaped hull of the heavy craft cutting
through the swells, his bow crashing against the occasional wave. Walter donned one of the Helly Hansen rain
slickers that Sami kept for his guests and went to stand at
the bow, scanning the horizon with a pair of binoculars
and pointing for Sami when he finally saw the sailboat.
Walter would, of course, step aside and let the Navy and
the Coast Guard do their jobs, but it was also, as far as he
was concerned, his case and his collar—come what
might, he wanted to see it through to the end.

DeLuca watched the arrest on a plasma screen at the TOC.
In addition to the UAV imagery, Scottie had patched in a
feed from the *Cuttyhunk*'s thermal imaging camera, which
was what a marksman on the *Cuttyhunk* used to locate
and then disable the sailboat's engine, firing a .50-caliber
shell through the hull and then the engine block. A second
shell was fired into the engine, just to be sure, and then a
third was fired at the rudder, disabling the *Aafia's Ark* to
prevent Jaburi from making any kind of run for it. The
stern of the *Livingston* housed a docking bay and a "moon
pool" large enough to tow the sailboat in and capture her
whole and afloat, but of course, Admiral Bishop explained,
"You don't pull a boat in until you know she hasn't been
rigged to explode and that those on board are fully com-
pliant."

     The thermal imaging, which could read body heat sig-
natures right through the hull of the sailboat as easily as if
it were made of glass, created a cartoonlike image that
showed a single individual down below, a bright orange

figure against a cooler blue background, the man scurrying at first when the shots were fired, then moving more calmly, contemplating his options, from the look of it. DeLuca had heard so much about Professor Jaburi that he was hoping to get a picture of his face before he was taken into custody, assuming he let them take him into custody.

He wondered about the man, so intent on destroying America—destroying the world, more or less—what motivated him? How was the horror of what he was hoping to accomplish not a deterrent? Did he really believe the *Alf Wajeh* mythology? Even after all of Walter Ford's notes, Jaburi was still a mystery. Was it possibly some kind of perverted desire to go down in history, the biggest mass murderer the world had ever known, or was it more complicated than that? The man had convinced himself that what he was doing was right, unlike most criminals who at some level knew and frequently admitted they knew what they were doing was wrong, but they just didn't give a shit. Jaburi thought what he was doing was right. Did he think he was doing God's bidding? He'd known Al-Tariq as a child—what had happened between them? Did he respect Mohammed Al-Tariq, or even love him, or did he simply fear him? Did he think Al-Tariq spoke for Allah? Or did Jaburi speak directly to Allah and regard himself as his chosen personal envoy? DeLuca imagined the latter to be the case, and that Jaburi, with his superior intellect, had probably considered himself "chosen" for some time.

But where did the hate come from? Who did he hate? Or what?

DeLuca could only guess, but his guess was Jaburi hated his own flesh, his own physical body. It was kind of

an intuitive conclusion, but it made sense: Jaburi's im-
maculate style of dress, the way he combed his victims'
hair—the physical body was something he needed to control. He probably felt separate from it, isolated or disconnected, a superior intellect transported around by an
inferior vehicle, like the queen of England getting a ride
in a rusted-out Ford Fiesta. Jaburi hated his body, its
urges, the things it made him do and think. Lots of people
hated their bodies, girls who starved themselves to death
or cut themselves with razor blades, men who castrated
themselves, hating their bodies. The question was, how
might such a psychosis manifest itself in a man, a brilliant
academic living in a world he thought was impure and full
of evil?

DeLuca considered. In all his experience as a police
officer, the craziest thing about crazy people, something
he'd found to be true with a remarkable consistency, was
that they all thought everybody else was as crazy as they
were. The "guy with the heads" who Walter Ford liked
to joke about, a mass murderer from Georgia who'd be-
headed his victims and planted the heads in his mother's
garden so that he could tell her, "Hey Ma—people look
up to you," had actually told the police that in his opinion, everybody wanted to cut other people's heads off—
everybody *thought* about it, they were just afraid to admit
it, and he'd simply had the courage to act on the normal
impulses that everybody had.

Crazy people thought that way.

So if Jaburi was crazy, and he was (brilliance was no
ticket out of madness or delusion, and often, it was the
ticket in), and if he thought that everybody thought the
same way he did, and if he hated his body, then he probably

thought everybody hated their bodies. Everybody was impure. Everybody needed cleansing. Everybody secretly wanted cleansing. The whole world, in other words, wanted him to do what he was about to do—everybody thought about it, but they were afraid to admit it or do anything about it. And he wasn't.

On the plasma screen, he watched the Coast Guard cutter *Cuttyhunk* close in on the sailboat, approaching within hailing distance, still upwind. He saw the LST pull to within a thousand yards, and he saw the Navy SEAL teams in their Scorpions, and then a boat he recognized as *The Lady J*. He wasn't surprised that Sami and Walter wanted to be on the scene for the arrest. He was surprised by Jaburi's behavior, watching as the academic climbed the stairs from his cabin and stood on the deck of the ship, his hands in the air. DeLuca had expected Jaburi to flee, or put up some kind of fight.

But he wasn't doing that.

"My name is Mahmoud Jaburi," Jaburi replied to the captain of the *Cuttyhunk,* who'd called to the smaller boat. The beam of the cutter's spotlight shone in Jaburi's face. "I work for the Central Intelligence Agency. You can ask a man there named Andrew Timmons. He will tell you. Or you can ask that man here, in the rain slicker. His name is Walter Ford, and he knows all about me. He has spoken to Agent Timmons. Ask him. He will tell you . . ."

The image from the Global Hawk circling the scene was remarkable, as good as if a movie crew were circling the ship in a helicopter. DeLuca watched. He saw Jaburi with his hands in the air. He seemed relaxed, unconcerned.

Cocky? DeLuca couldn't be sure. He saw Jaburi point to Walter Ford. He saw the spotlight from the *Cuttyhunk* shine on Jaburi's face.

"Can you get me a closeup?" he asked Scott.

"Just a second," Scott said, tapping at his computer keyboard. "Nope. That's as close as I can go. Maybe . . . nope."

"Get me as close as you possibly can, okay?" DeLuca asked his son.

"He's saying he has nothing to hide," Admiral Bishop said, listening on headphones to the radio chatter on the Navy's encrypted high frequency and relaying the communications. "He's telling the *Cuttyhunk* he works for the CIA. Who's the guy in the fishing boat?"

"He works for me," DeLuca said.

"Jesus," Abizaid said. "You people are everywhere."

But DeLuca wasn't listening, paying attention instead to the imagery coming from the Coast Guard's thermal imaging camera.

"Does anybody here know about thermal imaging?" DeLuca asked.

"I know a bit," Colonel Eagan said. "What's your question?"

"Well, look at the image of Jaburi. Now look at the image of my friend Walter. Or Sami next to him. These colors are correct, right?"

"The colors indicate temperature variations," Egan said.

"Right," DeLuca said. Jaburi was gesticulating. "So Walter and Sami are mostly orange with a little red in the core and then at the extremities they start to fade to yellow and green? Why is that?"

"Their body temperatures are cooler at the extremities," Eagan said. "These cameras are incredibly sensitive."

"Okay," DeLuca said. "So then why is Jaburi almost completely red?"

"Different people have different signatures," Eagan said. "I have boys who tell me they can read these things and tell whether or not somebody's angry."

"You're saying you think he's angry?"

"Well, no," Eagan said. "He wouldn't be that red. He's definitely warmer than the others. Maybe he's been exerting himself."

"Or maybe he's running a fever," DeLuca said. "Tell them to abort!" he shouted. "Tell them now—abort! Back off, don't arrest him—he's infected himself. He's got it, and he's trying to spread it!"

He watched, horrified, as Sami pulled his boat up alongside the *Aafia's Ark.* Jaburi still had his hands in the air. It looked as if he were arguing with the captain of the *Cuttyhunk,* pointing at Walter, then at the ladder hanging from the toe-rail, waving and inviting Walter aboard, Jaburi with his hands out to his sides in a gesture that tried to say, "Relax, you have nothing to worry about . . . trust me." DeLuca saw Walter talking to the captain about something, then Jaburi joining in a three-way conversation.

He saw Sami look over his shoulder.

"Answer your goddamn radio, Sami," DeLuca pleaded.

Jaburi and Walter continued to converse, the two men's body language casual and relaxed, DeLuca thought, the two ships no more than fifteen or twenty feet apart. Sami left the picture, then returned and whispered something into Walter's ear.

"Good, Sami, good—now back off," DeLuca urged.

Jaburi wiped his forehead with a handkerchief.

Walter and Sami disappeared into the wheelhouse, then the fishing boat reversed engines and separated from the sailboat, slowly at first, then engines full. The Coast Guard cutter and the rubber raiding crafts backed off as well.

"Jesus, Walter!" DeLuca said, breathing easier now. "Could you possibly move any slower?"

Epilogue

HE ASKED HIM THE SAME QUESTION IN PERSON a week later from his hospital bed at Bethesda Naval Hospital, where he'd been sent to recuperate and mainly to rest. He was taking medications to get the swelling down in the disk in his neck that was on the verge of rupturing. Phil LeDoux had, in fact, pulled rank on DeLuca for the first time in his life and ordered his friend to rest. For now, anyway, DeLuca felt like he could stand down. Of the twenty-four e-mail addresses, twenty had reported back, leading to the very quiet and highly secret arrests of more than two hundred terrorists. Of the remaining three addresses, two jihadis had turned themselves in, reporting that they'd lost their nerve and hadn't had the heart to activate the virus that had been sent them, meaning it was still live, at which point the bottles they turned over, still sealed, were handled very carefully indeed. The last terrorist was never found, simply missing from her apartment, but the bottle of "olive oil" was recovered, unopened, and neutralized.

Walter and his wife had driven down, to see their friend David. Sami would have come, too, but at the last minute he got a call from a group of Harvard professors who wanted to take one last trip while the bluefish were still running. DeLuca was tempted to tell Sami what he'd seen a week earlier, watching the arrest scene via the thermal-imaging feed, an image of Sami's boat and then, slowly circling it, a large school of fish, following one alpha fish twice the size of the others. A tech specialist with a degree in marine biology who was watching identified it as a school of migratory bluefin tuna. It was the thirty-thousand-dollar fish Sami had seen, and it looked like it was following him. DeLuca decided to keep that information to himself. It would only make Sami crazier than he already was.

He debriefed Walter Ford as best he could, filling in the details while Martha watched the television. By the second day, Jaburi had been too ill to rise from the berth in his cabin. Scottie said somebody at IMINT guessed, looking at the thermal images, that Jaburi's fever spiked at around 106 degrees. There'd been talk of sending over SEAL divers in Jack Brown dry-suits or boarding the ship with gowned-up NBC technicians to decontaminate and salvage the boat, but then the let's-just-blow-it-up-and-go-home argument won out, once all the risks were factored in. Seventy-two hours after the first shot had been fired, an eight-inch gun from the *Livingston* put Mahmoud Jaburi out of his considerable misery, obliterating the vessel with a thermobaric shell that created an instantaneous sixteen-hundred-degree plasma. Jaburi was no more. His ship was no more. *Alf Wajeh* was no more, just as Mohammed Al-Tariq was no more.

"So I'm still confused," Walter said. "If you didn't know Al-Tariq was alive until after you talked to Ali Hadid, how could he have known to put a reward on your head?"

"I don't know that he did," DeLuca said. "There's a lot of guys over there putting rewards on people's heads. Half of 'em are just plain assholes. The insurgency's not the half of it. Hopefully, the Iraqi cops we've been training will get it under control when they take over after we leave."

"David," Martha interrupted. "Excuse me, but I think you might know this man talking to Geraldo Rivera. I think he was in your unit. Wasn't that your unit?"

DeLuca looked up at the TV on the wall. He saw a familiar face, the words, "Lt. Col. Stanley Reicken, U.S. Army, 419th Counterintelligence Batt., Ret." at the bottom of the screen. He'd known they were going to ask him to resign, but the demotion was a pleasant surprise. He turned the sound up.

"Actually, Geraldo, I think they're wrong," Reicken was saying. "I was there. We are winning the hearts and minds of the Iraqi people. It's a slow process, but we're winning it. I personally supervised the installation of an electrical generator at a hospital in the town of Ad-Dujayl, and let me tell you . . ."

DeLuca turned the sound down again.

"To quote the Scarecrow in *The Wizard of Oz,* 'Some people with no brains do an awful lot of talking.'"

"Do you think that's true, David?" Martha asked. "Are we really winning the hearts and minds?"

DeLuca could have given her a more complete answer, but then he recalled Phillip LeDoux's orders—he was supposed to rest, and not upset himself.

"No, Martha, I don't think that's true," he said.

"So Bonnie's coming down tonight?" Walter asked, changing the subject. DeLuca nodded. "How're you with that?"

"She's called off the lawyers," DeLuca said. "They tell me the VA has a free marriage counseling program specifically for these sorts of things."

"Well that's good, then," Walter said. "Of course, you're not going to just rely on the VA program to save your marriage."

"No. Of course not."

"Okay, then," Walter said. "Martha, we should go."

"Can we bring you anything before we go home?" Martha wanted to know, eyeing the card sitting on the windowsill next to him.

"I'm good, Martha," he said. "Thanks anyway. Thanks for the flowers, too."

"Oh, wait a minute," Walter Ford said, reaching into the shopping bag he'd been carrying. "I almost forgot. This is from Gillian. I know she was saving this for you." Ford handed DeLuca the fifty-year-old bottle of McCallums that she'd locked in her safe. "When you get back, we thought we'd have a little service for her."

"I'll save this for then," DeLuca said.

After they left, he reread the card on the windowsill. It was from Evelyn, handwritten. It said,

Dear David,
I couldn't believe it when they told me you'd gone home. I'm so sorry I didn't get a chance to say goodbye, but then, that's been more the rule than the exception for me, these last few years, with people I care about. And the people I don't, I can't seem to get rid of. I hope they take good care of you—I know it's not like you, but do try to listen to the doctors and do what they tell you.

Now I must say, I believe you were quite a naughty boy, telling me about your "friend" who died in the "bombing" of "counterintelligence headquarters." But it has since been explained to me, and I understand. Your secrets are safe with me (all of them) so let's not not speak any more of it. They say the first casualty of war is the truth, and I'm afraid I may have inflicted my share of wounds to it myself (friendly fire, but that's hardly an excuse)—that's what happens in war, isn't it? That's just what happens.

It seems rather imperative, then, that I tell you, so that you know, that there are other truths I never fudge, and things I said to you that I meant completely and will always stand behind. There were things that happened that might not have happened, under other circumstances, but that doesn't make them any less true or meaningful in hindsight. You should know, I keep the friends I make and I protect my friends fiercely. And I consider you much more than a friend, David. I can't talk of love, though, can I? Too risky, isn't it? Too dangerous, and I know danger doesn't have much of an effect on you, but I'm going to let it go anyway.

So you be well, and perhaps we shall see each other again. We'll always have Sanandaj. We'll always have Balad. And we'll never pass this way again, they say, so there it is.

Be good.

Evelyn

P.S. I suspect you'll want to destroy this note. Go ahead—I won't mind.

She was right, of course. She was right about every-thing.

He tossed it into the wastebasket.

For an hour, he watched television. There were reports of a car bombing in Fallujah, an IED killing two soldiers at an intersection in Ar Ramadi, a mortar round that killed three Iraqi civilians in Samarra, and on and on it went. He was interrupted by a knock on the door. Phillip LeDoux stood in the doorway.

"Got a minute?" LeDoux said.

"Phillip," DeLuca said, smiling. "When did they let you out of the asylum?"

"I had to come in yesterday for meetings at the Penta-gon," he said. "Sorry I didn't call first but they told me you had visitors."

"Walter and his wife," DeLuca said.

"I'm sorry I missed them," LeDoux said. "Anyway, Dave, there are some other people in the hall who want to see you. I said I'd come in first to see how you were feel-ing. You up for more visitors?"

"Sure," DeLuca said, wondering who LeDoux could have brought by.

"Listen—there's something I wanted to say before they come in," LeDoux said. "You're going to be reading about this in the papers in the next couple months. You remember your friend Doc?"

"Yeah," DeLuca said. "Chaptered out on a sanity thing."

"Right on the details but wrong on the conclusion," LeDoux said. "Apparently he'd gone up the chain of com-mand about some things he said he'd seen going on in the prison at Baquba. Interrogators doing things to prisoners.

When nothing happened, he went off the reservation with the media. As I'm just now coming to understand it, some people were trying to have him declared insane to discredit him, but it's going to come out that everything he said was true. I'm having the whole thing investigated, including the coverup, but a lot of people are going to look really bad. I just wanted you to know. It doesn't really concern you, but I know Doc was a friend of yours."

"I appreciate it," DeLuca said. "He never said anything to us about prison abuse."

"I also wanted to tell you that the people in the hall *are* good people. I'll personally vouch for all of them. I may not always agree with all of them, but I wanted you to know my thoughts about them."

"If you'll stand by them, that's good enough for me," DeLuca said.

"Let's let 'em in, then," General LeDoux said. "By the way, I'd like you to meet Kathryn while you're in town, but we'll talk about that later."

First to enter was DeLuca's brother-in-law, Tom, who smiled and shook his hand. Tommy was followed by five men and a woman, who formed a semicircle at the foot of his bed.

"Sergeant David DeLuca, 419th Counterintelligence Battalion," General LeDoux said by way of introduction, "my old and good friend, I'd like you to meet, from your left, John Maitland, commander of INSCOM, Colonel Jose Canales, DIA Pentagon liaison, Warren Benjamin, deputy director of Homeland Security, Ross Schlessinger, deputy director of the CIA, Carla White, White House's National Security adviser, and Senator Danforth Sykes, from the Senate Select Committee on Intelligence."

"Senator," DeLuca said, trying to sit up. "Tommy. Everyone. You'll excuse me if I don't get up, but I don't have any pants on."

Tommy laughed, but the others seemed rather serious.

"It's good to see your spirits are up," Tom said. "How's your neck?"

"Not that bad, really," DeLuca said. "I gather you're not all here to inquire about my health."

"We're all hoping you get better," LeDoux said. "I've debriefed the committee as thoroughly as I could, but they wanted to meet you in person. We've got a little business to do here. Colonel Canales?"

"Sir," the colonel said. He looked way too young to be a full bird colonel, a clean-shaven Latino in his late thirties, DeLuca guessed. "Sergeant, it's a pleasure to meet you. Believe me, I've heard a lot about you. I think the general asked me to start because I'm going to be the good-news/bad-news guy here. So which do you want first?"

"Whichever you'd prefer, Colonel," DeLuca said.

"I'd prefer to keep the bad news to myself, but unfortunately, I can't. Here's the good news," he said, reaching into the briefcase he was carrying and extracting six hardshell clam cases, which he opened one at a time. "This is the Purple Heart. You were probably expecting that. This is the Bronze Star, with an attachment for valor. This is the Silver Star, also with an attachment for valor. In addition, you've earned a Soldier's Medal, a Legion of Merit, and an Army Commendation Medal. We're giving these to you because we wanted you to know, up front, that we recognize the work you've done and appreciate the sacrifices you've made. Your work in the Sunni Triangle was truly remarkable, and we wanted you to know that we know that."

DeLuca looked at the medals, then at LeDoux, wondering what the trick was.

"Thank you, sir," he said. "I think we had a lot of luck on our side."

"Well," Colonel Canales said, "judging by your record, either you're the luckiest man in the world, or your intelligence and skills have more to do with your achievements than luck. We don't give medals for luck."

"Okay," DeLuca said. "What's the bad news?"

Canales folded the clamshell cases and placed them back into his briefcase.

"The bad news is that these are yours, but we can't give them to you. Yet. We're going to have to hold them in abeyance."

"It's all top secret, Dave," LeDoux said. "TS/SCI until further notice. You can't talk about what you did. Ever."

"The president is also aware of your service," said Carla White, a woman of perhaps forty. "He asked me personally to tell you how much he appreciates it, but unfortunately, it's been determined that everything about Mohammed Al-Tariq and *Alf Wajeh* is too sensitive and impingent upon national security to allow for dissemination of any kind. We're just too vulnerable, and if we expose our vulnerabilities, we're inviting attack. We can't do it. We'd like to invite you to the White House and throw you a state dinner, but unfortunately, the best we can do is to thank you privately."

"That's all right," DeLuca said. "I've already had dinner."

"We do expect you'll receive the recognition you're due in the fullness of time," Ross Schlessinger, the CIA deputy director, said. "We just can't tell you when that might be. We keep a book at the CIA of the names of men who've done things we can never talk about, but we think it's important for them to know that we know."

"I'm not going to lose any sleep over it," DeLuca said. "There's obviously more though, right? You wouldn't all be here like this if all you wanted to do was pat me on the back and then tell me to shut up, I'm guessing."

"There's a bit more," Warren Benjamin said. "I don't know if you've been following the papers, but you're probably aware that ever since 9/11, we've been looking at intelligence and trying to figure out where we fucked up. And how not to fuck up again. So you're going to be hearing, in the next few months, or years, stories about all kinds of ways we fucked up, and some of them are going to be exaggerated or off base, but some of them are going to be true. The two ways that concern us most here are that there wasn't enough coordination between the various agencies, and there was too much reliance on electronic intel at the expense of human intelligence. Plain and simple, we need more boots on the ground—assisted by all the technology we can bring to bear, but boots on the ground."

"By the way," Schlessinger said, "if I may interrupt, speaking of intra-agency rivalries, I gather your people have told you about my man Timmons, the case officer who was running Mahmoud Jaburi. Timmons has been reassigned."

"It's a new world," Benjamin continued. "We don't really need guys sneaking around Moscow in black trench coats anymore. We need to adjust to the new map. It's not China or Russia anymore. It's Nigeria, and North Korea, and Uzbekistan and Kashmir and Sudan and Bali, and all the little countries and groups and organizations on the fringe of globalization who figure if they can't have a piece of the pie, they're going to take a shit in the pie so nobody else can eat it. Excuse the turd-pie analogy, but I think it fits."

"You've obviously never eaten an MRE," DeLuca said. "Turd pie is one of the better offerings."

"INSCOM is putting together a new agency," John Maitland, the INSCOM commander, said. "A special-access program, on a black budget. We're looking for people with exactly your skill sets to go into Africa and North Korea and wherever we need you to go and work the human intelligence so that we can find the new bad guys before they get organized. We're the new global police, whether we like it or not, and we're going to need global policemen like you to walk the beat for us. And to go undercover when you need to. So that's why we're here. We want to offer you a job."

"A job?" DeLuca said.

"Doing exactly what you were doing in Iraq, but with a wider agenda," Canales said. "Running small-scale missions and special ops crews and coordinating larger operations when need be. Hearts and minds. The things you already do well."

"Who would I be working for?"

"You're looking at us," LeDoux said. "Colonel Canales is your hands-on contact, under me, and I report to the committee. You'd have an unlimited budget, full hands-off authority, and all the toys you could possibly dream of. You'd be CI: Team Red. Red as in hot spot. You always said this would be a great job if the army would just let you do it right, so that's what we have in mind."

"My wife wants me to quit," DeLuca said. "We were talking about opening a bar."

LeDoux looked at Maitland, who nodded. Schlessinger nodded as well.

"We'll build you a bar," LeDoux said. "We really want to give you whatever you want, Dave."

"Can I keep my team?"

"We have a saying in Congress," Senator Danforth Sykes said. "'If it ain't broke, don't fix it, but if it breaks, blame the other party for not fixing it.' We want you to keep your team. I talked to Dan about you. You couldn't come with any higher recommendations, and I trust my son's opinion."

Dan had been transferred from Balad to the Landstuhl Army Medical Center in Germany, where the doctors had worked to repair his damaged kidney.

"How's Danny boy doing?" DeLuca asked.

"He's better," the senator said. "I have to say, on a personal note, I was upset when he said he wanted to stay in CI, but we've had a good talk about it and I've accepted his decision. It's been a bit remarkable, to his mother and me, how much he seems to have matured in the last year. What you'll be doing is important, Sergeant. I dare say vital. And my son believes you'd be the best person to head the team."

"You must be glad you found the WMD you've been looking for," DeLuca said. Maitland, Schlessinger, White, and Sykes all exchanged glances.

"We're not going to release that, at the present time," Carla White said.

DeLuca wanted to say, "Then before the next election,

perhaps?" but he held his tongue. Maybe he was just being cynical. It was none of his business—these were not the games he had any interest in playing.

"We're also prepared to give you a field promotion, here and now, with commensurate pay scale," Canales said. "You can take your pick. Sergeant first class, warrant officer, lieutenant if you want to join the officers' corps."

"No thanks," DeLuca said. "I'll take warrant officer."

"Well," Colonel Canales said, "General LeDoux predicted you were going to say that."

"And I want my team paid at least as much as the private contractors get paid."

"Not a problem," Canales said.

"Can you give us an answer now?" Maitland said. "Or would you like twenty-four hours?"

"I'm going to have to talk to my wife," DeLuca said.

"Of course," Carla White said. "We understand. The president has been saying he wants to recognize the sacrifices made by the families of our service members by building them a monument. He thinks we have enough monuments to soldiers and not one to stand for what their families have suffered and experienced. We've actually been looking at places on the Mall in Washington to do something."

"Well," DeLuca said. "That sounds a lot like political bullshit to me, frankly. I think the families would be more grateful if you fix the VA system."

He saw LeDoux try to stifle a smirk.

"We're going to do that, too," White said.

"My guy at USAMRIID says you probably stopped

somewhere between two and three hundred million deaths," Maitland said. "Just so you know."

"But why keep score?" DeLuca said. "I'll think about it. That's all I can tell you."

He knew, about five minutes after they left the room, that he was going to take the job. He didn't feel forced. Somebody else could do it if he didn't. He knew that. He was going to take the job, simply because right now, there was no better way for him to live, no other way that he could make the same level of contribution to the country that had given him a home, and a dream. Corny as it sounded, this was truly how he could be all that he could be. He thought about it for another hour, but he kept coming up to the same conclusion.

He wasn't sure how he was going to say it, but he knew approximately what he was going to say when his wife arrived, dropping her suitcase inside the door to his room.

She looked at him for a long time, tears welling up in her eyes.

"We have to talk," he said to Bonnie.

"That's my line," she said. "We'll talk, but right now, would you mind holding me? Because I really need you to."

"I might be a little rusty at it," he said.

"We'll start slow," she said.

"Good idea," he said.

She lay down beside him and rested her head on his chest.

About the Authors

DAVID DEBATTO has served in the active duty Army, Army Reserve, and Army National Guard as a German linguist, counterintelligence course instructor, and counterintelligence special agent. He served in Europe at the height of the Cold War in the late 1970s to early 1980s and in Iraq during Operation Iraqi Freedom in 2003 where his Tactical Human Intelligence Team (THT) hunted Saddam, WMD, and top Ba'ath party leaders. He is currently writing the second of this four-part series for Warner Books along with Pete Nelson as well as articles for major publications such as *Vanity Fair, Salon,* and *The American Prospect.* He is also a frequent guest on major television and radio news programs giving his analysis of breaking stories in the global war on terrorism. David lives in Massachusetts with his wife and two Bengal cats.

PETE NELSON lives with his wife and son in western Massachusetts. He got his MFA from the University of Iowa Writers' Workshop in 1979 and has written both fiction and nonfiction for magazines, including *Harper's, Playboy, Esquire, MS, Outside, The Iowa Review, National Wildlife, Glamour,* and *Redbook.* He was a columnist for *Mademoiselle* and a staff writer for *LIVE* magazine, covering various live events including horse pulls, music festivals, dog shows, accordion camps, and arm wrestling championships. He's published twelve young adult novels, including a six-book series about a girl named Sylvia Smith-Smith, which earned him an Edgar Award nomination from the Mystery Writers of America. His young adult nonfiction WWII history, *Left for Dead* (Random House, 2002), about the sinking of the USS *Indianapolis,* won the 2003 Christopher Award and was selected for the American Library Association's 2003 top ten list. His other nonfiction titles include *Real Man Tells All* (Viking, 1988), *Marry Like a Man* (NAL, 1992), *That Others May Live* (Crown, 2000), and *Kidshape* (Rutledge Hill, 2004). His novel *The Christmas List* was published by Rutledge Hill Press in 2004.